Recycling programs
for this product may
not exist in your area.

ISBN-13: 978-1-335-40650-7

Honor's Promise
First published in 2000. This edition published in 2021.
Copyright © 2000 by Sharon Sala

Dade
First published in 2011. This edition published in 2021.
Copyright © 2011 by Delores Fossen

Harlequin Enterprises ULC
22 Adelaide St. West, 40th Floor
Toronto, Ontario M5H 4E3, Canada
www.Harlequin.com

Printed in U.S.A.

HONOR'S PROMISE

NEW YORK TIMES BESTSELLING AUTHOR
SHARON SALA

CONTENTS

Sharon Sala is a *New York Times* bestselling author. She has 123 books published in romance, young adult, Western and women's fiction and in nonfiction. First published in 1991, she's an eight-time RITA® Award finalist. Industry awards include the following: the Janet Dailey Award; five Career Achievement Awards from *RT Book Reviews*; five National Readers' Choice Awards; five Colorado Romance Writers Awards of Excellence; the Heart of Excellence Award; the Booksellers' Best Award; the Nora Roberts Lifetime Achievement Award presented by RWA; and the Centennial Award from RWA for recognition of her 100th published novel.

Books by Sharon Sala

Secrets and Lies

Dark Hearts
Cold Hearts
Wild Hearts

Forces of Nature

Going Gone
Going Twice
Going Once

The Rebel Ridge novels

'Til Death
Don't Cry for Me
Next of Kin

Visit the Author Profile page at Harlequin.com for more titles.

HONOR'S PROMISE

Sharon Sala

This book is dedicated to mothers and daughters everywhere who've come to realize that the bonds of love are stronger than the bonds of birth.

and

To my dear son, Christopher, and his darling wife, Kristi Ann, who with the patience and understanding of their daughter, Chelsea Nicole, are learning what it's like to be parents.

Special thanks to EMT Dennis Dukes for his advice and expertise, and an acknowledgment of the dedication and sacrifice an EMT makes every day just for the welfare of the patient.

Chapter 1

Dear Mr. Malone, by the time you read this letter, I will be dead.

Trace Logan's feet came off the desktop with a thump, his casual posture gone as he continued to read the strange letter. Ordinarily he wouldn't be reading J. J. Malone's mail, but the boss of Malone Industries was at home, recovering from a fall off his horse. That in itself was not unusual, except for the fact that J. J. Malone was on the down side of seventy-six years old.

Trace frowned as his eyes caught the phrase, *I was the woman.* He couldn't believe what he was seeing. The words on the page yanked him to his feet. The overstuffed, oxblood leather chair went spinning around and around on its base like a merry-go-round gone crazy. *Took your granddaughter,* sent Trace to the wide expanse of plate-glass windows overlooking a portion of Colorado Springs's business district.

His eyes narrowed, and he tilted the page to catch the fading light as an approaching thunderstorm slowly blocked the sun's September rays.

Trace's heart was racing, his thoughts in a turmoil. He debated with himself as to the possible authenticity of the letter. *Knows nothing about it,* the woman wrote, ending with a final sentence, *And her name is Honor.* It was signed, Charlotte O'Brien.

"Damn," Trace muttered, and stared unseeingly through the tinted windows.

He barely remembered the incident. He'd been no more than eleven or twelve when it happened.

Mary Margaret Malone, only daughter of J.J.'s eldest son, John, who later died in Vietnam, was barely eight months old when she was snatched from her stroller in a park. It was the most publicized kidnapping since the disappearance of the Lindbergh baby years ago. But this time, no ransom note arrived, no phone calls or ominous threats were issued. There was no contact made whatsoever. The baby simply disappeared. After a time, it was assumed she was either dead or had been sold on the black market to some unsuspecting couple, desperate for a child they could not conceive.

J.J.'s hopes faded with each passing year until finally he'd ceased searching. Now, he rarely mentioned her passing through their lives.

Trace hurried back to his desk, searching through the shuffled papers for the letter's envelope. A Texas lawyer's return address in subdued but tasteful black script graced the corner. He frowned, tapped the envelope absently against the desk, and then pivoted decisively toward the office door.

"Irene," Trace ordered, "cancel my appointments for the rest of the day. I'll be at the Malone estate."

The secretary's perfectly drawn eyebrows arched in surprise, but she appropriately refrained from voicing her thoughts. She'd been J. J. Malone's personal secretary for many years. When Trace Logan joined Malone Industries over twelve years ago, he'd become part of her duties.

She sighed a long-suffering sigh as the office door slammed shut behind him, then started leafing through his appointment book, mentally preparing a plausible, professional excuse.

The wind whipped around the corner of the two-story Tudor-style mansion, blowing the first hints of moisture from the quickly moving storm front onto the windshield of Trace's car. He pulled into the paved driveway at the Malone estate and parked.

Patting his suit pocket to assure himself the letter was safely inside, he opened the door and made a dash for the house. He beat the deluge by two long-legged leaps as he entered through the rear entrance.

"Mr. Logan!" Trudy Sinclair cried, startled at Trace's unannounced arrival, and dropped the stalk of celery she'd been cleaning onto the hard, shiny surface of the gray flagstone floor. Little bits of leaf, water, and the long, thready strings she'd been stripping from the crisp green ribs went everywhere. She clasped her hand to her chest in dramatic surprise and promptly plastered the rest of the water and celery leaf on her apron front.

"Sorry, Trudy." Trace grinned remorsefully. He

watched the celery come to an abrupt halt against the work island in the center of the room. "I couldn't beat the rain to the front door, so I used the back. I didn't mean to scare you. Here, let me help you clean this up."

He bent down and began to gather the crisp, wet stalks when Trudy snatched them from his hands and pushed him toward the main part of the house.

"I don't need anyone messing about in *my* kitchen," she announced, clutching the celery to her already wet apron. "You just startled me. I'll clean it up myself, thank you. Mr. Malone is in the library. Go talk to him. Maybe you'll put him in a better mood."

Trace grinned again as Trudy's sturdy little figure bustled busily about the kitchen, quickly putting it back to rights.

"He wouldn't be in such a fix if he'd act his age," Trudy muttered, and shoved Trace the rest of the way from the kitchen. "The very idea," she continued accusingly, "riding horses at his age!"

Trace wisely left Trudy to her task and headed for the library. The smile disappeared from his face as he remembered the reason for his visit.

John James Malone was impulsive, hot-tempered, and rarely admitted to a failure or a mistake. And, he was too old to change. Trace was worried about how J.J. was going to receive the news.

He quietly entered the open double doors of the library and caught J.J. in the process of sneaking a cigar from the silver humidor on his desk.

"J.J.?" Trace said.

The tall, silver-haired man, balancing himself on crutches, jumped and dropped the lid of the humidor.

It went clanging to the floor and spun about in a whup, whup, whup sound until it came to rest at Trace's feet.

"Hellfire, boy," J. J. Malone said. He turned and glared, struggling to maintain his balance. "Now you've done it. *Sinless* Sinclair will have heard that lid and hide my cigars again. What the hell are you doing here this time of day? Is something wrong at the office?"

"Sorry, boss," Trace said. "This must be my day for surprises, in more ways than one." He slid his hand inside his suit coat and pulled out the letter. "No, nothing's wrong at the office. But..." and he hesitated, almost afraid now that he was here, to hand the man the letter. What if he had a heart attack? It was going to be a shock. He should have had Irene call J.J.'s doctor.

"But what?" J.J. urged, and slipped the cigar back into the humidor, quickly putting the silver lid back in place just as his housekeeper came bursting through the doorway.

She fixed him with an icy, disapproving glare, looked pointedly at the humidor, and then back at J.J. She sniffed the air suspiciously, and when she could detect no offending odors, she barked out, "Will there be anything you'd be wanting, sir?"

"Just a little privacy in my own home would be nice," J.J. muttered in return, then grinned mischievously as Trudy spun around and bustled back to the kitchen.

"Told you," J.J. said to Trace, and then his playful manner disappeared as he saw the odd, intense look on Trace's face.

Trace Logan was the son of his best friend, Conrad Logan. He'd taken him straight out of college and into the firm, more or less as a favor to Conrad. Trace had a razor-sharp mind and had quickly evolved into the hard, savvy man he was today. Due to J.J.'s accident, Trace was running Malone Industries singlehandedly... and competently.

"What is it, boy?" J.J. repeated. "Did we lose that government contract after all? I knew I should have called my man in Washington—"

"No," Trace interrupted. "It has nothing to do with business. It's personal, J.J. I opened a letter addressed to you."

"So?" J.J. questioned. "You know you have full authority to act on my behalf."

Trace pulled himself up to his full height of more than six feet, took a deep breath, and spoke as he handed the letter to his boss. "Maybe you'd better sit down to read this."

J.J.'s shaggy, white eyebrows shot upward as he cocked his head sideways.

"That bad, is it, boy?" He clumped awkwardly to his favorite chair by the fireplace and let himself drop backward with a thump. "Now, hand me the damned letter."

"I wouldn't call it bad news, sir. If it's valid, it could be the best news you ever had."

Trace handed him the letter, then lowered himself in the chair opposite the man he considered to be his second father. Trace watched J.J. pat his shirt pocket, locate his glasses, and slide them up his long, craggy nose. Then he looked at the return address on the envelope bearing his name, looked back at Trace's worried expression, and slipped the letter from the envelope. He cleared his throat, pushed his glasses to a comfortable position, unfolded the piece of paper, and began to read.

Trace watched the old man's face run the full gamut

of expressions. It went from shock, to disbelief, to sudden understanding, and then pure, unadulterated joy.

J.J. let the letter fall limply in his lap. He leaned his head back against the cushioned headrest and closed his eyes. His mouth worked spasmodically as he struggled with composure.

Trace could restrain himself no longer. He leaned forward and placed his hand on the old man's knee, curling his long, tanned fingers around the bony kneecap.

"Are you all right, J.J.?"

J.J. opened his eyes, unashamed of the tears that slipped from the corners, and sighed. He reached down and patted Trace's hand.

"Yes, son. I'm more than all right. I *knew* there was a reason I had to stay behind when my Meggie died. For the longest time I was so damned mad at God I didn't think it through. Yes, I was," he repeated, watching a frown appear on Trace's face. "First we lost baby Megan. She was named for my own Mary Margaret, you know. Then less than a year later that damned telegram came from the War Department telling us Johnny was gone. After that, my Meggie just quit on me. I couldn't do anything but watch her die from a broken heart."

J.J. fumbled around, digging in his hip pocket for a handkerchief. He looked up gratefully as Trace quietly handed him his.

"Thanks, boy," J.J. muttered, and blew noisily into the cloth as he continued. "There I was, Johnny and baby Megan gone. Then I had to let my Meggie go, too. Hell, yes, I was mad at God. There was no one left to be mad at but Him. Look at what's left of the Malones. You know as well as I that they're a sorry lot. My only other son is a priest. No babies there to carry on the

Malone name. And my daughter Erin is so busy being career person of the year that she has no time for family. Not even time for me."

"What happened to the baby's mother, J.J.?" Trace asked.

J.J. grunted loudly and gave his nose a final blow. "She up and married less than a year after Johnny's death and moved to Europe. I heard several years later that she'd been killed in a plane crash on one of her jet-set vacations. They're all gone. But…" His eyes darkened, and tears pooled again. J. J. Malone suddenly looked his age. "I've still got you, boy," he said huskily. "And now maybe my little Megan. You go to Texas, Trace. You find my Megan and bring her home."

"You read the letter, J.J.," Trace warned. "Her name's not Megan anymore. It's Honor, Honor O'Brien. And she may not want to come."

"You go find her," J.J. ordered gruffly, and pulled himself shakily to his feet, trying to balance on his injured leg without crutches.

Trace bent down, retrieved the crutches from beneath the chair legs, and handed them to his boss.

"I'll go," he promised. "And I'll find her. I'll even bring her back. But no one can say if she'll stay, sir," he warned. "No one." And then he was gone.

J.J. turned, and hobbled to the fireplace where a large, framed portrait hung in a conspicuous place of honor above the massive mantel.

"Well, Meggie love," J.J. spoke. "We're finally going to get her back. I just wish to God you were here to share my joy."

The laughing face stared silently back at the man beneath the portrait. The artist had captured to perfection her spirit, as well as her likeness. Masses of inky black curls tumbled carelessly around her face and neck, and the stormy gray eyes mirrored the sky outside. The turned-up nose and generous lips framing her laugh highlighted the single dimple at the left corner of her mouth. Mary Margaret Malone would remain, captured in spirit by the stroke of brush and oils, and stay on canvas, as she did in J.J.'s heart, forever young.

The numbers faded and blurred on the ledger page. Honor pinched the bridge of her nose, refusing to give in to the constant threat of tears that hovered behind her eyelids. They'd been there for almost a month now. Ever since her mother's death, she'd been fighting this near-overwhelming feeling of hopelessness. How was she going to get through the rest of her life without Charlie? She was all Honor had known for the first twenty-six years of her life. Now, Honor O'Brien had to figure out how to survive the rest of her life without her.

The busy sounds of customers coming and going filtered in through the office door where Honor was trying to work. Trucks and cars continually pulled in and out of the best-known all-night truck stop in west Texas. Charlie's had a reputation for the best mesquite barbecue in Texas. At least, that was what the truckers claimed. They were always ready to haul a load going down that way. If they did, it was a sure bet that they'd be stopping at Charlie's for some good eating, a chance to rest, and a visit with the two prettiest women in Texas.

Shock at the news of Charlotte "Charlie" O'Brien's illness and subsequent death had brought an outpouring of sympathy and support for her daughter, Honor. It had helped to know so many cared, but all the words in the world weren't going to get Honor through her grief. That strength had to come from Honor herself. And she was trying. It was just harder than she'd imagined.

She totaled the last column of figures, entered them in the ledger, and then slammed the book shut with a sigh of satisfaction. As usual, Charlie's was very much in the black. With her usual diligence and a little hard work, Honor would be able to live quite comfortably. Thanks to her mother's foresight, money was not a problem.

Suddenly, Honor realized the normal restaurant noise had ceased outside her office. An ominous silence sent her toward the door to investigate. And then the familiar strains of "The Tennessee Waltz" drifted faintly into the quiet.

"Oh, no!" Honor moaned, and stepped slowly into the shadowed hallway leading into the main dining area of Charlie's.

The place was nearly full, yet not a sound could be heard, except the music coming from the old jukebox in the corner of the room. People watched, puzzled yet honoring the sudden silence, while some regulars understood. Honor swallowed a sob at the sight of the middle-aged trucker crying unashamedly as he stared blindly at the flat black disk going round and round before his unseeing eyes.

She took a deep breath, rubbed a weary hand across her eyes and willed them not to tear, then started toward him, dreading the confrontation, yet knowing it couldn't be avoided. Slipping quickly through the maze of tables and booths, ignoring the stares and the whispers of concern, she hurried toward her uncle Rusty.

Russell Dawson was not actually her uncle, but he'd been her mother's suitor for as many years as she could remember. Rusty had proposed to Charlotte O'Brien on an average of six times a year. Finally he'd realized that Charlie had let him as far into her life a she ever would and loved her enough to take what he could get. He became the intermittent father figure in Honor's life. Every time he came through their area, he would announce his arrival with three long blasts of his truck horn. Charlie would come running, waving and laughing, and wind up being danced between the maze of tables to whatever tune was playing on the jukebox. The merriment would always end with "The Tennessee Waltz."

"Rusty," Honor said quietly, as she came up behind the stocky, balding man.

He was wearing his usual garb of blue jeans, two sizes too small, that rode beneath a pudgy stomach. His blue plaid western shirt was tucked haphazardly into the dangling waistband of the denim pants. And as always, the same shiny black cowboy boots, so well worn the pointy toes tended to curl upward. Honor was a good two inches taller than his five-foot-ten-inch stature, and she loved him dearly.

"Uncle Rusty," she repeated, and caught back a sob at the look of utter desolation in his eyes.

"How am I gonna make it without her, honey?" he asked hoarsely. He turned and patted Honor awkwardly on the arm.

"I don't know, Uncle Rusty," she answered shakily. "But I do know this. Momma would have a fit if she could see us now, feeling all sorry for ourselves."

Rusty blinked. He nodded, took a deep breath, pulled

a handkerchief from his pocket, and blew loudly. His pale-blue eyes twinkled at the noise, as he stuffed his handkerchief back in his pocket.

"You're right, girl. Damn, but Charlie would be havin' a fit now. Well, sweetheart, I wonder if you'd do your old uncle Rusty a favor?"

"You don't have to ask. You know I will," Honor answered softly, and kissed the bristly side of his unshaven cheek.

"Well, now," he said gruffly, trying hard not to break down again in front of all the silent witnesses to his misery. "Would you do me the honor of sharing this last dance? I hate to let the music go to waste."

Honor fought back the rising tide of despair. Her smile was frozen on her face as she stepped into his arms and gave herself up to the music and her uncle Rusty's need.

In and out they wound between the clusters of seated customers, dipping and swaying in familiar waltz fashion to the soulful strains of the familiar tune. More than one customer, aware of the significance of the dance, buried their faces in their hands.

Trace Logan pulled into the dusty parking lot of the busy restaurant, crawled wearily out of his rented car, and entered the air-conditioned comfort of the dining area just in time to see the drama unfold before his eyes.

His gut had twisted into a painful knot of shock as he saw a tall, leggy young woman enter the dining area from the back of the building. All he had was a glimpse as she wound her way toward the shorter, older man at the jukebox, but it had been enough to get his attention. Every place God had intended woman to curve had been generously exaggerated to perfection on her elegant height. The form-fitting blue jeans she wore, as well as the soft, clingy pink shirt that barely met the tiny waistband of her pants, added to her womanly aura.

Unaware he was holding his breath, he watched in fascination as the dance began. Suddenly, his breath escaped in a rush as his starving lungs yanked him back to sanity. He stepped backward and bumped into one of the bar stools. It met the back of his legs as he sank down on the leather-cushioned seat, unable to take his eyes from the dancers.

An odd, unreasonable anger made his mouth twist into a thin line of objection. He resented the older man's right to hold her that intimately as they waltzed between the seated patrons of Charlie's. The emotion startled him and made him take a second glance at the girl. What was there about the fleeting look he'd had that had drawn him so quickly into her spell?

And then the music stopped. Honor leaned down, hugged her partner gently, and whispered in his ear, "Come on over to the house, I'll fix you your favorite fajitas."

"The invitation will have to wait, honey," Rusty replied. "I shouldn't have taken time to come this far, but I couldn't help it. I have a load of perishables due in Los Angeles by tomorrow night. It'll take some truckin' to get there on time as it is. Can I take a rain check?"

"You know it," she answered. "And I'd better see your face back here soon or I'll come looking for you, Uncle Rusty."

"I promise," he said quietly. "You're still my little sweetheart, even if my best girl is gone." He cleared his throat, blinked watery eyes, and kissed her soft cheek. "Thanks for the dance, Honor." Then he walked quietly out the door, unaware of the curious look the tall man seated at the bar gave him.

Honor fought down a rising tide of tears as she walked quickly toward the heavyset man behind the bar.

"Hank, I want that damned song taken out of the jukebox. Call the service man now. I can't take any more surprises like that."

An overwhelming pain in her throat sent her stumbling into Trace's outstretched arms.

She didn't see the look of total shock come in his dark-brown eyes, nor did she see him struggling with words that refused to come from his lips. She was too busy trying to get outside into the anonymity of approaching nightfall. She wasn't going to let all these people see her cry.

"Excuse me," she mumbled softly, unaware of her key ring that fell at his feet, and pushed her way out of Trace's arms into the Texas night.

His arms felt empty as he watched her disappear through the door. Before his world had been turned upside down. He couldn't believe what he'd just seen. His search was over before it had begun. He would have to look no farther for the woman known as Honor O'Brien. The woman he'd just held in his arms was the living image of the picture that hung over J. J. Malone's fireplace in the library. Either that was the missing granddaughter or he'd just seen a ghost.

He shook himself, suddenly aware that he'd just let her walk out of his life, and started to follow her when his shoe kicked something metal. He looked down, startled by the sound, and reached for the ring of keys lying on the floor. He grabbed them and dashed out into the arrival of night.

She was standing to the right of one of the big eighteen-wheelers, using it as a shield. He could hear her sobs, and the utter desolation tore at his heart. If she was this devastated at the loss of her mother, and he could only assume this was the cause of her sadness, what was his news going to do to her? He didn't know how to approach her, or even what to say. Damn J.J. for sending him to do this! He didn't want this woman to hate him, nor did he want to frighten her. Suddenly, the approval of a total stranger was very important to the rest of Trace Logan's life.

"Miss!" he called out, as he walked toward her.

She looked up, startled and embarrassed at being discovered. But she couldn't seem to stop the flow of tears that had finally been released. A twinge of apprehension surfaced as the tall, dark man approached. He was obviously a stranger. Not many Texas workingmen wore such casual clothes with as much aplomb as this man.

The soft fabric of his dark slacks moved with the stride of his long, muscled legs. His shirt outlined the finely toned structure of his upper body. His face was shadowed in the quickly disappearing light, but she could see very defined, very appealing angles and planes and a hint of stubborn chin. A straight, perfectly formed nose sat just above the sexiest mouth she'd ever seen. His firm, shapely lips were twisted in an expression of concern. She stopped him with a motion.

"Do I know you?" she asked, and wiped helplessly at the tears that continued to flow down her face.

"No."

His voice came softly through the lowering darkness, straight into her heart.

"What do you want?" she continued, suddenly afraid of being caught alone, outside, with a total stranger.

"You dropped your keys."

He held them toward her and knew he'd frightened her with his uninvited presence.

"Oh," she said quietly, and held out her hand. The keys dropped into her palm with a familiar jangle. She breathed a quick sigh of relief as he took a step backward.

"Are you a nice man?" she asked, surprising herself by the need to keep him within her reach.

"My family thinks so," he said with a grin in his voice. And then he watched a strange, lost expression come over her face.

It was the word *family* that had done it. At that moment, Honor felt unable to cope with anything else alone.

"Good," she said with a choked sob as she stepped forward into Trace's arms. "I don't want anyone I know to see me cry."

His quick reflexes caught her, but he couldn't have spoken a word to save his soul. Shock warred with dismay, and quickly flared into a possessive feeling that scared the hell out of him. He knew in his heart, he wasn't going to be able to turn this one loose.

Honor refused to listen to the reasoning and common sense telling her what she already knew. She was doing the most foolish thing she'd ever done in her life. She'd just thrown herself into this handsome stranger's arms, with no thought of safety or reason, and had never felt so safe and comforted in her life. She let herself absorb his strength and reveled in the softly murmured words of assurance he was whispering in her ear. It was going to be all right.

Trace wouldn't let himself think of how she felt in his arms. He refused to acknowledge that she fit perfectly into every curve of his body as if she'd been molded to size. Her head rested just beneath his chin and he inhaled the faint but lingering scent of her shampoo. It was as fresh and inviting as the woman he held. How in hell was he ever going to get past this feeling? How was he ever going to be able to do what J. J. Malone had sent him here to do? He didn't want to think about the look of betrayal he knew she would wear when he had to tell her the truth.

"I'm sorry," Honor managed to whisper, as she pulled away in embarrassment. "I don't even know your name."

"It's Trace, Trace Logan," he answered softly, and wisely let Honor regain a measure of her composure.

"Trace? As in 'disappeared without a'?" Honor questioned, and smiled through her tears. She was desperately struggling to regain her sense of self and sanity.

Trace watched in fascination as he saw, even in the darkening shadows, the single dimple appear at the left corner of her mouth. He had to force himself to remember what she'd asked.

"Yes," he finally managed to answer. "As in disappeared without a trace. But it's actually a shortened version of my full name, Tracey. I just don't ever use it."

"Why not?" Honor asked. "I think Tracey is a perfectly acceptable name."

"Not when the name Richard precedes it," Trace drawled. "It's not easy being called Dick Tracey all your life. After five fights in as many weeks, my sixth-grade teacher wisely started calling me Trace. My family followed suit, and I've been Trace ever since."

"Well, Trace Logan," Honor whispered softly, as complete darkness finally swallowed them. "I want to thank you for letting me borrow your broad chest and strong shoulders. I desperately needed a leaning post, and I can say without hesitation, you were the most comforting stranger I've ever hugged. Thank you for being so considerate, even if you don't understand."

Trace started to speak, when he felt her lips at the corner of his mouth. His head turned like a magnet, needing to capture the imagined sweetness of her kiss. But he was a heartbeat too late as she sighed, touched his arm in appreciation, and disappeared into the night.

He meant to call out, but he forgot what he wanted to say. Instead he let her walk away into the Texas night, and stood for many minutes in silence as he struggled with a multitude of conflicting emotions.

He finally pulled himself together, fumbled in his own pocket for keys, and headed for his car, food forgotten in his need to get back to the motel room in nearby Odessa, Texas, and call his boss. He didn't know what to say other than he'd found Honor O'Brien.

Chapter 2

Trace walked into his motel room, slammed the door shut behind him, and slipped the safety chain through the slot. He threw the room key on the dresser and then sat down wearily on the bed. He ran his hands through his wind-blown hair in angry frustration and heartily wished he'd not been the one to open that damned letter. This was going to be nothing but trouble. Hell, it already was. The first woman he'd been attracted to in years, and he was going to ruin it with a phone call.

He looked at his watch, knew J.J. would be waiting for his call no matter what the time, and picked up the phone. He answered on the first ring.

"I found her," Trace stated shortly, allowing no hint of his personal involvement to cloud the issue. He listened to the old man's excited voice and then frowned at himself in the mirror as he continued. "Yes, it's her.

There can be no mistake about that. She's tall like you, and she's your wife's living double. I've never seen any two people look more alike."

He listened again, allowing J.J.'s excited orders to sink in before he continued.

"Remember what I told you before I left, J.J. She's not going to receive this news as gladly as you have. I can tell you for a fact that she's still grieving very much for a mother she obviously held dear. She's not going to like what I tell her. Hell, she may not even believe me. I don't know where to start. Just give me a few days. I'll let you know more later. Yeah, sure," he answered, in reluctant response to his boss's orders. "I'll keep in touch."

He hung up the phone, wearily began to undress, and headed for the shower, ignoring his empty stomach's complaints.

The porch swing creaked in a repetitive rhythm as Honor watched the steady stream of customers going through Charlie's.

Her home was just across the wide, graveled parking lot, far enough away for a little privacy, but close enough to dash over if the need arose. The staff at Charlie's was just like family. They'd worked for her mother for years.

There wasn't that much work to be had in the middle of nowhere, which was more or less where Charlie's existed. The closest town was Odessa to the north, and a little bit north and east was Big Springs. The towns were few and far between in west Texas, as were the homes. It was ranching land. The only other thing that had managed to make its mark in the area was the presence of the oil industry, whose fortunes rose and fell with predictable irregularity.

If there was a job to be had out here, it was kept with faithful attendance.

Honor loved the immense expanse of flat country landscaped with tumbleweeds and the ever-present clumps of sturdy mesquite that held on to its meager existence with fierce determination. Little else, except people, grew well here.

The night breeze felt cool against her freshly show-ered skin. Honor sighed, listlessly dragging her bare feet on the redwood floor of her front porch as she let the gentle wind rock the swing. She was unwilling to go back inside to the waiting emptiness.

Her breakdown earlier this evening had not come as a surprise. It had been long overdue. But she couldn't forget the tall, dark stranger, nor how she'd walked into his arms with no warning. It was so unlike her. And it had felt so right. She wondered if she'd ever see Trace Logan again and then scoffed at her own foolishness. She didn't know a thing about him; not even where he was from. He could even be married. She'd hardly given him a chance to refuse her cry for help.

Honor sighed as the phone inside the house began to ring. The only time it rang at this time of night was when she was needed at the restaurant. She hurried in-side, walking confidently through the unlit rooms with the sureness born of long years of familiarity.

"Hello." Her answer was soft and weary as she fum-bled for the light switch on the wall beside the phone and then forgot what she'd been about to do as the man's deep voice pulled at her memory. Instead, she stood qui-etly in the dark silence and listened to her heart race.

"Honor O'Brien?"

"Yes?" she answered hesitantly.

"This is Trace Logan. Remember me? From the parking lot?"

How could she forget him? Honor's breath caught in her throat. She took a deep, shaky breath before she spoke.

"Yes, I remember you," she said. "How did you know my name?"

There was a short silence before Trace managed to answer. "I asked someone at Charlie's," he said. "They also told me why you were crying."

"Oh!" came her quiet response.

"I know it's late. But I couldn't sleep. I kept thinking of you and... I just felt I needed to call. Are you all right now?"

Honor felt a smile beginning inside her heart. It quickly spread to her face as she gripped the phone tighter and held it a little closer to her ear.

"Yes. I'm all right. Thank you for asking."

There was an awkward silence and then Trace started to speak when Honor interrupted him with a question that made him nearly drop the phone.

"Are you for real, Trace Logan?"

"What do you mean?" he asked sharply. Surely she hadn't already discovered the true reason for his presence. A sick feeling pulled at the pit of his stomach.

"I mean, are you really this caring and this nice? Or do you have an ulterior motive?" Then she asked sharply in her usual forthright manner, "You aren't married are you?"

There was a quiet chuckle at the other end of the phone before Trace answered.

"Which question shall I answer first?" he asked with a smile in his voice.

Honor blushed. But it was dark, and she was alone, and it didn't matter anyway. She would still have asked the questions in the same manner.

"Well," Trace continued, "I don't know about nice and caring. Some of my business competitors would swear I'm not very nice. But I think they're just jealous."

Honor smiled.

"And," Trace said, "I really do want to know if you feel better. And no, I'm not married. Not now. Not ever." Trace took a deep breath and blurted out before Honor had time to ask any more dangerous questions, "Now, it's my turn. Will you have breakfast with me tomorrow? I find I'll be staying a bit longer than planned." He waited anxiously for her response.

The lift in her voice was evident. "Yes. I'd love to have breakfast with you," Honor answered, shocked at herself for wondering what it would be like to have breakfast *every* morning with Trace Logan…for the rest of her life. "But you better not be one of those 'bran and fiber' fellows. Charlie's specializes in the best home-made biscuits in Texas."

Trace burst out laughing. He couldn't help it. She was so engaging and so honest. He'd never met anyone who came across as openly as Honor O'Brien.

"It's a date," he finally managed to say past the last of his laugh. "What time?"

"You just get up and get here," Honor said. "I'll be waiting."

Trace's heart skipped a beat as her words registered in his brain. Dear Lord! He'd love to know someone like Honor would always be waiting.

"Great! See you in the morning," Trace said.

He knew he was just going to make matters worse by getting on a personal level with Honor. But heaven help him, he couldn't stop himself.

Honor hugged the phone to her breast long after Trace had disconnected, reluctant to sever the nonexistent link. She didn't know where this breakfast was going to lead, but at this moment Honor felt it was the most important meal of her life.

She was pouring coffee at one of the tables. Laughing at something one of the customers had just said when Trace walked into the restaurant. She was even prettier than he'd remembered. And in the light of day Honor looked younger than he knew her to be. That glorious black jumble of curls was pulled away from her face and fastened at the neck with a single strand of red ribbon. She wore little to no makeup. Her bright-red sundress stood her out in the crowd like a cherry on top of an ice-cream sundae. When she walked, the short, flared skirt wrapped teasingly around and between those long, long legs, and Trace felt his pulse accelerate. He furiously rejected the fantasies that popped into his mind. He couldn't afford to let them in. It might prove embarrassing in more ways than one. He still had to walk across the room.

Honor looked up and saw him standing at the entrance to the dining room. The smile on her face was instantaneous, as was that single dimple at the corner of her mouth. Trace watched, fascinated, as she hurried toward him.

"Hi!" she said.

If she had any sense she knew she should at least be

embarrassed by this meeting. But she couldn't quit looking at him. She'd known last night that he was nice-looking. Even that couldn't be hidden in the night shadows. But she hadn't realized just how striking he really was.

He had to be three or four inches over six feet. That she liked. She had to look down at nearly every man she met. His eyes were somewhere between fudge and chocolate-chip brown. His hair was just about the same thick, rich color and had a slight tendency toward curling. His features were just as she'd remembered. But his lips were not. They were better. She'd never seen a man with such an expressive mouth. She wondered what it would feel like to be kissed by those lips and then felt herself blushing. This had to stop.

"You better be hungry," she said cheerfully, as she grasped him by the arm and began pulling him toward an empty booth. "I am. I've been up for hours and I'd hate to embarrass myself by eating more than you."

Trace found himself laughing again at her exuberance and amazing lack of pretense. He couldn't remember when he'd been out with a woman who would even mention the fact that she'd ever experienced hunger pangs. Most of them were on perennial diets.

"Bring on the biscuits, woman," he teased, as he sat down in the brown leather booth. "I couldn't sleep for thinking of them."

Honor grinned. "Just let me turn in our order and tell Hank I'll be off the floor for a while. Do you want eggs, sausage, bacon?"

"Anything handy, just well done," he answered.

"This is Texas, mister. It doesn't come any other way."

She left him with a smile on his lips and hunger for more than breakfast warring with his good sense.

The meal was great. At least Trace thought it was. He couldn't really have said how it tasted. He ate everything put in front of him and didn't remember chewing a bite. All he could see was Honor's face and Honor's smile. He let her talk. Sometimes listening. Sometimes not. Sometimes just watching the animation of that beautiful face.

It was when she started asking personal questions about him and why he was here that Trace began to pay closer attention to what he was saying. This was where it was going to get tricky.

"So," Honor asked, "what brings you to this part of Texas?"

"My boss sent me to locate someone with whom he'd lost contact," Trace said.

"Who's your boss? And where are you from? It's obvious from your speech as well as your clothes that Texas is not home," Honor teased. "You haven't said 'y'all' or 'whut fer' even once."

Trace grinned. "I'm from Colorado," he answered. "I work for a man named J. J. Malone, of Malone Industries. I guess you could say I'm his second in command."

Honor raised her eyebrows in appreciation of his title, and then a look of pleased remembrance appeared on her face.

"My mother was from Colorado," she cried. "Colorado Springs, actually."

"It's a small world," Trace said quietly. "So am I."

This was beginning to get difficult. Now, anything he said was going to be construed at a later date as prying or lying. Either way, he was going to come out a loser.

"So, your mother was from Colorado," Trace remarked. "Do you have any other family here, or are they all still back in Colorado?"

"My mother was an orphan," Honor remarked, and then she smiled. "But I have Uncle Rusty. He's not really my uncle, but we claim each other anyway. And, I have more friends here than you could shake a stick at. That's Texan for a whole lot," she explained with a grin.

"I guess your father is dead?" Trace asked casually.

"Yes," she said, a sad, lost expression darkening her gray eyes. "He died in Vietnam, before he and Momma could ever marry. He didn't even know I existed."

Trace nodded sympathetically, while trying valiantly to hide his shock. So much of the story she was telling him was the actual truth. He wondered just how much of it was fabrication and how much of Charlotte O'Brien's life had run parallel to Honor's real parents. They'd probably never know.

"That's a shame," Trace said quietly. "*I* would have hated not knowing you existed, Honor. The luckiest day of my life was yesterday when I pulled into this parking lot."

For once, Honor was speechless. All she could manage was a blush and a silly, embarrassed grin.

"That's very generous of you," she finally managed. "I doubt very many strange women throw themselves at you in such fashion. I will say thank you once more, and then if you want to stay my friend, don't remind me again of how pushy I was. Momma would have had a fit. She didn't raise me like that, I swear."

"Looks to me like she did a pretty good job," Trace teased, delighted to watch that single dimple coming and going at the side of her face. "Do you look like your mother?" He hated himself for the questions he knew he was obligated to ask.

"No." She wiped absently at a damp ring her water glass had left on the tabletop. "Momma always said I looked like my father's side of the family. But because they didn't ever marry, she didn't have pictures. I used to get the feeling that they might not have approved of her. She rarely talked about her life before Texas and Charlie's."

Trace nodded. Everything fit. Charlotte's reticence to speak of her past. Her claim that Honor looked like the other side of the family. And conveniently estranged so that she never had to produce proof of their existence. Why did all this evidence make his heart hurt?

"When do you have to leave?" Honor asked. She hated the thought, but it was evident.

"Soon," he said quietly. Then he surprised himself as well as Honor as he reached across the table and grasped her hand.

"You said you came to locate someone for your boss," Honor repeated. "Have you found him?" She couldn't take her eyes off the path he was tracing on her knuckles.

"Yes," Trace answered. "I found who I was looking for." Then he quickly changed the subject. "What's your favorite thing to do?"

She answered with no hesitation. "Eat pizza and dance."

Once again, Trace's delighted laugh echoed in the dining room.

"If you can stand a busman's holiday, I would love to take you out to eat tonight. You'll have to name the place since I'm a stranger to the area. And, I don't know about the dancing…but I'm game to try."

"Pick me up about eight o'clock," Honor said, barely masking the urge to clap her hands in delight. "We're not far from Odessa. There's a great pizza place on the south side of town. After we eat, I'll show you how Texans spend Saturday night."

"Is that a promise or a warning?" Trace asked with a smile.

"All I have to say is, wear comfortable shoes."

Honor looked up at the influx of new customers pulling into the parking lot. "Well," she said with a smile and a sigh. "I better get back to work."

As she scooted out of the booth she turned abruptly. The skirt of her red dress flared, then wrapped around her shapely figure before it came to rest above her knees. Trace tried not to think of the tempting shape of the body beneath that dress.

"See you tonight?" she asked again, hating to break the merry mood they'd created.

'It's a promise," Trace said softly, and watched the joy in her eyes as she turned and walked away.

He was going to regret it, but he wanted one more night with Honor O'Brien before he had to tell her that she didn't exist. He quickly left Charlie's for his next destination, which was back to the lawyer who'd first directed him to Honor. He was going to need all the help he could get to finish the job ahead.

Honor was waiting on her front porch when she saw Trace's blue rental car turn off the highway into the parking area of Charlie's. Nightfall was only a thought away as she bounded off her porch and ran across the graveled lot to meet him.

Trace parked, opened the door, and had just emerged when he heard the sound of footsteps behind him. He turned to see Honor running toward him, her hand in the air, a smile of welcome on her face. Words were beyond him. He knew that if he went blind tomorrow, it would be enough to remember the sight of Honor coming to him with such joy.

He forced back the warning signals going off in his brain. This wasn't a wise thing to do, but he was operating on feelings, not good sense. For one of the few times in his life, Trace Logan let his heart overrule his head.

"Are you ready?" Honor asked breathlessly, and threw her arms around Trace's neck in a friendly, exuberant hug of welcome.

Trace choked on his speech as his arms tightened convulsively around her. She felt even better than she smelled, and she smelled heavenly.

"What perfume are you wearing?" he whispered in her ear, as he buried his face in the tumult of her curls.

"Passion," she said softly, and then leaned back to look him carefully in the face. "Don't you like it?"

"My God!" Trace muttered, and pulled Honor's arms from around his neck before his body betrayed him and embarrassed them both. "Like it?" he continued, and quickly seated her in the car. "It should probably be sold in a plain brown wrapper. On you, woman, it's dynamite."

"That's what it's supposed to be," she said, then grinned as she watched Trace's shaky hands miss the keyhole of the car's ignition. "Let's eat."

Trace smiled, rolled his eyes heavenward, and headed for Odessa in a cloud of dust.

They'd demolished all but one piece of the largest and best pepperoni pizza Trace had ever eaten. He was past being surprised at Honor's lack of pretense and didn't even offer to share the last slice. He knew better. He held up his hands in defeat and pushed it toward her. She didn't blink an eye as it went the way of the others she'd enjoyed.

"That was so good," Honor said. She sighed, pushed back her plate, and grabbed a handful of paper napkins to remove what was left of the pizza from her face and hands. "I haven't been here since just before Momma got sick."

The familiarity of the checkered tablecloths and dripped wax candles in ancient wine bottles reminded Honor of happier times. Tears brimmed.

Trace didn't miss the fact that her emotions were overwhelming her. "I know this is hard, Honor. But I'm glad you're letting me share this time with you."

He couldn't stop the quick, instantaneous feeling of panic that hit him in the gut every time her mother was mentioned. It didn't matter how many times he told himself that he was doing this out of love for J. J. Malone. It was only a matter of time before he had to confess his true reasons for being here. And when he did, everything that had bloomed between them was going to die.

Ignoring his guilty conscience, he grabbed the check and pulled her to her feet.

"Come on, woman. You've got a promise to keep. No more sad thoughts tonight. You promised to show me a Texas Saturday night."

* * *

The music was loud. Trace thought it was country, but at this decibel level it was hard to tell. Honor included Trace in the friendly chaos as she greeted old friends in the smoky darkness of Tilley's Texas Two-Step. It had the usual assortment of rowdy customers, a busy bar, and a better than mediocre band playing what Trace could only assume were the crowd favorites. Western music wasn't his favorite easy listening, but he was about to get a crash course in country music appreciation.

Honor grinned at the look of culture shock on Trace's face and leaned over, practically yelling in his ear just to be heard.

"What do you think?" she shouted, and watched his struggle with an answer that wouldn't insult her. She couldn't resist the laugh that bubbled up her throat and casually patted his arm as she pulled him toward an empty table. "It's all right," she yelled, "I'll ask you again later."

He was swept up into the most exuberant, exhausting, enchanting night he'd ever experienced. Honor patiently walked him through a round of dancing called Cotton-eyed Joe. It was performed with much yelling and cheering from the couples that stepped and scooted around and around the darkened dance floor.

Just as Trace felt he was finally getting the hang of the dance, it was over. Then she pulled him into another, and another, until he forgot what he was supposed to be doing with his feet and concentrated on how good it felt to be constantly holding Honor O'Brien close.

When the music slowed to a more sedate, familiar strain, Trace pulled Honor closely into his arms, ignored the persistent cowboy who kept trying to cut in, and swung her into the shadowy corners of the dance floor.

"This is more like it," he whispered in her ear. Her soft curves pressed against his chest as his hands slid below her waist and splayed in dangerous abandon across the flare of her hips.

Honor's heart pounded. But it was not from exhaustion. It was from the intense feeling of being in Trace Logan's arms. She could feel his heartbeat pulsing beneath her ear. It raced beneath her fingers as she slid her arms around his neck. Her body flowed against him as the music took them where they dared not go alone.

Trace felt her shiver and pulled her closer, stifling a moan as she acquiesced with no hesitation.

"Are you cold?" he asked softly, sliding his hands up her back and nesting them in the damp tangle of hair.

"No," she whispered in his ear. "Just..." she struggled for the right words "...just happy, I guess."

"Oh, honey," Trace moaned, and couldn't stop himself from the urge to taste the happiness.

His movements were slow, but Honor knew before he did that he was going to kiss her. She tilted her head just the tiniest bit and met his intentions with softly parted lips.

He swallowed her sigh as their initial touch melted into an electrifying caress of sensuality. Her response to his kiss was just as open and giving as her response to life. Trace tried to block out the images that flooded his mind of how generous and giving Honor would be at making love. He felt his body harden and his knees go weak. He pulled her tighter into his arms as the final notes of the last dance softly disappeared.

Honor knew what Trace was feeling. And she knew

that if he could see into her heart, an answering emotion would be lying there in wait.

"I guess it's time for me to take you home," Trace said, as he reluctantly released his claim on Honor's mouth.

He watched her blink in confusion and then look up at him with such a trusting expression, it made him want to cry. Tomorrow she was going to hate the sound of his name. He didn't think he was going to be able to survive that.

It was hard for her to answer; to find the words to express the joy this night had given her. Finally she spoke. "This has been the best night of my life, Trace Logan. I wish it never had to end."

She was puzzled by the expression that swept over his features, darkening his eyes with regret...and fear?

"Me, too," Trace growled. "Come on, before I forget I'm supposed to be a gentleman about these things." He pulled her gently toward the door.

The drive home was short and silent. Each of them seemed lost in the magic of their first date, both wondering if what they were feeling was shared or imagined.

It wasn't until Trace pulled to a stop in front of her darkened house that he forced himself to think of the consequences of continuing this night. He knew it was impossible.

Honor sat quietly in the shared silence of the car's dark interior and waited for whatever else the night would bring. She didn't want it to end, but she knew it had to.

"Come on, honey," Trace said softly. "I'll walk you to your door. I don't like to think of you entering a dark house alone."

She let him lead her silently up the porch steps,

handed him her key, and waited patiently as he turned it in the lock. She reached around in front of him as he pushed the front door inward.

"I'll get the light," she said quietly.

But Trace deftly caught her hand and stopped her.

He didn't speak. For a moment, neither of them moved. Then she was in his arms. Trace took one step in slow motion as he pulled them inside the privacy of her home and took the breath from her lungs with his kiss.

She burned. His mouth scorched, his hands branded. Suddenly, his kiss was not enough. She leaned back against the wall and pulled Trace into the ache he'd created.

Her soft little moan sent Trace's hands sliding down her back. He cupped the curve of her hips and pulled her fiercely against him, grinding her into the swelling pain in his own lower body. He knew he needed to stop, but the sensation of holding this magnificent woman so tenderly was driving reason out of his mind. He wanted everything Honor would share with him, but it was not his to ask. Not after what he was going to do to her tomorrow.

It was the thought of tomorrow that finally made him come to his senses, and he released his hold on her mouth and body with an angry rush of breath. Their foreheads met as he spoke harshly into the darkness.

"I shouldn't have done that, but I'm not going to apologize, woman. So don't ask me." He cupped her face in his hands and whispered against her lips, "Honor, these have been the most special two days of my life. Whether you believe me or not is immaterial. I can't put into words what I'm feeling. I don't even know if there are words to fit. But I do know this. No matter what else you will ever think of me, you have to know that I'm telling you the truth. I don't have the right to tell you what I'm feeling just now. Maybe tomorrow..." He let his words trail into the silence.

Honor was slightly puzzled by the strange, almost fatalistic tone of his voice, but she interpreted his reticence as consideration. After all they'd only just met. She could hardly believe that was true. She felt as if she'd known him all her life. But it was the mention of tomorrow that reminded her.

"I don't know when you have to leave," she whispered, and let her hand rest on his chest above his heartbeat. "But I hope you don't leave without saying good-bye. These past two days have been more than special for me as well. I have to go to Big Springs in the morning. My mother's lawyer called earlier today and asked me to drop in. I'll be glad when all this will and estate business is finished. Each time I am forced to discuss it, it just brings back all the feelings of loss. I guess time will help that too, but..." She shrugged in the darkness and Trace felt the fragile curve of her shoulders as she whispered, "You know what I mean."

Suddenly he had a horrible, dragging fear. He didn't want to turn her loose. He didn't want tomorrow to come. What if they disappeared tonight? What if he never went back to Colorado? He knew when she walked through the lawyer's door tomorrow, he was going to watch their future and her trust die. He couldn't face the thought.

"Oh, honey," he moaned, and pulled her back into his arms, hugging her desperately. "Remember! No matter what else happens between us, you are more special to me than you'll ever know."

Honor frowned in the darkness at the strangeness of his remarks. They sounded so final. When she thought to question him further, he turned and walked away. She started to call him back and then she stopped herself. Enough had passed between them for one night. Tomorrow was another day. She'd face it when the sun came up and not a moment sooner.

She watched Trace's car lights come on, watched him back out of the parking lot amidst the busy Saturday traffic at Charlie's, and then closed and locked the door.

"Yes, I've seen the lawyer," Trace growled into the phone, as he stared blindly at the ceiling above his bed. "She's going in tomorrow. Thinks it has something to do with her mother's estate."

"You sound mad, boy," J.J. muttered.

"You're right. I do sound mad. I *am.* I don't like being deceptive with someone, especially her. Hell yes, I like her." Trace shouted into the receiver. "How could I not? She's beautiful, honest, and trusting, and come tomorrow, she's going to hate my guts. Yeah, right," he muttered, as he hung up the phone. "I'll get a good night's sleep…but not in this lifetime."

J.J. frowned as he hung up the phone, and then an odd, engaging smile spread over his face. Wouldn't it be something if his granddaughter fell in love with Trace? It sounded as if Trace was halfway there already. He rubbed his aching leg and cursed roundly at the fates for throwing him off that damned horse. If it hadn't happened he wouldn't be waiting while someone else did his work. *Oh, well,* he thought, as he lay back down on his bed, *it'll all work out.* He'd waited too long to be disappointed now. Maybe by this time next week his granddaughter would be here where she belonged.

Chapter 3

The parking lot was full at the business plaza where Rolly Hawkins's law office was located. Honor kept one eye on the flow of traffic and another on the possibility of a vacant parking space as she made a second turn through the area. She saw an opening and turned the wheel of her shiny black Cougar before someone else beat her to it.

It was hot and windy. Not even a remote chance of rain teased the near-white cloudless sky as Honor dumped her car keys in her purse, slung it over her shoulder, and headed for his office. This visit was still a puzzle. She couldn't imagine there being anything left to sign. She thought she'd finished with all the paperwork weeks ago.

The secretary looked up, then smiled broadly as she recognized the approaching client.

"Honor! It's good to see you. Where did you get that

great outfit? I love it! I'd get one like it except I'm afraid my broad rear end and short legs wouldn't do it justice."

She looked longingly at the loose, flowing legs of the black-and-white striped linen slacks and the voluptuous curves barely hidden beneath Honor's soft, white blouse. She sighed loudly and rolled her eyes, exaggerating her distress.

Honor laughed and then replied, "Sometimes being tall isn't all that great, Judy. It's difficult to get romantic when the best view you have of your date is watching him go bald."

"Honey, you're a caution," Judy laughed, and then buzzed Rolly Hawkins's office. "Honor O'Brien is here, sir."

"Send her in! Send her in!" boomed a loud, raucous voice.

They smiled their good-byes as Honor walked into the inner office.

"Come on in here, girl," Rolly Hawkins said, as he greeted Honor with a hug and a peck on the cheek. He had to stretch, but he managed nicely. He never passed up a chance to kiss a pretty female. And he'd known Honor and her mother for years.

"Mr. Hawkins," Honor said. She returned the greeting and then casually seated herself across the desk from the rotund little man. "I was a bit surprised to get your call yesterday. I thought all this business was finished."

"Yes, well, sometimes dying is complicated," he said with an obscure smile, and looked down at his watch. "We'll get this meeting started just as soon as the gentleman arrives. And," he said loudly as the door to his office opened, "speak of the devil, here he is now!"

Honor turned and looked up at the tall, familiar figure of the man who entered the office. Her smile of amazement quickly disappeared as the sudden thought entered her brain: What possible reason would Trace Logan have for being here? One look at the solemn expression on his face told her she wasn't going to like the answer.

"Mr. Hawkins?" Fright tinged her question.

The look of concern and—pity?—on Rolly's face frightened her even more. She looked back at Trace, desperate for a word that would put her fears to rest. There was nothing but a similar expression of concern along with traces of guilt.

"I don't understand," Honor said, unable to disguise the tremor in her voice as Trace walked over to Rolly Hawkins's desk and handed him a long white envelope.

"Honey," Rolly Hawkins began. "You know I've been your momma's lawyer for years?"

Honor nodded silently and wadded her hands together in her lap. She wouldn't panic. There had to be a simple, logical explanation for Trace's presence. She wouldn't believe he'd be a part of any deception. She just couldn't.

"Just before Charlie went into the hospital the last time, she came to see me," Rolly said.

Honor couldn't mask her look of surprise. She hadn't known about that. She felt oddly betrayed. She thought they'd shared everything.

"And," he continued, "at that time she gave me some papers, including this letter, to be mailed after her death."

Honor swallowed hard, bit the inside of her lip, and stared blindly at a point just over Rolly Hawkins's shoulder. She could see Trace's face out of the corner of her eye. He looked as sick as she felt.

"What does that letter have to do with him?" Honor muttered, and looked accusingly at Trace.

Rolly Hawkins started to explain when Trace interrupted.

"Let me," he pleaded, and walked over to where Honor was seated. Kneeling before the hurt on her face, he grabbed hold of the knot she'd made of her hands.

"The letter Charlotte O'Brien had Mr. Hawkins mail was addressed to my boss, J. J. Malone. He'd be here himself, but he's still recovering from a fall."

Trace continued, his dark eyes pleading silently for Honor's patience and understanding as he worked the knots from her fingers and covered them with his own.

"The man your mother sent the letter to is your grandfather, Honor. I'm here on his behalf."

Her eyes widened and her mouth formed a perfect "O."

"My grandfather! I didn't even know I had one. But why all the secrecy? I knew I was illegitimate. I knew my father had family in Colorado. I don't understand why you're both acting this way. If he doesn't want to acknowledge an illegitimate child, I don't care. I've managed all these years without an extended family. I don't think I'll perish without one now."

Sarcasm tinged the panic she was trying to ignore. She didn't understand their pity.

"Your grandfather has no desire to ignore you," Trace replied vehemently. "Quite the contrary. In fact, he was ecstatic when he received the letter."

"Then, I don't understand," Honor said. Her heart thumped loudly against her breast.

"I know," Trace said softly. "There's no easy way to

tell you. I think the letter will speak for itself." He took the letter from Hawkins's desk and handed it to Honor.

She stared at the envelope in her hands and then back up at the two men who watched her with varying expressions of pity. She glared, took a deep breath, and yanked the letter from the envelope. With shaky fingers, she unfolded the paper and began to read.

Almost instantly tears pooled and began to flow down her flushed cheeks. Her mother's handwriting was unmistakable. It wasn't long before a quick frown pulled a tiny furrow across her forehead.

Trace watched the frown deepen, saw the shock, then the disbelief, then the pain and betrayal take physical possession of her body. She sat in frozen silence as her eyes grew stormy and her mouth tightened in the denial Trace knew would come. It was evident, and it was inevitable.

"This is a lie," Honor said quietly. Too quietly for Trace's peace of mind. "I can't believe you'd be a party to this, Rolly," Honor accused, as her voice grew stronger and her posture stiffened.

She stood up, crumpled the letter into a ball, and threw it at Trace's chest. "As for you, I guess I don't know what you're capable of. After all, you're nothing but a lying stranger."

Her anger enveloped him. At this point he couldn't do or say anything that was going to make her believe him, or make her understand.

"Now, Honor," Rolly Hawkins argued, "you know better than that. I have no reason on God's earth to lie to you. You're like a daughter to me."

"Daughter?" Honor shouted, and leaned over his desk. "That's a good one. I'm not your daughter! And you want me to believe I'm not even Charlotte O'Brien's daughter. If I'm to believe this bull, I don't even know who I am." Her voice broke, and she buried her face in her hands.

Trace leaned down, picked up the crumpled letter, and spoke softly as his heart broke into tiny, painful pieces.

"Your name is Mary Margaret Malone. You were born on July 4, 1965, to Johnny and Madeline Malone. You were snatched from your stroller while on an outing with your nanny when you were nearly eight months old. Your natural parents are dead. You have a grandfather, an aunt, and an uncle in Colorado Springs."

Honor gasped and turned to argue, when Trace's quiet repetition of facts convinced her that this was not a bad dream.

"No," she moaned, as her legs gave way.

Trace caught her just before she hit the floor.

"Here, lay her on the couch," Rolly said, and looked wildly around for help. There was none to be had. "Damn it, I knew this was going to be hard on her. She worshiped Charlie. And," he looked sharply at Trace as he gently lowered Honor's limp body onto the black overstuffed leather couch, "I don't care what you say, Charlotte O'Brien was a damn fine woman!"

"I'm sure she was," Trace said softly. He pulled his handkerchief from his pants pocket. "Here, dampen this for me," he ordered.

The lawyer quickly responded, and then handed the dripping cloth back to Trace.

"But the fact remains," Trace continued. "She stole someone else's child. Unfortunately, the child is the one who's going to have to suffer, and ultimately pay the price of the crime. Look where this has left Honor! Instead of finding a new family, she's just lost her mother twice. And," he muttered to himself, "I'm probably going to be the one she'll blame. In her eyes, I'm the one who tore her world apart. Dammit to hell, anyway," he said, and gently ran the cool damp cloth across her forehead and down her neck.

Honor moaned and her eyelids fluttered. She felt herself coming back through a long black tunnel, and struggled weakly as she fell from it, back into the light. And with the light came the memories. She wanted to cry, but the tears wouldn't come. They were frozen somewhere in her heart and mind.

"Honor..." Trace called softly, gently wiping the cloth across her forehead and down her cheek, trying to clean away the pain.

Honor heard her name, heard his voice, and slowly opened her eyes.

Trace watched her gray eyes cloud and darken like the thunderheads over the Colorado Rockies on a hot summer day. He braced himself for what he feared was coming. His fears were confirmed as Honor spoke.

"Get away from me," she said slowly, and began to push herself from the couch, away from Trace Logan's reach. "I don't want you to touch me. I don't want you to talk to me. I don't even want to look at your lying face. You snuck around, prying into my life with your casual questions and your false concern."

"I wasn't lying about being concerned, Honor," Trace said quietly. He couldn't defend himself further. He knew he shouldn't have become personally involved with her. But knowing and doing are two different things. And it was too late to worry about it now.

Honor glared, and then in a slow, dignified movement, turned her back on Trace and ignored him.

"Honor," Rolly Hawkins remonstrated. "I'm so sorry. I don't know what else to say except that it doesn't change your ownership of anything Charlie left to you. It's still legally yours."

He held up his hand, stopping the angry words she started to toss his way. "She also asked me to give you this." He opened his desk drawer and pulled out a faded blue book with an embossed flower border. "It's a journal. It was your momma's. Take it home and read it before you do anything else." He shoved it in Honor's hands. "You do what I say, girl. You go home, and you read your momma's words. Maybe they'll help. Maybe not. But it's the last thing you can do for her."

Honor grasped the journal tightly, picked up her purse from the floor by her chair, neither looked nor spoke to either man, and walked from the room.

Trace watched her go with a heavy, aching knot in the pit of his stomach. Then he turned to the lawyer.

"I'll be at the motel a while longer. If she contacts you, let me know."

Rolly Hawkins nodded and wiped his forehead in frustration.

"This is just a hell of a mess, boy," he said to Trace.

"Yes, sir," Trace agreed. "And for me, it's just begun."

Honor entered her house, closed the door, and slowly walked through the empty rooms, her footsteps echoing down the tiled hallway as she headed for the kitchen. She laid her mother's blue journal on the cabinet, put her purse on a bar stool, and picked up the phone.

"Hank," Honor said, as her bartender answered the phone. "I'm not feeling well. Will you call in some extra help? I think I'll take the day off and rest. Yes, thanks," she said quietly in response to his concern, and hung up the phone.

She walked back through the house, oblivious of her surroundings, and pushed open the door of her bedroom. Although her mother's taste had run toward western and southwest furnishings throughout the house, Honor's bedroom had escaped the same treatment. Instead of clay pots, mesa browns and reds for the furniture colors, and Indian artifacts hanging here and there, Honor's bedroom was like walking into a time warp.

A high, canopied, four-poster bed with sprigged muslin draperies stood in the middle of the room. A Persian-style carpet covered most of the shiny hardwood flooring. And an antique dresser sat against a wall, its oval, beveled mirror reflecting the image of the tall, dark-haired young woman who'd just entered.

Honor didn't even recognize herself. And then she smiled crookedly at the thought and at the stranger looking back at her in the mirror. "Of course I don't recognize myself," she said to the image in the mirror. "I don't know who I am."

The words were a death knell. She didn't want to be anyone else. She liked being Charlie O'Brien's daughter. She buried her face in her hands and turned away from the mirror, for the time being unwilling to face what lay ahead.

A numbness settled throughout her body. She stepped out of her shoes and began unbuttoning her blouse and slacks, letting them fall in unaccustomed abandon at her feet. Her underclothes were next as she turned to face the mirror.

The full-breasted, ivory-skinned body with the tiny waist and gently flaring hips looked familiar. She ran her hands across each feature of her body with an innocent, exploratory touch. She couldn't see or feel the turmoil raging around her heart, but it was there. She shook her head in a silent motion of denial, turned away from the mirror, and headed for the shower. The urge to wash away the last few hours was suddenly overwhelming.

It was late in the evening before Honor could bring herself to touch the blue journal. And when she did, she had to restrain herself from throwing it away. She didn't want to know; didn't want to face what was between the covers. But its very presence would not allow her to ignore its existence.

She took it to her room. Wearing an old, comfortably soft cotton nightgown, faded and shapeless from too many launderings, she finally crawled between the bedcovers and opened the book. A single page fell from the front fly leaf into Honor's lap.

My darling daughter, Charlotte wrote. *And for me, that's what you'll always be. If you are reading this letter, I expect you've already accused Rolly Hawkins of lying, rebuked the bearer of the letter I sent to J. J. Malone, and shut yourself in the house, away from the rest of the world, and the truth.*

Honor felt the blood draining from her head and leaned back against the headboard as the book fell limply from her hands. Her heart raced. Her stomach hurt. She didn't want to know this. She blinked back angry tears and pushed the pillows behind her into a more comfortable position. Anything to interrupt reading the rest of the letter…and the journal.

You have every right to be angry, but not with them. I'm the only one guilty of deception. And I selfishly

*chose a coward's way out of facing you. I waited
until it was too late to see your pain and anger, my
love. While I lived, I couldn't face losing your faith
and trust. What they have told you is true.*

Honor moaned aloud. The tears that had threatened
began to flow. This was going to kill her! Her hands
shook as she read the last few lines of the letter.

*I can make no excuse for why, other than, as
God is my witness, I was out of my mind with grief
at the loss of my own baby girl. The day after she
died, a telegram from the War Department destroyed what was left of my sanity. My sweetheart
was gone, my child was gone. I barely remember the next few weeks. The first clear memory I
have after receiving the telegram was seeing you
in your stroller, obviously unattended. I watched
your face light up. You laughed, held up your
arms to be taken, and so I did.*

*I began the journal after we came to Odessa. I
don't remember much about how or why, but what
was left of my world was glued back together by
your smile. God will forgive me. I know this, because he knows what's in my heart. I pray some
day you will be able to forgive me, too. Love,
Momma*

Honor put aside the letter, opened the first page of
the journal, and began to read.

April 9, 1966
*It's so warm here compared to Colorado. I'm glad
I came to Texas. Honor loves it. I let her lay in*

*her bed uncovered. She plays with her toes and
laughs as if she'd just tickled herself. She's such
a happy baby. I'm blessed.*

*April 15, 1966
I'm so lucky. I got a job today. Willis and Tiny
Lawson run a diner. Their waitress quit. There
are two rooms over the diner that Willis will let
me use. I took a cut in pay as payment for the
rent. Tiny loves my Honor. I have a job, a home,
and a babysitter. Everything is finally going to
be all right.*

Honor read silently, pausing only once to go to the
kitchen and pour a soda into an ice-filled glass before
going back to the journal and her bed. She hadn't eaten
all day. Food was the last thing on her mind, although
she was craving liquids. She supposed she'd cried just
about every drop from her body and it was simply demanding to be replenished.

As Honor read, the days and weeks of Charlotte's
story rolled into months, and then into years. She read
voraciously about a time in her life that she was too
young to remember. She became suspended between the
pages of her mother's journal and the truth it contained.

And then the entries grew fewer and far between.
Their lives were changing and growing. There was less
time to write. More time was devoted to work and a
growing daughter. It was the year she started to school
that sharpened her attention.

*May 5, 1970
I've got to remember to send for Honor's birth
certificate tomorrow. I'll need it for her school*

this fall. I don't know why I can't find it. I guess
I lost it when we moved. I don't remember much
about that time. So much sadness.

Honor gasped. It read as if Charlotte were innocent
of the knowledge of what she'd done. How could that
be? Surely she'd not deceived herself so well that she'd
refused, even to herself, to accept the truth? Honor desperately searched the delicate, faded script for an answer.

June 10, 1970
There's been a terrible mistake. I received my
Honor's birth certificate today. But it's wrong! It
has to be. I don't know how to fix it! It's too late.
Oh, God! My baby isn't dead. She's not! She's al-
most six years old. She's going to start first grade
this fall.

Honor's tears began again. It was obvious from the
rambling, disjointed thoughts Charlotte had written that
she was finally faced with unequivocal facts that she
couldn't ignore or hide. Not even from herself. She continued to read.

What have I done? Dear merciful God, what have
I done?

The entries stopped for two months. And then one
single entry ended the entire journal.

August 24, 1970
My daughter started school. What's past is past.

I'm not strong enough to undo what I've done. Only time...and God...will tell.

Honor closed the journal, thinking that was all of her mother's story, when a few phrases on a page at the back of the book caught her eye. She read her mother's last entry.

January 1, 1990
It's New Year's Day. But it's not a new year for me. It will probably be my last. It's finally come. My judgment; retribution for my one moment of weakness; call it what I may. I have cancer. It's inoperable, of course. God let me have these years with Honor, but I'm finally going to receive what, I suppose, is my due. I will never live to see her find love with that special man, nor see her children. I took her away from her family, kept her, and the secret, all to myself. Now, when I'm gone, she'll have no one. I've got to make it right. Maybe then God will finally forgive me. Or, maybe it's myself I need to forgive.

Honor closed the book, turned over, and turned out the lamp by her bed. Her fingers were shaking, her heart pounding. The book fell to the floor as she pulled a pillow from behind her back and buried her face in its fluffy softness. She was bruised, weak, and empty; disoriented by the emotions tumbling around inside her brain. Her hands clutched in the tangle of the sheet as she cried.

"Momma! Momma! What have you done to me? Dear Lord! What have you done?"

Her broken cries echoed in the darkness. She fell asleep, and as she slept, she dreamed. And when she awoke, she knew what must be done.

Trace lay flat on his back, and stared at the water stain on the ceiling above. He was nearly at wit's end, trying to think of a way to undo the damage he'd caused. Getting emotionally involved with Honor at such a crucial time in her life was disastrous. He'd promised J.J. that he'd bring her back to Colorado Springs, but now, because of his actions, Honor O'Brien wasn't even speaking to him. He had to find a way to undo the harm he'd caused. Her goodwill was vital if he was to fulfill his promise to J.J.

And her opinion of Trace, the man, was vital to his sanity. She'd been so open and loving, and then he'd had to watch her trust of him wither before his eyes. He didn't think he was ever going to get past that look of shock and betrayal on her beautiful face.

The phone rang. Trace grimaced. If it was J.J. again, he was going to hang up. He'd told him over and over that if he had any more news he'd call.

"Hello," he growled, and then swallowed the next angry retort hanging by a syllable on the tip of his tongue.

"I wasn't sure you'd still be here," Honor said shortly. She hadn't forgiven the man for his deception. But he was her only link with a journey that must be made.

"Honor!"

He sat straight up in bed. The tone of her voice hurt, but at least she was speaking to him. "Yes, I'm still here," he said softly. "Are you all right?"

"What do *you* think?" she asked angrily.

"I think you're scared," he answered, and heard her

sharply indrawn breath. "And I think you're mad. But you don't know for certain who to be mad at."

Honor ignored the pain in her chest and blurted out, "Are you leaving soon?"

"Will you come with me?" Trace retorted.

One long, silent moment hung suspended between them on the open phone line, and then she answered.

"Yes, it seems I must." But she quickly qualified her statement. "But I'm not staying. I'm just going back to fix what my mother…" Her voice shook. "What Charlie broke. After that, I make no promises."

"That's all I ask, Honor," Trace said softly. "That and a chance to make it right between us."

"There is no *us*," she said sharply. "I can leave by tomorrow. Come get me when you're ready to go. It'll take me until then to organize the restaurant staff."

A sharp click echoed in his ear. He didn't know whether to be worried that she still hated his guts, or whether to be glad that she'd made the first step toward reconciliation with her lost family. One thing was certain. J. J. Malone was going to be ecstatic.

Chapter 4

Honor didn't speak more than ten words the entire journey. They'd been through one small and two large airports, and were now on the last leg of their trip home. Not only would she not speak to him, she had refused to look at him. But she'd made the first step. She was here with him and they were almost home.

Trace sighed and shifted in his seat. He peered over Honor's shoulder, and then touched her arm before pointing out the tiny window by her seat.

"Those are the Rockies," he said against her ear. "We're almost there."

Honor turned with interest, forgetting her anger. Her words were rich with surprise.

"There's snow on the mountaintops." She leaned closer to the window. "And everything is so green."

Trace smiled.

"Will there be snow in Colorado Springs?" Honor asked. "I didn't think much about the weather when I packed. I may have to buy a few things."

"No," he answered. "Right now, there's only snow on the mountains. But it's almost October. It won't be long before we get snow. You'll love it! The trees are beautiful then."

"I don't plan on being here that long," Honor snapped, and withdrew back into her quiet, angry shell.

Trace bit the inside of his lip to keep from saying something he'd later regret. He already had more than enough regrets about the woman sitting beside him. He looked up as the stewardess came down the aisle, then muttered as he dug in the seat beside him, "Fasten your seat belt, Honor. We're about to land."

Her face lost all expression. Her hands shook as she reached for the seat belt and then struggled helplessly with the catch.

Trace leaned over, aware of her panic, and fastened the buckle in one clean movement before he leaned back in his seat. He didn't say a word.

Honor's heart was beating fast, too fast. She wanted to run, but there was nowhere to hide. She heartily wished she'd never left Texas. Her fingers gripped the armrest until her knuckles turned white.

Trace felt her panic. He would give a year of his life to make this easier, but he couldn't. All he could do was be there for her. If she'd let him. He threaded his fingers through hers and ignored her angry resistance.

Honor looked up in stubborn fury and started to argue. The expression on his face changed her mind. It was somewhere between a plea and warning. She pressed her lips tightly together, leaned her head back against the headrest, and closed her eyes. She couldn't look at the sympathy in those dark eyes. And she wouldn't acknowledge his presence, yet she could not refuse Trace or herself the comfort of his touch.

Then they were in a cab, en route to the rest of Honor's life.

The majesty of the mountains that surrounded Colorado Springs held her speechless. There were signs and billboards all along the highway proclaiming, by colorful advertisement, exactly what was available for the public to enjoy. There seemed to be everything from the view at Pike's Peak to enchanting depths of caves and caverns, all open for tourists' delights. There were train rides up mountains, and even a train ride available across something called Royal Gorge.

Honor couldn't ignore a twinge of interest and knew if she'd been here on vacation that she'd be having the time of her life. It was all so different from the flat, almost treeless plains of west Texas.

But her interest disappeared as the cab left the business district and started winding its way up a steep street through an obviously exclusive residential area. Nearly all of the homes they were passing were set back from the street. Their privacy was maintained with big iron gates, or fences and tall shrubbery. The area made Honor wonder, for the first time, exactly what her family did for a living. Earlier she hadn't stopped to care. It had been more than she could face just to admit that they existed. What they were, in society's eyes, had never occurred to her.

She had a sudden vision of how she would appear in her casual clothing and then instantly squashed the thought with another, more honest reaction. She really didn't care what kind of an impression she made on them. Charlie's opinion had been what mattered most in her life.

She sighed and relaxed against the back seat of the taxi. Suddenly all of her tension and apprehension dissipated. Honor didn't know why, but she knew she was not facing this crisis alone. The peace within had come after thinking of her mother. Honor smiled to herself and thought, *Maybe I'm not alone.*

Trace had watched Honor's face with each block they'd traveled. He knew when her interest had turned to fear. He'd seen a frown deepen the furrow between those stormy eyes. And then he saw Honor smile. He watched in fascination as the single dimple flashed an appearance before it disappeared. He couldn't resist asking, "What were you thinking of just now?"

Honor turned, and for several seconds remained silent as she gauged the true measure of his interest.

"My mother," she finally answered, and then with a shrug of near indifference, continued. "I just remembered that she had a reason for everything she did. I've been so angry about her letter and deception. I didn't want to know about this part of my life. But I was wrong. All I have to do is go along with this…" She hesitated, searching for the right word. "This new wrinkle in my life and then find a way to iron it out before I go on. I'll find a way. Momma always said there's a way out of the darkness. And the answer is usually inside yourself." She turned, gazing absently out of the window. "All I have to do now is wait and see what happens. Then I'll know what I have to do."

Trace couldn't answer. Her honesty and self-confidence were overwhelming. No matter what else Charlotte O'Brien had done, she'd done a remarkable job raising the woman sitting beside him.

The rest of the trip was completed in silence. When they turned into a long, tree-lined driveway, Honor didn't even flinch. She just took a deep breath and began gathering her belongings.

Honor watched the cab disappear down the winding driveway, then turned for a longer, more in-depth look at the understated elegance of the two-story home. It looked as if it should be sitting in an English countryside instead of perched on the side of a Colorado mountain. She smoothed down the skirt of her russet-colored suit and straightened the collar of the cream silk blouse. She caught Trace watching her with an apprehensive look. She felt obligated to assure him she wasn't going to cause a scene.

"It's going to be okay, Trace," Honor said sarcastically. "I won't embarrass you, or myself. Didn't your preliminary observation of me tell you anything?"

Her words stung. He knew she was still angry about his deception. He spoke before he thought. "You know damn good and well why I didn't say anything at first. What could I say? The first time we met, you wound up in my arms, crying on my shoulder. Just when did you expect me to throw my little news your way? Right before, or just after, I watched your heart break?"

Her face blanched. She tilted her head back in defiance as her cheeks registered the truth of his statement.

Trace resisted the urge to apologize. She had to see this from his point of view, too.

Honor knew that a lot of what Trace said was true.

But it still rankled that she'd let him get so close, so fast. It wasn't like her to be, for a lack of a better word, so *loose*.

She glared at Trace, saw his chin set in stubborn silence, reached in front of him, and defiantly rang the doorbell. It put an abrupt end to their doorstep feud.

"Oh, my! Lord have mercy!" Trudy Sinclair gasped, as she opened the door.

She couldn't quit staring at the pair on the doorstep. The young woman was a walking image of the portrait hanging in the Malone library. She'd known for two days now about the long-lost granddaughter's imminent arrival, but she hadn't been prepared for this.

"I know it's a shock, Trudy. But all the same, I think we better come inside," Trace said, and took control of the situation.

He put his hands on the little woman's shoulders, and gently moved her out of the doorway. Then he pulled Honor and her luggage into the hallway and closed the door.

"Oh, my!" Trudy repeated in shock.

"Trudy, this is Honor O'Brien," Trace said. He turned to Honor. "This place would come to a complete halt without Trudy."

Honor smiled at the housekeeper and held out her hand. She might be furious with Trace Logan and his deceit. But she saw no reason to include this sprightly little woman in the web of intrigue that her mother's letter had caused.

Trudy looked blankly at the offered greeting and then back at Trace. She couldn't remember anyone in the Malone family ever wanting to shake her hand.

Trace nodded slightly, the twinkle in his eyes assuring the housekeeper of the propriety of the gesture.

Trudy puffed her tiny self up to full stature and reached out.

"I'm pleased to meet you," Honor said softly.

"It's *my* pleasure, miss," Trudy answered.

"Please call me Honor. Where I come from, the only woman still referred to as 'miss' is Callie Walker. She's eighty-eight and never been married."

Trace threw back his head and laughed. He couldn't help himself. Trudy grinned, and then caught herself. She wasn't tending to her duties. Her duties were very important.

"Mr. Malone is in the library, as usual," Trudy said, pointing down the hallway. "You know the way."

She grabbed Honor's bags and called back over her shoulder as she started down the hall. "Let me know when you've finished your visit. Then I'll show you where your rooms are. Mr. Malone's quite excited about your arrival, Miss... I mean, Honor," Trudy corrected. "And, it's quite wonderful that you've been found. It's a miracle. That's what it is, it's a miracle."

She bustled away, pulling Honor's wheeled luggage behind her like a canvas pup.

"Come on, lady," Trace said. "You've just charmed the iron dragon. Meeting your grandfather is next on the list."

Honor looked away from Trace and refused to answer his smile. She didn't want to like him. She was still mad, wasn't she? And she *was* more apprehensive than she'd let on. No matter what she told herself, this meeting was going to change her life. And therein lay the problem. She'd liked her life just the way it was.

Trace read the worry on her face and wished with all his soul that he could take away the uncertainties and fears that had to be making her crazy. He couldn't imagine being dealt such a blow.

His hand slid up her back. Honor's resistance to his touch was instantaneous. Her shoulders stiffened, her gait quickened. It was all he could do to ignore the frown that marred her features as he guided her down the hall toward the library. Everything in him yearned to grab her and run, to do anything it took to soothe away the tension he felt in the muscles beneath his fingertips. But it wasn't feasible, nor possible. Right now Honor O'Brien didn't even consider him worthy enough to argue with.

"Come on, honey," he coaxed. "It won't be as bad as you think. I promise. I'm right here with you, all the way."

"And that's supposed to make me feel better?" Honor asked sarcastically. "Just what kind of loyalty am I supposed to believe you hold for *me?* I can't imagine that you assume I've forgotten the lies and deceit you used to get close to me."

"That's not true, Honor, and you know it," Trace said under his breath.

But they were too close to the library now to begin another argument. He took a deep breath, swallowed the words he wanted to shout in defense of himself, and ushered Honor into the room.

"J.J.!" Trace called.

A tall, white-haired man stared transfixed, lost in the dancing flames of the fireplace before which he stood.

J. J. Malone spun about, startled at the sound of voices. He'd been lost in thought and memories. His crutches had been replaced by a cane to ease the pressure of his slowly healing leg. But the sight of the pair in the doorway sent the cane falling limply from his hand. It clattered against the floor and landed at his feet. The tall young woman standing beside Trace Logan made him forget to breathe. Sounds muted and fell away as J.J. watched the reincarnation of his beloved Meggie looking at him from across the room.

The trio stood in uneasy silence, each uncertain how to break the tension of the moment when the portrait over the fireplace directly behind the old gentleman caught Honor's attention. Her gasp of recognition echoed loudly in the quiet. All eyes were instantly drawn to the shock on the girl's face.

She moved on instinct, drawn in spite of herself to the woman's image on the lacquered canvas.

J.J. watched her coming toward him, and resisted the urge to wrap her in his arms. She was here on sufferance. He knew that much. Trace had warned him over and over that she wasn't happy to discover this hidden part of her life. But he couldn't deny the surge of emotion that welled inside him, overwhelming in its intensity. Nor could he deny the tears that burned behind his eyelids.

"I kept telling myself all along that this was going to turn out to be a mistake," Honor whispered to herself, but both men heard her words. "I didn't know how, but I kept telling myself it would all work out. Now, I don't know. I just don't know."

She turned and looked around the room, desperation obvious in the torment of her face. There had to be an answer to this nightmare, or at least, an avenue of escape! But there was nothing except the look of pity on

Trace Logan's face. *Damn him! Damn them all,* she thought. *I don't want pity. I want to go home!*

Trace caught the terror in her gaze and started forward when her grandfather pointed toward the portrait and spoke, his voice shaking with suppressed emotion.

"That's my Meggie," he said gruffly, and gently allowed himself a lingering touch on Honor's arm as he turned her back to face the portrait. "She was your grandmother. You were named for her. I had no idea you would look so…" His voice broke. "I'm sorry. Old men get sentimental."

Honor suddenly realized that she wasn't the only one going through a traumatic ordeal. She turned and stared. The tall, elderly man stood before her, unashamed of the tears pouring freely down his weathered cheeks. Her heart was too gentle to include him in the anger. If her mother's letter was to be believed, she and the man were both innocent victims.

"Maybe now is the time for tears," Honor said quietly. She reached out and captured J.J.'s hand. "I think it's also the time for introductions. I'm Honor, sir. And, I'm glad to be here… I think." Her voice broke as she took a deep, shaky breath. "Thank you for having me. I know this time is going to be awkward. I could have stayed in a hotel."

J.J.'s voice regained its usual power as he interrupted. "You'll do no such thing, girl. There's no one in this house anymore except me and Sinless Sinclair. I'm tired of fending off her sneak attacks concerning my health and behavior. I'm old enough to take care of myself. And," he continued, "I'm not 'sir.' I don't suppose you'll be able to call me Grandfather just yet but I think we can both live with J.J. Don't you?"

Honor grinned in spite of the momentous occasion. The nickname he used in reference to the housekeeper struck her as funny. "I found Trudy to be quite charming," Honor said. "And I think I can manage to call you J.J."

J.J. sniffed and cleared his throat as he watched her dimple come and go. It unnerved him to no end. She was so like his beloved wife, it gave him chills. "Yes, well," he mumbled. "She's still a busybody."

Trace came up behind Honor and casually slid his hand up the middle of her back. He leaned forward to speak.

Honor shivered as his breath caressed the side of her face.

"I think you two need some time alone," Trace said. "I've done what I promised. I brought her back. Now, the rest is up to the both of you. Your granddaughter is more like you than you can imagine. It'll take me into the next lifetime to make her forgive me. Do what you can to make me look good, J.J. I don't want this lady mad at me any longer, okay?"

Honor was furious with the way Trace kept touching her. The stroke of his hand as it slid upward, coming to rest just below her hairline, brought back memories of a happier time. And yet, even as she wanted to scream at him in anger, she yearned to turn in his arms and bury her face against his strength. She needed to feel the sound, steady rhythm of his heart beneath her cheek and close out this nightmare into which she'd been thrust.

Trace moved away.

Honor panicked.

He was the only link she had between her old world and the new. Her look of despair was evident.

Both men instantly sensed what was going through her mind.

"You'll be just fine, Honor," Trace said quietly, reading the troubled depths in the stormy gray of her eyes. "I'll be back for dinner later tonight. Wait and see what happens, remember?"

Honor's heart raced as his hand slid down her back, lingering on the curve of her hip before he reluctantly stepped away. She bit her lip, and hoped she wasn't blushing. *Damn this man, he's making me crazy!*

Honor knew his reminder to "wait and see" was an echo of her own declaration. She took a deep breath, intent on regaining some measure of control. *What's the matter with me? I don't like Trace Logan. I don't even trust him!* But if she didn't like him, why was she acting like she couldn't function without him? She needed her head examined for more reasons than one.

"Of course, I'll be fine," she said. "What makes you think I won't? I'm a big girl. I don't need you to hold my hand."

She glared at Trace for mentioning their differences in front of J.J. She didn't need anyone running interference for her, either. She was plenty capable of sorting out her own thoughts regarding Trace Logan.

J.J. watched the interchange between the man he loved like a son and the granddaughter who'd just been restored to him. An idea took seed.

He hadn't become successful simply by accident. J. J. Malone was the champion when it came to subtle persuasion. More than once he'd encountered a reluctant competitor down on his luck and anxious to sell his business to anyone other than J. J. Malone. Before he'd finished the meeting, the man had been practically begging Malone to buy him out. He was a master at the game. Surely he could manage one man and one woman, when he'd held the fate of entire companies in his grasp.

"Certainly you'll be back for dinner," J.J. said loudly. "I'll tell Trudy myself. She always fixes *real* food when there's company for dinner. None of that tasteless garbage she feeds me when I'm alone."

He leaned over and picked up his cane, then hobbled out of the room, calling back over his shoulder as he left. "I'll be right back. Then we'll visit, girl. Then we'll visit. We've a whole lifetime to catch up on."

Honor watched his exit and then turned away, unwilling for Trace to see her uneasiness.

But Trace wouldn't let her pull away from him anymore. She was as far away as he could live with now. Something about this woman had taken hold of his every waking thought and his sleepless nights. He clasped her by the arms, turned her back to face him, and tilted her chin until their eyes met.

"Trust me, Honor," he pleaded. "Let yourself get to know this man. He's a fine old fellow. Honest as the day is long, and tough as your Texas boots. I think you'll like him. You're very much alike."

She nodded silently, refusing to speak. But not because she was mad. At the moment, it was because she was afraid she might cry.

Trace leaned down and gently brushed his lips across the softness of her mouth. He couldn't help himself. And he wouldn't have stopped himself if he could. He'd been wanting to do that all day.

Honor's mouth opened to protest, but it was too late. He'd already committed the deed.

Trace sighed as her lips softened and responded to the pressure of his touch. But he couldn't allow this to go any further, not now. Honor was too vulnerable. He didn't want her forgiveness out of panic and a feeling of need. He wanted her to come to him because she knew she couldn't face another day without him. That's the way he wanted to spend the rest of his life. He wanted to live long and happily, but not without Honor. It was unthinkable. He reluctantly released her and gave her a comforting, brotherly hug before he turned to leave the room.

"I'll see you later, honey," he said softly. And then he was gone.

It was several moments before Honor realized he'd called her "honey" again. It was even later before she realized she wasn't supposed to like it. Damn him anyway. It was hard to stay mad at a snake when it kept acting so decent. She turned her attention to the tapping cane and the footsteps she heard coming down the tiled hallway. It was time to deal with the issues at hand. And that meant letting herself accept the fact that this man coming back into the room with a beaming smile on his face was actually her grandfather.

Honor stood before the mirror in her room, putting the finishing touches on her hair and makeup. She couldn't remember when she'd spent this much time just getting ready to eat a meal.

Her visit with J.J. had gone much better than either could have hoped. She'd listened obediently to all of his stories, some of them rambling but all pertaining directly to portions of her life that she knew she must accept. She'd watched the sadness come and go as he detailed her disappearance, listened to his assurances of how long and hard they'd searched for clues that might lead to her recovery. But, he'd claimed sadly, they'd all led nowhere. Charlotte O'Brien had left no clues.

Honor listened, hardening her heart against speaking out in favor of her mother's actions. Now was not the time to defend what had taken place. She wasn't even sure that it was fair to try. But if things kept going favorably, before she left she wanted him to read her mother's journal. Maybe it would help. Maybe it would help them both.

She listened quietly, asking few questions, as J.J. then listed the events following her abduction that he felt ultimately resulted in his "Meggie's" death. Trace had already informed her that her natural parents were dead. But she had some curiosity concerning the aunt and uncle she'd yet to meet. She'd been assured that they would be present at the dinner tonight, and then the celebration would begin. The entire remaining Malone family would, once again, be complete.

It was all J.J. could do to allow Honor to leave him. He could not get enough of just looking at her. Finally, her pallor and the dark circles under her eyes made him realize what a strain the past few days had been for her. Reluctantly, he'd summoned the housekeeper, who'd eagerly taken her on a quick tour of the house before showing her to her suite of rooms.

Honor had been taken aback at the size of the home and the lack of staff in residence. She knew from experience that it took a lot of work to keep a home this size, but Trudy was the only staff member who lived on the premises. She'd prattled on about her duties until even Honor could tell the importance with which Trudy Sinclair regarded her responsibilities.

She sighed with relief as she came to her room, entered, and collapsed on the bed. The furnishings were so similar to those in her own home that the strangeness of her surroundings diminished. For the time being, Honor could regain some of the mental ground that she'd lost.

The events she was experiencing were so painful, and beyond the realm of her understanding. Emotionally, each passing moment became harder to face. Here, in the city where she was born, with the family who'd suffered, she had to come to terms with the fact she'd been stolen, that the woman she'd known and loved as "mother" had actually taken her away from a loving family, leaving them with nothing but grief.

A door slammed downstairs, jolting Honor's wayward thoughts back to the present. She frowned. It was too much. For the time being, she gave up trying to sort everything out. There were still too many unknowns.

Honor pulled a loose curl from her forehead and tried to push it back into place. It was no use. Her hair was behaving much in the same fashion as her thoughts: with abandonment and no regard for order. She sighed, stuck out her tongue at her reflection in the mirror, and took a long, last look at her appearance. She would do.

She needed to make a favorable impression, not for herself, but for her mother. She knew she would be judged by the way Charlotte O'Brien had raised her.

Her dress was short, and came just above her knees. The low, rounded neckline dipped daringly close to the lush swell of breast pushing defiantly against the confines of the soft, silky fabric. The bodice wrapped snugly around Honor's slender waist, while the skirt danced around her hips in a teasing flare.

But it was black.

And Honor knew you could never go wrong with black. It could be simple or classy. Tonight, Honor wanted class. That was why the only jewelry she was wearing were her mother's diamond earrings. They were two-carat studs and had been a gift from Rusty to Charlotte, on her fortieth birthday. They were Honor's most treasured possessions.

She pushed back her hair, tilted her head first one way then the other, watching the light catch in the brilliant cut of the stones, and smiled. They *were* big. But after all, she *was* from Texas. There, everything was larger than life.

She sprayed a touch of perfume, gave herself one final glance in the mirror, and started toward the closet to search for her shoes when a knock on her door made her turn.

Trace!

"I was going to ask if you're ready," Trace drawled, letting his eyes feast on the elegant beauty of the tall woman glaring at him with less than her usual venom. "But, that seems a bit weak. You don't look ready, Honor. You look dangerous. You've got my vote, lady. Actually, you've got more than that, but I don't think now's the time to discuss it."

"I suppose you have a good excuse for coming to my door. You could have waited downstairs with the others," she grumbled, caught off guard at seeing him standing so devastatingly close.

It was all she could do to ignore how well he wore clothes. The black dinner jacket and pants, obviously tailor-made, fit his tall, muscular frame to perfection. Honor sighed. If he was only ugly. Or bit his nails and picked his teeth. She'd have a much easier time remembering she was supposed to be angry and betrayed if she wasn't attracted.

"I know I could have waited," he said softly, as he stepped inside without waiting for an invitation. "But, I thought a friendly escort would be welcome."

Honor flushed and looked away. Here he was, being nice and considerate again. How did he know she was dreading a repeat of this afternoon? She'd managed the meeting with J.J. but that was just one man, one time. Tonight she was facing the rest of the family, and knew all too well that everyone would be watching every move she made. Just because J.J. was glad to see her didn't mean the rest of the family would feel the same.

"Oh, well," she muttered. "Under the circumstances, thank you."

"You're welcome," Trace said, masking his urge to smile.

She was the most vexing, taxing mix of femininity he'd ever encountered. Honor O'Brien was honest, independent, aggressive and compassionate. She was like Texas's state flower, the bluebonnet. Beautiful, sturdy.

"Well, I guess it's now or never," she said, and looked around, trying to remember what she'd been about to do when Trace had appeared.

"Don't you think you better put on shoes," Trace said, watching Honor's face flush an even darker shade of red.

"I was going to," she grumbled, and headed for her closet. "You interrupted me."

"Need any help?" Trace drawled again, watching

with extreme interest as Honor bent over, digging furiously through the bag on the closet floor.

"I don't need anything else from you, mister," Honor said, glaring back at the smirk on his face as she realized just what an interesting view she'd given him. "And just for the record, a gentleman would have turned around."

Honor watched Trace's eyebrows quirk, and watched in reluctant fascination as that damn sexy mouth of his twisted into a seductive smile.

"Who said I was a gentleman, Honor? You've called me everything else but."

Honor glared, stepped quickly into three-inch slingback pumps, looked him squarely in the eyes from her elevated height, and started to sweep by him in queenly fashion.

Trace slid his arm around her waist, guided her back around to face him, and whispered softly against her mouth.

"Since you've branded me a deceitful liar, I guess one more black mark against me can't hurt." He tasted the mutinous pout forming on her lips and groaned softly. "It can't hurt you, and will damn sure help me, lady."

His mouth slid hard across her lips and stopped her protest.

Honor was shaken. She'd wanted to object, but the kiss was so familiar and so devastating, she forgot to push away. Instead, she found herself being pressed between the wall at her back and the hard, muscled body of the man at her front. The man who was slowly but surely taking away her sanity. She moved against him. It was instinct that guided them together, but it was memories that tore them apart.

Honor splayed her hand across his chest and moaned, desperately tearing herself away from this big man's touch before it was too late.

"Honey, don't fight me. Not now, please," he begged softly.

Honor shook, blinking away tears of frustration as she sighed, allowing his hands to slide down the sides of her rib cage in a slow, teasing caress, meeting just long enough at the base of her spine to send cold chills rocketing through her system.

Trace felt the intake of her breath against his chest as she struggled with his audacity and knew he'd reached her limit...and his.

"Damn you, Trace Logan," she said thickly.

"I already have been," he answered quietly.

Trace pulled away, reluctantly releasing his hold on her tender curves. He traced the remnants of his onslaught on her carefully applied makeup, using his forefinger as a marker, then rubbed his thumb beneath her lower lip, removing the last little smear of lipstick he'd disturbed.

Honor stared, mesmerized by the look in his eyes and the touch of his hands, and tried to convince herself she still needed to hate. His deceit! His lies!

But the feeling wouldn't come. The only thing she could produce was an overwhelming sadness for the waste of what might have been. She flashed Trace a look he couldn't interpret and then muttered, "You need to do a little repair on yourself, mister."

Trace grinned rakishly, refusing to be daunted by her anger. She meant too much to him. He slipped his handkerchief from his pocket, wiped it across his lips, and then started to stuff it back when Honor took it from him and sighed.

"Be still," she ordered, rubbing at a spot he'd missed at the corner of his mouth.

Trace stood quietly, reveling in the feel of her hand on his face, inhaling the fleeting scents that emanated from her tall, elegant beauty, and resisted the urge to lay her down on the carpeted floor and lose himself in her mystery.

"Here," she said, as she handed the handkerchief back to him. "And don't push your luck again."

She flashed him a warning look as they walked carefully down the stairs. Her thoughts were whirling as they neared the sound of angry voices rising with increased volume. She took a deep breath, and pushed open the double doors with one motion. The angry tones evolved into understandable words as the door slid silently open.

"Father," the woman was arguing, lost in her tirade. "How could you be so foolish? This is probably nothing more than a scam to obtain money or social standing. You and I both know that Johnny's daughter is gone. Gone for all these years! These silly chases of yours had stopped. What made you start this futile search all over again? And what made you think for one moment that this horrible woman's letter was even genuine?"

Honor felt her ire building as she heard her mother's name being slung about with hateful abandon. It was nothing more than she'd expected. She pulled herself to her full height, tilted her chin in a position of defense, and gave it her best Texas drawl.

"Maybe I should have knocked."

Chapter 5

Honor watched the woman who'd been arguing so vehemently step backward in shock, then grope blindly
behind her for the nearest chair. She sank weakly into
its cushiony depths.

The tall, middle-aged man with a receding hairline
pulled at his collar, calling Honor's attention to his cler-
ical attire.

So this priest is my uncle, Honor thought, and
watched him make the sign of the cross as he stared
blankly at her presence. He turned in shock and gazed
for a long moment at the portrait above the fireplace,
before he turned his attention back to Trace and Honor.
He was the first to speak.

"Dear Lord!" he whispered prayerfully. "She looks
just like Mother." He looked angrily at his father, who
was wearing an expression of triumph. "You might
have warned us," the priest said in an accusing tone.

"It's quite a shock for Erin, as well as for me." Then he caught himself, ended his rebuke with a sigh, as if he'd done this many times in the past and knew it was as futile now as it had ever been. Their father, J. J. Malone, was a law unto himself.

The priest turned to Honor with a belated welcome and came toward her with outstretched arms.

"My dear niece. Found at last! What can I say? There are no words to express our joy. You must forgive our reticence, but I'm sure you understand. This is quite a shock! Quite a shock! Welcome home!"

For Honor, it was a bit too much, too late, but she graciously allowed the man his effusive welcome. She realized that because of her appearance, she was less of a stranger to them than they were to her.

"Thank you," Honor said, carefully extricating herself from the overwhelming exuberance of his hug. "You must be Father Andrew. What do I call you? Father, or Andrew, or..."

She looked to Trace for assistance, but he was no help. He'd pulled himself away from the center of attention, leaving Honor alone in the middle of the library to cope.

"Please, you must call me Uncle Andrew. I suppose you're used to calling your own parish priest, Father. But this is family and a time of rejoicing."

"I don't have a priest," Honor drawled, sensing this might become another small bombshell. She hadn't realized, but of course this was a very Irish, very Catholic, family.

Trace had an urge to grab Honor and dash out into the night. This was going to be a long, grueling evening, and from the signs so far, it was not going to be friendly. He ached for her. He knew how confused and strange all this must seem. Yet he knew Honor *could* stand up for herself. He saw J.J.'s expression darken as he absorbed Honor's announcement regarding her religious upbringing.

J.J. frowned. His voice boomed out into the awkward silence. "What do you mean, you don't have a priest? What's the matter, girl? Did that blasted woman raise you as a heathen?"

Honor gasped. J.J.'s frown would have frozen the feathers off a buzzard. It made her own ire rise magnificently to the occasion. "No, I'm not a heathen," she snapped. "I'm a Baptist."

"Practically the same thing," J.J. mumbled.

"Father!" the woman in the chair rebuked, as she rallied and pulled herself to her feet. She came toward Honor with a guarded expression on her face. "I'm sorry," she said politely. "Malones are not known for their tact. I'm certain this is not the welcome you were expecting."

"I wasn't expecting anything." Honor returned the delicate thrust of the woman's statement with a painless jab of her own.

The carefully groomed and formed eyebrows on Erin Malone's forehead rose to amazing heights as she let Honor's words soak in. She smiled a less than friendly smile and leaned forward, touching Honor's cheek with her own in an antiseptic welcome.

"Dear Megan... I'm your aunt Erin. But please, call me Erin. Aunt is so formal, and," she smiled coquettishly, and looked back at her escort, "it's so aging."

"Please call me Honor," she replied, not willing for anyone to mention legal names at this point. She had been raised as Honor, she wasn't ready to answer to any other name.

Erin looked as if she were about to argue when J.J. frowned, realizing that he'd almost let his little surprise get out of hand. Now that the shock of Honor's appearance had worn off, he was eager to get on with the evening. He'd also intercepted more than one angry look from Trace and knew it wouldn't take much more before he intervened.

"Of course, we'll call you by the name you were raised with, although it's not the one you were given at christening," he couldn't resist adding. He ignored Trace's look of warning as he stepped aside to introduce his daughter's escort.

"This is Hastings Lawrence. He's our family lawyer, as well as your aunt Erin's fiancé. Call him Hasty. He usually is."

J.J. slapped his leg and laughed aloud. By the expression on everyone's face, he was obviously riding an old joke to death.

Hastings Lawrence stepped forward, extending his hand in welcome. Honor had an instant impression of someone of whom to be wary. There was a forced joviality about the man that she didn't like. He slid her hand between his own and held it moments too long for propriety's sake.

He was several years Erin Malone's junior, but had done nothing to retain his boyish charms. He was soft, inclined to the pudgy side, and his perfectly groomed hair *almost* hid a large balding spot on the crown of his head. It was obvious that he didn't like looking up at Honor as they were introduced.

"Mr. Lawrence."

She pulled her hand away from his grasp as she turned and spoke to all assembled. "As I told J.J. earlier today, I know this is awkward. But maybe if we all do our best, we'll survive this visit as new acquaintances, if not friends."

"Visit?" J.J. bellowed. "You just arrived! I don't want to hear any hint of leaving tonight."

Honor ignored his remark, then silently thanked the fates for intervening as Trudy loudly announced that dinner was ready to be served.

Trace quietly took her arm and escorted her into the dining room before anyone else could volunteer. He privately thought that this evening was going to hell in a handbasket. He feared that Honor was feeling much the same way and had no intention of leaving her stuck between the family's constant bickering.

The meal was interminable. It was obvious to Honor, as the evening progressed, that Erin was spending the entire time trying to get her father to notice her. Honor knew Erin Malone had to be close to forty years old, but she'd obviously spent a good deal of time and money trying to hide the fact.

She was of average height, and the shortest person in the room by several inches. Her long dark hair was combed back away from her nearly round face in a severe, ultraconservative chignon that nestled at the back of her head. Her choice of clothing contrasted painfully with her hairstyle and makeup. It was soft, ruffly, and very feminine. The dark red slash of lipstick on her face made her other features fade in comparison. Honor thought Erin's eyes were hazel, but it was hard to tell because they were never still. Their gaze darted from Hastings, to her father, and then back again to her fiancé. Honor fancied she could almost see the wheels turning in her busy brain. Erin also totally ignored the fact that Trace existed, and only granted her brother Andrew and Honor an occasional crumb of conversation.

Honor felt Trace's presence, even without looking for him. It was solid and quiet. Because of him, she was able to field the probing line of questions thrown at her throughout the evening. Somehow, she knew if she fell flat on her face that he'd be there to pick her up. Even if she was mad at him. Even if she didn't like him.

Erin was passing on some obviously choice gossip about people Honor didn't know, and from the sound of the story, wouldn't care to. Honor turned to Trace as he sat quietly in obvious boredom and whispered very, very softly, "She doesn't like you a bit, does she?"

Her astute observation startled him. How did she do it? Honor invariably got to the heart of a subject with as little conversational clutter as anyone he knew. He couldn't resist a chuckle as he cocked one eyebrow at her in a rakish glance.

"You don't miss a thing, do you, lady?"

Honor grinned in spite of herself, and then realized it had grown exceedingly quiet. She looked up. Everyone was looking back. She shrugged.

"Sorry," she said, although she didn't mean it. She watched Erin mask her disapproval at Honor for taking the focus of attention away from herself.

J.J. smiled. He felt satisfied and complete now that his family was gathered about the table. If only his Meggie could be here to see this.

He'd watched for years as the Malone family dwindled in size instead of expanding as most families do. His daughter had foolishly let her reproductive years get away from her just for the sake of a career. There could be no children from Andrew, either. His long-lost granddaughter was going to be the answer to his prayers. She would put new blood into this moldering family. And from the looks of her, it would be a strong, spirited infusion. He also saw that Trace and Honor were back on speaking terms. *Good! Good!* he thought. He pushed himself away from the table, reached for his cane, and announced, "This is a nice night. Not too cool. There won't be many more like it this year. Let's have our brandy out on the terrace to cap off the evening. What do you say?"

It was obvious that no one ever argued with J.J.'s suggestions. They all filed dutifully outside without voicing an opinion.

Trace groaned softly, grateful for an excuse to get up from his chair. They'd been at the table for nearly three hours. It had been too long and cloistered. He was used to a more congenial atmosphere during meals and readily agreed to the move as he spoke. "I'll get the glasses, J.J. You show Honor just how beautiful a Colorado night can be. I'll be along shortly and continue her education…on Colorado, that is."

His teasing brought a blush, and he watched in satisfaction as Honor glared at his innuendo.

Erin looked at Trace, and then back at this interloper, this younger version of her life-long competition. Anger billowed. This wasn't fair. She'd spent her entire life trying to get her father to love her as much as he'd loved her mother, but it had never happened. He'd doted on his sons and his beloved "Meggie." Erin had gotten what was left over. It had never been enough. Now her nemesis was back, in a younger, more vibrant form. It was starting all over again. And it was obvious that she also had the attention of a man who had never given Erin the time of day.

When Trace had begun working at Malone Industries, Erin had sidled into his life, both in a business and personal fashion. She was several years older than he, but had never felt threatened by society's judgment of such relationships. Actually, Erin felt safer with younger men, more in control.

Trace had carefully listened to her business advice, aware that the boss's daughter was a force to be reckoned with, and wisely not allowed her anywhere near his personal life. It hadn't taken Erin long to get the message. She'd held a grudge ever since. She'd used Trace Logan as a weak excuse to herself as to why she'd never married. In moments of honesty she admitted only to herself it was because she was too selfish to share her time with anyone. She didn't want to lose her figure by bearing children, and she didn't want to watch some man grow old before her eyes, to know that she was bound to him by the bonds of her religion, until death did them part. Just the thought made her physically sick.

The group soon broke up into two clusters, leaving Honor on her own. J.J. and Hastings began to discuss business. Father Andrew cornered his sister. It was obvious to Honor that she was the subject of their conversation. The furtive glances they kept casting her way were anything but casual.

Honor sighed, rolled her eyes heavenward, and then forgot her weary disgust. The stars seemed to be falling in on her as she gazed up into the dark night sky.

She knew it was an illusion. Maybe it was because they were at a higher elevation. But regardless of the fact, the view was breathtaking.

Trace's voice startled her as he walked up behind her and cupped his body against the back of her own, molding himself to the softness of her curves.

Honor forgot what she'd been doing. All she could think of was how strong and unyielding he felt against her and how safe she felt with him behind her.

"So what do you think, lady? Are you still mad at me, or are you glad you came? Your reception has been less than I'd hoped for, but not unexpected. Erin, like her father, enjoys being in control."

Honor heard the concern in his voice and turned to face him, feeling her breasts brush against the unyielding muscles of his chest as he refused to relinquish his space.

As usual her honesty astounded him. She didn't mince words about any of them, yet she didn't criticize or condemn. She merely observed with startling clarity. "I feel as if I'm in a play and everyone is playing a part. None of this has been familiar or comforting. Not even particularly happy. I don't think anyone but J.J. is truly glad I'm here. I've disturbed a very settled, very unused portion of the Malone family, namely their emotions. But," she continued, "on the other hand, I didn't want to come, so I suppose this is no more than I could have expected. I didn't want to know them any more than they wanted to know me. Hell of a mess, isn't it?"

The poignancy of her voice pulled at his heart.

"I don't know whether to be sorry for what my mother did to them by taking me away, or thank my lucky stars that I didn't have to grow up here."

"I can't even begin to imagine what you're going through," Trace said softly, resisting the urge to pull Honor into his arms. He knew she'd object. And he didn't relish everyone watching him make a fool of himself. When it came to this woman, he had little to no control over his emotions. "But I can imagine how my part in this crisis has seemed to you. Honor, as God is my witness, I never meant to deceive you or hurt you. You've got to believe me!"

His vehemence startled her. She whispered back in frustration, "Don't ask for miracles. This is almost more than I can tolerate for one evening and still remain sane. What I can say is, I *do* know that this would have probably happened, with or without your intervention." And then her eyes grew stormy as she continued. "But you should have been honest with me from the very beginning, and you know it!"

The accusation hung between them, achingly obvious in its honesty.

"If I had, think of what we'd have missed, lady."

Honor blushed, thankful of the patio's shadows. She knew what Trace was referring to and was unable to argue with the truth of the statement. She shuddered wearily.

"I've had just about all of a good time I can take for one night. I need out of here. Will you help me make a graceful exit?"

He nodded and traced the curve of her cheek with his thumb. Her question and the quiver in her voice nearly broke his heart.

"Your answer may not be what my heart *wants* to hear, but I hear you. Just leave everything to me."

He took her by the arm with a firm yet gentle grip, and started back indoors, pausing to speak quietly to J.J.

"Honor wants to call home and check on her business. I'm going to show her to the den and then make my own exit. Thanks for the dinner. As usual, Trudy outdid herself. I've a lot of work to catch up on at the office, so I'll check in with you by phone tomorrow."

Hastings looked at Honor, gauging with interest the interplay between her and Trace. He couldn't resist the belittling comment that slipped through his slick smile.

"I didn't realize you had such a major role to play in your little business, Honor. Your grandfather has been informing me of your background since your abduction. I suppose your education has been varied to say the least. Growing up in a *café* was probably never boring."

Trace sucked in his breath at the rudeness. Fury dumbfounded him. But Honor's own words felled the lawyer with clean precision.

"You shouldn't be so…hasty." She purposefully lingered on the obviously hated terminology. "Don't assume anything about someone you just met, Mr. Lawrence. My little café is a twenty-four-hour, nonstop business. I have staff for three full shifts at a restaurant that seats nearly two hundred people. And, I've done the books for the business since my sophomore year at college. I graduated four years ago and have worked full-time with my mother and enjoyed it immensely. Naturally I'm concerned about something that we spent a lifetime building. Now if you will excuse me?"

His eyes narrowed and he masked his anger with an overdramatic display as he threw up his hands in mock surrender.

Honor had never wanted to slap someone's face so badly in her entire life.

"I'm going to say good night. I'm certain that I'll see you again before I leave. J.J., thank you for everything. See you in the morning."

She made up for her rather cool dismissal of the group by leaning forward and giving her grandfather a quick kiss on the corner of his chin.

And then they were gone.

Erin fumed. Tonight she'd lost more ground with her father than she had in the last twenty years. Father Andrew gathered his rather vague wits about him, let himself fall back into his otherworldly demeanor, and quickly uttered his own farewells. That left J.J., his daughter, and his lawyer alone on the terrace.

J.J. watched Erin's barely masked fury. His daughter had *that* look on her face again. Ever since she was a small child she'd craved, even demanded, all of his attention. No matter how fiercely he'd tried to show her his love, she was never satisfied. She imagined slights, fostered false accusations within her own mind, until he and Meggie had been helpless to change her behavior. They'd simply learned to accept it.

But now with the arrival of his long-lost granddaughter, he began to worry all over again. Surely Erin wouldn't do anything to harm the girl. After all, she was her own flesh and blood. Her brother Johnny's only child. Surely Erin had that much family spirit about her.

He turned to Hastings and spoke, pushing his fears back into the recesses of his mind where they belonged. "First thing tomorrow, Hastings, I want to begin a full audit of the company holdings. I'm going to be making some changes in my will and need an updated ver-

sion for the codicil. You know the routine. Start the ball rolling."

He grimaced and shifted his weight onto his good leg as he tapped the cane against the flagged terrace floor. "I think it's time I call it a night. Erin, my dear, I'll leave you two alone. Don't hurry if you're inclined to enjoy some time out here together. This is a night for romance and I'm way past everything but memories." He leaned over, patted her gently on the back, and gave her his usual brusque good-bye kiss.

Hastings felt the bile from his stomach boiling up into his throat. *My God! Not an audit! And not now!* But he could tell by the look on J.J.'s face that his mind was made up. He swallowed harshly, mentally shelving his panic. He'd deal with this later.

Erin wanted to throw something. But there was nothing at hand. As a result, Hastings received the brunt of her anger. He gathered her in his arms, perfectly willing to fulfill J.J.'s offer of romancing the boss's daughter when she shrieked wildly into his ear. "He's going to change his will," she cried, shoving herself out of Hastings's embrace. "She'll get everything, and all my years as the devoted daughter will be for nothing. She is the spitting image of Mother. That's all it will take. That's why she came. She's after his money. I know it! I don't know how, but we've got to stop this. And you're going to help me."

Hastings frowned, letting Erin ramble as she vented her anger. The best thing he could do was agree with whatever she said. But he had no intention of following J. J. Malone's orders. He had some problems of his own to solve. J.J.'s decisive move to change his will was going to send him straight to hell.

He'd spent the better part of his youth trying, with no success, to persuade the heir of the Malone fortune to marry him. If the fortune was going to be divided, he had to rethink his options. He knew there was no chance of Honor O'Brien considering him as a suitor. It was obvious that Trace Logan had beat him to that. *But,* he thought, *I'm not finished yet.* And he had some tracks to cover that only he knew existed. There would be no audit. Not yet!

He quietly escorted Erin to his car, letting the fury of her twisted imagination fall on deaf ears. He'd make his excuses tonight when he got to her apartment. He was in no mood to fake romance with Erin now. There was much to be done before business tomorrow.

Honor made her call to Charlie's, unaware of Trace's extreme distraction. He was bemused by her allure; entranced because it was so natural. Her face lit up as she obviously recognized whomever had answered the phone. Her sharp, decisive answers impressed him as she assumed the role of owner and quickly solved several problems regarding the business. She leaned her head back and laughed, unaware of the seductive sound of her voice. She kicked off her shoes, wiggling her toes in obvious relief as she continued her call, oblivious to Trace's fascination.

His body tightened. It was going to be difficult to stand and not give away what he was feeling. Honor laughed, and he wished it was at something he'd said. Her shoes fell off, and he wanted to personally remove the rest of her clothing. How in heaven's name was he going to be able to keep his hands off this woman and keep his sanity intact? She was infuriating, independent and intoxicating. And he was in trouble.

Honor hung up the phone and turned to face him with a lingering smile on her face. If he didn't have to move, he might get away with it. But something—probably hormones—pulled him up and out of the chair.

"Thank you, Trace," she said quietly. "It felt good to touch base."

Trace nodded and swallowed, trying to think of something to say that wouldn't get him into further trouble. Nothing came to mind.

Honor frowned. The least he could have said was, "You're welcome."

"What's the matter with you?" she asked.

"Nothing," Trace replied, wondering just how much of what he was feeling showed. Obviously not as much as he'd feared.

She shrugged. "You want to walk me to my room?" The question surprised them both.

"If I can," he mumbled, then groaned as Honor completely captured his wandering thoughts into a single, focusing ache when she bent over to retrieve her shoes. Her legs went all the way to…

Trace shuddered, wiped a shaky hand across his face, and followed Honor out into the hall and up the long, carpeted stairway.

"I'll sleep better now that I've called home," Honor said as they started toward her room. "The initial meeting is over. I can face whatever comes. Although I doubt if I'll prolong their misery or mine. I've met them. I'll visit a few days, but I'm going home as soon as I can book a flight."

She turned and leaned against her bedroom door.

"I don't belong here. At one point I might have, but no longer. One of my pet peeves used to be people who were always announcing that they must *find themselves*. I used to think that was an excuse for not wanting to get about the business of living. Now I'm not so sure. I don't know who I am, either."

Her voice tugged at Trace's heart. She was trying to sound so confident and secure about accepting this nightmare she'd been thrust into when she was actually struggling to stay ahead of the next surprise.

"You're the most together woman I know, Honor O'Brien. If you need any reminding about how you are, you just give me a call. I'll be more than happy to remind you."

His voice was deep and ragged as he struggled with his conscience and his libido. One kept telling him he'd already done enough to upset this woman, and the other kept telling him he hadn't even started.

"No," she argued. "I don't know who I am. Don't you understand, Trace? The real Honor O'Brien died nearly twenty-six years ago. And the real Mary Margaret Malone as good as died when she was eight months old. I'm no one. I'm just a patchwork of one small woman's mistake. She did her best to put me back together again, but I don't know if it was enough."

She sighed and leaned her head against his chest. "I can't think about any of this any more tonight. If I do, my brain is going to self-destruct. Thanks for the rescue," her dimple flashed, "and thanks for walking me home."

Trace slid his arms around her and pulled her up against his aching body until she relaxed and allowed herself the luxury of the contact. Her head came down and pillowed against the strength of his shoulder. They stood in the shadowed hallway as their heartbeats synchronized into one steady, pulsing rhythm. The evening's tension slid away as Honor relaxed in his arms. He rocked her against him and wished this night didn't have to end.

This is why God made women. Because it feels so damn good to hold them.

"I'll call you tomorrow," Trace whispered into the tumble of her curls beneath his chin. "If you haven't made plans with J.J., let me show you some of Colorado Springs. You gave me the cook's tour of Odessa, remember?"

"I remember more than you probably want me to," Honor said, looking up at the solemn expression on his face. "And I would love to see the sights, especially the caves."

Trace felt his heart sink as he grinned wryly. "Oh, hell, Honor. Caves are dark and damp and they have bats. You're a woman. Women are supposed to be afraid of stuff like that."

Honor knew instantly that she'd hit a nerve. "If you're uncomfortable doing that, we can do something else," she said, knowing full well he was going to deny it.

"You're a menace, you know that?" he growled. "I'll go into the damn cave, but I don't have to like it. Maybe you'll hold my hand if I get scared. What do you think?"

"I think that's the sorriest line I ever heard used just for the excuse to grope a woman, Trace Logan. I thought you'd be able to come up with something a little more original."

Her voice had lightened and the heavy sadness seemed to have disappeared from those stormy gray eyes. Trace would walk through a cave full of snakes just to hear her laugh again.

"I'm going to have to tell you good night, lady, before you discover any more of my unmanly weaknesses. I'm already brainless where you're concerned."

He leaned down, cupped her face in his hands, and breathed his good night kiss against her lips.

Honor felt her stomach muscles pull until she imagined a distinct link between her belly button and her little toe. Every instinct she had told her to reach behind her back, turn the doorknob, and pull them both into the anonymous darkness of her bedroom. But she retrieved her last rational thought just before it went over the precipice in her mind and ended their goodbye with a prediction.

"Tomorrow will be a better day. It has to. Today couldn't have been worse if we'd planned it."

Trace nodded, reluctantly released his hold on Honor, and began to walk away. When he got to the top of the stairs he turned. Honor was watching him from her doorway. He waved and smiled.

Putting his foot on that first stair step was the hardest thing he'd ever had to do. Every instinct in his body kept telling him to turn around and go back inside with that woman, close the door, and shut out the world. But he knew he couldn't. Because inevitably tomorrow *would* come and he was in no mood for regrets.

Chapter 6

Trace frowned as the phone rang again, threw his pencil down in disgust, and knew as he answered it that it would be a miracle if he finished this contract bid by the deadline. He quickly ended the conversation, knowing that he was going to have to work all day and all night just to get the bid in the mail on time.

He should have expected the mess on his desk. He'd been gone too long searching for Honor. Then he'd stayed too long after he'd found her. It had been all he could do last night to leave her standing at the doorway to her room. Every instinct he had told him to follow her inside, locking them in and the rest of the world out. Then he'd had to call Honor this morning to postpone their tour of Colorado Springs. He closed his eyes and sighed, recalling the soft, silky sound of her voice as she'd answered the phone.

* * *

"Hello," she mumbled, wondering for a fraction of a second where she was and who would be calling at this time of morning.

The deep, familiar drawl was instant orientation and sent a wave of longing spiraling through the pit of her stomach that had nothing to do with the resentment she was supposed to be feeling for Trace Logan.

"Good morning, Honor," Trace said softly. "Did I wake you?"

"Yes," she answered, and stretched, muffling a yawn.

Trace groaned and tried not to think of how Honor would look stretched out on a bed…his bed…soft and pliant, sleep-muddled and sexy as hell.

"Did you want something?" Honor asked puzzled by the persistent silence on the other end of the phone.

All her question did was pull another soft groan from the pit of Trace's belly.

"Are you all right?" she asked. "If you're sick, we can postpone the sightseeing. After all," she said quietly, "this trip wasn't intended to be a vacation."

"No, no, honey," Trace finally managed to say. "I'm not sick. But I am going to have to delay our sightseeing. It looks like this office went to hell in a handbasket while I was gone. I can't leave just yet."

"No big deal," she said, masking her disappointment with a blasé attitude. "Besides, your responsibilities toward me ended when you persuaded me to come to Colorado with you, remember?"

"Dammit, Honor! Don't start that stuff again," Trace growled angrily. "You know good and well what I think of you. At least you would if you'd quit blaming me for something I didn't start."

The silence stretched and Trace panicked, certain that he'd angered her into complete rejection. It was something he couldn't face.

Finally she spoke and her words surprised him. It was the first time he'd ever heard her admit that he might be lacking in culpability.

"I know," she finally answered. "But Trace, none of this is easy for me. Everyone keeps saying such horrible things about Momma. And I have to sit back and let them. I feel like a cuckoo's child; left in the wrong nest on purpose for someone else to raise."

"Look, honey," he said quietly, "if you get to feeling unwanted, just remember that I'm still around. And I can say without hesitation that I damn sure want you. Now go back to sleep. I'll call you later."

He hung up before Honor had a chance to argue or agree. She didn't know how she felt. One minute she wanted to curse the ground he walked on and the next she was resisting the urge to lay down on that same ground beneath him.

She rolled over on her stomach and buried her face in the pillow. *Oh, Momma, I need you! I don't know what to do!* And as suddenly as she'd asked, she knew.

Trace suppressed his wandering thoughts and buzzed the outer office for Irene to bring in the latest projected air freight costs. The sooner he finished, the sooner he could see Honor. He knew J.J. was at the doctor's office and hoped he would be released to come back to work. Even part-time would help.

It was nearly noon when he heard the door to his office open. He looked up and then smiled in pleased surprise as J.J. came striding in wearing a cocky grin and a pinstriped suit.

"Here I am, boy. Released with no restrictions. It's about time, for my peace of mind as well as Sinless Sinclair's safety. We'd spent just about all of the quality time with each other that we could stand."

"You don't appreciate Trudy," Trace rebuked with a smile, and then looked beyond J.J., hoping for a glimpse of Honor's tall, voluptuous figure and her smiling face.

"She's not here," J.J. said sarcastically. "I dropped her off downtown to do some sightseeing. Said she'd get a cab home. Damn, but she's independent."

"Not unlike others I might mention," Trace reminded him, trying not to show his disappointment.

J.J. continued, "I can see how I rate around here now, so I'll answer before you remember you didn't ask," he teased. "Well, Trace, my man, it's great to be back. Thanks for asking."

A red flush highlighted Trace's cheekbones. He satisfied himself with a grumbled rebuke.

"Shut up, J.J., I don't care if you are the boss. Grab a pen and paper and help me figure this bid."

J.J. smiled slyly and complied with the younger man's frustrated orders. They were soon both hard at work.

In spite of her resolve to keep Trace at arm's length, Honor had been disappointed when he'd called to cancel their sightseeing trip. But it had given her the perfect opportunity to follow up on a decision she'd made after his phone call. She was going to the library and pull every old reference she could find pertaining to her disappearance from the Malone family. She needed to understand their point of view. Maybe then she could come to terms with her reluctance to face the fact that she was a genuine Malone. She didn't want to face what her mother had done, and her cool reception at dinner last night had given her absolutely no incentive to pursue the matter further. Only an inbred sense of justice kept her from packing her bags and taking the first plane back to Texas. That, and a reluctance to tell Trace Logan good-bye.

Thanks to a very helpful librarian, it hadn't taken long to find the material she needed. Due to the age of the documents, most of it was on microfiche. She settled down in front of the tiny screen and began to read. Her face grew solemn, and more than once, tears welled and spilled over onto her cheeks. But she read on, lost in the pictures and stories of a family's tragedy, and finally an acceptance of their devastating loss.

The last article she read had an accompanying picture of J. J. Malone leaving the church after his wife's funeral. The anguish and suffering on his face were caught forever on the tiny black-and-white print. The story was full of the sequence of events that led to the family's run of tragedy and misfortune. But the truth could not be denied. It had all started with the disappearance of eight-month-old Mary Margaret Malone.

Honor turned off the microfiche reader and buried her face in her hands. Her shoulders shook with fatigue. Her eyes burned from the pressure of unshed tears.

"Oh, Momma," she whispered. "What am I going to do? You caused all this mess, then sent me here to fix it. I don't know how, Momma. I don't know how."

"Can I help you, miss?" the librarian asked, as she witnessed Honor's distress. "Are you all right?"

Honor looked up, her gray eyes brimming, and smiled crookedly at the woman's kindly face.

"I don't think I'll ever be all right again," she whispered, then caught herself before she said too much. The woman's curiosity was obviously getting the better of her as she glanced at what Honor had been reading.

"Thank you for your help," Honor said, then grabbed her purse and quickly exited the cool, quiet halls of the library for the hustle and bustle of Colorado Springs on a beautiful sunny day.

The air was crisp, but not too cool. The smell of pine from the tree-covered mountains surrounding the city wafted teasingly through the air, competing with exhaust fumes from the constant flow of city traffic.

Honor began walking aimlessly, looking now and then at the displays in the store windows. But she wasn't really seeing them. She couldn't get past the pain-filled expressions in the newspaper pictures. She couldn't forget the accusing stories of the journalists and their wild suppositions as to why no ransom note had ever appeared. Every trace of the Malone baby simply ended in the park on that day long ago.

A loud, familiar blast from a trucker's horn brought her sharply back to the present, and she turned quickly, half expecting to see someone she knew. She sighed with disappointment as a man with an unfamiliar face smiled and waved at her. She smiled back, knowing the friendly innocence of his greeting came from the long, lonely hours on the road and a yearning to communicate with another human being, if only for a moment.

Soon the trucker was gone, taking the friendly face and teasing smile with him. Honor found herself looking around in confusion. She was hopelessly, definitely lost. And she was exhausted. She looked down at her wristwatch and then blinked in shocked surprise. It was nearly three o'clock. Her stomach grumbled, reminding her that she'd missed lunch. She began searching the store fronts for a promising place to get a bite to eat. She continued walking, unaware that she was being followed.

It was only after the man saw the possibility of losing her in the crowd on the street that he increased his pace and caught up and then passed Honor. He turned just as she started into a sidewalk café and held out his arm, blocking her path.

"Excuse me, miss, but could I see some identification?" he said.

Honor looked startled and took a step backward, eyeing the stocky man's crumpled suitcoat and baggy pants. What gray hair he had left on his head was cut in an old-fashioned flat top. His pudgy cheeks made his small, close-set eyes nearly disappear behind their fleshy bulges. He looked to be in his early sixties and had at one time probably been quite tall. Now he was so stooped that it was hard to guess his height.

"Not until you tell me why you need it," Honor answered, and stared suspiciously.

The man put his hand inside his coat pocket and pulled out a leather-bound wallet. It fell open in his hand with a long, practiced plop. The badge caught the afternoon rays of the sun and flashed sharply in the corner of Honor's eyes. She breathed a sigh of relief. A policeman! She grinned, flashing her single dimple.

The policeman's eyes narrowed. He seemed to be searching his memory as he scanned each and every feature of her face.

"You scared me, Officer. I thought you were trying to mug me. You couldn't have turned up at a more opportune time. I seem to be lost. Maybe you could help?"

The man didn't change his expression nor did he change the nature of his request. Once again, he asked to see her identification. Honor complied with no hesitation. She pulled her wallet from her purse and willingly handed it over. He looked at the face on her driver's license and then back up at Honor, noted the address and then growled, "I wonder if you'd mind coming down to the station with me," he looked back at her license, "Miss O'Brien?"

Honor raised her eyebrows in shock. "It surely can't be a crime to be lost in Colorado Springs. I have no intention of going anywhere with you," she looked down at his badge, "Officer Lane. Not until you tell me what this is all about." She stood firm, a bit frightened of his suspicious manner.

The man knew he had no reason to make her come with him. How could he explain that when he'd first seen her, he thought he'd seen a ghost. It had been instinct that told him she might be the answer to solving a case that had haunted him for years. It couldn't be a coincidence that she was the mirror image of a woman who had belonged to one of Colorado Springs's foremost families. Before he could think of another excuse, the woman took away his decision to insist.

"If you have any questions regarding my presence here, you may want to call J. J. Malone. I'm visiting at his home,." Then she frowned and muttered, "Some welcome I've received from Colorado. This is getting ridiculous."

Lane's heart skipped a beat. She'd mentioned the

magic words and she didn't even know it. He put his badge back into his pocket, ran his thick, beefy fingers through his chopped-off hair and muttered, "You mean you're already staying at the Malone estate?"

"Yes, and if I can find a cab, I'm going to J.J.'s office. I've had more than enough *sightseeing* for one day."

"I'll be quite pleased to take you there myself," he replied. "There's a little matter of some unfinished business that I think J. J. Malone and I have to conduct." He grabbed Honor by the elbow and escorted her toward an unmarked car that looked just about as well kept as his clothing.

His badge and brusque manner got him past the security guard at the gate of Malone Industries and past the guard just inside the main door of the building. Before Honor knew it they were exiting the elevator on the tenth and top floor of the building where the offices of the president were housed.

The perfectly groomed secretary at the main desk looked up at the approaching couple and then stood abruptly, unable to mask her shock as she limply dropped the phone receiver onto her desk.

Honor had seen that look before and masked a sigh of despair. This day wasn't getting any better. Obviously this woman had also known the first Megan Malone, and quite well. She seemed to be in shock.

"Is J. J. Malone in?" Lane growled, refusing to relinquish his grasp on Honor's arm.

Irene nodded dumbly and then finally managed to speak.

"But you can't go in there. He's very busy."

She couldn't quit looking at Honor. She wanted to ask but couldn't bring herself to voice the question. It simply couldn't be! Megan Malone was dead. She'd gone to the funeral herself. So, if this wasn't Megan Malone, then who in the world…?

Honor stared angrily at the officer's grip on her arm, pried each finger off with sarcastic disgust, and then turned her back on the man. She'd had just about all she was going to take from this man. He wouldn't explain himself, yet had nearly dragged her to Malone Industries.

"Is Trace Logan in his office?" Honor asked sharply, and watched the woman's perfectly drawn eyebrows raise even higher on her forehead as she nodded her reply. "Then may I please see him? Just tell him Honor is here. He won't refuse to see us. I can promise you."

Irene looked down in surprise at the phone receiver dangling by its curly cord and quickly placed it back in its proper position. She leaned over, buzzed Trace's office, and then complied with Honor's request. She had barely lifted her finger from the intercom when Trace burst through his office door with J.J. following quickly behind.

"Honor!" Trace couldn't disguise the pleased surprise in his voice. But the expression on Honor's face and the stubborn look on the older man's face standing behind her brought him up short. Something was very wrong. Honor's chin began to tremble. If he'd had to fight snakes, he'd have been ready.

"What's wrong, honey?" he asked. He pulled her into his arms as she began to shake. The fury that exploded inside him surprised them all as he turned on the big man beside her with a vengeance. "What have you done to her?" he growled. "Better yet, who the hell are you?"

J.J. stepped forward and regained control of the situation. "I think I know why he's here," he said, recogniz-ing the elder man. "What I don't understand is how you found out so soon?" He smiled congenially. "I haven't even had time to think about calling the police on this matter. She just arrived yesterday," he explained, as they disappeared into his office.

Trace cupped Honor's face in his hands and took swift note of the look of weary shock in her eyes.

"I'm fine," Honor said, embarrassed at herself for acting so helpless where Trace was concerned. She pulled away from his protective grasp and began to pace the floor, waving her arms in furious abandon. "He just grabbed me on the street and started telling me I was going to have to go to the police station with him. I got lost, and I'm tired, and I missed lunch, and I'm sorry I've disturbed…"

Trace interrupted her, caught her by the shoulders as she paced past him and laid his finger against the pouting softness of her mouth. "You didn't interrupt a damn thing. Thanks to J.J.'s appearance earlier today, we had just finished. Besides, you don't have anything to be sorry for. I suspect this was something J.J. over-looked when he discovered your existence. Even I didn't think about what the police and, God forbid, the media will do with your appearance."

The look of dismay on her face made him regret his hasty words. Not one bit of this whole damn thing had been thought through. All they'd done was yank an unsuspecting woman from her home, thrust her into a strange, unfamiliar family that didn't seem to want her, and then wonder why she was less than receptive to the idea of being a Malone.

"Then she *is* related? Thank goodness. I thought I was losing my mind."

Irene's shaky remark brought them both to their senses as Trace smiled.

"No, Irene. You haven't lost your mind. That's just the reaction I experienced when I first saw her."

Honor stared at that slow, sexy twist of his mouth as he continued the introduction and ignored the smoldering fire in the pit of her stomach.

"Irene, I'd like you to meet Honor O'Brien. At least that's the name she thought was hers. This is also Mary Margaret Malone, J.J.'s granddaughter."

Irene gasped, grabbed her throat in dramatic dismay, and then grabbed a handful of tissues from her desk as she broke into tears. "Oh, this is just wonderful. I'm so pleased to meet you, dear. I'm not normally so distracted."

Trace smiled and patted Irene on the arm. "We're all glad she was found, Irene. I just hope she learns to feel the same about us. So far, it doesn't look like her welcome has been all it should have been."

Irene nodded, quickly excused herself to repair her makeup, and left Trace to deal with the front office.

"Come into my office, Honor. You'll be safe there. I'll just leave the paperwork on this bid with Irene and then I'll take you home."

His words were cajoling, his manner concerned, but there was nothing he could have said that would console Honor today. She'd had more than enough.

"I'll never be safe, Trace Logan. Thanks to that damn letter, my life is in a shambles. And the only home I have is hundreds of miles away. Thanks, but no thanks.

I'll find my own way home. The only thing you can do for me is call a cab."

"You know what, lady?" Trace said through gritted teeth. "I'm getting pretty damn tired of taking the blame for all the trouble you are going through. I didn't write that blasted letter and mail it. I didn't have anything to do with your disappearance when you were a baby. Hell, I barely remember hearing about it. I wasn't more than ten years old. I haven't done anything but try to make this nightmare as easy on you as possible. Well, if you don't need anything from me but a cab, it'll be my pleasure. If you need anything else, you're going to have to ask."

She turned, eyes flashing, head held high, and exited the offices as abruptly as she'd entered. Trace could only watch in dismay as she disappeared in a huff. He turned toward Irene's desk, his heart heavy with a sense of foreboding, and did as he'd promised.

He went back into his office and watched out the expanse of window overlooking downtown Colorado Springs until he saw Honor's tall, graceful figure exit the building. He watched her long, angry strides quickly cover the distance from the building to the outer gates, saw her speak to the guard, and then watched for several minutes until a bright yellow cab arrived. Then she was gone.

Trace had a sinking feeling that she didn't just leave Malone Industries. He had a distinct impression that Honor O'Brien had mentally, if not physically, just departed from Colorado.

By the time Honor arrived back at the Malone estate, she'd calmed down considerably. It wasn't her nature to hold grudges or stay angry for long periods of time. But she was more than tired. She was weary clear down to her soul. She couldn't wait to get inside, take a long, hot bath, and then fix something to eat. She was starving. She let herself into the house, walked quietly through the long, paneled hallway and up the carpeted stairs to the door of her bedroom. She had most of her clothes off before she ever started running her bathwater. When the last article of clothing hit the floor, she sank wearily into the tubful of steamy relief.

A long time later she heard the front door slam with sudden force and sighed. J.J. must be home. And he was probably angry that she hadn't waited for him. At the moment, she could care less. She debated about running some more hot water into her quickly cooling bath and then decided against it. Her stomach grumbled again and hunger won out over comfort. She pulled the plug with her toes and watched the water begin to swirl in a tiny vortex as it drained from the deep, old-fashioned tub. She caught a glimpse of her tall, slender form in the misty mirrors and sighed. Her personality was just about as distinct as her image. She felt disjointed in an abstract way. She could see herself, but not clearly. And that's just the way she felt inside. She knew she was in there. She just didn't know who to ask for.

"Oh, fudge," Honor muttered. "Right now I don't give a damn who's looking back at me. Whoever you are," she said to the foggy image, "if you're as hungry as I am, let's go get something to eat." She began to dress.

"Miss Honor!" Trudy gasped, as Honor walked into the kitchen. "Was there something I could get for you? All you need to do is ring." She pointed toward an intercom system on the wall.

"Pooh," Honor muttered, walking toward the huge double doors of the restaurant-size refrigerator. "The day I can't wait on myself is the day I need to stop eating. Do you have any ham?" Honor asked, poking curiously into the multitude of covered dishes and parcels.

Trudy Sinclair's first reaction was to fuss. She didn't allow anyone in her kitchen. It was her domain by right of passage. She'd withstood the insults of the Malone clan far longer than any of the other servants who'd come and gone.

After the death of J.J.'s wife, being in the house had become unbearable and most of them had departed for a more pleasant position. But something had made Trudy see past the anger and harsh words of the Malone family into the desperation of their actions. They were just lost. Megan Malone had been the anchor. Now they were just drifting. Trudy decided to tie down the remaining Malones as best she could. So she stayed and became, in her own way, indispensable.

She watched Honor's tall figure bent over in the depths of the refrigerator, digging curiously through her dishes. Something clicked inside her heart. This one was special. She could tell.

"Here," Trudy fussed, scurrying toward the open doors. "I think there's a piece of ham in this meat cooler."

"Oh, yes," Honor said gleefully, as she pulled out her prize. "Great! I'm starving. And I can't think of anything that sounds better than some ham and eggs and homemade biscuits." She turned toward the stove with the paper-wrapped meat in her hands. "Do you mind?" she asked, knowing that this *was* Trudy's kitchen. "I'm quite competent in here." She indicated the appliances with a sweep of her hand. "We use stuff like this in my restaurant. And I've certainly taken my turn at chef more than once when an emergency arose. I promise I won't make a mess that I don't clean up." Her anxious, hesitant expression won Trudy's heart.

"You just have at it, honey. If you can't find something you need, just ask."

She bustled busily back to her chore at the sink. She had been cleaning some vegetables for J.J.'s evening meal. Soon both women were busily engrossed in their own meal preparations.

When J.J. burst into the kitchen, his angry voice booming into the silence, it startled them both.

"Trudy!" he yelled. "Have you seen Honor? She stormed out of my office and I can't find her anywhere."

"If you'd calm down and turn around," Honor said quietly, "you'd find me a lot faster."

The look of relief on J.J.'s face was obvious. "My dear," he said as he turned toward her, "you frightened me. I thought you'd gone back to... I mean, I thought you might be—"

"I know what you thought," Honor interrupted, as she stirred the long wooden spoon into her bowl of biscuit dough. "And don't think it didn't cross my mind. But," she grinned, as she turned the dough out onto a bread board and began to knead it lightly, "my stomach got the better of me. I was too hungry to run away. Maybe tomorrow." She reached for the cookie cutter she was using to cut out her biscuits.

"What in hell are you doing?" J.J. bellowed, as he realized that Honor was actually in the kitchen...cooking her own food.

"I'm fixing my supper," she answered mildly. "Where

I come from, the evening meal is not dinner, it's supper. And the noon meal is not lunch, it's dinner. And," she continued, briskly cutting the soft, fluffy dough into perfect circles and placing them on the greased baking sheet, "I like to cook, and I'm good at it. And I was hungry for biscuits, ham, and eggs."

J.J.'s eyes lit up. He hadn't had such plain, simple fare in years. Possibly not since he'd become successful and his Megan had hired a cook instead of preparing the family meals herself. It had been so long since he'd sat in a kitchen and listened to the chatter. Smelled the wonderful, homey smells of food cooking and listened to the pots bubbling away as the women worked. A sharp, painful longing pierced the crusty armor of his heart. He tilted Honor's face toward him, looked with pride at the smudge of flour on her chin and down the front of her borrowed apron, and sighed in contentment.

"I think you're gong to be good for me, girl. I think you may be good for all of us. Sometimes a body forgets what matters most in this world." His sharp blue eyes teared, but he blinked furiously, refusing to allow them access to any more of his buried emotions. "Do you think you made enough for all of us? I can't remember when I've had eggs, biscuits, and ham."

Honor looked at J.J. Then she turned and looked at Trudy's face, saw her argument disappearing, and smiled at them both. "I think I made enough to feed an army. My eyes must have been bigger than my stomach. Momma always said they were. I'd be happy to share."

Trudy's insistence that she not be included was ignored, and soon three places had been set at the kitchen table. A platter of fried ham, a bowl of fluffy scrambled eggs, and a plate of golden-brown steaming hot biscuits became the focal point of the evening. Trudy located a jar of homemade preserves, some butter, and a jug of milk. The food was delicious, but it was the camaraderie between the three that was special that night. For the first time since his Meggie died, J. J. Malone didn't feel lonely. And Honor felt, for the first time since her arrival, that there just might be a possibility of learning to belong here, just as she had in Odessa.

Her conscience had been rebuking her all evening. She knew she'd been particularly rude to Trace. He'd come to her defense so quickly when she and the policeman had entered the offices. He had instantly assumed the role of protector and she'd just as quickly attacked him and his motives when she knew good and well that he was not to blame. She was ashamed of herself. Honor didn't know why she kept pushing Trace away. It wasn't like her to be so suspicious or unforgiving. Tomorrow, she told herself, she'd call him. If it was okay with J.J., she'd even invite him for supper. She smiled and mentally corrected herself. It would have to be *dinner* while she was here with the Malones. They weren't *supper* kind of people.

She finished her nightly grooming routine, laid her hairbrush down on the dresser, and crawled into bed. She sighed, closed her eyes, and wished heartily that she was back with the *supper* kind of people right now. If she were home, she'd be doing the books, or possibly filling in for one of the staff. She wondered if they were busy or if they'd had problems that couldn't be resolved. She made a mental note to call Charlie's first thing tomorrow. If she had to, she'd be on the first flight home.

Just before she drifted off to sleep, she nearly let herself drift back into the sadness and regret that she'd experienced after visiting the library. But she refused to allow herself to feel any responsibility for the events that had followed her disappearance. She had to keep telling herself it just wasn't her fault. And try as she might, she couldn't fault her mother as stringently as she knew she should. She'd loved Charlie O'Brien too much. Soon she was asleep and as she slept, she dreamed.

And in her dreams she stood alone, sandwiched between shadowy figures whom she recognized but could not touch. Behind her was the fading image of her mother, small, blonde, and gentle, urging her to take a step forward. In front of her stood several tall, judgmental figures, accusing, pointing, demanding more of her than she could give. She struggled beneath the covers, trying in vain to turn around and go back with her mother. But she couldn't seem to move.

Then she heard his voice, deep and gentle, persuasive and compelling. She saw his tall, strong figure standing beside her. She imagined that she could feel his touch sure and strong. She relaxed. She knew as she fell into a deep, dreamless sleep that no matter what happened, no matter who demanded things of her that she was unwilling or unable to give, that if she would let him, Trace Logan would be beside her. And that would be enough.

Chapter 7

Honor wandered aimlessly through the Malone mansion, mentally noting the absence of personal mementoes in the empty rooms. Such a huge, opulent home and so devoid of the things that give meaning and pleasure to life.

A phone call home had assured her all was running smoothly at Charlie's despite her absence. It was obvious that Hank, her bartender, and several of the day staff were more than curious about her prolonged stay. It was also obvious that rumor had already spread of Charlotte O'Brien's secret, even back home. She hadn't denied nor acknowledged anything to which Hank had alluded, but his vehement assurance that nothing could change their opinions of Charlie made her feel better. It had gone a long way toward healing the ache in Honor's heart.

Her sleep had been troubled. She suspected it was her

conscience telling her what a fool she'd been to alienate Trace when he'd been the only person who'd shown sincere concern for her since this whole nightmare had begun. It was past time to apologize. She hadn't been raised to hold grudges. And she couldn't forget the hurt that had appeared in Trace's eyes when she'd stormed out of Malone Industries.

Of all the people involved, Trace Logan was the one most innocent of any blame. He wasn't part of her family, past or present, and yet he'd been the one she'd made to suffer most.

Honor went to the phone and made her call.

"Malone Industries," a woman's voice answered.

Honor bit her lower lip in frustration. She'd forgotten all calls would go through a switchboard.

"Trace Logan's office, please."

When Irene answered, Honor repeated her request. "May I speak to Trace Logan, please?"

"I'm sorry. He's on another line," Irene answered in a businesslike manner. "Would you care to leave a message?"

She muffled her dismay. She'd been ready to apologize, and all she kept getting were receptionists.

"Just tell him Honor called," she said softly. "He has my number."

She hung up too quickly to hear Irene urging her to hold.

He'd been so angry yesterday and his accusations had been all too true. She had been blaming him for the past few days of turmoil when none of it had actually been his fault. He'd just had the misfortune to be the one who'd first made her aware of her mother's deception.

That was at the bottom of most of her anger. She and

Charlie had shared everything. At least she'd believed that to be true up to the day Trace Logan had knocked a hole in her world and let out all the safety and trust. It was just going to take time to patch the hole. The trust would come later.

Honor wandered through the kitchen area, saw a note from Trudy indicating her whereabouts and what time she would be home. J.J. was at the office and wouldn't be home until evening. There was nothing to do and no one to talk to. It was with no small amount of relief that the doorbell's ring set Honor hurrying to answer its melodic summons.

"Erin!" Honor said, unable to disguise the surprise in her voice.

Her aunt was the last person she'd expected to come calling. She hadn't seemed pleased that Honor even existed.

Erin smiled a cool, casual greeting, waved an antiseptic kiss toward Honor's cheek, and escorted herself into her father's home.

"My dear!" she gushed, while the smile in her voice didn't quite meet her eyes. "I've come to take you to lunch. Father said he'd left you all alone. He's just too wrapped up in that job for his own good."

Honor hid her shock at the invitation and refused to acknowledge an inward warning signal that told her Erin Malone was not sincere. She mentally rebuked herself. It wasn't like Honor to be so suspicious and she decided to give her aunt the benefit of the doubt.

"Come, come," Erin urged, looking down at her watch. "I've made a reservation at my favorite restaurant." When she saw Honor's hesitation, she added, "Father knows where we're going. He said he might even be able to join us."

"Well," Honor relented. "Just let me get my purse. Will these clothes do or should I change?"

Erin looked coldly at the tall, fashionably dressed young woman wearing a crisp, winter-white pants suit and her mother's face and pushed back the frown that threatened to wrinkle her high, round forehead.

"You look fine," she replied, and then couldn't resist a rude dig. "People as tall as you can wear any old thing off a rack and still look smart. Your little suit will suffice. Come, we need to hurry."

Honor let the remark pass unheeded but made a mental note to be on guard. Somehow she didn't think this lunch was quite the family outing Erin proclaimed it to be.

She exited the Malone house and missed Trace's call by minutes.

Trace slammed the phone down in disgust, mentally cursing the fates that tied him to his job and told Irene to keep trying the number until she reached Honor. He had to talk to her. He regretted his outburst the moment it had happened, but by the time Honor had exited the offices in anger it had been too late to take it back.

The restaurant was crowded, yet Erin was treated with obvious deference. Honor supposed money and prestige talked no matter where one lived. The food was fashionable, not memorable, but it didn't matter. Honor wasn't hungry and had the most overwhelming urge to bolt and run. She'd never felt so exposed. She watched her aunt's agitation and noted how her eyes kept flashing nervously as her gaze swept the crowded room. Honor watched her nod occasionally at someone she would recognize, and once Erin even smiled and waved at a couple across the room. But she made no move to include Honor in her inner circle of acquaintances or even introduce her to any of the people who'd stop to say hello as they passed their table. She would simply excuse her rudeness with an offhand remark and a shrug.

"Those are just old family friends. No one you'd know or be interested in. After all, you're only here for a visit, right?"

Her casual question was punctuated with a near-lethal stare as she waited for Honor to disagree.

Honor was spared an answer as she saw Erin's face light up. She knew without turning around that the reason she'd been duped into coming here had obviously just arrived. And she had a terrible suspicion that it wasn't J. J. Malone who'd just come into the restaurant.

"Darling!" Hastings Lawrence gushed, as he leaned over and kissed his fiancée on the cheek. He raked Honor's cool beauty with a sly gaze and then wisely gave Erin his undivided attention. "Sorry I'm late, ladies. But duty comes before pleasure and I had to finalize a contract. I'm certain you both understand. Am I forgiven?"

Erin looked sharply at Hastings as he greeted Honor and then pulled herself back to the situation at hand. This was no time for jealousy. Hastings's slow nod to her as he walked behind Honor's chair assured her that all was going according to plan. She sighed with relief and then fidgeted through the dessert that Hastings insisted on ordering. Her niece sat in regal silence across the table from them. If Erin didn't know better she'd think Honor was suspicious.

Erin glared as she watched Hastings actually scrape his dessert plate for the last crumbs of his cherry cheesecake. She told herself that her imagination was just playing tricks. There was no way Honor could know what she had planned. It wasn't much, but Hastings had agreed it was a good idea. And it was all she could think of on short notice. For her piece of mind, it had better work and it had better be good. She was intent on making Honor's stay as short and uncomfortable as possible. She wanted her world back the way it had been before they knew Johnny Malone's daughter still existed.

Hastings Lawrence had agreed with alacrity to helping Erin with her little scheme. In fact it had been his sly innuendoes that had given Erin the idea. Anything that removed Honor O'Brien from the picture could only help him. If he couldn't think of something fast, he'd be unable to stall the audit. It was only a matter of time before J.J. asked him about its progress.

Hastings didn't have much time to cover the tracks he'd been carelessly leaving for years. Ideally, just calling off the audit would solve everything. But if the possibility existed of causing a permanent rift between J. J. Malone and his newfound granddaughter, he was willing to pursue it. He needed time to hide the tracks of his greed.

Erin signed for the check and without further delay, led the way from the restaurant. They had no sooner exited when a crowd of people started shouting the Malone name. They pressed forward, some armed with flash cameras, some with video equipment, all intent on the same thing: a scoop on the resurrection of Mary Margaret Malone.

Honor stood numbed with shock as they trapped her against the outside wall of the restaurant. She couldn't move and she wanted to scream. This was no more than she deserved for trusting someone her instincts told her was false.

Honor turned her head slightly, searching the crowd for her aunt. When their eyes met, Honor knew by the expression of glee on Erin's face that she'd planned this. And by the look on Hastings's face, he'd helped, too.

Honor smiled a slow, secretive smile that wiped the pleased expression from Erin's face. She'd expected Honor to panic and run. But she'd underestimated her niece. Honor might be a Malone by birth, but she'd been bred a Texan. And they didn't run from trouble.

Honor turned back to the shouting crowd of newsmen and photographers. "Excuse me," she said calmly, and began forcing her way through the crowd toward the curb, ignoring the shouted questions and microphones shoved in her face.

Erin panicked, unable to hide her surprise as her niece began to leave. She followed suit, desperately pushing her small self through the tight fit of bodies who kept angling for a picture or a statement. Honor reached the curb, hailed a passing cab, and then stood in wait until Erin and Hastings had worked their way to the street.

Believing that Honor was holding the cab, Erin started off the curb when Honor raised her hand and spoke to the crowd. They quickly hushed, waiting for the words from the long-lost heir that would give them their scoop.

"Gentlemen...and ladies." Honor lingered on her choice of words, since the behavior of the crowd suggested they were obviously anything but. "If you're so desperate for a story, I suggest you interview my dear aunt and her fiancé. He's also the family lawyer. I'm sure they have plenty to say with regard to my appearance."

Erin's mouth went slack as a red flush of anger spread from the neck of her dress upward into her plastered hairline. Her niece leaned forward and whispered in her ear.

"It's all yours, sweetie," Honor drawled. "And you'd do well to remember the Alamo. Texans don't run, they fight." She slid into the cab with one smooth movement and closed the door in their faces.

The cabdriver moved into the stream of traffic as the crowd of people swelled around Erin Malone and her fiancé. One thing Erin did note in her fury before she was engulfed by the clamoring crowd: Honor O'Brien had never looked back.

"Do you have all the papers?" J.J. asked, as he continued to dig through the stack on his desk.

"Yes," Trace answered, and snapped the lock shut on his briefcase.

He had less than two hours to go home, pack a few clothes, and make his flight to Washington, D.C. But he needed to hear Honor's voice before he left, assure himself that she wasn't still angry. He still had not been able to get a phone call through to her and couldn't stop the sensation of dread that overwhelmed him when he thought about leaving Colorado without making peace with her.

He could barely face the thought. But if she couldn't see past her anger to the relationship they'd begun to build before she'd discovered her mother's secret, then maybe, as much as Trace hated to admit it, she'd never be able to forgive him. And if she couldn't forgive him, there was nothing on which to build a relationship. Yet Trace refused to consider that possibility. In this short space of time, Honor had become more important to him than any woman he'd ever known.

From the first time they'd met when she'd collapsed in his arms in tears until yesterday when she'd turned away and stormed out of his office without a word, he'd been in a fog. And if he didn't pull himself together, Malone Industries was going to lose a very important contract.

That was the reason for the hasty trip to Washington, D.C. If he didn't go soothe a few feathers, Malone Industries was going to lose a tremendous amount of revenue. The loss would be staggering. Trace had no choice but to leave.

His exit from the office was abruptly halted at J.J.'s shout of anger. "What's the…" he began, but didn't have to finish his question. He could see for himself. The television was on, and Honor's distress as she faced the crowd of reporters filled the entire screen. Someone had captured her on film from the moment she'd exited the restaurant until she'd disappeared in the cab. The camera caught the look that passed between the two women as Honor leaned over and whispered in Erin's ear. There was no audio with the film, but it was unnecessary. The expressions were there on their faces for the world to see.

The string of oaths that erupted from J.J.'s lips were echoed in Trace's heart. They both knew who was responsible.

"Oh, my God!" Trace muttered. This would just about be the last straw for Honor. He cursed the day he'd ever persuaded her to come back to Colorado with him.

"Irene!" J.J. yelled into the intercom. "Get Erin and Hastings in here. I don't want excuses. I want warm bodies—in my office now!"

"Yes, sir!" she replied, and hastened to do his bidding. Whatever those two had done now, she wouldn't want to be in their places for anything.

"You'll miss your flight," J.J. growled, as he paced behind his desk.

"I'll get another," Trace said quietly. "I'll make the meetings tomorrow. But I'm not leaving...not just yet."

J.J. turned, his sharp eyes missing nothing of the blank, expressionless look on Trace's face. He felt a twinge of remorse for Erin and then stifled at the thought. Daughter or not, he knew just how Trace felt and nodded his approval for what he knew would probably amount to a verbal holocaust. He'd seen Trace Logan in action before, and he was deadly.

Both culprits of the media leak worked in the Malone Building but on different floors; Erin on the second floor in Marketing, and Hastings on the ninth floor in Legal. But they'd obviously conferred before walking into J.J.'s office because they arrived together.

Erin entered wearing a belligerent expression; Hastings more prudent with an innocent, expectant air. Both came to an abrupt halt as Trace stepped in front of them. The low, ominous tone of his voice did nothing to ease their nervousness.

"I caught your little act on television today," he growled, and then forestalled Erin's interruption with a single look.

Erin shivered in spite of herself at the cold, flat expression of distaste in Trace's eyes. Wisely she refrained from defending herself and settled for glaring back at him instead.

Trace turned his attention to Hastings.

The lawyer's nervous behavior was evident as he ran his finger inside the collar of his shirt and looked around for someone to step in and stop this conversation from happening. No one moved. The balding spot on the top of his head turned bloodred and he began to sweat.

"Listen, you sonofabitch," Trace said. "I'm on my way to D.C., and while I'm gone you better pray that nothing like what just happened to Honor today ever happens again. You better hope to God that she doesn't so much as get a hangnail. Because if she does, I'm holding you responsible." He touched the lawyer's shirt front with his forefinger, jabbing the button just over Hasting's heart with repetitive regularity. "Do you hear me? You don't want to ignore what I've said. You don't want to make me mad." His words got quieter and quieter, until his last sentence was barely above a whisper. Hastings looked like he was going to be sick.

"How dare you!" Erin gasped, and looked to her father, trying to judge his reaction to Trace's threat. Her heart sank as she saw him frown. He wasn't looking at Trace, he was looking at her.

"Shut up," Trace ordered, barely sparing Erin a glance.

Erin shook with rage. She wasn't used to being thwarted.

"You've no right speaking to me like that," Erin cried, as indignation and fury warred with each other inside her trembling body.

"You're right," Trace said quietly, "I don't have the

right. I'll leave that to your father." He gave Hastings a last, long look of warning, ignored Erin's existence, gathered his belongings, and left.

"Close the door," J.J. ordered.

Hastings hurried to comply.

Honor arrived at home only to find more journalists camped at the edge of the Malone estate, hoping for a glimpse of J. J. Malone's granddaughter. Ignoring the requests for an interview and the shouted questions, Honor paid the cabdriver and quickly hurried inside the house. This was definitely something for which she'd been unprepared. But she knew that if she'd just thought this whole trip through, she should have expected it.

The atmosphere inside the mansion was not much better, but for different reasons. Honor found Trudy in the library, distraught from the news that her only sister, who lived in a retirement village in Denver, had been in an accident. She was near tears, torn with the need to be near her sister, yet aware of the impending mess that the Malones were going to have to face in the coming days. She'd also seen the film clip and was well aware of the reason for the newspeople outside the home. She didn't know what to do but burst into tears. So she did.

Honor took the decision out of Trudy's hands by making a phone call. Within the hour she had booked Trudy on a flight to Denver, helped her pack, and called a cab to take her to the airport.

"I don't know what Mr. Malone will say," Trudy sniffed, as she clutched her bag and watched out the window for the cab's arrival.

"I do," Honor replied. "He'll say, Have a safe trip and call when you get there. And that's what I expect you to do. Please," Honor urged. "Don't worry about this mess here. It was to be expected. And don't worry about J.J. I can cook. Lord knows I've had enough practice at that. As for the rest of this..." She shrugged. "It'll soon blow over. I'm just a seven-day wonder that will soon be forgotten."

"Well," Trudy muttered, embarrassed that she'd allowed herself to come undone in front of Honor. "I won't soon forget you, dear," she said with vehemence. "I don't know what I'd have done without you. I couldn't seem to make a decision."

"I understand," Honor said, giving Trudy a gentle hug. "Tragedy does that to a person. Believe me, I know."

Trudy looked startled, then nodded and blew her nose loudly before proclaiming, "Here comes my cab. I'll call."

Honor watched as the cabdriver deftly maneuvered through the people and vehicles congregated at the boundary of the Malone estate. Then it disappeared.

She stared at the mass of news vans, photographers, and passersby and promptly burst into tears. *My God, Momma! Look what you have done to me!*

Trace took the curve into the Malone estate in dangerous fashion. He didn't even slow down for the photographers standing in the street, ogling through cameras outfitted with telescopic lenses for a *one of a kind* shot of the resurrected heiress. He ignored their startled expressions and angry words as he drove rapidly to the house.

The front door was locked, and no amount of ringing on the doorbell got him an answer. He headed for the service entrance. It was unlocked, but Trudy was nowhere in sight. What in the world had happened to this family?

"Honor!" His voice echoed frantically throughout the entire downstairs as he ran from room to room. But she was nowhere to be seen. Had she and Trudy simply vanished? There was nowhere left to look but her bedroom. If she wasn't there, he was calling J.J. and then he was calling the police. If he'd obeyed his first instincts when he'd seen the tape on the television, he'd have done it then. She needed protection. He headed for the stairs, taking them two at a time.

Honor rolled over on her back, swiping quickly at the fresh set of tears that had just begun to fall. She staggered from her bed as she heard her name being called. The tone of voice was frantic, but it was too faint for her to tell who was searching for her. She opened the door to her room just as Trace bounded to the top of the stairs.

Thank God! he thought, and then his stomach took a dive toward his heels. *She's been crying.*

"Trace?" Honor's shaky voice was his undoing.

"Honey? Are you all right?" he asked.

She took a deep breath as another stream of tears slid from her eyes. "No."

The quiet, broken word was all it took. She was in his arms. "Where's Trudy, sweetheart?"

"Gone. Her sister had an accident."

Trace's heart twisted at the forlorn look in her stormy gray eyes. That beautiful, expressive mouth, so often laughing, was knotted in an expression of defeat. He couldn't bear it. He lifted her into his arms, carried her to her room, and kicked the door shut behind him.

"I'll take you home."

The statement was what she'd been waiting to hear.
It was the ultimate gift of his feelings. He wanted her
happiness first, before his job, before his boss's desires.
He would take her home!

And then his arms tightened around her shoulders
as he carried her to the bed and turned and sat, holding
her lightly across his lap, gentling her with softly whispered word and touch. A slow warming swept over her.
Honor knew that no matter where she went or how long
it took her to get there that she'd never be home unless
she was in Trace Logan's arms.

"Oh, Trace," she whispered, and pressed her mouth
against the wild, angry pulse in his neck. "As long as
I'm with you, I'm already home."

He was stunned. Her words had come at a time when
he'd feared that she would never speak to him again.
He was overwhelmed. He was in love.

"My God!" His deep, harsh groan swept against her
cheek as he fell backward upon her bed, taking her
with him.

Honor stared down at his eyes, melting with an emotion that sent shivers of anticipation sweeping through
her system. Suddenly she was aware of being aligned
face to face, breast to chest, stomach to...

Trace was hard. Instantly...achingly. His hands slid up
across her shoulders and cupped her face. They stared for
one long single moment. Not speaking. Barely breathing.

"You know what's about to happen?"

His voice was harsh, his touch gentle.

Honor sighed, laid her head upon his shoulder, and
closed her eyes. "It's been a long time coming, Trace.
And I think I'm tired of waiting."

"No more," he whispered. "No more waiting."

Clothing slid away. Piece by piece. First hers, then his. Sometimes gently, sometimes too slow. But when Trace slipped the last piece of lingerie from her hips and leaned back on one elbow to look at what he'd uncovered, he was overwhelmed.

She was so much more than what he'd imagined, and he'd imagined perfection. Every curve of her body accentuated and highlighted the next. And when his eyes slid down past her stomach to the temptation awaiting him, he groaned.

Honor feasted her eyes on his broad, muscular shoulders, the hard, flat belly, and the symbol of his need for her. He was so much man and she was so ready to belong.

"Trace, I'm afraid."

"No," he muttered, and buried his face in the valley of her breasts. "Please don't be afraid of me. I'd die before I'd let anything hurt you."

"No, darling," she whispered, as her hands slid across his back and down his hips. "I'm not afraid of you. I'm afraid that when this happens, I'll never be able to let you go."

"Let me go? You don't have an option, sweet lady. You couldn't lose me if you tried. You're the one who better be sure, because I keep what I take."

Honor gasped, as he slid over her and then between her legs. His weight marked his possession as he pressed her into the mattress at her back. His hands swept across her body as he captured her lips with a groan. Suddenly the need for talking had ended and the time for loving had begun. She was caught up in a world where only she and a man's hands, a man's mouth, and a man's body existed. And then that world exploded with one uplifting motion that sent the two separate lovers into one downward spiral of completion.

Trace groaned. He heard a clock down the hall chime the hour and knew that he would have to leave. He could hardly bear the thought. Honor had given herself so completely that he knew he'd never be the same. She was in his blood.

"Honey?" His soft whisper against her ear turned her toward him with a quiet sigh.

"I love you, Dick Tracey."

He grinned. "You better. Them's fightin' words."

"No fighting…just loving," Honor whispered. Her mouth found his chest.

"Wait, sweetheart," he cautioned. "Don't start anything that I can't finish. If you're staying here, then I have to catch a plane to D.C. tonight. If I don't, your grandfather's business will go straight to hell. His accident and my absence have severely weakened the core of the company's reputation."

Honor sighed and lay back on the bed. She stared solemnly at the look of promise in his eyes and the words of promise on his lips. He'd asked. She'd been the one to say that she would stay. For the moment, it was all she could do.

"I'm staying," she said quietly. "But when will you be back?"

"I don't know for certain," he said, as he rolled from the bed and began to dress. "But as soon as I get to my hotel I'll give you a call and leave my number. I don't want you to go through any more incidents like today alone."

Honor watched a hard, secretive expression come and go on his face and wondered what he'd said to Erin and Hastings as he continued.

"I doubt if you'll have any more trouble. But just in case…" He bent down, pressed a hard, swift kiss on her pouting lips, and promised, "All you have to do is call. I'll be here. Remember what I said? What I take… I don't let go…ever."

Then he was gone and Honor was left with his promise on her lips and a lilt in her heart.

Honor headed for the kitchen to make a foray through Trudy's larder. After Trace had come, she'd lost track of time. She glanced nervously at her wristwatch and knew that her grandfather would be arriving soon. She'd promised Trudy she would take care of him. Honor believed in keeping promises. She just didn't know that she would be so quickly tested when J.J. brought Erin and Hastings home with him.

She found them waiting for her arrival in the library and watched with amusement as they all turned in unison at her entrance. It was obvious that they'd come only under duress.

Erin looked away as Honor entered and Hastings busied himself with pouring a glass of wine. She struggled with the urge to call out *At Ease,* and then decided silence would be a wiser course of action. She would let them do all the talking. She was curious as to just what they could possibly say that would make this evening even passable.

J.J. hurried to Honor's side as he spoke. "My dear, are you all right?" His voice was anxious, his eyes filled with concern.

Honor surprised them all by choosing to ignore the day's events. After what had happened between her and Trace, she was hard-pressed to feel bitter about anything.

"Of course," she said. "But I can't say the same for Trudy. I just put her on a plane to Denver. Her sister has been in an accident. She'll call later."

J.J.'s bushy eyebrows rose in arched surprise. This wasn't exactly what he'd expected Honor to say. He'd expected anger, a sense of betrayal from what was supposed to be her newfound family, even fear. But this blasé attitude about herself and her genuine concern for his housekeeper floored him.

"Well, I'll say!" he muttered. "Too bad about her sister. I suppose I'll have to call one of those temporary services and get some help until she returns."

"Only for the cleaning," Honor said. "I'll do the cooking. It's no big deal."

Erin felt her stomach twist into a tighter knot of dismay. This would only put Honor in greater standing with her father. And after the dressing down she and Hastings had taken today, she could only stand back and allow it to happen. Erin was selfish and jealous, but she wasn't a fool. She'd nearly gone past the bounds of her father's forgiveness and that was something she couldn't face. No matter what anyone else thought about Erin Malone's tough, hard-nosed attitude, she still craved her father's love and approval.

"Are we having company for supper… I mean, dinner?" Honor asked, and then looked pointedly at the pair standing in guilty silence beside J.J.

"That's entirely up to you, my dear," J.J. growled. "These two have something to say to you. And then if you want, they will be on their way. I think we've all pushed the limits of your patience and endurance for one day."

Honor turned and waited. She wouldn't make this easy for them. They didn't deserve it. Erin was the first to speak. And when she did, Honor had the strangest sensation that even though the apology was grudging, it was sincere.

"I'm sorry, Honor," she said, and looked at her father with a lost, almost childlike expression on her face.

He nodded for her to continue.

"What I did today was spiteful and hateful, and I can honestly say that I wish it had never happened."

"Absolutely," Hastings echoed, while looking at his fiancée with a sinking heart.

It was obvious to him that Erin would probably take no further part in antagonizing Honor. He stifled a snort of disgust and pasted his benign, lawyer face on for the assembled company. As far as they were concerned, he was just a spineless puppet for Erin Malone's whims and fancies.

Little did they know that he harbored and fostered a very cunning, devious personality that yearned for the money and power that belonged to J. J. Malone. He'd been the one to manipulate Erin into calling the press and she didn't even realize it. He wasn't finished yet. There were other ways and other people that could help him reach the goals he had set for himself.

"Okay," Honor said. "If there's going to be two more for dinner, I'll add water to the soup." She headed toward the kitchen. "I'll call you when it's ready. Try to be nice to each other."

The evening went better than any of them could have

dreamed. Erin didn't want to admit it, but if she gave this young woman half a chance, she'd probably like her.

Honor was courteous but kept her opinions of Erin's sincerity to herself. She'd given her the benefit of the doubt once, and it had been spit back in her face. She would be slow to trust again.

All the way to Washington, D.C., Trace struggled with his conscience and his heart. He knew he had tremendous responsibilities toward Malone Industries, but his heart told him he was doing the wrong thing. He should have stayed in Colorado with Honor. Every instinct had told him that her troubles weren't over. The incident at the restaurant hadn't been life-threatening, but the undertones had been more than malicious. Someone was setting out to cause her as much mental stress as possible. He knew all the facts pointed to Erin Malone and her intense desire to be number one in her father's eyes. But this wasn't quite what he would have expected Erin to instigate.

His thoughts kept jumping from one family member to another. Who else besides Erin had anything to lose if Honor became an important member of J. J. Malone's family again? Father Andrew was virtually out of the picture. His life and his world were the church. By choice, he'd have it no other way. That only left Erin. But this stunt had merely made her look bad in her father's eyes, and Erin was smarter than that. She would have chosen another method that wouldn't implicate her so quickly.

Who did that leave? Trace wondered. There were no other family members, not unless one wanted to count Erin's fiancé. Trace started to dismiss that thought out of hand when something made him stop and take a harder look at this incident. Just what would Hastings Lawrence have to gain if Honor O'Brien had never been found?

A thoughtful expression darkened Trace's eyes. He ran his fingers through his hair and down the back of his neck, twisting at a knotted muscle just below his collar. He had a feeling that he'd better finish his business in D.C. as quickly as possible. Something told him that Honor might be facing more than the press before this was over.

He heard the pilot announcing their arrival and quickly buckled his seat belt. He was suddenly very anxious to get off the plane and to a telephone. He needed to hear Honor's voice.

Chapter 8

After Trudy's abrupt leave-taking and yesterday's events, J.J. would not hear of Honor staying at the mansion alone. So after a quick breakfast, they both departed for Malone Industries and missed Trace's phone call.

Trace frowned, hanging up after letting it ring for nearly a minute, and grabbed his briefcase. He would be late for his first meeting but was desperate for word of Honor's well-being. After what they had shared yesterday, he was overwhelmed by the immensity of his love for her. The distance that was between them now was nearly impossible to bear.

He caught the hotel elevator on its way down, squirmed himself in beside the people who were tightly packed into the tiny interior, and swallowed his frustration.

The elevator reached the ground floor, spit out its

load into the hotel lobby, and then started back up for more of the same. Everyone who'd just exited the elevators was now racing toward the front doors, competing for the cabs that were lined up for possible fares. Now Trace had little time to dwell on what was going on back home. Trying to get a cab at this time of day was something like being in the front line of the Boston Marathon. You *could* see daylight in front of you, it was what was behind you that made you worry.

Finally he succeeded and barked out his destination. His day had started in turmoil; he just prayed that it would end on a happier note. He would find some time later in the day and try calling again. Honor O'Brien was making him crazy.

Irene was pleased to see J.J. bringing his granddaughter to work with him. She yearned for a chance to get to know her better. Megan, J.J.'s wife, had been a good friend of hers. Looking at Honor was like looking at Megan all over again. She quickly volunteered to be Honor's guide through the building. They left J.J. with a cup of steaming hot coffee and one of his favorite sweet rolls.

The morning passed quickly. All too soon it was time to break for lunch. Honor had qualms about going out into the public eye again. But J.J. solved that problem with a suggestion to eat in the company cafeteria.

Irene rolled her eyes and made a delicate but sarcastic comment as they started out the door.

"I'll have the Alka-Seltzer ready when you two return. I'd rather skip lunch than face that buffet of instant heart disease."

J.J. frowned and made a face as they exited the office. Once he made a decision, it was next to impossible to deter him from his goal. And his goal was saving his granddaughter from any more harassment. At least he knew they'd be safe within the confines of his own building.

Irene pulled her sack lunch from a drawer and began to eat. The phone rang. She swallowed hastily and mumbled her response.

"Malone Industries, J. J. Malone's office. How may I help you?"

"Irene? Is that you?" Trace asked. She sounded strange.

"Oh! Mr. Logan. Yes, it's me. I was just having a bit of lunch. You just missed Mr. Malone. He and his granddaughter have gone to get something to eat."

Trace sighed with relief. Now he knew where Honor was.

"Will you tell them I called, give Honor this number," he said, and then hesitated before he added, "And tell her I love her."

"Sir?" Irene questioned.

"Just write it down."

"Yes, sir!" Irene smiled to herself.

She jotted down the message, underlining the part about loving, and finished her lunch. Several more phone calls came in and she gathered the stack of messages, along with J.J.'s mail, and put them on his desk.

"Irene!" Hastings Lawrence called, as he stuck his head into the office door. "Has J.J. returned from lunch? I've some papers he needs to read."

"No, but I expect him soon."

"Well, if you don't mind, I'll just wait in his office. They're important and there's a deadline on getting them signed."

Irene nodded her approval. It was common practice between J.J. and his lawyer. She had no reason to refuse the man. But she'd been unaware of the seriousness of the conflict between the two yesterday. Letting the lawyer into the office played an innocent part in the loss of contact between Trace and Honor.

Hastings walked around J.J.'s desk, playing an imaginary game with himself that this was his office and his company. As he laid his papers on J.J.'s desk, he noticed the stack of phone messages atop the mail.

Trace Logan's name caught his attention. With no qualms of the propriety of snooping, he took the message, read it and, erupted in fury. He loved her? The bastard was confident enough of his position to have it written down for all to see? He felt the ground tilting beneath him. Time continued to slip away and take Hastings's safety with it.

He heard voices, knew J.J. was returning from lunch, and hurried around the desk. He quickly took his seat opposite J.J.'s chair and sat waiting for his boss with an innocent, expectant expression on his face.

When Honor walked in with J.J., he nearly lost his composure. Only years of suppressing his true thoughts stood him in good stead. No one, not even Honor, knew how surprised he was to see them together.

He's teaching her the business. Erin was right! He was going to put this woman in the company.

If his panicked thoughts were correct, his chances for promotions just took a nosedive. And then rational thought took over, and he silently admitted to himself that it wouldn't matter if he married Erin Malone tomorrow. None of this mattered if he couldn't stop the audit.

He'd not only be out of business, he'd be incarcerated for more years than he cared to imagine.

His mind whirled. He had to find a way to stop this audit! There would be no reason to stop it unless he could cause some sort of rift between J.J. and this damn Amazon claiming to be his granddaughter. He knew that was virtually impossible. And he shuddered thinking about the threat Trace Logan had left ringing in his ears.

Hastings didn't have the guts to flaunt the physical threat. But he had to do something. If he couldn't cause trouble between these two, maybe there was another way. He wasn't ready to admit defeat.

J.J. frowned as he saw his lawyer waiting inside his office. He was still angry about Hastings's part in what he considered a betrayal of loyalties. But the lawyer's bland demeanor and the reason for his presence quickly made J.J. forget his anger.

It was business as usual. Honor took the opportunity to escape into Trace's office, away from Hastings's shifty eyes. She didn't like him. And from their first meeting, hadn't trusted him.

She closed the connecting door and walked over to the long leather couch against the wall of Trace's office. The scent of his aftershave was faint, but lingered enough on the furnishings and one of his jackets to give Honor a sense of his presence. It was enough to make her long for his deep, gentle voice, that sexy mouth that twisted into a heartbreaking smile whenever he saw her, and feel the comfort of being held securely within his tender strength. Yesterday flooded her memory. The emotions that he had pulled from within her. The depth of commitment they had shared.

She walked over to the coat rack, took down his jacket, slid her arms inside the sleeves and wrapped all that she had of Trace Logan around her. She closed her eyes and inhaled deeply, remembering.

Her heartbeat accelerated and then skipped a beat as she saw the huge, overstuffed leather couch against the wall. She could imagine Trace's long length stretched out on that piece of furniture. She tried *not* to imagine herself beneath him.

Her eyes burned, her heart ached, but there was no tall, dark man with chocolate-chip eyes to take away her loneliness. She knew it had been her choice to stay. She sighed and remonstrated herself. *Feeling pitiful is not your style, Honor, my girl.*

She sank onto the leather cushions, pulled Trace's jacket tighter around her, and stretched full-length along the couch. She told herself she'd only rest a minute; maybe close her eyes just until they quit burning. But the minute stretched into several and then into an hour.

When J.J. finally had time to miss her, he found her sound asleep in Trace's office. He quietly closed the door and let her sleep. As long as he knew where she was, she could do any damn thing she pleased. He was overwhelmed with the joy of knowing that he had Johnny's daughter back. He gave instructions to his secretary to hold all the phone calls and then went back to work.

It was late afternoon when Honor awoke and, soon after, accompanied her grandfather home. She wondered about the absence of Trace's promised phone call, but her confidence in their love gave her no reason to worry. When he found time, he'd call.

This was the order of their routine for the next couple of days. It wasn't until the third day after she'd started accompanying her grandfather to the office that she realized the harassment had started again. But in a way she would never have expected.

"Irene... Hastings just called. He needs those contracts you were working on. Are you finished with them? I told him Honor would bring them down to legal."

J.J. was all business now that Trace was gone. He'd forgotten just how much of the workload Trace had assumed until he was no longer there to take it.

Honor had willingly offered to run errands for Irene. It was the least she could do under the circumstances. J.J. still wouldn't let her stay home alone, and Trudy wasn't due back until the weekend. She was bored to tears at the office, concerned by the absence of contact between her and Trace, and gladly welcomed anything she could do to make the day pass quicker.

Irene nodded, gathered the papers scattered on her desk, and handed them to Honor. "Just give them to anyone in the front office. They'll see that he gets them," Irene said. She'd picked up instantly on Honor's dislike of Hastings Lawrence.

Honor smiled and started out the door. This was nothing she hadn't done many times during the past few days. So she was more than surprised when she entered the elevator, pushed the button for the correct floor, waited for the car to move, and it didn't! When nothing happened, she pushed the button again. This time the car started to move, and Honor sighed with relief.

The thought of getting trapped in one of these mobile closets made her teeth ache. She looked up, watched the number light up on the floor she wanted, and then watched in dismay as it passed and continued downward, moving faster and faster with each floor it passed.

"No, no, no," Honor muttered to herself, dropped the stack of papers she was holding, and started punching the emergency button over and over with frantic force. Nothing happened. The car continued to slide toward what Honor knew could only be disaster.

Trace! The thought of him coincided with the instant jolt of the car as it came to a sudden stop. She fell backward, catching herself with outstretched arms, and felt a twinge of pain as she leaned hard on her left wrist. Just when she began to breathe a sigh of relief, the lights went out.

It was the blackest black Honor had ever experienced in her life. She literally could not see her hand in front of her face. She held her breath, instantly afraid that the car would begin to move again. She knew if it did that she was too close to the bottom for another safe stop. This time it would crash.

Afraid to move, she lay quietly on her back, willing her heart to a normal rhythm, and waited for help to come. Someone had to have heard the screeching gears when the car finally stopped. Or surely they'd discover what had happened when they tried to use the elevator. All she had to do was wait.

It was the sound of footsteps on the roof of the elevator car that alerted her of someone's presence. Someone was coming to help.

"Thank God!" Honor muttered. "Here!" she called. "I'm in here! Please help me!"

The footsteps stopped. Honor knew she'd been heard. Nothing happened! No one answered her! That was when she began to worry. And when she heard the tiny opening being removed from the roof of the elevator above her head, her heartbeat quickened. What did this mean? It was easy to imagine the worst when nothing but blackness swirled around her. Panic made the thick, dark air harder and harder to breathe. Honor struggled with the need to scream aloud in fear. But she sensed this was connected to the episode outside the restaurant several days earlier and wouldn't give whomever was above the satisfaction. Her fears were confirmed as she heard the harsh, gulping breaths before he began to whisper. His soft, raspy words sucked the air from her lungs as fear wrapped itself around her heart and squeezed. Then her heart began to race and she scooted as far into a corner of the car as she could get.

"Go home, bitch!" he whispered. "Get out while you're still in one piece. Next time you won't be so lucky."

"Who are you?" she asked, and pulled herself quietly to her feet. If she was going to be attacked she wasn't going to be on her back when it happened.

But there was no answer. Just the sound of the plate being replaced in the roof of the elevator car, then sliding sounds, as if he were crawling or climbing. She couldn't tell.

The car jerked, the lights came on, and as if nothing unusual had happened, started back up to the floor Honor had chosen when she'd first entered the elevator. She watched in silent fear as the door opened and then breathed a frantic sigh of relief. There was no one there. She bent over, quickly gathered the scattered papers to her breast, and ran from the elevator as if the hounds of hell were at her heels.

She knew she must look like she'd been hanging out

the window of a freight train as all eyes in the main office of the legal department turned to her. But she didn't care what they thought, and she offered no explanation.

"Here," she said, thrusting the jumbled stack of papers into the receptionist's hands. "I dropped them. Tell Hastings he'll have to sort them again."

She was gone as quickly as she'd entered. And when she arrived back at her grandfather's offices, she ran past Irene's desk into Trace's office and closed the door behind her with a bang. She grabbed his jacket from the coat rack, threw it over her shoulders, and wrapped it and herself into a ball in the corner of the long leather couch.

"Trace," Honor whispered through tightly clenched teeth, trying desperately not to cry, "I need you to come home. Dear God, I need you here, now! I can't deal with this mess by myself. Do you hear me, Trace Logan? I need you! Why haven't you called?"

She wrapped her arms around her tightly drawn-up knees, buried her face against Trace's jacket and began to shake. By tomorrow, unless she was very much mistaken, she was going to be very, very sore. The fall she'd taken in the elevator had been a hard one, and her wrist was already beginning to throb. She just hoped it wasn't cracked or broken. How would she explain it to J.J. if it was?

She could wait no longer for Trace's call. She would find him herself. She knew the name of his hotel, called information, and soon had a number. But when she dialed, the reception was less than desirable.

"Burlington Hotel," the man answered.

"Please," she gasped, struggling unsuccessfully to

control her panic. Her voice shook as she continued. "I need to speak to Mr. Trace Logan."

"Logan? Logan?" Silence and then a bit later an answer. "Sorry…not in his room at present time. Leave message?"

Honor sighed. This person didn't speak much of the English language. But she was desperate. She had to try.

"Tell him that Honor called. That it's an emergency. He must call me soon. I'll be waiting." And then she whispered to herself, "And praying."

"Yes, yes," the man mumbled. "Honor will be served. Of that you can be assured."

She had her doubts, but there was no need chiding him. She started to ask him to read the message to her when he disconnected.

The remainder of the day was uneventful, but Honor couldn't rest. She kept imagining that everyone she passed in the halls was the mysterious stranger who'd caused the near-tragic accident. She knew it was silly. She hadn't seen a thing, and she hadn't recognized the voice. It had been nothing but an evil whisper. She knew one thing for certain. She wasn't getting back on the elevator alone.

Trace slammed the phone down in disgust, wiped a hand across his weary eyes in frustration, and yanked open the door of the phone booth. When he got home, the first thing he was going to do was insist that the phone system at the Malone home have Call Waiting. Either no one was home or the damn phone was busy. Honor must think the absolute worst. And he'd been more than a bit surprised that she hadn't tried to call him.

He'd checked his messages daily, and the only one

he'd received made absolutely no sense. It had been something about hastily obeying the call to worship. He'd tried to question the desk clerk, but no one could clear up his confusion. He finally decided that it had been meant for someone else and tossed it away.

His anxiety about his prolonged absence from Honor was increasing. He'd expected to hear from her before this. But he'd cleared up nearly all of the misunderstandings regarding Malone Industries. If all went as planned tomorrow he'd be on his way home.

And when he got there, he and Honor were going to have a very long talk about their future. And then they weren't going to talk at all. He smiled to himself, and headed for the conference room.

Going to the office had taken on a whole new meaning of the word "boredom" for Honor.

She'd started to argue with her grandfather about continuing to accompany him to work and then could tell by the size of the crowd outside the Malone mansion and the look on his face that she was going to have to spend another day with him as bodyguard.

"Let's go, girl," J.J. called.

Honor sighed as she kneaded at a lingering soreness in the lower portion of her back. At least she'd suffered no lasting effects of her episode in the elevator. Evidently no one had noticed a thing at Malone Industries and that was just the way she wanted it. She'd called entirely enough attention to herself just by showing up in Colorado Springs. Mentioning the fact that she was now being terrorized would feed the flames of her existence to new heights with the newspapers. Trace would call, and then he would know what to do. Until then she'd just wait.

She searched the hall table for her purse, picked it up and stuffed it under her arm, took one final look at her appearance and decided that if this red-and-black plaid jacket and matching slacks were too flashy that it was just too bad. She hadn't planned on staying this long and was running out of choices. And now that this mess with the media had occurred, a simple shopping trip was out of the question.

Trudy would be home tomorrow, and that would be the last of J.J.'s excuses. She could stay home and await Trace's return in comfort.

She knew J.J. secretly liked having her go with him. It had given them an opportunity to get to know each other better. And she knew that when it came time for her to leave, he was going to put up one big argument.

Last night during dinner, Honor had finally admitted to him that she'd gone to the library and read about the history of the Malones and her disappearance. Afterward, he'd shown her a wealth of family pictures rich with images of a family that had rejoiced at her arrival into the world. The picture of a tall, dark man holding his baby carefully against his chest and the slender, dark-haired woman leaning against his arm, looking up in laughter, would be the only image she would ever know of her parents. But she could feel nothing more than sorrow for what might have been. The memory of Charlie was too great. Her love too overwhelming. The loss too fresh.

"So what do you think now, girl?" J.J. had growled softly, as she'd closed the cover of the last album.

"I don't know what to think, J.J. But I have something I want you to read. And then you tell me what *you* think. Okay?"

He nodded his approval and waited in the library for Honor's return. When she came back, she was carrying a blue leather-bound book clutched tightly to her breast. She walked to his chair, took a deep breath, and then handed him the book. He started to open it when her words ceased the motion.

"It's Momma's journal. The lawyer had it and gave it to me after Trace's arrival. Maybe after you read it, you'll understand a little bit of why she did it."

"Do *you* understand?" J.J. growled.

Honor was silent for a moment, and then with her usual honesty, replied, "Sometimes I think I do. And then sometimes I want to cry with the useless waste of it all. But I loved her, J.J., I loved her very much. That hasn't changed."

"Fair enough," he said, and opened the cover. He began to read, and when he did, Honor left. She couldn't watch him see into her mother's soul.

A long time passed before J.J. came looking for her. He found her in the kitchen making cookies and raised his eyebrows at the mess of flour and bowls scattered on the cabinet. "Trudy will have your hide."

"No, she won't," Honor said. "She likes me. Besides, I'll clean it up. I had to do something. This seemed the most productive and it took no thought."

She turned and stared, waiting for him to say something about the book he carried in his hand. Finally, she blurted it out. She could wait no longer.

"So, what do you think of Charlotte O'Brien now?" Her voice shook. She felt as if his pronouncement of the contents of the journal were vital to how their relationship would progress from this moment on.

He shook his head regretfully and laid the journal in a safe place away from the mess on the cabinets. "It didn't help at all, girl. Until I read this, I had a clear picture in my mind of some vindictive, vicious woman who'd taken my darling granddaughter. Now I don't know what I feel except an overwhelming sadness that somehow this could have all been avoided if she'd just had someone who cared."

A sob pushed its way past the lump in her throat as she threw her arms around J.J.'s neck. It was the first spontaneous emotion she'd shown toward him since they'd met.

"I knew you'd understand," Honor whispered in his ear, and placed a kiss on his weathered cheek. "Here..." She pulled away, and grabbed a plate filled with the fruits of her labor. "Have a cookie, Grandfather. What Trudy doesn't know won't hurt you."

He grinned, took a handful of the forbidden treats, and was on the way to his room to go to bed when he realized that she'd called him Grandfather. Elation, joy, and even a bit of sadness for the many years wasted before he was able to experience this overwhelmed him.

He started to go back when he realized she'd done it as unconsciously as he'd accepted it. A slow, warm feeling started around the region of his heart and spread to every portion of his body. This was more than he'd dreamed of and less than he wanted. Before he was through, he'd have this family back together the way a family should be.

Honor cleaned up the kitchen, knowing Trudy would soon be home, and went to bed, satisfied that a step in the right direction had been taken tonight. She felt better than she had in a long time. Now if Trace would come home, she'd really feel at ease. She slept soundly, unaware that this would be the last night of peace that she would know for days to come.

Honor started down the long, quiet hallway as she exited the secretary pool at Malone Industries. She was still filling her time posing as an errand girl for her grandfather's office. She had just delivered a multipage defense contract that was to be copied and then collated. Her thoughts were jumbled, her emotions mixed. A phone call last night, just before she'd gone to bed, had stirred old memories and made her more than a bit homesick.

Hearing her uncle Rusty's voice filled with dismay and concern had nearly been her undoing. He'd tracked her location through Hank, the bartender at Charlie's, and it was evident from the bits and pieces of conversation he'd let slip, that he was fully aware of his Charlie's part in Honor's present situation. It was also evident that he wasn't any too happy about her presence in a place he knew nothing about and with people he'd never met. He still considered Honor *his* girl, and nothing was going to change that.

"When are you coming home, honey?" Rusty had pleaded.

"I don't know, Uncle Rusty," Honor hedged. "I check in at Charlie's nearly every day. Everything seems to be running smoothly whether I'm there or not. I feel like I just haven't quite done what Momma intended for me to do when she sent that letter. I'll tell you one thing. This

has certainly been building my character." Her wry remark, referring to an old adage that Charlotte O'Brien
had used over and over when referring to dealing with
troublesome situations, made them both laugh.

"Well," he finally concluded, before he hung up.
"You have my number. If you ever need me, sweetheart, I expect to be called. You're all I have left of
my Charlie, and I don't intend to lose you, too. Do you
hear me?" His voice was gruff, and Honor knew he was
probably close to tears.

It was no more than she'd experienced. She missed
all her friends back in Odessa. She was also more than
upset that Trace had not returned her call. He'd promised. And after her scare, she'd needed him desperately.
She couldn't understand his lack of communication.

"Going up?" the man behind Honor asked, and
stopped her reverie with a rude awakening.

She jumped, unaware that she'd been standing in
front of the elevator, staring at the closed doors. Evidently he intended to use the car, but she had no intention of getting on that thing again, especially with a
strange man.

"No! No, thanks," she mumbled, and turned away,
searching the hallway for the lighted Exit sign leading
toward the stairway. She would take the stairs.

The stairwell was cold, the air-conditioning obviously funneling through the upright tunnel like air
through a pipe. Her steps echoed up and down the free
space of the stairwell, making it sound as if an army
of men were marching beside her. She shivered, partly
from the cold, partly from the eerie feeling of being so
isolated in such a narrow space.

Honor scoffed at herself, decided that this sensation was just a holdover from being stranded in the tiny elevator car, and continued upward when a door from the floor behind her opened. She turned in sudden fright.

"Honor!" Erin Malone called. "I haven't seen you in days. I wasn't certain you were still here."

Erin was ill at ease, but still willing to try to make conversation with Honor. Her conscience had been bothering her badly ever since the evening they'd spent together, and she was surprised at the pleasure she felt when she'd seen Honor ahead of her on the stairs. The girl had been more than decent toward her, and, she told herself, Johnny *had* been her favorite brother.

"Oh!" Honor said, obviously breathing a loud sigh of relief. "I didn't know it was you. You startled me."

Erin frowned. She read more into Honor's innocent remark than Honor meant to impart.

"Why so jumpy?" she asked, as she stood at the foot of the stairs, looking up as Honor paused on the steps above. "Have you been having more problems with the press?"

"No…not with the press," Honor hedged, and started to walk down a few steps when she saw Erin's expression change.

She saw Erin's eyes change direction, saw her look of recognition, and saw her start to smile. That was when Honor felt the breath on her neck and the hands at her back. There wasn't time for fear, only the shock of falling through space and the look of horror on Erin Malone's face as she came hurtling toward her. After that, nothing.

"Megan! Honey! Do you hear me?" J.J.'s voice was frantic, his hands gently searching the crumpled heap of his beloved granddaughter at the bottom of the seventh-floor landing. "The paramedics are on the way. Please, Meggie, don't leave me," he pleaded, in tears at the sight of the huge bump forming on her forehead.

Erin knelt at his side, her heart twisting in horror at what she'd unwittingly witnessed. She was torn between jealousy at the term of endearment J.J. had just used when talking to Honor and the shock of watching her fiancé actually push Honor down the stairs.

Hastings had watched Honor fall through the air, watched her roll and bump down the last few steps, and then had given Erin a strange look of warning before he disappeared through the door at the top of the stairs. Why had he done such a thing? Erin hadn't indicated a desire to participate in anything so horrifying. She was more than a bit fearful of the fact that he'd done this in front of her; implicating her by presence if not actual participation, and then staring at her so harshly. If she didn't know better she would have read that warning look he gave her as, *You're next if you tell.*

Erin shuddered, heard the hurried footsteps coming down the seventh floor corridor, and rushed to open the Exit door.

"In here!" she called, and held the door open for the paramedics to pass with their equipment.

"Can you hear me, miss?" the EMT called aloud, as he made a quick but thorough examination of the young woman who'd suffered the fall.

She was beginning to regain consciousness, and they had to complete their initial examination quickly. He had to immobilize her before she moved and caused herself possible permanent injury. A cervical collar was placed around her neck and a long spine board was carefully slipped beneath her before the move was made to a stretcher where she was then strapped safely in place.

"What?" Honor mumbled, as she struggled through pain and darkness that kept pulling her back into its grasp.

"You've had an accident," J.J. said, as he began to walk beside her stretcher. The paramedics were wheeling her toward the elevator that would take her down to the waiting ambulance. "Don't worry, Meggie," he whispered brokenly, awkwardly patting at her strapped arm. "I'm right here beside you."

Honor felt the pain returning full force, and with it the memory of what had preceded. She opened her eyes to see the bright fluorescent lights overhead, flowing into one long continuous stream of yellow as the stretcher moved on silent wheels quickly down the corridor leading toward the elevator. She saw her aunt's worried expression as she ran to keep up with the movement of the paramedics. Honor focused on the guilt she knew she would see in those nervous, darting eyes and spoke as they all came to a stop at the elevator.

"I'm not Meggie," Honor said through tightly clenched lips and ignored the look of pain on her grandfather's face. Her gaze turned toward her aunt. She spoke softly, her words for Erin Malone only. "And it was no accident."

X-rays revealed no broken bones, nor permanent injuries of any kind. But she knew before the doctors ever told her that she was going to hurt like hell. There wasn't a bone in her body that didn't ache, or a muscle that didn't cramp. The fall had been hard, but the lesson Honor learned even harder. She was a fighter all right, but she was no fool. She knew her aunt had seen whoever had pushed her. Honor wasn't convinced that Erin had known it was going to happen. She could still remember the look of surprise on her aunt's face. She also saw it turn to horror just before she fell. But she didn't care whether Erin had instigated it or not. She obviously hadn't said anything to her father about the incident, and her silence was good enough for Honor. If her presence in Colorado was all that threatening, they could have their life back just the way they wanted.

Honor leaned over, winced, and moaned aloud as pain shot through her body all the way to the top of her head. She stifled the cry, then reached for the telephone and pulled it into her lap. She blinked from the pain, thought for the few seconds it took to recall the number, and then made her call.

The man answered on the second ring, and Honor spoke before he had finished identifying himself.

"Uncle Rusty," she whispered as she began to cry. "Will you come get me?"

His shocked response to her condition and quick assurance were what she needed to hear. He was on his way out of the door before Honor could tell him good-bye.

Honor disconnected, painfully set the phone back in place on the bedside table, and turned her head into the pillow. The tears that had flowed so freely while talking to her beloved Rusty had stopped and frozen around the building pain inside her chest.

She was being rescued, but not by the man she'd expected to help her through the mess he'd brought her into. Trace Logan had promised he'd be with her every step of the way. He'd taken her to bed and taken her love, and left with promises he hadn't kept. There'd been no calls, no letter, no nothing. Honor stifled the betrayal she felt and told herself it didn't matter. She should have known better. The door opened, and Honor knew without looking who had just entered.

"How are you feeling, dear?" J.J. asked, careful not to slip and call her Meggie. It had obviously angered her beyond his understanding.

"I'm alive," Honor muttered, and stared blankly at Erin who stood quietly beside her father, beseeching Honor with some strange, silent plea not to tell what had happened.

"Your uncle Andrew is on his way over," J.J. said, trying to instill some measure of civility back into this obviously hostile conversation. Her anger puzzled and frightened him.

"I don't need a priest," Honor said angrily. "I just need to go home."

"And you shall," J.J. responded, relieved by her request. "But the doctor insists that you spend the night for safety's sake. We wouldn't want you to suffer any unforeseen consequences."

"I've already suffered the consequences," Honor snapped, and then winced at the pain it caused when she'd raised her voice. "I don't intend to do it again. I'm going home," she repeated. "But not back with you. I'm going home to Odessa. My uncle Rusty is already on his way. I've had just about all the welcome I can take from the Malones. I don't need any more."

"I don't understand," J.J. said, shocked beyond words at her anger. They'd been on such good terms before this incident.

"I know you don't," Honor said, suddenly weary of

talking, weary of looking into the faces of strangers. She wished she'd never heard of the Malones or Colorado. For the first time since her mother's death she was bitterly angry. Angry at Charlotte O'Brien for dying and starting this nightmare, angry at Trace Logan for finding her, loving her, and making promises he didn't keep, angry at being born into a family such as this. "If you want answers, talk to your daughter. I don't intend to talk about this again."

J.J. looked startled and then turned angrily toward Erin.

"Come with me," he ordered. "This discussion will not take place in front of Honor. She's suffered enough at our hands."

Then he turned with a heavy heart, looked at Honor's angry face, and knew it was over. His chance to regain his granddaughter had just resulted in not only losing her, but from what Honor had just implied, at the hands of his own daughter. If she had any connection to what had just happened, he couldn't bear to think of the implications this created.

Honor watched them leave, listened to the door click as the latch slipped into place, and hardened her heart against the pain. She didn't need them.

Chapter 9

The elation Trace felt when his plane landed in Colorado Springs quickly disappeared when he entered his office and saw the expression on Irene's face. Something was very wrong and he had a sinking sensation that Honor was involved.

"Where's Honor?" he asked sharply, and felt his stomach pitch as Irene grabbed at a tissue and started to cry.

"Gone!" she answered. "It was just terrible. One minute she was fine, the next she'd fallen to the bottom of the stairs." She dabbed at her eyes, and then pulled another tissue from the box on her desk.

"She fell down what stairs?" he asked, trying to make sense of his secretary's hysterics and not give in to the panic he felt at her words.

"The stairs here in the building," Irene mumbled

from under her wad of tissues. "It was just fortunate that Miss Malone saw it happen and called for help."

"Erin Malone was present?" Trace asked quietly, as a foreboding began to enter his jumbled thoughts.

"Oh, yes!" Irene repeated. "And she called Mr. Malone right after she summoned the paramedics. They took Honor away in an ambulance, and then this morning when Mr. Malone came to work, he was so sad. He said that Honor was gone, that he'd lost her for good." Irene sniffed, and blew her nose. "I don't know quite what he meant by that, but he was very withdrawn and told me to hold all his calls."

Trace absorbed the information with building panic and fury. He knew he shouldn't have gone away and left Honor here to fend for herself. Some instinct had warned him that something like this might happen. He'd put his job and his so-called duty to J. J. Malone ahead of his feelings for Honor, and this was what had happened. He'd let Honor down, when he'd promised just the opposite. But why hadn't she called? The hurt that came with that question was more than he could bear.

A slow-burning rage began to build inside his chest. He looked up as the door to J.J.'s office opened and the older man stepped out. Trace couldn't mask his shock. J.J. looked as if he'd aged ten years in the last five days.

"What in hell happened while I was gone?" Trace growled, ignoring the pain and suffering on his boss's face.

'She's gone, boy," J.J. whispered, and ran a shaky hand across his eyes. "She's gone and it's all this damned family's fault."

Trace absorbed J.J.'s words and drew his own conclusions. By the expression of guilt on J.J.'s face, they were obviously correct as he asked, "It was more of Erin's doing, wasn't it?"

"I'm not sure," J.J. replied. "I've never seen her like this. She acts scared, but she won't talk. I don't know what to do."

"Well, I sure as hell do," Trace muttered, then dropped his coat and briefcase. He started out of the room with a look of grim determination on his face.

"Now, listen here…" J.J. began, when Trace interrupted.

"No, *you* listen," he said. "I'm going to find out just what happened to Honor. I'm the one who talked her into coming back here in the first place. I promised to help her, and all I did was leave her to the wolves. Dammit, J.J., she means everything to me. If Erin is the key to the answers I need, she's going to tell me what I want to know, and I don't care what it takes to make her talk. Do you understand me? If you aren't ready to accept that, then you can fire me."

J.J. stood silently, his position as boss and Erin's father warring with the understanding of Trace's desperation. And it was obvious from the way Trace was acting that more had developed between them than friendship.

Trace turned his back on his boss and walked out of the office. Someone had hurt the woman he loved, and someone was going to pay. He stalked through the reception area and into her office without waiting to be announced.

Erin looked up, exasperation turning to panic as she saw Trace barging through her door. The people sitting around the conference table looked on in shock, waiting for Erin's explosion. It never came.

Trace ignored everyone else in the room as he focused entirely on Erin's pale face and the fear in her eyes.

"Get out," he ordered quietly, speaking to the others.

"What's the meaning of this?" one of the men began to argue.

"I said, get out!" Trace repeated, and when he spoke, stepped aside and motioned with his hand for them to exit now.

Something told them this was not the time or the place to argue. They filed out quickly, darting curious looks at the angry man and the panic-stricken woman they were leaving behind.

"You couldn't leave it alone, could you?" Trace whispered as he walked to where Erin was sitting and leaned over, blocking her exit by placing a hand on either arm of the chair.

"I don't know what you mean," she began, when his look silenced her next words and nearly stopped her breath.

"Yes, you do, you bitch. I can't believe you'd do this to your own family. Even I didn't think you were capable of this." He watched the panic spreading in her eyes as she sat frozen in position, afraid to move or speak. "I want to know about Honor's fall. And I'll know if you're lying to me, woman. So don't try it."

J.J. slipped quietly into his daughter's office, listening with a heavy heart as Trace forced the information from Erin that his own pleas had been unable to elicit.

Trace saw something in her eyes that surprised him. Erin Malone looked like she was about to come unglued. "It wasn't an accident, was it?" he said, and then wondered where that question had come from. He hadn't known he was going to ask it.

Suddenly Erin began to shake. She wrapped her arms around her stomach, as if holding herself together to keep from flying apart. Her eyes filled and her breath came in short, aching gasps. How had this gotten so out of hand? She'd never meant for any of it to happen. It wasn't her fault. Not this. She began to sob.

"I didn't know he was going to do it," Erin mumbled and swallowed hard before she continued. "I swear I didn't. I was beginning to like her. If you don't believe me, ask Father. We had dinner together. I apologized about the newsmen. I didn't know he was going to do it," she repeated incoherently and started to slide downward in her chair.

Trace yanked her hard and sat her upright. He wasn't ready for her to fold on him yet. What she'd just said made his blood run cold. God in heaven, his instincts had been right. It hadn't been an accident.

"Who did it, Erin?" Trace growled and shook her sharply. The expression in her eyes told him what she could not. "It was Hastings, wasn't it?" he whispered quietly.

"I saw him step through the door behind her. I thought he was looking for me. I started to speak when he just stepped up behind her and pushed. She fell." Her voice quavered and then became so faint Trace had to lean over to hear the rest of her statement. "It seemed to take forever for her to fall. I tried to catch her, but I couldn't get up the steps fast enough." Her breath came in short, loud gulps as she continued her story. "Then when she'd stopped falling, he just stood at the top of the stairs and stared at me." Erin began to mumble and grabbed at Trace's arms to emphasize her point. "It was as if he was warning me not to tell. He scared me. I didn't want him to hurt her. I swear to God, I didn't."

Trace stepped back from Erin, looking at her as if she were a stranger. "You mean you saw him push her and didn't say a thing to anyone? You just let him get away with it?"

"Erin!" J.J.'s shocked tone of voice echoed in the waiting silence of the room. "Why in the name of all that's holy didn't you say something? No wonder Honor was so bitter. She knows you kept silent on purpose. Damn you, girl, I don't blame her. I don't blame her one bit." His voice was loud and shaking. He stalked toward his daughter and she shrank back in fright.

There had to be more to this incident than Hastings Lawrence just trying to stay on the good side of his reluctant fiancée. Trace stopped J.J. with a look. "I want to know what Hastings Lawrence has to lose by Honor's existence."

His question surprised both father and daughter, and each looked at the other in blank dismay. Finally, Erin spoke hesitantly. "I don't understand what you're getting at."

J.J. interrupted. "I think I do. You remember the first night Honor came to us, after dinner when she'd gone to make her phone call?" He looked to Trace to remind him of the sequence of events that night. When Trace nodded, he continued. "I asked Hastings to begin an audit so that I could make some changes in my will. Maybe he thought Erin wouldn't get as much as he'd hoped. I've suspected for years that her money was a good portion of his supposed devotion."

Erin looked furiously at her father, angry beyond words that J.J. would even voice such a suspicion.

A knowing expression appeared in Trace's dark eyes as he spoke. "There's been no order given for an audit. I would have known, even before I left. It always goes through me, remember?"

J.J. looked stunned. "But I told him nearly two weeks ago. There's no reason why it hasn't been initiated in that length of time."

"What if it was the audit that started all of this and not the actual update of your will? What if he thought that by making her angry enough to leave you would decide not to change your will and there would be no need for an audit?" Trace asked.

Erin began to argue. Her fear was overridden by the ridiculous notion that Hastings would worry about company audits.

"That's preposterous," she muttered. "Hastings had nothing to hide. And besides, he was in Legal, not Accounting. He didn't have access to the monies. At any rate, he doesn't need it. He always has plenty of his own."

"My point exactly. And maybe it isn't the actual company money he's worried about," Trace said. "He has access to everything your father owns. J.J., I suggest you do some checking on your own and order the audit immediately. I've got another plane to catch, and this time I just may not be back. As for Hastings Lawrence, you either bring charges against him…or I'll deal with him my own way."

His threat left nothing to the imagination as he glared at the pair who stood in stunned silence, too shocked to argue with his ultimatum.

Honor paced the darkened living room of her home, unable to bring herself to turn on any lights, not even a table lamp. She knew hiding wasn't going to solve her problems, but for the time being it made her feel better. It was all she was capable of doing. And she was home! Being cared for by people who loved her was reassuring, and here she was safe.

Rusty Dawson had seen to that when he'd arrived in Colorado Springs and quickly hustled her from the hospital. He'd taken it upon himself to retrieve her belongings from the Malone estate. He'd wasted no words on preliminary introductions or etiquette, nor had he minced words about his opinion of the Malones in general.

J. J. Malone could not argue with the truth, no matter how painful, and had quietly assisted the angry little truck driver. Then he watched with brooding sadness as the last remnants of his granddaughter's fleeting presence disappeared with Russell Dawson.

Rusty had Honor back in Texas and in her own home before she had time to absorb the change of residence. He'd announced that he was taking charge of Charlie's until Honor was well. He reminded her that he'd done it more than once for Charlie. She acquiesced with little argument.

It was only after she'd entered her empty house and walked quietly through the dusty rooms that it hit her. She was home all right, but she didn't feel as satisfied as she'd imagined.

It was a long way from the wooded mountains and the multitude of lakes and rivers. It was a long way from the new friends she'd made before the terror had begun. And it was more than a long way from Trace Logan. It seemed a lifetime ago when he'd held her in his arms and wiped away the last tears of sorrow she'd shed for her mother.

Honor felt betrayed by her so-called family and forgotten by the man who'd promised to love her. But it didn't change the fact that Trace Logan had made a place for himself in her heart. And the place was still there, empty and aching.

She walked over to the window and pulled away the curtains, searching for answers that weren't there. All she could see were the lights of cars coming and going on the highway in front of Charlie's, and once in a while, a beam of light that would flash on the wall of the hallway when a car turned into the restaurant parking lot.

She let the curtains fall back into place and sighed softly. It wasn't like her to be so moody or so bitter. But she'd never experienced such a devastating sequence of events in her entire life. She'd survived the Malone family. But she didn't know if she was going to survive losing Trace Logan.

A single tear worked its way to the surface and struggled furiously through the thick brush of Honor's eyelashes before it escaped down her face.

"Damn you, Trace Logan," Honor muttered. "You made me like you. You made me love you. Now I'm supposed to just forget you ever existed? I can't do that. I don't know how."

A car came to a more than abrupt stop in the parking lot. Honor winced at the sound of flying gravel. She hoped that it had missed the other cars parked in orderly fashion. It wouldn't be the first time there'd been a wreck at Charlie's.

She heard the sound of someone running on the gravel through the parking lot, heard footsteps leap past the first two steps on her front porch and then someone hammering at her door in a demanding manner. Her heart jumped, and she stepped back into the darker shadows of her living room. Then she heard the voice. It was angry and loud and even a little worried, and she hadn't expected to ever hear it again.

"Honor!" Trace called. "I know you're in there. Rusty told me where you were. For God's sake, sweetheart, open the door."

Elation at the fact that he was here warred with the fact that he was too late. Where had he been when she needed him? She debated for a moment at the wisdom of even answering the demand. And then his last plea drove every reason she had to be angry out of her heart.

"Baby, I just need to see for myself that you're okay. I won't hurt you. I won't let anyone hurt you again."

"That's what you promised when you took me away the first time," Honor accused quietly, as she opened the door. She heard Trace's sharply indrawn breath as the truth of her words hit home.

They stood facing each other in the darkness, each silhouetted by the faintest presence of lights. Silence hung between them like a curtain in the doorway until Honor stepped back and allowed Trace to enter.

He pushed the door shut behind him and squinted in the darkness, letting his eyes slowly adjust to the lack of light.

"Why didn't you return my call? Why didn't you call me when you were hurt? What the hell did I do to you to make you run away from me, too?"

The anguish in his voice twisted a knot in the pit of her stomach as the meaning of his questions slowly soaked into her shocked consciousness.

"I didn't get your call," Honor said. "And I did call you, after the first time. But you didn't return *my* call. I was so scared. You promised you would come. That all I had to do was call. Well, I did. But you never came."

Trace groaned. What a confusion of hurt they'd caused each other…and all because he'd left Colorado when his instincts told him otherwise.

He pulled her fiercely into his arms. He couldn't help himself. Just the sound of her voice was not enough to assure him that he'd finally found her again. He needed the touch and the heartbeat against his chest to assure him that she was really there. But her muffled moan of pain and stiffened posture quickly reminded him of why she'd left.

"Oh, God, baby!" He released her with a groan. "I forgot about the fall. Please, honey. Don't pull away from me. If I can't hold you, will you just hold me?"

His tender request shook her resolve to resist. She hesitated for only a moment, then sighed in defeat as she leaned forward, resting every inch of her aching body against the solid strength of his waiting arms. Trace's body was shaking beneath her touch as she slid her arms around his waist. And when she laid her head beneath his chin, she heard him whisper brokenly, "I'm so sorry I left you. I'm even sorrier that you had to go through all that hell alone. It'll never happen again, I promise. Just give me a chance to make it up to you."

His lips brushed across the top of her head as he tangled his fingers in the hair cascading down her back. He pulled, tilting her head gently away from his chest, and as her face turned toward him, he found her mouth in the darkness as surely as if they were bathed in light.

She could feel every curve and every angle of his lips as they pressed against her mouth in gentle torture. His groan heightened the pressure as he maneuvered her sigh into his mouth with desperation. As her knees weakened, she unconsciously tightened her hold around his waist. It was all the encouragement he needed. His body betrayed him as he hardened against her and Honor moved against him, yearning for what he promised.

"This isn't a very good idea, lady," Trace muttered against her lips, and pulled away with a groan. "We're starting something here that you're in no shape to finish."

He threaded his fingers through the heavy fall of her hair at the nape of her neck and lifted it away. His lips searched, located, and claimed the pulse point he had felt beneath his fingers, and his tongue traced the length of its beat until he reached the collar of her blouse. A tiny moan escaped from Honor's lips and Trace stopped, once again reminding himself that it was more than a miracle she was even able to walk.

"It's too dark in here, lady," he whispered against her lips, and felt them open beneath his words. "The feel of you against me is more than I can take. Where's the light switch?"

Honor sighed, leaned her forehead against his shirt front, and felt along the wall behind her.

The living room was bathed in light. Both Trace and Honor blinked blindly, trying to adjust their eyesight to the illumination. And when he could finally see, Trace felt a horrible rage take hold of his senses. If he could get his hands on Hastings Lawrence now, he'd kill him.

"No," he muttered, and started and then stopped himself from touching the fading bruises on her forehead and down the side of her face. "No, no, no!" he said between clenched teeth. It was as if denying their existence would make them go away.

"It's not as bad as it looks," Honor said quietly, and looked at Trace for assurance. "They're already fading."

She put her hands on his arms, felt the muscles tighten, and rubbed her hand softly up and down them, trying to work out the anger beneath her fingertips.

Trace's eyes grew darker, and a muscle in his jaw jerked as he tried to speak past the fury welling up inside him. "Take off your blouse," he ordered, and then began unbuttoning it before Honor could argue.

She gasped and tried to block his intention, but it was no use. She'd never seen Trace so determined or so angry. And she knew when her blouse came off he was going to be worse.

"I'll do it," she finally agreed, as his fingers trembled trying to maneuver the tiny buttons through their respective holes. She watched his face as she slowly slipped each button free and hesitated as the last one released the hem of her blouse.

He watched, an enigmatic expression on his face as little by little, the extent of her injuries was revealed. His breath came out in a grunt when Honor shrugged one shoulder out of her blouse, letting the soft pink, much-washed fabric dangle down her back. Trace gently pulled at the remaining sleeve. It, too, came free, leaving Honor bare from the waist up.

The bruising was worse down her back, especially along her spine where she'd borne the brunt of her fall. Trace touched the ridge of her backbone, running his fingers gently along the edge of her injuries and wanted to cry. This was all his fault. If he'd stayed in Colorado Springs, she wouldn't have suffered like this.

Honor saw the guilt and the pain on his face. "Trace, please don't," she whispered, and started to put her blouse back on.

Trace stopped her, pulled Honor into his arms, leaned against the wall, and buried his face in the tangle of hair at her neck. "Don't," he pleaded. "Just let me hold you, baby. I won't hurt you…and I swear to God neither will anyone else, ever again."

"I don't blame you," she sighed. "You didn't push me. I'm not sure who did. I only felt the hands at my back and the breath on my neck just before I fell."

"Hastings Lawrence pushed you," Trace muttered, knowing her reaction was going to be extreme. Honor's gasp didn't stop his angry statement. But what she said after that did.

"Then he's probably the one responsible for the incident in the elevator, too," she muttered to herself, and then her feet left the floor as Trace lifted her into his arms. She started to object when she saw the look on his face.

"What about the elevator?" Trace asked too quietly, as he remembered her casual remark about trying to contact him *the first time*.

Honor didn't answer.

Trace was too calm. Honor sensed his barely contained fury. He bent down, lifted her into his arms, and started down the hall with her.

"Where are you taking me?" Honor asked.

"To bed," he answered.

Honor sighed and wrapped her arms around his neck and buried her face against his cheek.

Honor felt the downy softness against her back as Trace laid her on top of the comforter covering her bed. He slid down beside her and buried his face in the bare curve of her neck and shoulder. He was shaking, but Honor suspected it was not from fatigue. She could feel the fury building inside him as he loomed over her in the shadows.

His hands slid up the flat surface of her belly, lingering momentarily at the waistband of her jeans, and then he sighed before falling back onto the pillow beside her head and covered his face with both hands.

Trace hurt so much he didn't know where to start. He'd betrayed her trust. And he felt betrayed that she hadn't called. How was he ever going to make up leaving her alone when she'd needed him so desperately?

"What about the damned elevator, Honor?" he asked again.

"It was the reason I began using the stairs," she whispered and slid an arm across his chest before laying her head against his heartbeat. "A couple of days before I fell…was pushed," she corrected herself, "I got in the elevator and pushed the button. It began to fall. I thought I was going to be killed."

A none too silent curse escaped from Trace's lips as he wrapped his arms around Honor and pulled her across his chest. He needed to hold her. He'd come so close to losing her and never even known it.

"Nothing I did seemed to work. Not the emergency button, not the alarm, not anything. But as suddenly as it started, it stopped. Then the lights went out and someone got on the top of the car and whispered some pretty ugly threats through the opening in the roof." Honor shuddered, and felt Trace's strong arms cradling her gently against his strength.

"Why didn't you call me, Honor?" Trace asked softly.

He kept stroking lightly over and over her injuries, as if love could take away her pain. "Didn't you know I would come? Don't you know how much you mean to me?" His voice was deep with hurt.

"I did call. I left word with the desk clerk that it was an emergency and that you should call Honor immediately."

"Oh, honey," he whispered, as he gently smoothed his hand across her hair, "I would have come. And I think I know what happened. I *did* get a message. But it was so strange...all garbled. None of it made any sense, and when I questioned them at the front desk, no one could give me an answer."

Honor remembered her own concern about the lack of communication between herself and the clerk with less than a proper grasp of the English language. It wasn't his fault!

Trace turned his head and listened intently.

"Someone's coming," he said. "Are you expecting company?"

"It's probably Uncle Rusty," Honor said, and started to get up from the bed when Trace stopped her movement with a hand against her bare midriff.

"Wait here," he ordered, covered her with a spread from the foot of the bed, and hurried out of the room before Honor had time to argue.

She heard her uncle's familiar voice and the deep, gruff timbre of Trace's reply. But she couldn't decipher what they were saying. If she had, she would have been even more afraid.

"I thought you'd be here about now," Rusty said, looking around the room with a sharp, all-knowing glance. He saw Honor's pink shirt lying in a heap beside the wall and turned a fierce, angry glare toward Trace. At this point, no matter what Honor had told him, he trusted no one from the Malone family nor anyone representing them. He walked past Trace, picked up Honor's blouse, and turned back with an angry question in his eyes. Trace's words surprised and relieved him, all at the same time.

"Have you seen her back?" Trace growled, and shoved his hands into his pants pockets. The dark-blue weave of the fabric on his slacks stretched beneath his balled fists, pulling it taut against the muscled strength of his tall frame.

"Yes, son," Rusty replied, instantly relieved that he'd deciphered the reason for a portion of Honor's clothing laying on the living-room floor. He dropped the pink blouse on the back of a chair. He'd been just as appalled when he'd seen the extent of Honor's injuries. "But they're healing, and so is she." Then he took another turn around the room, as if checking to see if they were truly alone before he spoke. "Where's my girl?" he asked.

"In her room," Trace answered, and then caught a sense of something else. "Why? What's wrong?"

"One of the truckers just pulled into the lot and thought he saw someone messing around Honor's car. He didn't know anything about what she's been going through and just mentioned it in passing when he came in to eat. He thought someone might be trying to steal it."

Trace jerked and started to the front door to check for himself when the older man's words stopped him cold.

"I already looked. Someone's cut her brake line. She wouldn't have gone more than a half mile before she'd be in a world of hurt when it came to stopping that car." He walked toward Trace and glared in his face, his bright-blue eyes piercing Trace's conscience. "Now, I want to know what in hell is going on around here? I'll take a tire iron to the man who lays another hand on my girl. Do you understand me, boy?"

Trace knew the man felt he was to blame, if not completely, at least partially. He had been the one who'd taken her away. He couldn't find it in his heart to disagree. However, what Rusty Dawson just told him changed everything. She wasn't even safe here. But he knew a place where she would be.

"I'm taking Honor away tonight while it's still dark." Rusty Dawson's frown was wiped away by Trace's declaration. "I know who's doing this. But right now I can't prove it. The only eyewitness is too scared to talk. There's a place where Honor will be safe until the man is found and brought to justice."

"I don't like it," Rusty growled, and paced the living-room floor. He knew Charlie would have been appalled to know that her letter had started all of this. This was ugly and scary and didn't belong in their world.

"I know you don't, sir," Trace answered quietly. "Neither do I. But as God is my witness I'll protect Honor with my life. I have no choice." He turned and walked toward the window and pulled away the heavy fall of curtain. Like Honor, there were no easy answers awaiting Trace's search, either.

Rusty sighed and leaned against the wall. "What's between you two?" he asked, hating to hear the answer. He'd lost Charlie, he didn't want to lose Honor, too. Not yet.

"I'm not going to lie to you, Rusty. I love Honor, and

I believe that she loves me." He turned and faced the older man's angry frown. "She's my world, and I'll do anything it takes to keep her safe."

"In the long run," Rusty said, "it's all up to my girl. But I have to know where you're taking her."

Trace nodded, and the two men quickly made their plans.

Rusty was to contact Honor's grandfather, and he, in turn, would have a set of instructions that must then be followed before Honor would be truly safe. Rusty left with determination in every step.

Trace had his own set of plans to be made. He knew he had little time to accomplish them. If Hastings had already started to work his evil here in Texas, Trace had to hurry.

He started back down the hallway and met Honor coming from her bedroom, pulling a thin, button-front shirt over her bare shoulders.

"You'll need something warmer than that," Trace said gruffly, and gently turned her around. "We're leaving tonight. And we need to hurry, lady."

Fear wiped away the smile in her eyes as a sense of his urgency invaded her heart. "What's wrong?" she whispered, and pulled the shirt tightly around her waist.

"He's been here," Trace said, and watched her eyes grow stormy and her chin stick out in mutinous rebellion.

"I'm not running away," Honor argued. "Not again. This is my home."

"I can't protect you here, honey," Trace said. "And he's getting serious. He just cut, or had someone cut, the brake line on your car."

Honor's anger swiftly changed to fear and melted

the bones in her body as she slumped against the wall. This was a nightmare.

"Come on, Honor. There's a place where you'll be safe. I'm taking you there tonight." Trace slid his arms around her shoulders and gently walked her toward her room. They would need as many warm clothes as she owned and there was no time to waste.

"Where will you be?" Honor asked, as she tried to swallow the tears that thickened her speech.

"Right beside you, baby," Trace promised, and leaned forward, sealing his promise with a kiss. "All the way."

Honor looked up, saw the truth and something else in Trace Logan's eyes that made her hurry. Whatever, or whomever, was waiting for her beyond the walls of her home might just have gotten more than they'd bargained for. Trace looked ready to kill.

Chapter 10

The sun was almost at the horizon of a new day, but it was obviously not going to reign long as a line of thunderheads rolled over the mountain ahead of Trace's four-wheel drive vehicle. He maneuvered the narrow tree-lined road with ease as he searched its border for the familiar landmark that stood at the entry to his property. A quiet sigh of relief slid through his lips as the tall, skeletal branches of the dead tree standing guard at a graveled side road came into view. They'd made it! And with little time to spare! The inclement weather was rolling in with a vengeance. Trace knew from many years of experience with Colorado weather that one didn't want to be caught on a mountain road in a thunderstorm. If a falling tree didn't get you, a disappearing road bed would. He rubbed the back of his neck wearily and ventured a quick glance at Honor who'd managed to curl herself into a ball and go sound asleep after they'd disembarked from the flight Trace had chartered out of Odessa. This way, there had been no public airport to deal with or tickets to purchase. There was no easy way to trace their exit from Texas.

As Trace turned off the blacktop onto the graveled side road, the sound of the tiny rocks bouncing against the underside of his vehicle awoke Honor with a start.

Trace frowned. "Sorry," he said, as Honor sat straight up in her seat and looked around with a soft, befuddled expression on her face.

"Where are we?" she mumbled, rubbing her fingers against her eyelids, trying to rub away the dry, burning sensation.

"Home," Trace answered quietly.

The sound of the word and the sound of his voice were like pouring a warm, soothing oil on the turmoil inside her heart. Honor looked at Trace, so solid and so near and felt for the first time in weeks that everything was going to be okay.

She leaned back and watched the driveway widen into a yard surrounding the most enchanting home Honor had ever seen.

"Oh!" escaped her lips, as she glanced upward and watched the impending storm clouds mirrored in the expanse of windows on the face of the cedar-and-glass two-story home.

The house blended into the thick, wooded area as if it had been birthed on the spot. The peaks and gables on the rough, cedar shake shingles struggled for domination among the tall stands of pine and aging oaks.

"Do you live here?" Honor finally managed to ask.

"Not year round," Trace answered. "But it's mine.

And not many people know it. This is one place I can come to and not be chased down to solve a problem at work." He pulled the four by four under the carport just as the heavens unloaded. "Made it, and just in time," he said.

He reached behind the seat, grabbed the bulky suitcase bearing Honor's quickly packed wardrobe, and headed up the steps with Honor in tow.

"Welcome to my home," Trace said softly, and resisted the urge to touch her again.

In some way, he still felt cheated by the fact that he wasn't the one who'd come to her rescue. He supposed if he was honest with himself, he was jealous. Rusty Dawson's relationship with this leggy beauty was entrenched in years. He'd had only a few weeks and still felt on shaky ground.

"This house is beautiful. I feel like I should be carried over the threshold or something," Honor said, and then nearly swallowed her tongue at the wild, dark expression that leaped into Trace Logan's eyes.

"What you better do is not put any more ideas into my head, lady. There are already more there than you're ready for."

Honor stifled a grin, knew when she'd pushed too far, and sedately walked past him into the house.

"Trace..." she said softly, as she entered the vast space encompassing the living area of the house. "It's beautiful."

Her eyes ran up the length of the tall cathedral ceiling and caught on the polished wood rails surrounding the open upstairs balcony that overlooked the living area. Everything was natural finishes and natural woods. It blended in with the magnificent view so perfectly it gave one a sensation of still being outdoors yet able to enjoy all the modern comforts.

Lightning flashed and, directly following, came the deep, angry rumble of thunder echoing against the neighboring mountain peaks. The storm was right on top of them. Honor jumped and then flashed a guilty look at Trace, who stood watching silently as Honor absorbed his home.

"I'm not scared of storms," she said quickly. "I just wasn't expecting that."

"You're not scared of much, are you, Honor? I, on the other hand, wake up in a constant cold sweat imagining that I've lost you."

His terse remark reminded Honor that Trace was still more than put out with the fact that she'd called her uncle instead of him for help. She sighed and followed him up the stairs, knowing it would take more than an apology from her to get back in his good graces. But he was wrong about one thing. She *was* scared of the dark and of the possibility of losing Trace Logan.

Trace dumped Honor and her baggage in a large, airy room with a sloping ceiling, muttered something about food and heat, and left. Honor let him go, knowing that a little space and silence would do wonders for a disgruntled man's disposition.

She began to unpack and was doing fine until she began opening drawers and doors to put away her clothes. She shuffled through their contents with a sense of panic. Unless Trace was into wearing lace and lingerie, some other woman had a claim on him that Honor had known nothing about.

She turned angrily, certain that she was justified in being furious after the commitment of loving that had passed between them, and stomped from the room, her unpacking momentarily forgotten. She found him in the basement fiddling with an enormous contraption she assumed was the boiler that heated the house.

"Is there something you'd like to tell me about the clothes in my room?" Honor yelled, as she cleared the last three steps in one giant leap.

Trace jumped up and backward from his crouched position, startled by her presence and tone of voice, and bumped his head on a low-hanging rafter. A long string of unintelligible curses slid from between his tightly clenched teeth as he grabbed at the top of his head and shoved a hand through his hair.

"For pity's sake," Trace groaned. "What did you do that for?"

"I didn't do anything," she muttered. "I didn't even touch you," she argued. "I only asked you a question… which by the way, you conveniently neglected to answer."

"What the hell did you say?" Trace muttered, a bit relieved that nothing but a rapidly forming knot was under his fingertips.

"Whose clothes are in my room?"

Trace felt a quickening in the pit of his stomach, and a tiny flash of awareness began growing into a relieved certainty. If she was angry at the presence of women's clothes in his home, that meant she was jealous. Good! But he wasn't buckling under this quickly. She'd worried him to death with no thought of his feelings and now when she was upset, demanded an instant answer.

"Patsy's," he finally answered, watching her face for a reaction.

"Oh!" she muttered, shocked by his quick, open answer to a question she expected him to ignore. "Well, I just wondered," she said, and then waited for him to elaborate. When he volunteered nothing further, she spun about in frustration and started back up the stairs, certain in her heart that some other woman he'd never mentioned had a prior claim she couldn't fight. She got halfway up the stair steps before her curiosity and anger got the better of her.

"So! Who the hell is Patsy?" Honor yelled back down the stairs.

"My baby sister," Trace said, and hid the glee he felt as he saw her anger turn to instant embarrassment.

"Well! I hope you enjoyed that," she muttered, and stomped back upstairs to finish unpacking.

Trace sat down on an overturned box of Christmas decorations and watched Honor's backside and long legs disappear through the doorway. He rubbed his head, wincing as his fingers grazed the knot on top, and began to grin. The grin became a smile, the smile, a full-fledged laugh that he quickly muffled. She was already angry enough. He didn't need to rub it in.

Hastings watched his fiancée's apartment building, the frustration level building inside him until he could barely control his fury. The man he'd hired to tamper with Honor's car had called with the news that the job was completed. But he doubted it would do any good because Honor O'Brien was gone and no one seemed to know where.

Hastings saw Erin come out of her apartment building and then stand just under the doorway, sheltering herself from the rain while obviously waiting for a cab.

He jumped out of his car and dashed across the street before she had time to realize what was happening.

"Where is she?" he growled angrily, as he stepped between Erin and freedom, pressing her against the building in a threatening manner.

She trembled, knew instantly who he was referring to, and knew her answer was only going to make things worse.

"I don't know," she said. "And I wouldn't tell you if I did. Why in God's name did you push her down the stairs? She might have been killed!"

"That was the whole point, baby," he whispered, and pushed himself against Erin in a suggestive manner. "Then it would all be yours."

"I don't want it all at that price," Erin argued. "You're crazy," she added and tried unsuccessfully to move him away.

"Not crazy," he whispered, and casually wrapped his hand around her throat. "Just careful." Then his gaze shifted to the rapidly throbbing pulse beneath the palm of his hand and watched the panic flare in her eyes. "Did you tell?" he asked, referring to Honor's fall.

"No! Of course not," she cried, and struggled within his grasp. Her life depended on making him believe her sincerity.

"Good girl," he growled, and pressed a hard, punishing kiss against her lips. "See that you don't." And then he was gone.

Erin tasted blood from her bruised mouth and shuddered. This man was unlike the man she'd bullied and cajoled for years. He was hard, forceful and dangerous. She didn't know him at all. With panicked relief, she saw her cab coming up the street and dashed out into the rain. She had to get to work and tell her father about this, and then she was going to disappear. She had a friend who'd moved to Lisbon some time ago. Portugal was supposed to be nice this time of year. Maybe it was time to see for herself.

Honor stood at the immense expanse of window overlooking the front yard and stared into the darkness. A gust of wind blew a sheet of rain hard against the glass just as a bolt of lightning illuminated the night. Honor blinked and jumped back in surprise. For a girl from west Texas who saw less rain per year than she'd seen today alone, it was definitely culture shock.

She pulled the tail of her sweatshirt down and rubbed her hands against the matching white sweat pants. She shivered in spite of the roaring fire in the fireplace and the heat emanating up into the floor vents from the boiler below.

"If you're cold, come away from the window," Trace drawled, and patted the cushioned seat beside him.

Honor shook her head and sighed, then sauntered toward the fireplace, ignoring Trace's invitation. Instead, she curled up on the braided rug in front of the fire. She was still miffed about Trace letting her have that fit and a bit worried that he'd made absolutely no personal overture toward her since their arrival, not even a hug.

She didn't know that he was fighting every instinct he had not to peel her naked and bury himself in her softness. She didn't know that he kept seeing a replay of the array of bruising on her body and feared that he would hurt her.

Her eyes were stormy, a mirror image of the sky outside as she turned her face up to Trace and spoke.

"Are you still mad at me?" she asked, fiddling nervously with the inseam of her pants as she sat crosslegged before him.

She didn't give him time to answer as she jumped to her feet and started poking about the gallery of framed portraits and snapshots lining the massive mantel above the fire.

"Who's this?" she asked, and pointing to a picture of a tall young man who greatly resembled Trace Logan.

He could keep his distance no longer. "My brother, Ron, his wife Carol and their family." He took the picture from her hands and placed it back in line, then took her by the hand and led her down the minigallery of Logans, naming each as he went along. "These are my parents, Conrad and Susan. They are in Denver, visiting my brother, Ted and his family. He and Julie have twin boys. And this is Patsy, my baby sister."

He looked at Honor, cocked his eyebrows in a mocking gesture and ignored the flush that rapidly spread across her cheeks. "This is Patsy, her husband, Carl, and their daughter, Trish. She's nearly three, and quite a handful. We usually all meet here for the holidays. It's the only place large enough to hold us."

"You're so lucky," Honor said quietly, and pulled her hand away from his grasp. "I always wanted to belong to a large family but there was only Momma and me." She turned away and stared into the fire. "Then, when I discovered I actually did belong to a family like that, look what I got."

Her eyes were brimming with unshed tears as Trace came up behind her and made her turn and face him, still careful of her fading bruises.

"I won't be mad at you, if you won't be mad at me,"

Trace whispered in her ear. "And, I know where you belong."

She smiled against the bulky softness of his sweater, and buried her face in the curve of his neck, inhaling the scent of his cologne, the woodsmoke from the fire, and Trace the man.

"Where do I belong, oh, wise one?" she teased, and felt his body tense against her.

"In my arms, in my heart, and," he reluctantly withdrew before he continued, "from the looks of the dark circles under your eyes, you also belong in bed."

"Who's going to tuck me in?" Honor asked. But all she received for her trouble was a glare from Trace as he ushered her upstairs to her room.

Leaving Honor alone was the most difficult thing Trace had ever attempted. And so far, that's all it was—an attempt. He had to make it through the night before it became an accomplished feat. He walked quietly through the downstairs rooms, carefully checking the locks on the windows and doors before retiring. He was at the bottom of the stairs when a tremendous crack of lightning flashed through the wide expanse of glass, nearly blinding him by its intensity. The thunder that followed actually rattled the windows. Then the lights went out!

Trace jumped, startled by the violent sequence of events, and knew before he ever heard her scream that Honor would be scared to death.

She had just emerged from her bath when the thunder came crashing down through the mountains. It was when the lights went out and she saw nothing but total darkness that she lost it. She could deal with darkness in her own home, it was even comforting and familiar. But not this.

The scream that erupted from her throat scared her nearly as much as the storm. She hadn't been expecting it, either. It was too much like being stranded in the elevator.

Honor reached in front of her, blindly searching for something to which she could orient herself. But it was no use. She couldn't assimilate the unfamiliar surroundings by touch alone and she couldn't find the doorway. So she did the only sensible thing. She wrapped her arms around herself, refused to move another step, and screamed again, only louder.

"I thought you weren't afraid of storms," the deep, familiar voice teased, as he opened the bathroom door on her second scream.

"I'm not," Honor cried, as she flew straight toward the sound of his voice and into his arms. "But I'm afraid of the dark."

It took little more than a heartbeat for Trace to realize Honor was wet and shaking and bare as the day she was born. The knowledge and the sensuous sensation of touching her slick, satiny body did two things to his resolve to leave Honor untouched this night.

The first thing was, he totally forgot why he'd ever considered it necessary, and he couldn't remember the second thing, either. Nothing but the feel of her soft, damp skin beneath his fingertips registered in his brain. He groaned, wrapped his arms around her, pulling her soft, generous curves as closely against him as breath would allow, and tried desperately not to stagger from the feel of her bare hips pressed against the blossoming ache below his belt buckle.

Honor knew the moment her bare skin brushed against his clothed body that what she'd done in fright would have consequences resulting from love. There was no mistaking the increasing urgency of Trace's body against her or the near-desperate way he'd caught and stopped her frantic flight.

"Oh, my God!" Trace muttered, as he ran his hands along her rib cage, feeling his way down past her tiny waist to the gentle flare of her soft, shapely hips. His hands splayed and then pressed as he fitted her between his legs. He groaned against her lips, still damp from the dew of her shower, and covered them with his own in deliberate devastation.

Honor moaned as an ache began in the pit of her stomach. Were it not for the fierce, unrelenting hold of Trace's arms, she would have fallen to the floor. It felt as if the bones in her legs had suddenly disappeared.

She groaned against his mouth and struggled briefly in his grasp before she pulled her arms free and found the object of her search. The hard metal buckle at his waist came undone despite the violent tremble in her hands. There was only a piece of braided metal between her and heaven as she fumbled blindly for the tab of his zipper. It was just about then that she felt her feet leave the floor. Suddenly she was in her bedroom, on her back, on the floor, on a rug, and under Trace Logan. She could vaguely see his clothes coming off faster than the rain outside was coming down.

"Shouldn't we be on the bed?" Honor whispered, as she felt Trace's hard, muscled body sliding down beside her.

"Too far," he muttered, just before he buried his lips in the damp valley between her breasts.

Honor felt his mouth, then his teeth, and finally his tongue begin an exploration of her that drove sanity into the night with the storm. There wasn't a place untouched or untasted on Honor's body. And she knew if someone threw a match into the room, she'd ignite. Her skin, heightened to an unbelievable sensitivity by his sensuous foray, was burning beneath his touch as Trace moved over her body with skilled perfection, seeking out the places that made her moan...and the places that made her gasp...and the place that stopped her breath. It was there that the search ended and another journey began.

Trace had reached every limit of endurance he'd ever imposed upon himself. He knew if he didn't take her now he'd lose his mind. He slid his knee between her legs and felt her open instantly to make room for him. Raising himself on arms that trembled and ached from the self-imposed restraint, he paused only briefly at what he knew would be heaven.

Honor felt his weight shift, realized that this wild, insane ache was going to get worse before it got better, and shuddered as he touched the center of her being. She arched upward, unable and unwilling to wait any longer, wrapped her long legs around Trace's hips, and pulled him down, down, into the fire he'd started inside her body.

The motion shocked, the sensation came without warning, and before he had time to think, Trace spilled himself into Honor's body with shuddering, aching thrusts. He felt the answering warmth of her own release as tiny muscles convulsed around him and then fell on top of her in shocked exhaustion. It was long moments later before he could speak, and when he did, it came out in the form of a low, regretful laugh, before he buried his face in her neck and rolled her over on top of him.

"I haven't lost control like that since I was seventeen,"

Trace whispered with a smile in his voice, and gently traced her body as it rested against him in the darkness. "But I should have expected it from you, lady," he drawled, before he tangled his hands in her hair and pulled her down into his kiss. "You've made me as uncertain now as I was then, maybe even worse. Hell, I haven't had good sense since you cried in my arms the night we met."

"I wondered even then what this would be like with you," Honor whispered against his mouth, and moved suggestively against his already rejuvenating manhood. "I can honestly say, my imagination wasn't as good as the fact."

"I didn't have a chance, did I?" Trace teased, as he rolled Honor off his body and then stood before pulling her to her feet.

"Where are we going?" Honor asked, as she slid against his searching thrust.

"Umm," he mumbled incoherently, as he grabbed desperately at her seeking hands. "If I can get you there," he groaned, "to bed. And then I think I'll tuck *you* in, only this time let *me* do the tucking. I promise it'll last longer."

He sealed his promise with a kiss and proceeded to fulfill his pledge with delicious deliberation.

It was much later that night, when the electricity came back on with startling clarity, that they realized the possibilities still open to them. Trace turned off the lights, cradled Honor's sleepy body beneath him, gently caressed her love-swollen lips, and then proceeded to rock her back to sleep in a manner as old as time.

Chapter 11

Cool air teased at the bare skin of Honor's back where the covers had slipped. The sensation made her scoot farther down into the bed, searching to regain the warmth of the night. But the farther she scooted the colder it got. Her eyes reluctantly opened, sleepily searching for the reason. It only took a second for last night's memories to come rushing back into her consciousness. And with them came the answer to why she was cold. The house was freezing and Trace was nowhere in sight.

Honor jumped out of bed, grabbed some underwear and a red sweatsuit from her partially unpacked suitcase, and quickly dressed, sighing in relief as the soft, fleecy interior of the outfit began warming her chilled body. With a pair of socks in one hand and her tennis shoes in the other, she left the room in search of food and Trace, and not necessarily in that order.

The floor was cold beneath her bare feet and Honor wondered, as she sat downstairs on the bottom stair step and tied her last shoelace, what had happened to Trace and last night's comforting warmth? She wandered through the entire downstairs, listening for signs of him until finally her impatience ended the search.

"Trace! Where are you?" she called loudly, and then waited for him to answer.

Another gust of cool air wafted through the house. She shuddered. But this time not from cold...from fear. Something was wrong! After last night, no one could make Honor believe that Trace was gone without so much as a note. She started back through the house again, and this time something told her to repeat the search in a quieter fashion.

An odd, repetitive noise had penetrated Trace's sleep. He reluctantly unwound himself from Honor's warmth, careful not to disturb her rest as he slipped across the hall into his own room. He dressed quickly. The house was too cool. He made a mental note to check the thermostat when he went downstairs.

His denim pants and old gray sweatshirt were clothes reserved only for leisure time. And he wondered as he hurried down the hallway why he didn't allow himself more of this so-called leisure. This trip had started out as a mission to keep Honor out of harm's way. But it had taken a power failure to put his life and priorities quickly in place. This had become a proving ground for what he hoped was the rest of his life. He wanted Honor to trust and love him just as much as he loved her. She had to get past her resentment of the fact that he was the original bearer of bad news. And if last night was an indication, she was developing a fantastic case of amnesia.

Just as soon as possible, if all his suspicions proved to be correct, charges would be filed that would probably remove Mr. Lawrence from their lives, and society, altogether. Trace had no way of knowing that the wheels of justice had already been set in place by J. J. Malone. Or that Hastings was on the run.

Trace noticed that the sound that awakened him had stopped. Yet he thought nothing of it as he began a cursory investigation of doors and windows. Last night's storm had been fierce, even by mountain standards. Almost anything could have broken or blown loose.

He could find nothing obvious inside the house to account for the odd noise he'd heard. He started through the kitchen toward the back door and then stopped. His eyes widened in surprise and then narrowed thoughtfully as he saw the basement door standing ajar.

"What the...?" he muttered, and walked toward the gaping door. He pulled it back slowly, leaning forward to peer down the long, darkened tunnel of stairs. Then he stood quietly, listening. Nothing seemed or sounded out of place. He shrugged, stepped back, and started to pull the door shut when something fell to the floor below with a crash.

Trace yanked the door back and hit the light switch at the top of the stairs. Nothing happened. No lights and no further sounds were heard. He muttered a soft curse, knowing that he had better places to be and much better things to be doing with Honor than fiddling around with the boiler again. But his caution overruled his heart as he retrieved a flashlight from the cabinet drawer beside the door and started down into the basement.

* * *

Hastings had known his plans to prevent discovery were over when he'd called the office yesterday without identifying himself and asked to speak to Erin. When he'd been told that she'd taken an extended leave of absence and left the country, a warning had gone off in his brain.

The bitch! She'd told! He just knew it! His suspicions were confirmed when he then asked to be transferred to Legal. He disguised his voice and shrewdly asked to speak to himself. He didn't have to guess what it meant upon being told that Hastings Lawrence no longer worked for Malone Industries. He hung up in sick panic.

His first instinct was to run. Obviously the least they could charge him with was assault. The worst was attempted murder and embezzlement. His fury soared. He cursed loud and long at the fates that had resurrected that damned granddaughter and ruined long years of careful planning. And his anger grew as he thought of Trace Logan's threats and interferences that had set off this chain reaction of disasters. He'd run all right! But not before he made them pay. Now all he had to do was find Honor O'Brien, and when he did, he'd find Trace Logan, too. Of that he was certain.

The storm's aftermath had left broken branches, loose rocks, and, in some places, ankle-deep mud. But Hastings didn't notice the destruction or the sharp bite of the sharp, misty wind that cut across the treetops on the mountain. He chortled gleefully as he hitched his backpack to a more comfortable position. There was Logan's vehicle right where he'd guessed.

Hastings had been a visitor here only once and had

forgotten about the house until he'd begun wracking his brain for places Trace Logan might go to hide.

Hastings knew no one would expect him to hike in. But he'd been quite adept at backpacking during his college days. And, he thought smugly to himself, he hadn't lost his touch.

He stopped at the edge of the trees bordering the house and grounds and stood for several minutes watching carefully. Finally he was convinced that they were probably still asleep. He was also convinced that Trace had Honor O'Brien with him and thought it a stroke of luck that the two people who destroyed his dreams were in the same place at the same time.

Hastings crept quietly up to the house and began investigating possible points of entry. His logical, meticulous mind allowed for every avenue of exploration. He was rewarded, on his third time around the house, when he finally spied a basement window that was completely concealed by overgrown shrubbery. Crawling on his hands and knees behind the bushes, he slipped off his backpack, and in no time, had gained entrance into Trace's house.

It was dark and warm in the room, with the big black boiler competently channeling its heat throughout the house. Hastings sat on the bottom step of the basement stairs and warmed himself before venturing farther, comfortable in the knowledge that he was undetected. His plan had been vague as to how he was going to dispose of these two people who had become his nemesis. But he'd come prepared.

He dug into his backpack, pulled out a flashlight and began his investigation. The flashlight's beam was narrow and weak, and he shook it slightly, as if trying to shake out more light. It only succeeded in making the light go out completely. He then wasted precious time disassembling the flashlight and putting it back together again before he had it in working order. When he located the breaker box that controlled all of the power to the house, the power ceased instantly with a flick of his finger.

"Now," he whispered softly to himself, as he started toward the boiler with a handful of tools, "let's see what we have here."

Hastings was a shrewd man, but his was not a mechanical mind. He fiddled and tapped on every gauge and lever of the boiler. The possibility of an explosion made to look like an accident would be the perfect way to solve his problem. But all his poking and prodding brought no satisfactory results. Ironically, by shutting off the electrical power first, Hastings had unknowingly stopped his own plan for succeeding. The boiler's fans and even the main switch all worked from electricity. When the power was off, the boiler was incapable of any function whatsoever.

Hastings muttered a curse of frustration and gave the boiler a final thump with his wrench, unaware that the floor vents that carried the warm air throughout the house also carried the sounds of his frustrated vandalism. But the same floor vents had in turn alerted Hastings to the fact that someone was moving about upstairs. His heart missed a beat as he heard sounds of a door closing and then footsteps overhead. He stopped all motion and stood silently waiting, his mind awash with tension. Adrenaline rocketed through his body as a confrontation became more and more apparent.

Suddenly, he knew how to draw them to him. Using

the narrow beam from his flashlight for guidance, he quickly ran up the basement stair steps, listened for a moment to assure himself that no one was yet in the vicinity, then pushed the door that led down to the basement ajar. An open door was perfect bait, especially when it had been closed the night before. He went back quicker than he'd come up, panic fueling his movements as he searched for a place to hide.

When someone came to investigate, he would be waiting. Stairs had become a perfect instrument of destruction for Hastings. He was not big and strong. But he needed more than his cunning to succeed. Why not take advantage of the stairs' proximity? He pushed aside a stack of empty boxes under the stairs and leaned as far back into the shadows as he could get...and he waited!

The air is cooler down here than it should be, Trace thought, as he used the flashlight beam to help him negotiate the long, steep flight of steps leading down to his basement.

"Damn!" he muttered, envisioning how cold this house could be with no power. If the electricity was off for an extended period of time, he'd have to hunt for the portable kerosene heaters.

Something moved below and Trace's senses sharpened. That was not the wind! Every possible caution that he should have used earlier before he started down the steps came rushing into his brain. He turned the narrow beam of light to the open stairwell beneath his feet, but it was too late! Someone grabbed at his feet, yanking his balance out from under him. His body flailed outward, grabbing at nothing but air as his body was propelled by gravity outward and downward. Trace's shout of fury was drowned out by a cackle of laughter. He recognized the laugh and the danger, but it was too late. He threw the flashlight backward in an attempt to distract his assailant. It connected with a loud thump, but it was too late to help Trace.

He started to shout Honor's name in warning, but there wasn't enough time between the thought and the distance to the concrete floor. He hit the bottom step with his shoulder, and the floor with his head. Then he rolled limply on his side as the darkness claimed him before the pain had a chance to register.

Hastings stepped out from under the open stairwell and kicked Trace's flashlight aside. He rubbed gingerly at the swiftly swelling knot over his right eye and watched in satisfaction as a bright-red stain began pouring onto the sleeve of Trace's gray sweatshirt. One of his arms was outflung as if trying to break the fall, the other lay under his head where the deep, ugly gash in his forehead was emptying his life onto his shirt and the floor beneath him.

Hastings watched, satisfied that the fall would be mortal, then just to aid the process, kicked him sharply in the rib cage. There was absolutely no reaction, nor indication of life from the big man at his feet. He grunted in satisfaction and began gathering his tools.

"You'll never threaten me again, you bastard," Hastings muttered. Now all he had to do was get rid of the bitch upstairs, and he was home free.

He blinked rapidly, trying to clear the vision of the eye that continued to swell. But it was no use. And he didn't care. He could see well enough with the uninjured one to tell that Trace Logan had just spent his last day on earth.

By the time Hastings had gathered all of his gear, carefully repacked it in the backpack, and stuffed the backpack through the basement window for later retrieval, the house was thoroughly chilled and his eye was swollen shut. He stepped over Trace's limp form, started upstairs, and then turned for one last check. He leaned over and ran his fingers along Trace Logan's neck, smiling at the fluttering, fading pulse. He knew that with a little luck and time on his side, Logan would soon be dead. It was perfect! When Logan's body was discovered, it would look as if he'd just tripped and fallen, then died from the injuries and exposure.

Satisfied that all was well, he patted his jacket pocket, assuring himself that the gun he'd retained from his backpack was still in place. He had other plans for Miss O'Brien Malone. They'd never find her body. There were caves all over these mountains. He'd seen several on his way up. But his reverie was interrupted by Honor's voice as she called out Trace's name.

Hastings looked around wildly, unwilling to be caught down here with her. She was too big for him to remove if he had to do away with her here and he still wanted all of this to look like an accident. He ran quickly up the stairs and shut the door behind him as he silently entered the kitchen. He didn't want her wandering down where she didn't belong. His heart raced and his fingers twitched as he pulled the gun from his pocket. One down, one to go.

Honor slowed down the urge to shout Trace's name again. She didn't know why but some instinct told her that silence was imperative. Her hands shook as she reached back blindly, and when she felt the solid strength of the wall behind her, leaned against it and listened.

She knew by the amount of daylight outside that it was way past sunrise. But the sky was still cloudy, promising another dreary day. From her vantage point in the downstairs hallway, Honor could see all of the living room and a portion of the wall that separated it from the kitchen and dining area. Her gaze was focused on the outside view. For some reason, she'd imagined that if there was any danger it would be coming from outside, not inside with her. But when she saw the reflection of the man in the wide expanse of living-room windows and realized that he was already inside the house with her, she panicked. Then when she saw the gun and who was holding it, she had to stifle the moan of fear that slid up her throat. Honor looked around, desperate for an answer to the situation, and took the nearest exit until she had time to think. The patio doors behind her led onto the outside deck. If she could get them open without alerting Hastings, maybe she could use the density of the woods to her advantage. She had to get away and she had to get help. She couldn't let herself think about why Trace hadn't come to her rescue.

The well-oiled lock slid back with little more than a tick as Honor pulled the glass door open just enough to squeeze through. She quietly but quickly pushed it back in place, swallowed the sob of fear that threatened to choke her, and ignored the steps on the other side of the deck. She would have to walk across the deck in plain view to reach them. There was only one other choice. She would have to jump down from the elevated structure. It was high, but it was safer and quicker.

"God help me!" Honor muttered prayerfully. She

jumped, fell to her hands and knees, and then with no thought for the hide off her hands that she'd left behind, dashed toward the welcoming cover of the forest.

Hastings heard nothing of Honor's exit and wasted precious time carefully searching the entire two-story house before he realized that she'd somehow eluded him. And if she was gone, that meant she knew there was a reason to run. And that meant she'd somehow discovered his presence.

"Dammit! Dammit!" he yelled loudly, shoving furniture about with wild abandon. This wasn't how he'd planned it. He rubbed gently at his forehead as the ache behind his eye ballooned into a pounding throb of pain.

It was only when he backtracked through the house that he discovered the unlocked patio door. As he pushed it roughly aside, more of the cold, damp mountain air came sweeping into the house. But Hastings could have cared less. He leaned over the side of the deck and smiled. Footprints shining in the muddy yard like breadcrumbs in the forest were going to lead him right to little Miss O'Brien. He lowered himself carefully over the side and headed into the woods, his one good eye on the ground below.

J. J. Malone paced the floor in his library, staring blindly at the bookshelves and once in a while at the smiling portrait of his Meggie. But there was no joy in looking at her face today. He was more concerned with the fact that Trace hadn't called.

Rusty Dawson's message had been frightening. When J.J. had discovered that Honor's life seemed to still be in danger, he'd called the police and then hastened the audit himself. Trace had been so insistent and so certain that it would give them some badly needed answers. From all the preliminary reports that J.J. had received, it seemed Trace had been right. Hastings Lawrence had been dipping into a slush fund and playing around with J.J.'s properties and securities as if they were his own. It seems he'd bet a lot more than time on the possibility of being married into the family. Hastings had been borrowing money on properties that didn't belong to him, investing the money, and when and if the investments paid off, pocketing the profits before he paid back the embezzled amounts. The problem was, he'd neglected to pay back as much as he'd borrowed, and his scheme was about to cave in on him. All because of the arrival of J.J.'s long-lost granddaughter.

And there were other more urgent reasons for J.J.'s concern. Rusty Dawson had assured him that Trace would be calling as soon as they'd arrived in Colorado. He knew where Trace was taking Honor. Rusty had informed him of every step of the plan he and Trace had made before they'd ever left Texas. But there'd been no call, no contact whatsoever. There was simply no answer at Trace's home.

J.J. frowned as he recalled Erin's hysterics as she'd burst into his office yesterday. It hadn't taken him long to ferret out the fact that Hastings Lawrence was behind her concern, and when he'd listened closely, he echoed her panic. This had already gone way beyond corporate crime. This was personal. Hastings Lawrence had attempted murder, twice, and was nowhere to be found. That's when he'd called the authorities, again. And that's when he'd been told that Hastings Lawrence had disappeared.

Trudy Sinclair walked into the library with a tray of steaming-hot coffee and a look of determination.

"I don't know just exactly what's wrong," she snapped, as she placed the tray on his desk. "But I suspect it concerns your granddaughter. I've heard bits and pieces of what's been happening, both while I was gone and after I returned. And it's been nothing but bad. Bad, I tell you!" She glared at her boss, just daring him to dispute her right to speak her piece. "She doesn't deserve what's been happening. And," she said dramatically, as she pointed to Meggie's portrait, "she'd have a fit if she saw you doing nothing but twiddling your thumbs."

Satisfied that she'd made her point, she bustled out, uncaring if J. J. Malone fired her or not. She'd come to think a great deal of the young woman in the short time she'd been with them and couldn't bear to think of any more harm coming to her through this family.

J.J. wanted to shout. He wanted to call her back and accuse her of being a meddling busybody. But his conscience wouldn't allow him the luxury. She was right. He had already alerted the authorities about Hastings Lawrence. But it wasn't enough for J. J. Malone. He needed to be involved. He called the police, asking them to go to Trace's home in the mountains and check on their safety, and then made another call for himself.

"Andrew!" he ordered, as he heard his son's voice answer on the third ring. "We've got trouble, boy. Come and get me. And this time you need to bring more than your car. You better bring a world's worth of prayers."

It was cold, so cold. And the pain! When he tried to claw his way out of the persistent tendrils of darkness, the pain would rocket through his body and send him spiraling back into unconsciousness. But something kept pushing, something kept him from letting go. If he could just remember what, maybe he could pull himself back to the real world. Stormy eyes, gray as the rainy sky, kept urging him forward, beckoning first with sleepy passion and then pleading with tearful persistence. Someone needed him. He had to fight the need to sleep, to sleep forever.

Voices! He could hear voices! Trace struggled valiantly to call out, let them know he was here. He needed to help…someone…help… Dear God! Memory came flooding back with the pain. Honor! She was in danger.

"Father, this doesn't look good," Andrew said, as he and J. J. Malone entered Trace's house.

The patio door was standing wide open, furniture lying broken and in wild disarray and no one in sight. He muttered a quick prayer and headed for the telephone, leaving his father to stand in stunned silence.

J.J. couldn't face the implications. He knew he was too old for all that had taken place in the past month. A lesser man would probably have had a stroke. At the moment he felt angry enough to precipitate one.

"The authorities are already on their way," Father Andrew said, watching his elderly father for signs of distress.

"Quit staring, dammit," J.J. growled. "I'm not going to fade out on you yet. I'm too mad to die. Come on, Son. Let's check this place out."

He led the way through the house, careful not to disturb what might turn into a crime scene, yet missing nothing that could tell him what might have happened to his granddaughter and the man he regarded as another son.

They began upstairs, searching frantically for a sign of Honor or Trace. Nothing!

"You take the east side, I'll take the west," Father Andrew said, as they began a sweep of the downstairs rooms.

And it was Father Andrew who got the fright of his life when he entered the kitchen at the same time Trace opened the basement door and fell into the room.

"Merciful God in heaven!" he whispered, made the sign of the cross, then yelled loudly for his father. "Here! In the kitchen. Come quickly, Father. I've found one of them!"

J.J. took one sick look at Trace's condition, ordered Andrew to make another phone call, and this time for the ambulance. Trace was covered in blood.

J.J. knelt at Trace's side, his hands shaking as he began searching for other injuries besides the gash in his head.

"Honor..." Trace muttered, weakly pushing against the hands that pulled at his clothing. He'd managed the stairs by determination alone. There was no strength left for anything but an argument now.

"Lie still, boy," J.J. ordered gruffly. "It's J.J., and Andrew is with me. Help is on the way, Son. Don't move. You've got a bad cut on your head."

"Honor..." Trace repeated, relief flooding his body as he recognized his boss's voice. Someone had to find Honor.

"She's not here, Son," J.J. said, hesitated, and then continued. This was no time for delicacy. Honor's life might be in danger. "Do you know where she is?"

"No." Then Trace mumbled out a name that made J.J. sick. "Hastings. He was here. Heard him…" Trace's voice faded away with consciousness.

"The police…they're here," Father Andrew shouted, and ran toward the door to let them in.

He prayed that the ambulance wouldn't be far behind, then added another prayer that Trace Logan would be the only one needing its services. Please God, they find his niece alive and well. He didn't think his father could take any more.

Honor ran until her heart hurt and her breath came in deep, ugly gasps. She looked back, searching the thick, wooded area for signs of pursuit. She could see nothing but trees and rocks, and more trees and more rocks. Then her stomach did a flip-flop as she looked around in panic for a familiar landmark. There was none. She was lost! She didn't even know which way to go to get help. Was she going up the mountain, or down? There were so many trees. And no path! There was nothing for a girl from west Texas to use for bearings. She'd never been in such dense woods and had no idea how to orient herself.

"Oh, God!" she muttered, sank limply onto an enormous dead tree lying in horizontal grandeur on the forest floor, and put her head in her hands. "Momma, if I live through this I may never forgive you for sending that damn letter."

The mention of her mother's name sent a sense of peace flooding through Honor's panicked mind. She shivered, and looked up startled, half expecting to see her mother standing before her.

"Okay," Honor muttered again. "I get the message. Quit feeling sorry for yourself, Honor. Think, dammit!"

And suddenly, she knew. Last night's storm had been torrential. The rain that had fallen would have run downhill. All she had to do was look for signs of runoff. And it wasn't long before she found a channel cut into the hillside between two large boulders. Water was still trickling through the narrow gash in the earth with persistence.

"Yes!" Honor cried, then looked around fearfully, afraid that she might have been overheard. She still could see no signs of anyone, but that didn't mean a thing. The trees were so dense that she and Hastings could walk up on each other and never know until it was too late…for Honor.

She started downhill, unable to run as swiftly as she had before. Now there was the possibility that she would run headlong into Hastings Lawrence's lap. Yet she could do nothing else. Every thought in her heart was for Trace and the fear that even if she succeeded in eluding Hastings, and even if she was able to summon help, it would be too late.

Hastings saw her before she saw him. It was the red sweatsuit. Honor may as well have announced her whereabouts with a loudspeaker. Hastings smiled to himself, wincing as the movement of facial muscles pulled at his swollen eye, and slipped behind a large boulder. He frowned as his shoes sank into mud over his ankles and then shrugged. He drew his gun, held his breath, and aimed. It was his decision to lean forward just the tiniest bit that saved Honor's life.

When Hastings leaned, everything leaned but his feet. They were stuck! He couldn't stop his momen-

tum as gravity sent him falling flat on his face into the
mire. Hastings bit his lip, sucked mud, and to make
matters worse, the gun went off. It was all the warning Honor needed.

Her pulse raced into overdrive as she dived for the
nearest cover. *Oh, God! Oh, God! He was right on top
of me and I didn't even see him. Where the hell do I go
from here?*

Honor looked around, saw Hastings's predicament
as he struggled wildly to his feet, his facial features entirely obscured by the mountain mud that was sticking
with gooey persistence.

But she didn't need to see him to know he was mad.
She could hear every furious curse he was using on
himself, the gun, and Honor O'Brien. And she'd just
had an idea. She pulled off the top of her red sweatsuit
while Hastings was trying to rub the mud from his face,
and stuffed it into some thick undergrowth, making it
seem as if Honor herself were hiding within. Then she
grabbed a couple of softball-size rocks from beneath
the same bushes and backed away, betting her life on
the fact that Hastings would be *hasty,* key in on the red
shirt, and come rushing forward.

Hastings struggled wildly to his feet, digging mud
from his good eye and spitting mud from his mouth
so that his curses had somewhere to go besides back
down into his churning gut. When he was finally able
to see through a veil of muddy tears, he got the shock
of his life. He'd expected Honor O'Brien to be long
gone when his gun had discharged. But he could still
see a bit of that red sweatshirt through the dense undergrowth. Maybe his luck was finally turning. It was just
possible that the shot had found its mark after all. He

dashed forward, expecting to find a cowering woman, if not a wounded one. But he never reached the bushes.

He saw it coming from the corner of his eye, but he reacted too late. The first rock caught him up beside the head on his good eye and he staggered backward in pained surprise, grabbing at the spot above his left eyebrow that felt like it was falling off his face. He screamed in pained fury and turned his gun toward the direction the missile had come from. But he was too late. And once again his reactions were far too slow and way off course.

This time when Honor let fly, she aimed for more tender territory. She drew back, squinted her eyes, and aimed for just below his belt buckle. The rock went hurtling toward its target and then connected with stunning force into Hastings Lawrence, eliminating the threat of any future heirs. She watched in satisfaction as he froze in agonized shock and turned a beautiful shade of red beneath the mud on his face. The red quickly faded into stark white as he dropped the gun and grabbed at his quickly swelling anatomy.

"Noooooo," he moaned, doubled over, and once again fell face forward into the mud.

Only this time he didn't taste anything but the bile that boiled up his throat and spewed onto the ground. He couldn't think, he couldn't talk, and worst of all, he couldn't walk. And he knew from the look on the face of that damned Amazon who was coming toward him with her shirt in one hand and a stick in her other that she wasn't through with him yet.

The last thought he had before Honor bopped him on the head was that he probably should have taken his chances and just gone to prison. It would have been a lot less painful. He just wasn't cut out for this.

Honor had no qualms about rendering Hastings unconscious. If she'd followed her instincts, she'd have cracked his evil head in two. But she resisted, allowing herself the one blow. She nudged him with the stick. When he didn't respond, she bent over, quickly slipped his belt from the loops, and with moves she'd learned from an old boyfriend, tied Hastings Lawrence like a bulldogged calf in a rodeo. She yanked her shirt back over her head and shivered. She was chilled to the bone. She picked up the gun and began to run. She had to get to Trace!

The county sheriff had arrived, taken a quick assessment of the situation, and called for backup. This looked like a tough one. They were going to have to hurry if they hoped to find J. J. Malone's granddaughter before this Lawrence fellow did. The Malones were old family in Colorado Springs. Besides that, it was the principle of the thing. The police had been unable to find the granddaughter the first time she'd disappeared. It was a matter of pride that they didn't let it happen again.

He swiveled in his tracks as he heard sirens coming up the driveway and knew it was probably the ambulance, and none too soon. Trace Logan had lost a lot of blood.

"Sheriff!" one of his deputies called, pointing toward the back of the house. "Someone coming...on the run."

The men assembled in the yard turned en masse and saw a tall, leggy young woman taking the steep slope off the mountain as if the hounds of hell were at her heels. Then the sheriff blinked in stunned surprise and breathed a sigh of relief. If he was any guesser, his job just got a lot easier. It looked as if J. J. Malone's granddaughter had just found *them*.

Honor couldn't believe her eyes. She wasn't lost any longer. She'd seen the top of Trace's house and keyed on the shingled roof with fierce determination, although her stamina was almost gone. Her legs were burning, her lungs about to burst. She'd long ago given up trying to swallow. There was no spit left to worry about. She came off the slope, and a swift surge of relief swept over her at the distinctive emblems on the doors of the cars below. Police! They were saved!

She would have called out, but her legs gave way and she sprawled face forward in the wet grass.

"Are you hurt? Did he harm you in any way?" the sheriff asked, as he helped Honor to her feet.

"Trace?" Honor managed to gasp. "What happened to Trace?"

"Where's Lawrence? Did you see him? How did you elude him, lady? From the shape Logan was in we didn't expect to see you walking, let alone running."

His statement gave breath to Honor's lungs as she heard him mention Trace's name. "What shape? Is Trace hurt? Where is he?"

"Inside. But I suspect when he sees your face, mud and all, he's going to be just fine. You tell me about Lawrence and that's the last question you'll hear from me today. Everything else can wait. Where did you see him last?"

"He's about a quarter of a mile up the mountain. This is his gun."

"What?" the sheriff asked, shocked that she could

be so specific. "How can you be sure he's still there? And how did you get his gun?"

She smiled. "Because I tied him up before I left," Honor replied, and started toward the house. "You don't need to hurry. He's got mud up his nose, his eyes are swelled shut, and he's just passed the test for eunuch of the month." She added as an afterthought, "He's probably suffering from a concussion, too. I expect you'll need to administer first aid before handcuffs."

The sheriff looked on in stunned amazement as the tall young woman seemed to get her second wind and bounded away from him, her goal obviously set on the men in white who were carrying a stretcher toward the waiting ambulance.

Chapter 12

Still damp from his shower and wearing nothing but a
towel twisted carelessly around his hips, Trace looked
into the mirror and then winced as he tried unsuccessfully to comb his hair over the place where his stitches
had been. He'd gotten too close to the scalp.

There was nothing he could do about the new scar
on his forehead. It was visible for all to see. But when
his mother got a look at the length of the cut that disappeared into his hairline, he knew she was going to cry.
He smiled to himself as he remembered Honor's reaction. His mother couldn't hold a candle to the amount
of tears that Honor had shed.

Trace could barely remember the ambulance ride.
Hell! He didn't remember much that took place after he
started down the basement steps. But he did remember
seeing Honor come flying toward him across the yard

as the attendants loaded him into the ambulance. He'd
never felt such relief at the sight of her dirty face and
muddy red sweatsuit.

Honor had taken one horrified look at Trace covered in blood and fainted. When that happened they
just loaded Honor into the same ambulance on another
stretcher and headed for the hospital with J.J. and Father Andrew following closely behind.

The next thing Trace remembered was Honor crying and hiccuping as she sat by him in the emergency
room, holding his hand while they stitched his head
back in place.

All thoughts of the last few days went by the wayside
as Trace looked into the mirror and saw Honor walk into
the room behind him holding an outfit in each hand.

"Honey," she asked, swinging the clothes by their
hangers, "which outfit should I wear to meet your family?"

"I like that," he drawled, pointing to the black silk
teddy Honor was wearing and watched, mesmerized by
the appearance of her dimple as his words registered.

"Oh, you do, do you?" Honor asked. She dropped the
outfits at her feet, shrugged one tiny spaghetti strap of
her teddy off her shoulder, then watched the look of passion flare in Trace's eyes as she slid the other strap down
her arm. The teddy hung, suspended on the thrust of
Honor's breasts before gravity pulled it down her body
into a puddle of midnight around her feet.

"If you like it that much, then it's yours," Honor
drawled. "But you're going to have to come and get it."

And then she was in his arms and in his heart and in
his blood. Nothing mattered but her hands on his body.
Nothing existed until he claimed her lips with his own

searching mouth and drank life back into his tortured lungs. Trace groaned, shaking from the intense, instant need that Honor always triggered in him. Her body filled his hands as her love filled his soul. She was everything, and without her he'd be nothing.

His legs grew weak as his body hardened. His hands slid down between their bodies and began a searching journey all their own that sent Honor's sanity flying.

She meant to cry out at the pleasure he was giving her, but she needed her breath to survive. She'd started to touch Trace in much the same way he was touching her, but she needed her hands clasped around his neck to keep from falling. Instead, she leaned weakly against the wall, held on for dear life, and let Trace Logan into her body and into her heart.

He'd meant to take her to bed before he'd taken her body, but once again it had been too far and *he* was too far gone. Trace felt Honor opening beneath his fingers as he teased and caressed her satiny warmth. But when the heat between them nearly burned his fingers and he felt the sweetness flow, he couldn't think of moving to a bed. The only movement he was capable of was inside Honor, and so he did. With a groan of need, he slid his hard, aching manhood between her legs and thrust upward, moaning softly into her ear as the sensation made his bones melt.

"Look at me, Honor," he pleaded, pausing as he allowed her body to adjust to his swelling presence. "You look at me when I love you. Then you'll never have to wonder who you are again. You're my lady, my love, and my life." And then he began to move.

Honor watched, eyes brimming with tears and love, lips parted in sweet agony as she drew breath and life from their joining. The room spun as a building pressure began to overwhelm her. Suddenly she could see nothing, feel nothing, but those dark eyes and his body, moving…moving…moving. And then there was silence.

Sometime later, the sounds of cars coming up the drive and horns honking their arrival brought them both off the bed they'd finally located, onto their feet and frantically searching for clothes.

"Oh, Lord!" Honor moaned, as she jumped on one foot, trying to stuff her other leg into a pair of slacks. "I shouldn't worry about what to wear to meet your family. Just about anything would be better than this."

Trace laughed joyfully, planted a hard, hungry kiss on her worried mouth, and pulled a thick white sweater over his head.

"I'll go first," he said. "Take your time, love. It'll take them a bit of time to unload and unwind. Come down when you're ready."

Honor smiled, nodded gratefully, and then caught a glimpse of herself in the mirror as Trace left the room. It didn't matter what she wore. She was still going to look like she'd just gone ten rounds through a carnival's tunnel of love. Her hair was in tangles, her eyes wide, and her lips looked red and swollen. And she'd never been happier in her life.

As Trace had predicted, his mother had taken one look at the place where his stitches had been and burst out crying. His dad had just rolled his eyes at his wife's hysterics and started unloading their car. Just then three other cars pulled into the yard and his brothers Ted and Ron and their families and his sister Patsy and her family began spilling kids and clothes onto the yard.

Everyone was laughing, glad to be together again, and thankful that Trace, a beloved member of the family, was safe and well. They continued their loud, boisterous meeting as the Logan menagerie moved into the house.

"My God, Son!" Conrad Logan muttered, as he dropped his heavy bags onto the living-room floor. "What in hell happened at Malone Industries? When J.J. called telling us you'd been hurt and Hastings Lawrence was responsible, I couldn't believe it. I knew J.J.'s granddaughter had been found. Heard it on the news. Called myself to congratulate him. But then all that good news turning to this..." He stopped his rambling, pulled his eldest son into his arms, and gave him a tight hug, pounding him on the back in gentle roughness. "Just glad you're all right. Damn glad!"

His sister grinned and blew him a kiss, dumped her sleeping baby onto the sofa, and went back outside to retrieve her lingering husband and the rest of the luggage. She'd save her welcome for later. Trace smiled at her and winked as he acknowledged his father's concern.

"Thanks, Dad," Trace replied, returning the hug. Then he went to help his brothers, who were struggling with their own mountains of luggage.

"Damn, Dick Tracey," Ted teased, while Ron looked on in delight at the old nickname. "I leave you alone and what do you do? Nearly get yourself killed. And, by the way..." he drawled. "Who's this Honor O'Brien?"

Trace took a deep breath, all the foolishness disappearing from his demeanor at the mention of her name. "She's mine," he muttered.

"So, it's that way, is it?" Ron asked. "Well, old man, welcome to the club."

They laughed easily and then were distracted by the

flurry of children all shrieking their delight at being released from the cars and the long rides from Denver. The children's noisy exuberance woke Patsy's baby, and between her cries and the children's shouts of joy, pandemonium reigned.

It was that scene that greeted Honor as she started down the stairs. That, and the way Trace was laughing. She'd never seen him like this, so at ease, and so confident that he was an accepted member of this loud, happy family. It stayed her progress. And so she watched, a lonely figure in blue as she hesitated to interrupt, afraid she would not be accepted when she so desperately wanted to belong.

"Dear Heavenly Father," Susan Logan gasped. She was the first to see the tall, dark-haired woman in matching blue slacks and sweater sitting on the stairs... watching. "It's Meggie!"

Everyone pivoted toward the direction Susan Logan was looking.

"No, Mother," Trace answered quietly, as he walked up the stairs to meet his love. They came the rest of the way down the stairs together. "This is my Honor."

'But she looks just like... I know you told us... I just didn't expect..." Her voice quivered, her eyes filled.

Trace's father stepped forward and went to meet them. He paused, looked deeply into Honor's face, saw the anxiety and the need for reassurance and saw the ghost of another woman he'd lost to his best friend, J. J. Malone, more than forty years ago. *Some things do come full circle,* he thought, and pulled Honor into his arms.

"Welcome to the family, Honor O'Brien."

Trace's mother shocked her entire family when she pulled herself together without shedding another tear.

"Yes, my dear! Welcome!" she cried, and warmly clasped Honor's hand between her own. "Come," she urged, pulling Honor with her toward the sofa. "You must tell me all about yourself. Your grandmother and I were best friends. I hope we can be, too."

The last of Honor's fears disappeared as she was absorbed into the Logan clan as if she'd known them for years. And so the day passed.

It was nearly sundown, the tired children already in their beds as Honor stood on the deck alone, entranced by the night sounds and how quickly night came to the mountains. She watched the sun slipping closer and closer to the crest of the ridge, and then right before her eyes it was gathered into the waiting arms of the trees to be hidden until it would burst forth on the opposite side of the mountain the next morning. Instantly the sky turned into a magical, myriad display of colors as the last rays of the sun reluctantly released their hold on today.

Honor shivered, wrapping her arms around herself, aware of the chill of night air yet reluctant to go back inside.

So much had happened to her since Charlie's death. So many surprises, so many choices to be made. But she knew in her heart that she'd made the right ones. Peace filled her. Charlotte O'Brien *had* done the right thing… finally. Honor was not alone. Not anymore.

"Cold, baby?" Trace whispered in her ear as he came up behind her and wrapped her in his arms. He nuzzled through the dark tangle of curls at her neck, found just the spot he was searching for, and branded her with his kiss.

"A little," Honor replied. "But I was just thinking

about how happy I am and how fortunate we both are to have survived the past few weeks. I talked to Uncle Rusty earlier. He'll be out later next week."

"I know," Trace said. "That's good. He's now part of this family, too." Then he grabbed her by the hand, urging her inside to the warmth and the waiting family who'd been primed for a surprise.

When they entered the house J.J., who'd arrived some time after the Logan clan, was deep into the discussion of Hastings Lawrence with Trace's father. Honor knew by the look on Trace's face that he was going to make some wise remark. He still crowed about Lawrence's downfall and the manner in which he'd been felled.

"I saw him coming out of the courtroom yesterday after his arraignment," J.J. remarked. "He wouldn't look at me. And he was still in a wheelchair. Quite subdued."

"From what I hear he'll be lucky if he ever gets out of that chair. He was doing fine as long as he had stairs to use for weapons. It was when he ran out of stairs and ran into Honor that he ran out of luck," Trace drawled.

Everyone burst out laughing as Honor blushed and then shrugged innocently.

"Enough about that slimy weasel," Trace said. "I have an announcement to make." He pulled Honor under his arm and hugged her as he continued. "Mom, you and J.J. have exactly six weeks to plan the biggest wedding Colorado Springs has ever seen. By Christmas there will no longer be an Honor O'Brien. She'll be Honor Logan."

He stopped them before pandemonium broke loose as he finished. "And, there's just one more thing I have to do before this day is over." He pulled a small, flat, gaily wrapped box from behind his back and handed it to Honor.

"Here, love. This is for you. And I think you'll know just where it belongs." He leaned forward and placed a gently reassuring kiss on the dimple by her mouth.

Honor's eyes widened and her heart thumped an extra beat as Trace laid the little package in her hands. She tore away the wrappings. Her excitement faded into shock and then into the most overwhelming joy she'd ever experienced as she pulled a small silver frame from within the layers of tissue paper.

She tried to speak, but the word wouldn't come. She could only look at the image staring back at her through a veil of tears.

"Oh!" she finally whispered. "Oh, Trace! Only you would know what this means to me. Only you!"

She threw her arms around his neck and kissed him soundly in front of God and everybody before turning to the mantel over the fireplace behind her. She walked down the length of the mantel where the many, many pictures of the Logan family rested in all their glory and placed the small silver frame she was carrying in line with all the rest.

It was a photograph of Honor and her mother. And they were smiling into each other's faces in some secret, conspiratorial manner, as only mother and daughter can do.

Trace had done what no one else had been able to do since her world had fallen apart. Right or wrong...he'd given her back her mother...and he'd given her love.

* * * * *

Delores Fossen, a *USA TODAY* bestselling author, has written over one hundred novels, with millions of copies of her books in print worldwide. She's received a Booksellers' Best Award and an RT Reviewers' Choice Best Book Award. She was also a finalist for a prestigious RITA® Award. You can contact the author through her website at deloresfossen.com.

Books by Delores Fossen

Harlequin Intrigue

The Lawmen of McCall Canyon

Cowboy Above the Law
Finger on the Trigger
Lawman with a Cause
Under the Cowboy's Protection

HQN

Lone Star Ridge

Tangled Up in Texas
That Night in Texas (ebook novella)
Chasing Trouble in Texas

A Coldwater Texas Novel

Lone Star Christmas
Hot Texas Sunrise
Sweet Summer Sunset
A Coldwater Christmas

Visit the Author Profile page at Harlequin.com for more titles.

DADE

Delores Fossen

Chapter 1

Kayla Brennan sure didn't look like a killer.

That was Deputy Sheriff Dade Ryland's first thought when his glare landed on the blonde who was running down the staircase. His second thought went in a different direction.

A *bad* one.

More specifically to her dark purple dress that hugged every curve of her body. Real curves. Something that always got his attention even when it shouldn't.

Like now, for instance.

Sex and Kayla Brennan shouldn't be occupying the same side of his brain.

He'd seen her before, of course, from a distance. Just over a year ago at the Silver Creek sheriff's office where she was being questioned about her husband's suspicious fatal car accident. That day Dade watched her from the doorway of his office. But she'd been pregnant then and had hidden those spicy blue eyes behind a pair of designer sunglasses. She'd shown no emotion of any kind.

Unlike now.

He saw just a flash of fear before she closed down. That pretty face became a rock-hard wall.

Dade cleared his throat and kicked up his glare a notch, hoping both would give him an attitude adjustment. It did. But then it wasn't hard to remember that this curvy blonde might be partly responsible for the death of someone he loved.

"I heard the doorbell," Kayla announced. She paused on the bottom step when she spotted Dade in the doorway, and her attention flew in the direction of the other man in the foyer. "Who's he?" she demanded.

Because Kayla apparently didn't recognize him, Dade tapped the badge clipped to his rawhide belt. "*He* has a name, and it's Deputy Sheriff Dade Ryland." He nudged the other man aside and stepped into the foyer so he could close the door.

Her left eyebrow rose, and her gaze slipped back to Dade. "You're a deputy?" She didn't wait for him to answer. "You look more outlaw than lawman."

Yeah, he got that a lot, but Dade wasn't about to let Kayla get away with the observation. "You'd know all about outlaws, wouldn't you?"

She flinched a little. Just enough to make Dade wonder exactly how raw that nerve was he'd hit.

Her flinch quickly turned to a scalpel-sharp glare, and she was almost as good at that particular expression as he was. "What are you doing in my house?"

House. That was a loose term for what was actually

the Texas-sized mansion on the outskirts of his home-town of Silver Creek. A mansion she'd inherited when her husband had been killed. Dade had been raised nearby in a big ranch house with sixteen rooms, but he was betting the Brennan place was double that size.

The same probably went for Kayla's pocketbook, al-though Dade had some one-upmanship on her in that particular department. His family had earned their money through hard, back-breaking, honest work on the ranch. Kayla had married her millions, and those millions were as dirty as she no doubt was.

"I'm here on official business," Dade informed her. He glanced at the bald, gorilla-sized man who moved a few steps away. Dade knew his name was Kenneth Mitchell.

Kayla's so-called bodyguard.

Probably more like a hired gun as dirty as the woman paying his salary, and that's why Dade kept his hand on his gun tucked in his shoulder holster.

"The deputy says you're in his protective custody," Kenneth relayed to Kayla. His bulky body strained against his black suit, just as the muscles in his face strained against his skin.

She studied Dade, her eyes narrowing. "How did you know I was here? I led everyone to believe that I'd be at my house in San Antonio."

Dade shrugged, figuring the answer was obvious. "The district attorney, Winston Calhoun, called the sheriff and told him."

The way she pulled in her breath let him know that the answer had not been so obvious to her after all. "Mr. Calhoun assured me that he would keep my where-abouts a secret."

Dade tipped his head to the badge again. "He didn't exactly announce it to the press. He told me because you're in my protective custody."

Her eyes narrowed even more. "Protective custody?" she repeated. "How do you figure that?"

Dade walked closer to her. "Easy. You're the state's material witness, and the D.A. wants you alive long enough to testify against your father-in-law."

There it was in a nutshell, but that didn't begin to cover what Dade wanted from this woman. Yes, he wanted her to testify against her late-husband's scummy father, Charles Brennan. He wanted her to take the stand and spill her guts about the extortion and murders that Brennan had committed. While she was at it, Dade wanted to know if Brennan had killed his own son—Kayla's husband.

But those were just the icing.

What Dade really wanted her to admit on the stand was that she'd had some part in another crime.

Ellie's murder.

Dade had to take a deep breath as those memories crashed through him.

Ellie hadn't been just his sister-in-law and his twin brother's wife. Dade had loved her as deeply as he did his blood family. Kayla Brennan and her scumbag father-in-law were going to pay for killing Ellie.

"Don't worry," Kayla said with a sappy sweetness that couldn't be genuine. "I didn't come out of hiding just to let someone silence me."

No, but Kayla had come out of hiding after nearly a year. So she could testify, she'd told the D.A. But Dade wondered if there was more to it than that. He knew the

D.A. had been trying to contact her for months, and she hadn't responded.

Until three hours ago.

Then, Kayla had called D.A. Winston Calhoun and told him that she would testify against her father-in-law in an extortion and racketeering trial. A trial that could send Charles Brennan to jail for several decades.

Hardly the death sentence Dade wanted for him.

However, Dade was willing to bet that Brennan had no plans to spend one minute behind bars, much less a decade. And he probably wouldn't. From what Dade had read, the case was weak at best, and witnesses kept backing out or disappearing.

But now Kayla had arrived on the scene.

Dade couldn't believe Kayla had doing her civic duty in mind. No, this was probably some kind of revenge move to get back at her father-in-law. No honor among thieves in the Brennan clan.

"I wasn't worried about you," Dade corrected. "Just doing a job I was ordered to do." And he had indeed been ordered by not just the sheriff, who was his brother, but by the D.A. Kayla was a star witness in every sense of the word, and a lot of people wanted her alive.

She made a sound of sarcastic amusement and breezed past him to head toward the double front doors. "I'll stay alive so I can testify, and I don't need you or anyone else in your family to protect me. That's why I hired Kenneth."

Dade stared at her. Well, he stared at her backside anyway because she was already walking away from him. Her low thin heels made delicate clicks on the veiny marble floor.

"I don't care how many guns you hire," Dade informed her. "You're still in my protective custody."

Kayla stopped and glanced at him from over her shoulder. The corner of her rose-tinged mouth lifted just a fraction, but it wasn't a smile on her face. "Protective custody, you say? Right. Those two words don't go together when it comes to you or any member of your family. The Rylands hate me."

Dade didn't deny it. "We have reason to hate you."

"No." She huffed, causing a wisp of her hair to move slightly. "You have reason to hate someone for your sister-in-law's murder, but I didn't have anything to do with it."

"Got proof of that?"

"Do you have proof to the contrary?" she fired right back at him.

He leaned in a little. "If I did, your butt would be in jail right now."

Another smirk. A short-lived one. She turned away so that he couldn't see her face. Her head lowered slightly. "Well, because I'm here and not in the Silver Creek jail, you obviously have no proof. So you can leave."

"I wish." Dade went closer while keeping an eye on Kayla's bodyguard. "Nothing would make me happier than to walk out that door and leave you to deal with the wolves, but I have my orders."

"You can take your orders and get out." She reached for the doorknob, but Dade snagged her wrist with his left hand.

The wrist snag obviously didn't sit well with her bodyguard because he reached for his gun. Dade reached for his, too.

"Stop this!" Kayla practically yelled. She jerked her hand away from Dade and shook her head. "Please," she said. Her voice was softer now but edged with the nerves that were right beneath her skin. "Just leave."

Dade's nerves were too close to the surface, too, and touching Kayla certainly hadn't helped. He felt ornerier than usual, and that wasn't good because he was the king of ornery. Best to go ahead and lay down some ground rules.

Dade aimed his index finger at Kenneth. "You draw that gun and I'll shoot you where you stand. Got that?"

Oh, the man wanted to argue all right. Dade could see it in his eyes, but he knew what was in his own eyes—determination to finish this damn job so he could get the heck out of there.

When Kenneth finally eased his hand away from his weapon, Dade turned back to Kayla. "Where's your baby?"

She pulled back her shoulders. "That's none of your business."

He tapped his badge in case she'd forgotten. "This isn't personal, lady. I'm asking because I need to establish some security measures." He got closer, violating her personal space and then some.

Not the brightest idea he'd ever had. His chest brushed against her breasts, and he got a fire-hot reminder that Kayla was a woman.

Dade held his ground and met her eye-to-eye. "Where's your son?" he repeated.

She didn't back down, either. "He's sleeping upstairs. Now tell me what this is all about."

Dade ignored her question. "Is your son away from the windows?"

She stepped back and her breath rattled in her throat. "Why?"

Dade gave her a flat look. "Because my protective custody extends to your son, Robert."

"Robbie," she corrected, although she looked as if she wanted to curse for giving him even that little bit of personal information about her child. A kid who was supposedly just eleven months old. A baby. And it was because of the baby that Dade had quit arguing about this assignment so he could drive out to the Brennan estate.

He didn't care a rat's you-know-what about Kayla, but he would do everything within his power to protect an innocent child.

Even her child.

"The deputy's trying to scare you," Kenneth interjected.

"Yeah, I am," Dade readily admitted. He looked at her again to make sure she got what he was saying. "And if you have any sense whatsoever, you'll be scared because you can't believe Brennan is going to let you get anywhere near that witness stand tomorrow morning."

Her bottom lip trembled a little, but she kept her chin up and her expression resolute.

"Your baby's safety is one of the main reasons for the protective custody," Dade informed her. "I have to take your son and you to a safe house. Sheriff's orders."

She started the head shaking again. "I've already had someone upgrade the security system, and I can hire more bodyguards." Kayla looked at him. "I wouldn't have come back here to Silver Creek if I hadn't thought I could keep my son safe."

Dade made sure they had eye contact again. "You thought wrong."

She glanced out the sidelight window. "I don't believe that. Charles wouldn't do anything that would risk hurting Robbie."

"That's a chance you're willing to take?"

She didn't answer that. "Besides, I don't trust you any more than I trust Charles."

Dade couldn't blame her. The Rylands hadn't exactly been friendly since Ellie's murder. Things would stay that way, too, but it wouldn't stop Dade from doing his job.

Kayla stepped closer to him. So close that he caught her scent. Not perfume but baby powder.

"I'll call my attorney," she said with her voice lowered. "But I'm certain you can't force protective custody on me."

She was right. Well, unless he thought she was going to run. But because she'd arrived voluntarily, he didn't exactly have reason to believe she would leave.

"Think about your son's safety," Dade reminded her.

"I am." And she turned and opened the door. "I can keep him safe without so-called help from the Rylands."

Fine. Dade had warned his brother and the D.A. that this wouldn't be an easy notion to sell, and both had told Dade that somehow he had to convince Kayla otherwise. Well, he'd failed, but he darn sure wasn't going to lose any sleep over it.

Dade was barely an inch out the door when Kayla slammed it so hard that he felt the gust of air wash over him. It mixed with the blast of chilly February wind that came right at him. He waited a second until he heard her engage the lock. He waited an extra second to see if she would change her mind, but when she didn't re-open the door, Dade cursed and headed off the porch and toward his truck.

Hell.

He really didn't want to go back to the sheriff's office and tell his brother, Grayson, that he'd failed. Not that Grayson was likely keeping count or anything, but Dade figured he already had too many failures on his records. Far more than the other deputies in Silver Creek. Still, he couldn't force a hardheaded woman to listen to reason.

Dade opened the door to his truck, moved to get inside and then stopped. He lifted his head, listened and looked around.

The area surrounding the circular drive and front of the estate was well lit so he had a good view of pretty much everything within thirty yards in any direction. But it wasn't the lit areas that troubled him. It was the thick clusters of trees and shrubs on the east and west sides of the estate.

He waited, trying to tamp down the bad feeling he had about all of this. But the bad feeling stayed right with him, settling hard and cold in his stomach.

Dade cursed, shoved his truck keys in his pocket and headed back for the estate. He didn't relish going a second round with the curvy Kayla, but he would for the sake of her son. Dade turned. Made it just one step.

And that's when the shot rang out.

Chapter 2

Kayla was halfway up the stairs, but the sound stopped her cold.

A sharp, piercing blast.

The sound tore through the house. And her.

She froze for just a second, but Kenneth certainly didn't. He drew his gun.

"Get down!" Kenneth shouted. "Someone just fired a shot."

Kayla's heart started to pound, and her breath began to race. She had no intentions of getting down. She had to get to her baby. She had to protect Robbie.

There was another shot, followed by someone banging on the front door.

"Let me in!" that someone shouted. It was Deputy Dade Ryland. He was cursing, and while he bashed his fist against the door, he continued to yell for them to let him inside before he got killed.

Her first thought was that Dade was responsible for the shots, but that didn't make sense. He'd come here to warn her of danger, and if he'd wanted to shoot at them, then he could have done it in the foyer at point-blank range. Still, that didn't mean she trusted the deputy.

"You need to get down," Kenneth warned her again, and he headed to the door to disengage the security system and let in the deputy.

Dade didn't wait for the door to be fully open. The moment Kenneth cracked it, he dived through nearly knocking down her bodyguard in the process. The deputy had his gun drawn and ready, and he reached over to slap off the lights. In the same motion, he kicked the door shut.

"Lock it and reset the security system," Dade ordered Kenneth. He took out his phone from his jeans pocket and called for backup.

Even though he'd turned off the lights in the foyer, Kayla had no trouble seeing Dade because the lamp in the adjacent living room was blazing. Dade's eyes were blazing, too, and he turned that hot glare on her.

"I heard your bodyguard tell you to get down. What part of that didn't you understand?" Dade barked.

"I have to get to my son," she barked right back, and Kayla continued up the stairs. Or rather that's what she tried to do, but the third shot wasn't just a loud blast. It ripped through the window in the living room, spewing glass everywhere. And worse, the bullet tore into the stair railing just a few yards below her.

She froze. Oh, mercy. Someone wasn't just shooting. The person was actually trying to kill her.

"Now will you get down?" Dade demanded.

Without warning, Dade aimed his gun into the living

room and fired, the blast echoing through the foyer. He shot out the lamp, plunging them into darkness. It took a moment for her eyes to adjust.

Even over the blast still roaring in her ears, Kayla heard a sound that robbed her of what little breath she had left. Robbie started to cry. He wasn't alone. The nanny, Connie Mullins, was with him, but Kayla didn't want to count on the petite sixty-year-old woman when it came to a situation like this.

A situation that had turned deadly.

Kayla refused to think of the possibility this could end with her death. And that wouldn't even be a worst-case scenario. Worst case would be for Robbie to get hurt.

Dade pointed to the living room where he'd just shot out the light. "Can you see the SOB shooting at your boss?" he asked Kenneth.

Her bodyguard shook his head, and both men glanced up at her as she started to crawl toward the nursery.

Dade cursed. "Cover me," he said to Kenneth. The order barely made it out of his mouth when he came barreling up the stairs, his cowboy boots hitting against the hardwood steps.

But that wasn't the only sound.

More shots came. One right behind the other. Each of them ripped through the expensive carved-wood railing and sent splinters flying in every direction. That didn't stop Dade. He made it to her, crawling over her to shove her as low as she could get.

"Robbie," she managed to say.

Dade's gaze slashed to hers. "If you go to him, the bullets will follow you."

That was the only possible thing he could have said to make her stop.

Kayla froze, and the full impact of that warning slammed into her as hard as the bullets battering the foyer. Oh, no. She'd put her son in danger. This was the very thing she'd tried to avoid, the very reason she'd come out of hiding, and she had only made it worse.

Again.

The anger collided with the fear, and she wanted to hit her fists against the stairs. She wanted to scream out for the shooter to stop. But more than those things, she just wanted to protect her baby.

"Is your son with a nanny?" Dade asked.

Kayla managed a nod. She'd asked Connie to wait in the nursery when she heard Dade ring the doorbell. "In there," she said, pointing to the first door off the left hall.

"Are they near a bathroom with a tub?" he also wanted to know.

Another nod. "There's one adjoining the nursery." And Kayla hated that she hadn't thought of that herself. "Connie?" she shouted.

"What's going on, Kayla?" the woman shouted back.

"I'm not sure," Kayla lied. "Just take Robbie into the bathroom and get in the tub." The porcelain tub would be their shield against the bullets.

Robbie was still crying, and the sound of her son's wails let her know that Connie was on the move. Robbie's voice became more and more faint until Kayla couldn't hear him at all.

That didn't help her nerves.

Hearing him had at least allowed her to know that he

was all right. Still, she didn't want him out in the open in the nursery in case this attack continued.

As if to prove to her that it would, more bullets ripped through the foyer.

"How long before backup arrives?" Kenneth shouted.

"Too long," Dade answered. "At least fifteen minutes. This place isn't exactly in city limits."

Kenneth cursed and took cover behind a table. Kayla silently cursed as well. In fifteen minutes they could all be dead.

"I have to move you," Dade informed her. Other than a glance that had an I-told-you-this-could-happen snarl to it, his attention volleyed between the living room and the front door.

Kayla shook her head. "But you said I can't go near Robbie."

"You can't. But it's only a matter of time before the shooter changes positions." He tipped his head toward the front. "There are a lot of windows, and he'll have a clean shot once he moves."

Not *if* he moves but *once*.

"I'll roll to the side, just a little," Dade instructed. "And without standing up, I want you to get to the top of the stairs. Duck behind the first thing you see that can provide some cover."

Kayla managed to nod, and the moment that Dade lifted his weight off her, she did as he'd ordered. She covered her head with her hands and scrambled up the stairs as fast as she could.

The shots didn't stop, and one plowed into the wall above her just as Kayla dived to the side of a table. She'd barely managed that when Dade came barreling toward

her. He hooked his arm around her waist and dragged
her away from the table, away from the wall.

But also away from the nursery.

He hauled her toward the right, the opposite side
from where Robbie and the nanny were, and Kayla was
thankful that Dade had given her son that extra cushion
of security. However, there was no cushion for Dade
and her. They were off the stairs, yes, but the bullets
continued to come at them. Dade flattened her on the
floor and crawled back over her.

Kayla was well aware of his body pressed hard
against hers. His breathing, too, because it was gusting in her ear. But she also felt his corded muscles and
the determination to keep her alive.

That didn't mean, however, he'd succeed.

And that both frightened and infuriated her.

Just like that, the shots stopped. Kayla held her
breath, waiting and praying that this was over, but it
was Dade's profanity that let her know it wasn't.

She glanced back at him, and her gaze collided with
those steel grays. He barely looked at her, but in that
glimpse he managed to convey his concern and his disgust.

He hated her.

All the Rylands hated her. And Kayla couldn't blame
them. Guilt by association. Her father-in-law had probably caused Ellie Ryland's death. And so far, he'd gotten off scot-free, thanks to a team of good lawyers and
a technicality in some of the paperwork that had been
used in his original arrest.

"What?" Dade snarled.

It took her a moment to realize he was talking to her,
and she knew why. She was staring at him.

"Nothing," Kayla mumbled. And she forced her attention away from the one man who should disgust her as much as the shooter outside. But much to her dismay, what she felt wasn't total disgust.

Yet more proof that she was stupid.

She had noticed Dade Ryland's storm-black hair. It was a little too long, and his five o'clock stubble was a little too dark for her to think of him as handsome. No. It was worse than that. He wasn't handsome.

He was hot in that bad-boy, outlaw sort of way.

Well, she'd already been burned by one bad boy, and she wasn't looking for another. Not now. Not ever again.

Dade gave her another glance, and she could have sworn he smirked, as if he could read her mind.

"You see the shooter yet?" Dade called down to the bodyguard.

"No."

"The shooter's probably moving," Dade growled. He levered himself up just slightly and re-aimed his gun toward the front of the house.

Kayla could do nothing other than hope this would end with her baby unharmed. She'd been a fool to come back, a fool to respond to Charles's latest threat.

But what else could she have done?

She had to get out from beneath the hold Charles had on her. She had to try to make a safe, normal life for her son. But instead, she'd gotten this.

"Someone told Charles I was here," she mumbled. "Probably the D.A. or a Ryland." She hadn't meant to say Dade's family name so loudly, but by God it was hard to tamp down the anger while bracing for another attack.

"No one in my family is responsible for this," Dade informed her. "Lady, you got into this mess all by yourself."

She wanted to argue, but the sound stopped her. In

the distance she heard sirens. No doubt the backup that Dade had called. Even though she didn't like the idea of the place crawling with any more Rylands, it was better than the alternative.

She hoped.

Beneath them in the foyer, Kayla heard her bodyguard moving around. Maybe so he could try to spot the shooter. Dade moved, too. He used his forearm to push her face back to the carpet, and he maneuvered himself off her. This time not just an inch or two. He reared up and took aim at the front windows.

He fired.

The blast roared through her ears, and she had no time to recover before there was another shot. Not from Dade. This one came tearing through the foyer but from a different angle than before. This bullet took out one of the front windows and sent glass flying through the air.

Dade had been right. The shooter had moved. And now Dade and she were in his direct line of fire.

For a few moments at the beginning of the attack, Kayla had hoped the shots were meant as a warning. A way to get her to grab Robbie and go back into hiding. But this was no warning.

This was an assassination attempt.

Dade sent another shot the gunman's way, and she put her hands over her ears to shut out the painful noise. However, she could still hear them. And the siren. It grew closer and closer as the gunman's shots came faster and faster. He wasn't panicking, and he definitely wasn't running. He was trying to kill her before the sheriff arrived.

"Stay down," Dade warned her. He shifted his gun toward one of the other front windows and fired.

This time, Kayla heard another sound. A groan of some kind, following by a heavy thud. Had Dade managed to shoot the gunman? Maybe.

Kayla looked up and followed the direction of Dade's aim. There. Through the jagged shards of glass jutting from the window frame, she saw something.

A man.

He was dressed head to toe in black, and it was only because of the porch light that she could see his silhouette. She could also see his gun, and he took aim at Dade and her.

Kayla yelled for Dade to get down, and she latched onto him to pull him back to the floor. But he threw off her grip and fired at the shadowy figure.

The man fired a shot as well and then clutched his shoulder. She couldn't be sure, but she thought this time maybe Dade had managed to shoot him.

Dade must have thought that too because he headed down the stairs, taking them two at a time while he kept his gun trained on the person on the porch. Kayla could only watch with her breath held and her heart pounding so hard that it might come out of her chest.

The man on the porch fired.

She yelled to warn Dade, but her warning was drowned out by another shot and the sounds of the approaching sirens. She heard Dade curse as if in pain, but what he didn't do was get down. He raced toward the door, threw it open and fired again.

But so did the gunman.

Oh, God.

She realized then that if this assassin managed to kill Dade that he would come after Robbie and her next. Of course, Kenneth was down there, somewhere, but if the gunman got past the bodyguard, then Kayla would have no way to defend her baby and herself.

Kayla cursed herself for not bringing some kind of weapon with her. But she wouldn't need a weapon if this goon tried to get to her baby. No. Pure raw adrenaline and the need to protect her child would give her the strength to fight whoever came through that door.

She stood, preparing herself for whatever she had to do, but instead she saw the blue swirls of the lights from a police cruiser. Red lights, too, maybe from an ambulance. The vehicles tore across the lawn and screamed to a halt. There were no more shots, just the noise of the men who scrambled from those vehicles.

Kayla waited, the seconds clicking off like gunshots in her head, and when the waiting became unbearable, she began to make her way down the stairs. The foyer was still dark, and the only illumination came from the jolts of red and blue lights from the responding vehicles.

"Kenneth?" she called out, her voice hardly more than a hoarse whisper. He didn't answer. "Deputy Ryland?" she tried.

No answer from Dade either.

Kayla inched down the steps, praying this ordeal was indeed over but also bracing herself for whatever she might see.

She didn't brace herself enough.

There was blood on the floor of the foyer. In the darkness it looked like a pool of liquid black, but she instinctively knew what it was.

And there, slumped in the doorway was Dade Ryland.

Chapter 3

Dade looked down at his left arm and cursed. This was not a good time to get shot.

Hell.

Using the doorjamb for support, he got to his feet and tried not to look as if his arm was on fire. He figured he'd failed big-time when he saw Kayla. Her eyes were wide, her face way too pale.

"You've been shot," she said, the words rushing out.

Was that concern he saw and heard? He had to be wrong about that. No, this was probably just a reaction to the blood. And there was no doubt about it, there was blood.

"Check on your bodyguard," Dade barked, and he pulled back his shoulders so he could face the responders who were coming right at him.

First, there was his brother, Sheriff Grayson Ryland.

Tall and lanky like most of his five siblings, Grayson might not have been the biggest of the half-dozen people who came out of the cruisers and ambulance, but he was automatically the center of attention and the one in charge. Grayson commanded respect just by stepping onto the scene.

Another brother, Mason, stepped out from a vehicle, too—a weathered Ford truck that had been red once, maybe twenty years ago. Mason, like Dade, was also a deputy sheriff but worked only part-time because he also ran the family ranch.

Dressed in his usual black jeans, black shirt and equally black Stetson, Mason made his way toward the estate. Not with Grayson's speed, authority or concern. Mason always looked as if he were stalking something. Or headed to a funeral.

"You're hurt," Grayson said, and he used his head to motion to the medics so they'd hurry to Dade. Grayson also kept his gun trained on the man sprawled out on the porch.

The dead man.

Dade had managed to take the guy out, but not before the SOB had fired a shot into Dade's arm. Talk about a rookie mistake, and he hadn't been a rookie in fourteen years, not since he'd joined the Silver Creek sheriff's department on his twenty-first birthday. Considering that being a cop was his one-and-only desire in life, he always seemed to be screwing it up.

Like now, for instance.

The gunman who could have given them answers was as dead as a doornail. Added to that, Dade had nearly let Kayla Brennan be gunned down, her bodyguard had been shot, or worse, and the jagged slice on his arm from the bullet graze was hurting like hell.

Grayson stooped down and put his fingers to the gunman's neck. "He's dead."

Yeah. No surprise there. "You need to check on Kayla's bodyguard," Dade let his brother know. He would do it himself, but he wanted a chance to catch his breath and get ahead of the pain.

"Kayla?" Grayson questioned, standing upright. He aimed a questioning glare at Dade, and Dade knew why. *Kayla* was way too personal to call someone who might be responsible for a family member's death.

Grayson was right, and Dade silently cursed that, too. He was a sucker for a damsel in distress, and while he wasn't sure about the damsel part, Kayla was definitely in distress.

And so was her baby.

With his glare morphing into a disgusted scowl, Grayson flipped on the lights and walked past him and into the foyer where Kayla was kneeling down next to Kenneth.

"He's still breathing," Kayla announced, and that sent two of the medics scurrying in the bodyguard's direction.

One medic, however, Carrie Collins, a leggy brunette in snug green scrubs made a beeline toward Dade.

"I'm okay," Dade tried to tell her, but she latched onto his arm to examine it.

"I'll decide if you're okay or not," Carrie answered.

Like Kayla, there was way too much concern in her voice and expression. In this case, though, Dade knew why. Carrie and he had once been lovers, but that wasn't just water under the bridge. The water had dried up nearly a year ago. Too bad Carrie didn't always remember that.

"You need stitches," Carrie mumbled, her forehead bunching up. "And probably a tetanus shot."

But Dade tuned her out and put his attention on Kayla, Grayson and the unconscious bodyguard. Grayson caught onto Kayla and moved her away from the man so the medics could get to work, but it was obvious Kayla had tried to help her employee. Her hands and dress were covered with blood.

Kayla looked down at her palms, which were shaking almost violently, and she shuddered. Now that the lights were back on, Dade also saw the tears well up in her eyes.

Dade's feet seemed to have a mind of their own because he started toward her. So did Mason. Mason grunted and glanced down at Dade's arm.

"You scratched yourself," Mason remarked with zero sympathy in his tone. "Don't expect me to do the paperwork for this goat rope."

It was just what Dade needed to hear. Sarcasm without sympathy. He knew his brother loved him. Well, Dade was pretty sure of that anyway. But Mason wasn't the sort to cut anyone any slack.

Unlike Kayla. Blinking back tears, she made her way toward Dade with her attention fixed on him. "I thought you'd been killed."

Dade was aware that both his brothers were watching and listening. "No. You didn't get lucky this time."

She flinched as if he'd slapped her, but quickly regained her composure. "Lucky?" she challenged. "Right. Well, let's just say I'm grateful you did your job and put yourself in front of bullets for me." Her voice trailed off to a whisper. "Thank you, Dade."

Dade was one-hundred-percent positive that his brother hadn't missed the way his given name had just purred right off her sympathetic rose-tinged lips. Or maybe the purring and the sympathy were his imagination.

Oh, man.

Kayla was going to be trouble with a capital *T.*

"I have to check on my baby," she let them know.

Dade snagged her by the arm. "Have the nanny and Robbie stay in the bathroom, okay? This might not be over."

As expected, the fear returned to her eyes. She swallowed hard, nodded and raced up the stairs.

"I'll need to question you when you come back down," Grayson called out to her.

Without looking back, she gave another shaky nod.

Dade wanted to hit himself in his fire-burning arm just to get his mind off this asinine need to comfort and to play nice with the one woman he shouldn't want to comfort or play nice with.

The three of them watched her make her way up the stairs, and Dade waited for the lecture from his brothers. A lecture that would no doubt include a reminder to think with his brain and not with what was behind the zipper of his Wranglers. But the lecture didn't come.

Not verbally anyway.

Grayson stepped away to give the medics some instructions, and then he took out his phone to call the county medical examiner, something Dade should have already thought to do.

"Did the dead guy give you any warning before he started shooting?" Mason asked.

Dade shook his head. "Kayla…" He considered calling her Ms. Brennan, but heck, the damage had already been done. "She refused protective custody, and I was on my way back to town when I figured out something was wrong. The guy opened fire before I could get back inside."

Mason stayed quiet a moment, but his forehead bunched up. "She refused our help." It wasn't a question. Mason sort of growled it out in a disapproving way.

Dade shrugged and then winced when that sent another shot of fire through his arm. "Understandable. She doesn't trust us. Just like we don't trust her."

Mason made a sound, one of his grunts that could have meant anything. Or nothing at all. "I'll keep watch outside. We don't need any more of Charles Brennan's henchmen showing up here tonight."

No, they didn't. And it could happen all right. Dade figured there was no way Brennan was going to let Kayla get anywhere near a witness stand.

"I need to clean that wound," Carrie let him know.

"Later." Dade moved to the side so the medics could take the bodyguard out on the gurney. Grayson had finished with his call and Dade wanted an update. Thankfully, Carrie didn't follow him.

"The M.E.'s on the way," Grayson relayed. "And the rest of the deputies. Once they arrive, we can get *Kayla* and her baby out of here."

Dade glanced at the pool of blood and the shards of glass on the glossy marble floor. Maybe that would convince her to accept protective custody and leave for someplace safer.

If a safe place actually existed.

"Did she say why she changed her mind about testifying and came back to Silver Creek?" Grayson asked.

Dade shook his head and looked in the direction of the footsteps he heard. Kayla was making her way back downstairs, and she was no longer wearing the blood-soaked dress. She'd put on black pants and a gray blouse. She'd also adjusted her attitude. No more threat of tears or sympathetic looks. She was sporting a first-class glare.

"How's your son?" Dade asked, pleased that he would have to deal with the real Kayla rather than the damsel.

"He's fine," she snapped and then turned her attention to Grayson. "Someone obviously leaked my location," she accused before she even reached them in the foyer.

"Seems that way," Grayson admitted. "I suppose you think it was one of us."

"I do."

Dade stepped in front of his brother so he could finish this fight. "We have better things to do than endanger a witness. So that means the leak came from your side. Who knew you were coming here?"

She folded her arms over her chest. "You mean besides the Rylands?"

"Yeah, besides the *cops*." Dade didn't budge an inch. He met her eye-to-eye and practically foot-to-foot. But when she glanced down, Dade looked as well and saw the drop of his blood that had spattered onto one of her high-priced shoes.

"You need stitches," Grayson grumbled.

"I need answers from Ms. Brennan," Dade grumbled right back. But he did step slightly away so he wouldn't bleed on her fancy clothes.

And speaking of clothes, she'd missed a button on the blouse. Why he noticed that now, he didn't know.

Wait, yeah, he did know.

His male brain was too alert to the fact that Kayla was a woman. A woman with a gap in her blouse that allowed him a peek of the top of her right breast.

Dade did a double take.

She had a tattoo, a little pink heart right there on the swell of her breast.

Kayla made a soft sound of outrage, obviously noticing what had caught his attention, and she quickly buttoned her blouse as if she'd declared war on it.

"Your son's nanny knew you were here," Dade reminded her. He rolled up his shirt sleeve to put some pressure against his grazed arm.

She gave him a flat look. "My nanny is not responsible for this. She was in just as much danger as we were."

Dade couldn't argue with that. "So who else knew?"

Kayla wearily touched her fingers to her forehead. "My sister, Misty Wallace, but she wouldn't have told anyone."

Grayson and Dade exchanged glances, and Dade knew that Grayson would verify that as soon as he could.

Kayla noticed that glance and must have realized what it meant. "Don't waste your time with my sister. I trust her with my life, and she would die rather than tell Charles where I am. Instead, investigate the D.A.," she answered, her voice edged with anger.

"Winston Calhoun's not in the business of killing witnesses, either," Dade let her know, although he would check to make sure the D.A. hadn't accidentally said the wrong thing to the wrong person. "I've known Winston my whole life. We can trust him."

"Maybe not," Kayla disagreed. "Is he rich like you and your family?"

"No." And Dade didn't like where this was going. "But not everyone can be bribed."

"My former father-in-law has a knack for finding a person's weak spot and getting his way." There was no smugness in her statement, and a frustrated sigh left her mouth.

He couldn't argue with that, either. "What about your sister, then? Is Misty dirty rich like you?"

Oh, that got a rise out of her. The anger flashed through her eyes. "This isn't about Misty. It's about Charles and whomever he could have bribed."

"Maybe," Dade concluded. "Then I'll go back to my original question. Who knew you were coming here? A boyfriend? A lover?"

She shook her head and looked ready to slug him. "No, on both counts."

"Your driver, then." Dade tried again.

"I drove myself, and I didn't tell anyone else where I was going." She paused. She glanced around the foyer, her attention landing on Dade's bloody arm. "I came here because I thought Charles would believe this was the last place I'd be."

"Obviously you got that wrong," Dade grumbled.

"Obviously," she grumbled right back.

"Why did you change your mind about testifying?" Dade pressed when she added nothing else.

Kayla dodged his gaze. "You wouldn't believe me if I told you."

Because she was staring at the floor, Dade ducked down a little to make eye contact. "Try."

She lifted her shoulder, stepped away from him. "I wanted to do the right thing." Kayla paused. "This morning, I got a threatening email from my ex-father-in-law."

Dade and Grayson exchanged another glance. "You told the D.A. about this?" Grayson asked.

"No, what would have been the point? Charles's threats are nothing new and never specific enough to bring charges against him. But this time, something inside me...snapped." She paused. "Or maybe for the first time things got crystal clear." Her gaze came to Dade's again, and she blinked back tears. "After reading that email, I knew the only way I could get this to stop was to testify and make sure Charles is put away for the rest of his life."

Oh, hell. There it was again. Sympathy. It was burning as hot as the gash on his arm. Grayson obviously wasn't immune either because he gave a heavy sigh.

"And that's the reason I need you in protective custody," Grayson concluded. "I want to take you and your baby to a safe house so that Brennan can't get to either of you. Brennan is out of jail on bond, and we're trying to keep an eye on him. But you know better than anyone, he can hire guns to do his dirty work."

Kayla stared at Grayson. Then stared at Dade, too. "After what happened tonight, how can you possibly keep my baby safe?" she asked. Her voice broke on the last word.

Dade was about to assure her that he would do his best, but Grayson's phone rang. He glanced at the screen and mumbled some profanity before he stepped away to take the call.

"I still don't trust you," Kayla whispered to Dade.

He nodded. "Yeah, I get that." He pointed to the blood on the floor. "But you've got a very short list of people you can trust right now."

She must have known that was true, but she still didn't agree.

"That was one of the medics," Grayson relayed, putting his phone back in his pocket. He walked back across the foyer toward them, his attention nailed to Kayla. "Your bodyguard died on the way to the hospital."

That was all he said. Grayson didn't offer any details or reiterate that she could have been the one in that ambulance.

Kayla pulled in her breath, and what little color she had drained from her face. She gave one crisp nod and turned toward the stairs. "I'll let the nanny know that we're moving to a safe house tonight with Dade—Deputy Ryland," she corrected, her voice now chilled with that ice-queen tone.

Dade didn't exactly celebrate because it had taken way too long to convince her to do the right thing. Now, he only hoped it *was* the right thing. After all, she'd just put her son's and her lives right in his hands.

"I think we might have found our leak," Mason said, stepping into the doorway.

That got everyone's attention. Kayla stopped on the bottom step and turned to face him.

"I checked the dead gunman's phone." Mason held up the bagged cell for them to see. "About a half hour before this guy started shooting, he made three calls." He aimed his usual surly expression at Kayla. "First one was to some guy named Danny Flynn, a lowlife who likely works for your ex-father-in-law, Charles Brennan."

"He does," Kayla admitted. "I remember that name."

Well, that wasn't exactly a bombshell. Everyone knew how much Brennan wanted to stop Kayla. Of course, Brennan would deny any association with the employee who'd gotten the call, but the cops might be able to break the employee and get him to confess.

"You said you'd found the leak?" Dade prompted.

Mason glanced at the screen on the dead man's cell. "We got two possibilities. The next call the gunman made was to Misty Wallace."

The breath seemed to swoosh right out of Kayla. "My sister?"

"Your sister," Mason confirmed.

Kayla frantically shook her head. "But Misty wouldn't tell Charles or anyone else where I was going."

"Right," Mason grumbled. "That call to her says otherwise." He went to Grayson and handed him the phone so that his brother could also check out the screen.

From his angle Dade couldn't see what caused both his brothers' eyes to narrow.

Kayla had a white-knuckled grip on the stair railing. "Who's the third person he called?"

"What kind of game are you playing, Ms. Brennan?" Grayson demanded.

"What do you mean?" And her shock sure as heck sounded sincere.

But Dade didn't take her sincerity of the head shaking at face value. He leaned in so he could see the name of the last person the gunman had called.

Hell.

What was going on?

Chapter 4

Kayla was trembling, but that didn't stop her from marching across the foyer to see what had caused the Rylands to turn those accusing stares on her. And then she saw the cell phone screen.

No, it couldn't be. But it was.

It was her name and number.

"Why did the gunman call you?" Dade demanded.

"He didn't," Kayla answered as quickly as she could get out the words.

"The phone says otherwise," Mason Ryland growled.

"Then it was faked somehow." She hated the quiver in her voice. Hated even more that she cared one iota what these Rylands thought of her, but by God she'd had no part in this attack. "I wouldn't have hired someone to shoot into a house where my son was staying."

The trio exchanged glances. A united brotherly front

against her. They didn't just look alike—they had the same scowls. And they were also waiting for more of an explanation. However, Kayla didn't have one.

"Where's your phone?" Dade asked after first giving an impatient huff.

She glanced around but didn't see it and remembered she hadn't seen it upstairs, either. Just moments before Dade's arrival, she'd been searching through her purse for it. "I must have left it in my car." She pointed to the side of the estate where she'd parked.

Even though none of the lawmen came right out and accused her of lying, it was clear from their deepening scowls they didn't believe her.

"I'll look for it," Mason insisted, and he strolled out, leaving her to face the remaining two.

"I didn't speak to the gunman," Kayla tried again. "And if he called me, it was to set me up."

"Why would he do that?" Grayson asked.

Kayla didn't have to think too hard to come up with an answer. "Maybe to try to discredit my testimony. Charles could have hired the gunman to do that because if he could prove I had an association with a killer, then it might make a jury less likely to believe anything I say."

Another exchange of glances before Grayson spoke again. "Or *you* could have hired the gunman to make Brennan look guilty of attempted murder. A crime that could put him away for life and not just the twenty years he'd get for the other charges."

Oh, mercy. As theories went, it wasn't a bad one, and Kayla had no idea how she would convince the Rylands that she was innocent.

"Maybe your sister is the one who did the hiring."

Dade tossed that out there, not tentatively, but it wasn't a roaring declaration of Kayla's innocence, either.

But what had she expected?

Yes, Dade had saved her life. Had even been wounded in the process, but to him she was lower than dirt. Well, except for those heated looks that he hadn't quite been able to suppress. Kayla was too familiar with those looks. Her late-husband, Preston, had certainly given her enough of them, and she was painfully aware of where that had gotten her.

"I'll call my sister," Kayla mumbled and started for the house phone that was on a table in the foyer. Of course, to get to it, she would literally have to walk through her dead bodyguard's blood.

"Here," Dade offered, handing her his cell.

Kayla took it, her hand brushing against his. Not a gentle hand, either. It was rough. No doubt from the physical labor of ranch work.

The adrenaline was playing havoc with her body and memory so it took her a while to remember Misty's number. She began to press it in when she heard Robbie. Not crying, but he was making fussy sounds, and those sounds were getting closer. Kayla looked at the stairs and saw her nanny, Connie, making her way toward them. The petite brunette looked completely weighed down with Robbie in the crook of her left arm and a suitcase gripped in her right hand.

Kayla stopped the call so she could go help, but Dade motioned for her to finish it. Instead, he hurried to the stairs, took the suitcase himself and set it on the floor. Robbie was rubbing his eyes and fussing when his attention landed on Dade. The fussing stopped, and much to Kayla's surprise, her son mumbled something indistinguishable and reached for the lawman.

Her surprise grew to shock when Dade reached out as well and eased Robbie into his arm.

"I have two other suitcases upstairs," Connie let him know, and she looked at Kayla. The nanny's eyebrow lifted to verify if it was all right for Dade to have hold of her son.

It wasn't all right, and Kayla moved to do something about that.

Just as her call to Misty went straight to voice mail.

"I'll get the suitcases," Grayson offered. "Show me where they are," he directed to Connie, and the two started up the stairs.

"Misty," Kayla said when the voice mail instructed her to leave a message, "call me immediately. I have to talk to you. It's important. I need to know if you told anyone where I'd be staying."

And with that done, Kayla hurried to Dade and practically wrenched Robbie away from him. That didn't make her son or Dade happy. The baby immediately started to cry, and Dade winced when she bumped against his wounded arm.

"Sorry," she mumbled. Kayla eased Robbie's head against her shoulder and began to rock.

Dade gave her a flat look after he was done wincing. "I wasn't going to kidnap him."

"I know. It's just…" But she had no idea how to finish that explanation. At this point it would sound petty if she admitted that she didn't want her son in a Ryland's arms. "Misty didn't answer her phone, so I left a message."

Dade waited a moment, his stare drilling through

her, and she earned another of those impatient huffs. "You do realize I'll be around the baby and you while you're in my protective custody?"

Kayla was sure she blinked. "But you're injured. I thought someone else would guard us." Preferably someone who wasn't a Ryland.

"No...." He stretched out the word. "This isn't an injury. It's a scratch, and it won't affect my aim if I need to take out another gunman."

Another gunman. That sent an icy chill through her. Thankfully, it was a chill her son didn't seem to notice because he finally calmed down and started to go back to sleep. But Kayla knew there would be no sleep for her in the immediate future.

And she knew who to thank for that.

"I need to make another call," she told Dade, and she didn't wait for his permission to use his cell. Nor did she have to try to remember this particular number. She'd seen it countless times on her own phone.

Charles Brennan answered on the first ring.

"Dade Ryland?" Charles greeted, though he sounded more amused than concerned. "Why would the deputy sheriff be calling?"

"No, Charles. It's me," Kayla informed him.

Dade rolled his eyes and reached for the phone, but she moved away from him and held on tight to both Robbie and Dade's cell.

"Did you send someone to kill me tonight?" she demanded from Charles.

"I don't know what you mean."

She listened for any differences in his voice. Anything that would confirm that he was behind this attack. But he sounded like his normal arrogant self.

"Someone hired a gunman to come after me," Kayla clarified, even though she was certain he already knew what she meant.

"And where are you exactly?" Charles asked. Still no change in his inflection.

Even though she doubted Dade had actually heard Charles's question, he got right in her face, and his scowl intensified. Something she hadn't thought possible.

"I'm at a place where I won't be much longer," Kayla answered. "And I want you to stop this now. Robbie could have been killed tonight."

"What?" Charles barked, and it had a cold, dangerous undercurrent to it.

"You heard me. The idiot you hired could have killed us all. Call off your dogs, Charles, and take your punishment like a man."

"I wouldn't have sent an idiot after you." And there was the change of inflective. It sounded as if he were telling the truth.

Sounded.

But Kayla had learned the hard way that Charles was capable of deception in its purest form. He certainly hadn't denied that he'd hired a hitman.

"The gunman phoned one of your goons," Kayla informed him, even though Dade gave her a have-you-lost-your-mind look. "I want you to call whomever it takes to make this stop."

Charles didn't answer right away. "I'll get back to you." And he hung up.

Dade threw up his hands and winced again. "Did it occur to you to ask me before you made a call to our number-one suspect?"

"I thought I was your number-one suspect," she snarled and thrust his phone at him.

He opened his mouth, probably to confirm that she was, but he didn't. Dade just shook his head, snatched his phone from her hand and stuffed it into the front pocket of his jeans. "That call accomplished nothing."

"Well, it made me feel better," Kayla fired back. It didn't. Nothing would make that happen, not with her bodyguard dead and the body of a hired assassin on her front porch.

Dade mumbled some profanity. "Don't do anything else that might end up helping your father-in-law, understand?"

Oh, that stung. She would never help Charles. *Never.* "Look, I know you don't believe me, but we're on the same page when it comes to my late-husband's father. It's possible Charles was responsible for your sister-in-law's death. Likely, even. But you couldn't possibly want him in jail more than I do."

Dade met her eye-to-eye. "Wanna bet?"

Kayla didn't dodge him. She held her ground. "As long as Charles is free, I'm not. And neither is my son." Because she needed it, she brushed a kiss on Robbie's forehead. "It's not my fault that Charles isn't behind bars. If you want someone to blame, blame the cops who investigated Ellie Ryland's murder."

Dade didn't flinch, but it was close. Probably because his brother had been in on the investigation. Heck, all the Rylands had, even though it hadn't been their jurisdiction. In fact, the case had gone to the FBI when the lead investigator had uncovered some evidence of Charles's money laundering that was linked to a federal case.

"The FBI's search warrant was screwed up. It didn't include the storage facility at his estate," Dade reminded her. "And that meant all those files and records that were seized there couldn't be used to convict Brennan. To add insult to injury, there was no more proof to arrest him, much less get a conviction."

Kayla knew all of this by heart because she'd read the reports too many times to count. "Then blame the FBI. Blame Charles's team of lawyers who challenged the warrant in the first place. But know this—if I get the chance to put Charles away, I'm taking it. Not for you. Not for your late sister-in-law. But for my son. When are you going to believe me?"

The fit of temper and energy went as fast as it came, and Kayla felt beyond drained. Maybe that's why she hadn't heard Mason come back into the house. And he wasn't the only one to reappear. Grayson was at the top of the stairs, a suitcase in each hand, and all of them were staring at her again.

"Maybe we'll believe you when there's proof that you're innocent." That came from Mason—the dark and dangerous Ryland. The one who made her more nervous than even Dade. "Your phone wasn't in the car. I searched every inch of it."

Kayla wearily shook her head. "Then I must have lost it or left it at the condo where I was staying."

"Convenient," Mason mumbled.

"No, it's not," she argued, knowing it wouldn't do any good. "I wish I could produce the phone so you'd know I had no part in this."

"Call her cell," Grayson said, making his way down the stairs. "The number is there on the dead gunman's phone."

Kayla huffed and was about to tell any Ryland who would listen that calling her on the missing phone would be useless. She didn't have it with her in the house, and she honestly had no idea where it was. But she decided just to let them have their way.

Mason lifted the gunman's phone so he could see the numbers through the plastic bag, and he used his own cell to make the call.

Kayla's heart nearly stopped.

Because the moment that Mason finished pressing in the numbers, the sound shot through the foyer.

While the rest of them watched and while Kayla held her breath, Mason followed the sound.

He didn't have to go far.

Just a few feet away from her.

There, under the foyer table, at the edge of the pool of blood, her missing cell phone was ringing.

Chapter 5

Dade listened to Grayson's latest request and silently cursed.

Yeah.

This was going to be fun.

He snapped his phone shut, dropped it on the console between Kayla and himself and continued the drive to the safe house.

"We need your fingerprints so we can compare them to those on the cell we found in your foyer," Dade relayed to her. He whispered so he wouldn't wake Robbie.

Both the baby and the nanny, Connie, were asleep in the back seat of the SUV, and Dade wanted it to stay that way. They were less than ten minutes from the safe house, both clearly exhausted, and he'd have to wake them soon enough.

When Kayla didn't answer, Dade glanced at her. She

was leaning against the window, her attention fastened to the side mirror. No doubt looking for another gunman who might try to follow them. Dade had done the same thing since he'd started the half-hour drive from her estate to the old Wellman ranch and had thankfully seen nothing but a coyote and a deer on the narrow country road.

"Fingerprints," she mumbled. "I have a juvenile record. You can probably get them from that."

"A juvenile record?" Dade hadn't meant to sound shocked, but he was.

"I was fifteen and stupid. I went for a joyride with a boy and didn't know he was driving a stolen car. When the cops stopped us, he told them we stole the car together."

All right. He had to think about that a moment. "I'm surprised a rich girl like you couldn't hire a good lawyer and get the charges thrown out." Dade hadn't meant it to sound so callous, but he had seen it happen too many times.

She gave him a look that could have frozen hell. "You know nothing about me. *Nothing.*"

That was true. Until tonight Kayla had been the woman married to the mob. The daughter-in-law of a slimeball killer. And now she was Dade's responsibility.

Among other things.

She was also a woman, and he kept noticing that. Like now, for instance. Even though she was giving him that hell-freezing look, he could also see the fear and the weariness. Oh, and her hot body. He didn't want to think for one minute that it played into this, but he was afraid it did.

So did that little baby sleeping in the car seat behind him.

Dade might have been a bad boy with a badass reputation, but that kid had nearly turned him to mush when he'd reached for Dade in the foyer. The kid had something his mom didn't—complete trust that Dade would take care of him.

"My fingerprints will be on the phone," she reminded him. "Because it belongs to me."

"Yeah, but Kenneth's shouldn't be on it. Should they?"

"No." She paused a moment. "I'd been looking for my cell right before you arrived, and I'd just asked Kenneth if he'd seen it. He said no."

Well, that was a start. "So, if his prints are on it, then it could mean he was in on the attack."

Kayla shook her head before he even finished. "That doesn't make sense, either. If the gunman had called my cell and Kenneth had the phone on him, I think I would have heard it."

"Maybe it rang when you were upstairs with your son." And maybe Kenneth hadn't wanted her to hear it because he wanted to set Kayla up, to make her look guilty.

She shook her head. "If Kenneth and the gunman were both working for Charles, then why didn't Kenneth just kill me before you arrived? He had plenty of chances. And then why would the gunman have killed a fellow hired gun?"

Dade didn't have answers to her questions, but he hoped to remedy that soon. His laptop was in his bag, and he intended to spend most of the night working.

"The dead gunman's name is Raymond Salvetti," Dade told her. "Ring any bells?"

She sat up straighter in the seat and repeated it several times. "No. He has a record?"

"Oh, yeah. That's why Grayson was able to make such a quick ID."

Kayla blew out a long breath. "Did you connect him to Charles?"

"Not yet."

And maybe never.

Because Brennan would have known there was potential for the hired gun to be caught, he could have hidden the paper trail that would connect him to a possible killer. Still, that didn't mean they couldn't link Brennan to the dead bodyguard or to Danny Flynn, the other man the gunman had phoned. Flynn hadn't been at his residence when SAPD had checked, but his name and picture had been sent out to law-enforcement agencies throughout the state. Plus, Kayla could recognize the moron if he showed up.

Dade took the final turn down the ranch road and drove the last quarter of a mile to the house. He watched Kayla as she took in the place. It didn't take her long because there wasn't much to see—a simple wood frame house and two barns surrounded by acres of pasture and trees. There was no livestock, no other people, and there hadn't been since Pete Wellman died three years earlier. He'd had no heirs, so Grayson had bought the place as an investment.

"Wait here a second," Dade ordered. He brought the SUV to a stop directly in front of the porch and the front door. Mason had already been out to put things in order, but Dade wanted to be sure.

He got out, went to the front door and unlocked it. Dade was pleased to hear the security alarm kick on. He disarmed it temporarily and did a walk-through. A living-dining combination. A kitchen. Three bedrooms. Two baths.

Tight quarters.

Especially because Kayla had a unique way of reminding him that she was around.

When Dade was satisfied that the house was indeed safe, he went back to the SUV to grab the suitcases. There were five total, and by the time he'd gotten them all inside and in place, a drowsy-looking Connie had already taken Robbie to the room that Kayla and the baby would share. Dade's room was in the middle. Not by accident either. He wanted to be able to hear if anything went wrong.

Once they were all inside, Dade didn't waste any time resetting the security system. He was certain they hadn't been followed, but he didn't want any surprise visitors in the middle of the night. Just in case, he left on his shoulder holster and gun.

"Does the bandage on your arm need to be checked?" Kayla asked.

Dade was in the process of removing his jacket. And wincing. That's probably what had prompted her question. "No, it's fine."

He'd slathered the wound with antibiotic cream and bandaged it at the sheriff's office when they'd stopped to pick up the SUV and other equipment.

Kayla stared at him as if she might challenge him and then fluttered her fingers toward the bathroom. "I need to take a shower." And with that, she walked away.

Dade watched her.

In fact, he couldn't make himself look away. Well, until she glanced over her shoulder at him. Then, his attention flew to the bag he'd put next to the sofa. Time to get his mind on the investigation and off Kayla's backside. But man, the woman had some curves.

Dade grabbed a soda from the fridge that Mason had stocked, took out his laptop and sank onto the sofa. There were already emails and reports about the shooting. Of course, with two dead bodies there would be a lot more to follow.

He fired off an email to Grayson to let him know about Kayla's juvenile record and the possibility of getting fingerprints from that. Grayson answered almost immediately with a thanks.

Dade scanned through the rest of the reports until he got to an attachment with Kayla's name. It was the file with everything Grayson and the San Antonio police had gathered on her. Because Kayla and he would be joined at the hip for the next few days, Dade opened it so he could find out more about this woman who had his body zinging.

Kayla Wallace Brennan was thirty-one, four years younger than him. Born in Houston. Parents divorced when she was a kid. One sister, Misty. Kayla married Preston Brennan when she was barely twenty-four, and their marriage had lasted nearly six years. Six years was a long time to be under the influence of a mob family. A woman could pick up all kinds of nasty habits.

Dade scrolled down.

And his fingers froze on the keys.

There were pictures of Kayla. Not the cool, rich ice queen with a great butt. They were police photos taken three years ago. Her hair had been pulled back, no makeup, and the camera had gobbled up a dozen or more images of the bruises on her face and upper body. Her right eye was practically swollen shut. Her bottom lip, busted open.

Dade got a rock-hard knot in his stomach.

He skimmed through the report that followed the pictures, and that knot in his stomach tightened. Kayla hadn't been mugged. According to the report, her husband, Preston, had done this to her during a domestic dispute.

A day later, Kayla dropped the charges.

Hell's bells.

Dade had seen that happen before, but he hadn't thought this had gone on with Kayla.

That stomach knot quickly turned to raw anger. Preston had been a big guy, muscles on top of muscles, and he'd used his wife for a punching bag. Dade cursed some more and then nearly jumped out of his skin when he heard the sound.

A loud thump.

He came off the sofa, drew his gun and hurried in the direction of the sound. Dade braced himself to come face-to-face with a gunman or maybe even Charles Brennan.

But it was a naked Kayla against the wall.

Okay, she wasn't naked exactly. She had on a silky white bathrobe that had shimmied off her shoulder all the way to the top of her breast, and it was that naked part of her that grabbed his attention more than the clothed parts.

"I slipped," she mumbled and quickly righted the bathrobe. No more peeks at her breast and that tattoo. "My legs are like jelly."

Dade understood that. He suddenly felt a little wobbly, too. And aroused. Something he quickly pushed aside. But he did reholster his gun and catch onto her arm to steady her.

"It's the adrenaline crash," he let her know. "You should probably try to sleep it off."

She nodded, raked her hair from her face. "I just need a drink of water first."

Kayla eased out of his grip and stepped around him. At least she tried. But the hall was narrow, and they brushed against each other despite their efforts to avoid one another. Heck, she might as well have kissed him because that's the punch he felt in his body.

Dade put some distance between them and followed her. Best to get back to work. But he didn't succeed with that either because Kayla suddenly froze, her attention knifing right to the photos on his computer screen.

She made a sound, something small and helpless that came deep from within her throat. It was a split-second response before she steeled up again.

"Why are you looking at those?" she asked, but her voice wasn't nearly as steely as she was trying to appear to be.

"I was going through your files." And Dade left it at that. It seemed a sick violation of her privacy, but those pictures told him more about Kayla than he'd ever wanted to know.

She swallowed hard and went to the fridge to get a bottle of water. She gulped some down as if her throat were parched. "Preston had a mean streak," she mumbled.

Yeah. And even though it was stupid, Dade wished the mean-streaked moron was still around so he could beat him to a pulp. "So why did you stay with him?" Dade asked before he could stop himself.

Her forehead bunched up, and the corner of her mouth lifted. A dry half smile. "What you really want to know is why I let him do that to me." She drew in her breath. "Because at first I loved him. I thought he would change. And then I began to believe I deserved to be hurt."

Even though it pulled at his arm wound, Dade put his hands on his hips. "You thought you deserved *that?*" He didn't wait for her to answer. "Because you didn't. No woman deserves it."

She nodded. Hesitated and then nodded again. "I figured that out eventually and was in the process of filing for a divorce when he was killed in the car accident."

Again, Dade had to adjust everything he knew about this woman. Here she'd been a battered wife, pregnant, and yet she'd planned to divorce a man who would have likely tried to kill her.

"I'm sorry he did that to you. Real sorry," Dade mumbled.

She tried to shrug and then blinked hard. The tears were right there, threatening to spill. He debated if he should do anything, but his feet started toward her before the debate even had a chance.

Kayla whispered a soft "no" when Dade reached out. But she didn't step back, and that made it easy for him to ease his good arm around her and inch her to him. She went board stiff but still didn't move to stop him.

"This isn't a good idea," she reminded him, even though she was sniffing back tears.

"Yeah. I don't always lean toward the *good idea* approach. I'm more of a go-with-your-gut kind of guy." And with that, he pulled her to him.

"I don't want your sympathy," Kayla insisted, still sniffing.

"Okay, because I'm also not good with that. This is just a little human kindness, that's all. You've been to hell and back, and I'm guessing that started a long time before today. Before those pictures were taken."

"That sounds like sympathy to me," she complained.

Dade didn't argue and he didn't let go of her. "Then we'll strike a deal. We can still dislike each other. Heck, it can border on hate. I won't give you any sympathy, but we'll call a truce."

She made a sound of disagreement and eased back so they made eye contact. "A truce that involves hugs." Now, she stepped back, but that didn't seem to make her any happier. "I'm very vulnerable right now. I'm scared, and I have a horrible knack for allying myself with the worst person possible."

Dade cocked his head to the side. "You talking about Preston now or me?"

She froze a moment. "You. Preston can't hurt me anymore, but you, well, you can."

And he instinctively knew she wasn't talking about physical violence. He had never hit a woman, and if he got his hands on Kayla, the last thing he'd want to do is hit her.

"*I* would be a mistake," he said, but he didn't say it under his breath as he'd intended. It was plenty loud enough for her to hear.

The corner of her mouth lifted just a fraction and then lowered just as quickly. "The worst kind."

Yeah. He was in trouble the size of Texas here. Because now they weren't indirectly talking about something beyond truces and protective custody. They were talking about this damn attraction.

And sex.

Dade cursed. "I wish to hell I hadn't seen your tattoo."

Or those pictures on the computer. And while he was at it, he wished her scent would stop sliding through him. She smelled like a fairy princess, all flowery and soft.

A smile barely touched her lips. "The tattoo is a relic from my youth. And I wish you hadn't seen it, either."

That was what she was saying, but her eyes were warm now. Not that riled spicy blue. This was more like the color of the sky. Calmer. Welcoming.

She opened her mouth, closed it and then motioned toward the hall. "Good night, Dade."

He didn't argue. He'd already said enough stupid things, and if she stayed, there would only be a greater opportunity for more stupidity. However, she only made it one step before Dade's phone buzzed.

"It's Grayson," he said, glancing at the screen. Dade answered it and hoped like the devil this call was good news. Any good news would do.

"Thanks for the email about Mrs. Brennan's juvenile record," Grayson started. "Her prints were there, and we were able to do a quick comparison. It's her prints on the cell, and the account is in her name."

It was exactly as they'd expected, and it certainly didn't make her guilty of anything other than owning a cell phone. "Any other prints?" Dade didn't exactly pray that there would be, but he considered it.

"Just smudges," Grayson let him know. "Nothing we can match."

Damn. Not good news because the phone was pretty

much a dead end. If Kenneth had indeed had the cell when the gunman called, then that was a secret that Kenneth had taken to his grave.

Dade locked eyes with Kayla who was hanging on to his every word. "What about the dead gunman's cell? Anything on it that'll help?" he asked Grayson.

"No breaks there. We're still looking for Danny Flynn. But we did locate the other person the gunman called."

"Misty Wallace?" Dade questioned, and that drew Kayla's full attention. She walked closer, and Dade went ahead and put the call on speaker.

"Yeah. San Antonio PD picked Misty up about twenty minutes ago," Grayson let Dade know.

SAPD. That meant his twin, Nate, had likely been involved in that pickup. Dade hated that Nate had to be part of this, but of course, he would be. Brennan was possibly the man who'd murdered Nate's wife. There was no way his brother would step back from this investigation.

"Nate will bring Misty here tomorrow morning so we can question her," Grayson added.

Kayla's fingers were trembling when she touched them to her mouth.

"Is Misty talking?" Dade immediately asked.

"Not to SAPD, but she says she'll talk to us. And she has a message for her sister. Misty wants you to tell her that she's sorry."

"Sorry about what?" Kayla said under her breath. It wasn't very loud but apparently loud enough for Grayson to hear.

Grayson grumbled something under his breath, too. "She wouldn't say, but I intend to find out."

Chapter 6

Kayla heard the sound, and her eyes flew open. It wasn't the sounds of bullets like those in her nightmares. This was laughter. And it was coming from the other side of the house.

"Robbie?" she called out and then remembered Connie had come and gotten him when he woke up earlier. The nanny had told Kayla to get a little more rest, and apparently she had.

She threw back the covers and spotted the sunlight speckling across the room from the tiny gaps in the blinds. She checked the clock on the nightstand—already seven-thirty. Not late by many people's standards, but she'd overslept.

How the heck could that have happened?

Here they were in the middle of a dangerous situation, and she'd slept in like the diva Dade already thought she was.

Kayla changed out of her gown and put on the dark blue pants and top that she practically ripped from her suitcase. She used the hall bathroom to finish dressing and raced toward the laughter. She soon found the source.

Her son.

Dade was at the kitchen table, Robbie in his lap, and her son was giggling because Dade was playing airplane with the spoon of oatmeal. Her son devoured the oatmeal the moment it made it to his mouth.

Kayla made eye contact with Connie who was near the stove pouring herself a cup of coffee. The nanny, who looked as if she had also dressed in a hurry, simply shrugged.

"Mommy's up," Dade announced, and he sent another spoonful of oatmeal Robbie's way. Another giggle. And her son lapped it up.

"I'm sorry," Kayla told Dade. "I should have been up to feed him."

Dade just shrugged as well. "I have a niece, Kimmie, who's just a little bit older than Robbie, and I feed her a lot of mornings."

So that explained why the bad-boy cowboy looked perfectly natural with flecks of oatmeal on his jeans and chest-hugging black T-shirt. Robbie hadn't escaped, either. He had oatmeal smeared into his blond hair.

"I can take over," Kayla insisted. But when she looked in the bowl, she realized that Robbie had finished.

"Da-da-da," Robbie babbled, and he slapped his hands on the highchair tray.

Kayla was mortified and was about to launch into an apology for that, as well.

"He's trying to say Dade," Connie quickly explained.

Dade lifted his shoulder again. "That seems a little easier to say than Deputy Ryland."

Maybe, but it was downright unnerving to hear those sounds come from her son's mouth. More unnerving to see the big grin that Robbie doled out to Dade.

"Let me get him washed up," Connie insisted.

"I can do it," Kayla offered.

But Connie glanced at Dade. "I think the deputy and you have some things to discuss."

Yes, they did. Misty, for one, because her sister had been brought in for questioning and had issued that vague *I'm sorry.* Kayla had tried to call her sister more than a dozen times before she went to bed, but Misty hadn't answered.

Connie eased Robbie out of the highchair and brought him over to Kayla so she could get a morning kiss. She got one all right, complete with oatmeal smears and a smile that could have lit up the night. Kayla had no choice but to smile back.

"I love you," she whispered to her son, and Robbie babbled back a string of sounds that could have meant anything. But Kayla knew he was telling her that he loved her, too.

"He's a fun kid," Dade said, and he got to his feet.

"Yes, but he's usually shy around strangers." Probably because Robbie hadn't been exposed to many, but he'd taken to Dade as if he'd known him his whole life.

Dade looked at her, as if waiting for more, but she didn't want to talk about how good he was with her son. Kayla also didn't want to stare. She failed at that. She stared. And wondered how anyone could look that good with flecks of oatmeal on them.

She reached up and plucked a piece of it from Dade's hair. "Robbie's a messy eater."

"Not as bad as Kimmie. Once she crammed a handful of strained peaches in my ear. Couldn't hear for hours." With that, he smiled.

Oh, mercy.

He was hot with his usual bad-boy scowl, but that smile made her weak at the knees. Kayla stepped back, cleared her throat and changed the subject. "When will Grayson question Misty?"

Dade's smile faded as fast as it'd come, and he checked the wall clock over the table. "Soon. They're setting up things now so we can watch. My laptop is already on, and I've connected to Grayson's computer at his office."

She glanced at his computer screen to verify that it was indeed on, and there on the screen was what appeared to be an office. An empty one.

"Watch?" she challenged. "But I thought I'd be able to see Misty in person."

"Not a chance," Dade informed her. "We aren't leaving this safe house unless it's an emergency."

Of course. That made sense for security reasons. But Kayla had wanted to see her sister and not through a computer screen.

"We'll be able to hear and see them," Dade verified. "They can hear and see us, as well." He grabbed a cup of black coffee from the counter and headed to the sofa.

Kayla poured herself some coffee, but when she joined him, she immediately saw the dilemma. The sofa wasn't that large, and with his computer perched on the coffee table, the only way she would see the screen was to sit right next to Dade. So, that's what she did, and Kayla tried not to react when her arm brushed his.

He reacted, though.

Dade winced. And that's when her attention shot down to the bandage. "I should check that."

She didn't wait for him to agree because he wouldn't have. Kayla eased back the bandage, afraid of what she might see. The gash was an angry red color and the area around it was swollen.

"I'm taking antibiotics," Dade reminded her.

He tipped his head to the prescription bottle on the end of the coffee table. It was sitting on top of a first-aid kit. Kayla dug through the kit and came up with a tube of antibiotic cream.

"This isn't necessary," he complained.

"It is," she complained right back. "You wouldn't have been shot if you hadn't been protecting me."

That was true, and Kayla didn't regret her decision to tend his wound. But what she hadn't considered was that touching Dade posed some problems of its own.

His arm was rock-hard, and even though he wasn't heavily muscled, he was still lean and solid. A cowboy. And for some strange reason that made her smile.

"What?" Dade questioned. He dipped his head so his eyes could meet hers.

Not a good idea, either.

Because it put them breath to breath and nearly mouth to mouth.

Everything seemed to freeze. Except her heartbeat. It jolted like crazy, a reaction she quickly tried to get under control.

Dade didn't tear his attention from her. Kayla didn't move either. She just sat there, her fingers smeared with cream and poised over his arm. And in that moment, she had a terrible thought.

What would it feel like to kiss Dade?

A glimmer went through his cool gray eyes that let her know he was thinking the same thing.

"Is there a problem?" someone asked.

Kayla jerked back so fast that her neck popped.

There, on the screen, was Lieutenant Nate Ryland. She recognized him from the investigation and from his picture in the newspaper. This was Dade's fraternal twin brother. A brother who no doubt hated her to the core. And God knows what he must have seen in Dade's and her eyes.

"Kayla was checking my arm," Dade volunteered. "How much longer until the interview?"

Nate didn't answer right away. He kept his attention on Kayla. Was it disgust she saw? Or worse, was it that painful for him to look at her?

"A few more minutes," Nate finally said. "I was just checking to make sure we'd be able to see and hear you. We can," he mumbled. "By the way, Grayson had to give your location to the D.A."

"Why?" Kayla and Dade asked together.

"Winston said he had to talk to her about the trial."

Dade didn't like the idea of anyone knowing their location. Judging from Kayla's expression, neither did she. "Can't it wait?"

"Not according to Winston," Nate answered. "He has to file some papers in court today or it could jeopardize the case."

Well, Dade didn't want that, but he also didn't want to put Kayla at further risk. "Warn Winston to be careful," Dade insisted.

"I will," Nate assured him. "For now, though, I'll get Ms. Wallace in here."

"Wait," Kayla blurted out. But then she fumbled with what to say. "I'm sorry about your wife," she finally got out.

Nate stood there, his jaw muscles working against each other. It felt like an eternity. Finally, he nodded. "Thank you." And he walked out of camera range.

Kayla held her breath, wondering if Dade was going to blast her for daring to bring up the topic of Nate's dead wife. But he merely pressed the bandage back in place, reached over and muted the sound on his computer. He also handed her a tissue so she could wipe the ointment from her fingers.

"I'm very protective of my brother," Dade threw out like a warning.

"I understand." And she did. Kayla often felt that way about Misty. "But Nate doesn't appear to be a man who needs protecting."

"Not now."

She shook her head, wondering if they were still talking about Ellie's murder.

"Things were different when we were kids," he mumbled. Dade huffed, paused, huffed again. "Something happened when Mom was pregnant with us, and Nate was born with a lot of medical problems."

Ah. She understood that, too. "So you fought his battles for him?"

"Yeah. Sometimes literally." He stared down at his hands and scraped his thumbnail over one of his knuckles. "The kids used to rag on him at school. But Nate, he was smart. A lot smarter than the kids who tried to bully him, so he could usually talk his way out of a butt whipping. Still can." Now, Dade looked at her. "He's the youngest cop in SAPD ever promoted to lieutenant. He's a big gun there."

"He's a survivor," Kayla mumbled.

Dade shrugged. "Losing Ellie nearly killed him."

And therefore it had nearly killed Dade. Kayla could see how much Dade loved his twin brother, and whether he realized it or not, he was still fighting Nate's battles. Still making sure that she wasn't a threat.

Kayla was about to assure him that she was no threat, but Dade spoke first. "Last night I did some digging into your sister's recent—"

He stopped when there was movement on the laptop screen, and Dade turned up the volume. Kayla wanted to know what Dade had been about to tell her, but she knew it would have to wait when she saw Grayson lead Misty into his office. Her sister dropped down into the chair directly in front of the webcam.

Misty did not look like a happy camper.

That was reasonable, because she was essentially in police custody and had been the entire night. Her short blond hair looked as if it hadn't been combed, and her sister wore no makeup. A rarity. It made her look much younger than twenty-seven. She looked more like a schoolgirl waiting out detention.

Misty's eyes zoomed right in on Kayla. "I can't believe you let them bring me in like this."

Kayla felt as if Misty had slapped her. All that anger in her voice, and she was glaring not at Dade or Grayson but at Kayla.

"Kayla was nearly killed," Dade responded before she could find her breath.

"Well, I didn't have anything to do with that," Misty

fired back. But when she looked at Kayla again, her glare softened a little. "I'm sorry if you were almost hurt, but I'm not responsible for it."

"Not almost hurt," Dade again. "She was almost *killed* by a man named Raymond Salvetti who phoned you just a half hour before the attack."

Misty gasped. Hopefully because she was surprised by that revelation. It had to be that. Because Kayla couldn't believe that her sister would betray her. Their relationship wasn't perfect, but her sister loved her.

Kayla hoped.

Frantically shaking her head, Misty looked up at Grayson. "Someone did call me last night, and I didn't recognize the number so I let it go to voice mail. I swear, I don't know any gunmen."

"Maybe you do," Dade countered. "Think hard. Did you know Raymond Salvetti?"

Misty didn't hesitate even a second. "I don't have to think hard. I don't know anyone like that. Charles set this up. He would do anything to get to Kayla, and he probably hired this Salvetti guy."

"Yes," Kayla agreed. "But for him to do that, he had to know where I was staying. Salvetti came to the estate, Misty. He knew I was there."

Misty did more of that frantic head shaking. Kayla wanted to hold on to each one of them as the truth. "I didn't tell anyone where you were staying. You told me to keep it a secret, and I did. I swear, I did."

"How did you let Misty know that you'd be at the estate?" Grayson interrupted. He looked at Kayla. "In person? Phone? Email?"

"Phone," Kayla and Misty answered in unison. It

was Kayla who continued. "Where were you when we had that conversation?" she asked Misty.

"At a bar on St. Mary's. But no one heard our conversation."

"You're sure?" Grayson pressed.

"Positive." Misty shoved her hands through her hair and groaned in frustration. "If you want to point the finger at someone other than Charles, you need to look in your own backyard. That Silver Creek D.A., Winston Calhoun, and his assistant, Alan Bowers, have been bugging me for months. Both have been trying to find Kayla. Well, I'm betting both of them knew she'd be at the estate."

It was true. Both men did know. And Kayla hadn't ruled either or both out as the leak that had led the gunman to her. Like Dade had apparently done last night, she needed to do some digging because the Rylands might not think of friends and neighbors as potential felons. But Kayla knew for a fact that Charles could be very persuasive. He had a knack for finding people's weak spots.

"Why would you think for one minute I would put Kayla in danger?" Misty demanded. She volleyed a glare between Dade and Grayson.

"Money," Dade volunteered, and he gave Kayla an *I'm-sorry* glance. "I dug into your financials last night, and I found you've recently come into some money. Ten thousand dollars to be exact."

Kayla heard the sound of shock escape from her throat. So that was what Dade had been about to tell her. Oh, God. Misty and she hadn't come from money, and even though Kayla gave her sister a monthly allowance to cover living expenses, Misty went through it as quickly as she got it. And Misty hadn't always spent the money wisely. Sometimes, she'd even used it to buy drugs. That's why Kayla hadn't just doled out more.

Ten grand was a huge sum for her sister, and Misty had to have an explanation. She just had to, and Kayla waited with her breath held.

Misty huffed. "I'm an artist," she snarled at Dade. "And I sold some paintings. That's all there is to it."

"You've got receipts for the sales, of course?" Dade remarked.

Her sister's eyes widened, and she lowered her head until she was staring down at her lap. "No, not exactly. It was a private sale. A cash deal."

Kayla's heart dropped, as well. Her sister had never made that much money from her paintings, and a sale like that should have caused Misty to call her immediately.

"I need the name and contact info for the buyer," Grayson insisted. He grabbed a notepad and pen and slid them Misty's way.

Misty's attention stayed fixed to her lap. "I don't have it, but I can get it, I suppose."

"You suppose?" Kayla questioned. She tried very hard not to get angry about such a casual comment. "Misty, someone tried to kill me and maybe Robbie, too. You have to cooperate with the police. I need answers so I can keep Robbie safe."

That got Misty's attention aimed back at the webcam. "I don't have answers!" she shouted. "The person who bought the art didn't contact me directly. He went through a friend of a friend and said he wanted the deal to be secret, that he didn't want his soon-to-be ex-wife to know he was draining their accounts." She moved closer to the screen. "Can't you see, Kayla? Someone's trying to set me up."

"Then, prove it," Dade fired back before Kayla could say anything. "Get the name of the art buyer from your friend of a friend."

Misty's forehead bunched up and she mumbled something Kayla didn't catch. "Give me twenty-four hours," she bargained. She began to chew on her thumbnail. "And I think it's time I called a lawyer."

Dade and his brother exchanged a glance. "Twenty-four hours," Grayson confirmed. "If I don't hear from you, I'm hauling you right back here, and it won't be just for questioning. I'll arrest you for obstruction of justice and any other charge I can tack on."

"Thanks a lot, Kayla," Misty snarled, and she jumped to her feet. She practically ran out of the office.

Grayson leaned closer to the screen. "I'll call you if I find out anything."

A few seconds later, the screen went blank. Kayla's mind, however, didn't. It started to spin with plausible explanations, none of which she hoped would point to her sister's guilt.

"Charles could have set up that art deal to incriminate Misty," Kayla tossed out there. "He knows she's the only person I trust, and he might want to take that from me."

She expected Dade to counter her theory with a reminder that Misty had looked guilty of something. Or that her sister hadn't mentioned this art deal before now.

But he didn't say any of that.

Dade simply slipped his arm around her shoulder and eased her closer to him. Kayla thought about his shoulder. That this might be painful for him, but she couldn't refuse the comfort he was offering her. She'd had to stay strong for so long. All on her own. And it felt good to have a semi-ally.

"Grayson is a good cop," Dade reminded her. "He'll get to the bottom of this."

Yes. Dade was a good cop, too, and she was afraid that *bottom* would incriminate her sister. "I feel the same way about Misty as you do about Nate. I've always protected her."

Dade stayed quiet a moment and gently rubbed his fingertips on her arm. "You're positive she didn't sell you out to Brennan?"

Kayla wanted to be angry that he would even ask. After all, she'd had no trouble feeling that anger during Misty's interview. But it wasn't anger she felt this time.

It was fear for what Misty could have done.

"Charles could have manipulated her," Kayla suggested. "He could have made her believe that telling him my whereabouts would be the only way to keep me alive."

"But wouldn't she have admitted that to you, especially after I told her that you'd nearly been killed?"

Kayla hoped that would be true, but she had to shake her head. "She might be too afraid to tell me."

She braced herself for Dade to huff or roll his eyes, but he didn't. Maybe because he had five siblings, he understood the sometimes-delicate dynamics of family.

"Misty doesn't know how bad things were with Preston and Charles," Kayla continued. "She knows I witnessed some illegal activity. That I overheard conversations about money laundering and such. But Misty believes those were rare occurrences. They weren't."

Dade stayed quiet a moment. "Exactly how much did you witness?"

"Too much," she mumbled. "I overheard and saw enough to convict Charles of dozens of felonies."

"Good thing, too, because I doubt there's any physical evidence to nail him."

"There used to be," Kayla admitted. "He had files at his office and heaven knows what stashed in safe-deposit boxes under fake names." She had to take a deep breath because that was a reminder of just how dangerous her former father-in-law was and continued to be.

Dade turned slightly so they were directly facing each other. "Protecting Robbie and you comes first. I can't put Misty or anyone else ahead of that, understand?"

"Yes." It's exactly what she wanted Dade to do—to protect her son at all cost.

And Dade would. She didn't have to second-guess that. Mercy.

How much her life had changed in these short hours. Just yesterday, she thought of Dade and all the Rylands as the enemy, but she no longer felt that way about Dade.

That could be a major mistake.

"Yeah," she heard him say and realized he was studying her eyes as if he knew exactly what she was thinking. Maybe he did because he looked away, cursed and mumbled something.

"What?" she asked.

He cursed again. "This," he answered.

This was bad. Because Dade turned back to her, leaned in and touched his mouth to hers. It was quick. And dirty. It packed a punch of a full-fledged French kiss.

"Hell," he mumbled. "If I'm breaking the rules, I might as well break 'em hard."

And he did.

His hand went around the back of her neck and he dragged her to him. Not just the lip contact but some body-to-body contact as well. Her breasts landed against his toned chest muscles.

Oh, he was good. Too good. His mouth blazed against her and sent a jolt of fire through all the wrong parts of her body.

She'd been right about Dade. He could melt chrome with that mouth and seduce her straight to his bed. Something that couldn't happen.

Kayla repeated that to herself. Several times.

Finally, she managed to pull back. Or maybe she was successful only because Dade pulled back as well.

"There are about a hundred reasons why that can't happen again," he insisted. And he inched away from her so they were no longer touching.

Kayla couldn't argue with that, and she could even add some reasons of her own. "I can't get involved because my last relationship nearly destroyed me. Besides, when you look at me, you'll always think of Nate's dead wife."

He made a sound of agreement.

And then Kayla heard another sound.

One that she hadn't expected to hear. Apparently, neither had Dade because he sprang from the sofa, and in the same motion, he drew his gun from his shoulder holster. He hurried to the window, and Kayla followed, but Dade only pushed her behind him.

"Hell," Dade mumbled. "We have a visitor."

Chapter 7

Dade drew his gun and pushed Kayla behind him. No one should be here, but there was a black four-door sedan barreling up the dirt road toward the ranch house.

"Who is it?" Kayla asked. Her voice wasn't just trembling, it was downright shaking.

Dade kept his gun and his attention nailed to the car, and it didn't take him long to figure out who their *visitor* was. Or rather *visitors.* Because he instantly recognized the two men who exited the car when it came to a stop in front of the house.

"It's the D.A., Winston Calhoun, and the assistant D.A., Alan Bowers," he said.

She drew in a hard breath. "They're here already?"

"Is everything okay?" Connie called out to them.

"Yeah," Dade answered, but he had no idea if that was the truth. "Just stay put with Robbie."

When he started across the yard, Winston ducked his head down, probably because of the icy wind. He carried a leather briefcase and was dressed for work in an iron-gray business suit that matched the color of his hair and the winter sky. He was a good twenty years older than Dade, and Dade had known the man his entire life.

He couldn't say the same for Alan.

The thirty-something-year-old had moved to Silver Creek about a year and a half ago when he'd gotten the job at the D.A.'s office. He was lanky to the point of being wiry, with hair so blond that he looked more at home on the beach than he did in cowboy country. Like his boss, Alan wore a suit, so this obviously wasn't a social call.

When the men made it to the porch, Dade reholstered his gun, disengaged the security system and opened the door. "This had better be important," he snarled.

Winston spared him a glance, but his dark eyes went to Kayla. Yeah. Something was definitely wrong, but Winston didn't say a word until both Alan and he had stepped inside.

"Charles Brennan's lawyers just requested a trial delay," Winston announced.

Kayla didn't make a sound, but Dade could feel her reaction. Every muscle in her body tensed.

"Please tell me he won't get it," Dade insisted.

Alan lifted his bony shoulder, and Winston shook his head. Dade just cursed. Kayla and Robbie sure as hell didn't need this.

"You could have told us this over the phone," Dade pointed out. "Rather than risk someone following you."

Alan's mouth tightened. Probably because he was insulted that Dade had just slammed him for what Dade considered to be an unnecessary visit that could turn out to be a big-time security risk.

Winston, however, had no visible reaction. "This visit is important," he declared. "And for the record, no one followed us. We were careful."

Winston set his briefcase on the table near the door and extracted a manila file. "I need to get Kayla's signature on the statement she gave me over the phone two days ago." He handed her both the file and pen.

"Of course." Kayla's voice was still shaky and so was her hand. And Dade knew why. The statement and her signature would be needed if for some reason Kayla couldn't testify.

In other words, if Dade failed to do his job and Brennan killed her.

"I'd like to read through this first," Kayla said, her attention already on the first page. She sank onto the sofa.

"It's all there," Alan informed her. He made a nervous gesture toward the papers. "We just need your signature so we can leave."

Kayla lifted her eyes. Met his. "I'd still prefer to read it."

Dade was about to second that and even insist on it. Not because he didn't trust Winston but because this entire visit was well beyond making him feel uncomfortable. However, before Dade could say anything, Winston latched onto his arm and pulled him aside. Alan stayed near Kayla.

"We haven't been able to link the dead gunman, Salvetti, to Brennan," Winston whispered. "But we have been able to link Brennan to Danny Flynn, the guy the gunman called. Flynn did some handyman work at Brennan's estate."

None of this surprised Dade. "Any proof that Flynn orchestrated the attack last night?"

"No. But get this—Brennan says Flynn's trying to set him up because he fired him."

Of course Brennan would say that. He would say and do anything to cover his butt.

Dade heard Robbie make a sound. A squeal, followed by a fussy protest. And Kayla nearly jumped off the sofa.

"I'll check on him," Dade told her. Best for her to finish reading the statement so he could get Winston and Alan out of there.

Dade headed down the hall, and it didn't take him long to spot the baby. Connie had him in a snug protective grip, but Robbie clearly wanted to get down. Dade went closer, and when the baby reached out for him, Dade pulled him into his arms.

Without thinking, he brushed a kiss on Robbie's forehead.

That was something he often did to his niece, Kimmie, but he regretted it now. That kiss earned him a raised eyebrow from the nanny who clearly didn't trust him. Robbie, on the other hand, was loaded with trust. He babbled something to Dade and dropped his head on Dade's shoulder.

Heck.

Dade didn't want to feel the warmth of holding this child in his arms. Because Kayla was still his family's enemy. There couldn't be anything between them.

Well, except for his feelings for her son.

And that kiss, of course.

But Dade was reasonably sure he'd be disgusted with

himself about that later. Too bad the attraction he felt for her kept putting off that *later*.

Dade tried to hand Robbie back to the nanny, but when the baby fussed again, Dade kept hold of him and returned to the living room to check on Kayla. When she spotted them, Dade got another raised eyebrow. Dade looked at Robbie to see his reaction, and the little boy gave him a big toothy grin. Dade couldn't help but grin back.

"I'm finished." Kayla scrawled her signature on the last page of the statement and handed both the pages and the pen back to Winston. She didn't waste even a second taking Robbie from him.

Dade had expected those raised eyebrows from their guests, but he was a little miffed that Kayla would have that reaction, especially because they'd set fire to each other's lips just minutes earlier.

"I'll let you know if Brennan gets the trial delay," Winston assured them. He tipped his head in a farewell gesture, and the two attorneys headed to the door.

Dade followed them, closing the door behind them and resetting the security alarm. He turned to ask Kayla about that raised eyebrow reaction, but she spoke before he could.

"You trust both of those men?" she asked. It didn't seem like an accusation exactly, but there was concern dripping from her voice.

"I trust Winston." But then he had to shrug. "I don't really know Alan. Why, did you get bad vibes from him?"

"From both of them," she corrected. "But then I'm getting bad vibes from almost everyone."

He stared at her. "Even from me? I noticed you didn't care for my holding your son."

She opened her mouth as if she might leap to dispute it, but then Kayla shook her head. "It's not that." And she repeated it. "Your brothers hate me, and I don't want to do anything that would hurt your relationship with them. I figured the D.A. would report back anything and everything he saw here."

Oh, he would. Maybe Alan, too. But Grayson had already seen the close contact between Kayla and him at the start of the interview with Misty. Grayson wasn't stupid, and he no doubt had already noticed what was simmering between Kayla and him.

"It might be too late to do that kind of damage control." Dade went closer, caught onto Robbie's foot and gave it a jiggle. He was rewarded with a grin.

"Is everything okay?" Connie asked from the hall.

"Yes," Kayla quickly answered. "I'll keep Robbie with me for a while and give you some time for reading."

The nanny made a sound of approval, but Dade doubted she'd get much quality reading time. The attack from the night before was too fresh on all their minds.

Kayla grabbed the diaper bag from the coffee table, took out several small stuffed animals and sank down onto the floor with Robbie so he could play. Dade checked out the window.

Nothing, thank God. Maybe it would stay that way.

He maneuvered himself so he could keep watch but sat on the floor along with them. Robbie seemed to approve because he handed Dade a blue horse and then laughed when Dade made a neighing sound.

"You're good with kids," Kayla said sounding more than a little surprised.

Dade shrugged and took out his wallet. He opened it to show her a picture of his thirteen-month-old niece, Kimmie. The picture was there all right, front and center, but something fell out.

A tarnished silver concho.

Kayla grabbed it before it could hit the floor and stared at it. The concho was a blast from the past that he didn't need, and Dade had forgotten it was even there.

"It's the symbol for the Ryland ranch." The double back-to-back Rs were prominently displayed. "My father gave me and each of my brothers one before…well, before he left."

One look in Kayla's suddenly sympathetic eyes, and he knew she'd already heard at least bits and pieces of this tragic story. Boone Ryland had run off and abandoned his six sons twenty years ago, and that had been just the beginning of things gone wrong for what was left of the Rylands.

"Twenty years," Dade mumbled, "and the gossip hasn't died down."

Kayla didn't deny she'd heard gossip. She reached out, touched his arm and rubbed gently. Her touch was warm and curled through him, but it was also a reminder that the events twenty years ago would always be a stab to his heart.

He took the concho from her, shoved it back into his wallet and put it away. Out of sight but never out of mind.

Kayla cleared her throat and eased Robbie back into her lap when he tried to crawl away. "Nate's child is your only niece or nephew?" she asked.

Dade was a hundred-percent thankful for the change in subject. "Yeah, but Grayson and his wife have one on the way." He kept his attention fastened to the window.

"Grayson looks as if he'd be a good father," she remarked. Her forehead bunched up. "Not your other brother, though."

He knew exactly which brother she meant. "Mason." And he couldn't disagree with her. "Mason is a hard man to figure out. Hard on himself. And others. After our dad left, Mason took his concho, shot it with a .38 and then nailed what was left of it to his bedroom wall. Said it was the first thing he wanted to see when he got up in the morning so he'd remember how much he hated the old man."

When Kayla didn't say anything, he glanced at her. Her mouth had dropped open a little. "That doesn't sound…healthy."

"Not much about our past was," he admitted. He sure hadn't planned on spilling his guts this way, but he didn't stop, either. "Plain and simple, my father gave us those conchos to relieve his guilt, and then he destroyed us, especially our mom. She committed suicide on Grayson's eighteenth birthday and left a note begging him to keep the family together."

Kayla touched his arm again. Probably to give him another of those soothing rubs, but Dade moved away. "Grayson succeeded."

"Yeah, I guess. He's happy now anyway." One of six wasn't exactly a good track record, but before Grayson's wife, Eve, had come back into his life a few months earlier, the Rylands had been batting a thousand in the bad-relationship department.

Kayla stayed quiet a moment. "So what about you—have you always kept your concho in your wallet?"

This wasn't a story he was used to telling, not out loud anyway, although he remembered it like it was yesterday. "When we were fourteen, Nate and I threw ours in Silver Creek. But like a bad penny, mine turned up. Grayson's wife found it about a week ago when she was out taking some pictures for a newspaper article she's working on."

Kayla's mouth dropped open again. "She found it after all these years?"

He shook his head and waved her off. "Don't go there. This isn't some kind of cosmic sign for me to forgive my father." Dade bit back the profanity of what he really wanted to call Boone Ryland because Robbie was in the room. "It was just blind luck she found it, that's all. And first chance I get, I'll toss it right back in the creek. Heck, maybe the Gulf of Mexico. Doubt anyone would find it then."

The silence came. Of course it did. He'd just saddled a mountain of old baggage on Kayla. Right about now she was probably thinking he needed some big-time therapy, and she was no doubt regretting that kiss, too.

"Don't throw the concho away." Her voice was a whisper now. "Give it to me."

Dade was sure he looked at her as if she'd sprouted horns. "Why?"

She flashed him one of those half smiles, the ones that weren't of the happy variety. "So I have something to remember the man who saved my and my son's lives."

Good grief. That wasn't a good reason because it seemed intimate. Or something. It definitely didn't seem *right*.

"Plus," she continued. The smile was gone now, and her chin came up. Second-guessing her request, he figured. "If you want cosmic justice, what better way to get it than to give your enemy the guilt gift from a father you despise?"

Dade just stared at her, and she stared back. Robbie did, too, as if he was trying to figure out what was going on.

"Forget I said that," Kayla added. She tried to chuckle. Failed. "I won't need anything to remember you."

Yeah. Dade felt the same about her. Kayla would be in his dreams—hot, uncomfortable dreams—long after this assignment ended. It'd been a while since he'd wanted a woman as much as he wanted Kayla.

Dade could already feel his hands on her. Could taste her. Could hear the sounds she'd make when he was deep inside her. And that hard ache went through his body and begged him to kick this attraction up a notch.

But he couldn't. Because of her safety. And because of that cute little kid staring up at him.

Dade stood and took out his wallet. Then, the concho. He tossed it into Kayla's lap. Quick, like stripping off a bandage that had been in place way too long.

She picked up the silver-dollar-sized concho the way a person would handle fine crystal and closed her fingers around it when Robbie reached for it, as well. She gave her baby a kiss instead.

Yet another too-intimate moment that he shouldn't be experiencing with Kayla. He'd be thankful when this trial was over so he could put some distance between them.

And Dade was almost sure he believed that.

"A car," Kayla said at the same moment Dade heard the sound of the engine.

Hell. What now? Maybe Winston had driven back to tell them that Brennan had gotten the delay he'd requested. If so, Dade was going to give them instructions on how to use a phone to relay information.

Dade hurried to the window next to the door and looked out. He groaned, but inside his reaction was much worse.

Kayla latched onto Robbie and hugged him close to her body. "Who is it?"

"It's trouble," Dade let her know, and when he drew his gun he was afraid this time he might have to use it.

Chapter 8

Kayla tried to brace herself for the worst, and the worst would be Charles. However, he wasn't the person who stepped from the car.

It was her sister, Misty.

Dade glanced back at her as if expecting an explanation, but Kayla didn't have one. "I didn't tell anyone including Misty, where we were staying."

"Well, someone did, unless it's blind luck she found her way out here," he snarled. "Go to the bedroom and wait. Keep Robbie quiet if you can. Maybe she's just on a fishing expedition and doesn't actually know you're here."

Kayla was about to insist that Misty was no threat. Old habits died hard, and she had a lifetime habit of defending Misty. But the truth was their location had likely been compromised. Now the question was how?

"Carrie Collins," Dade spat out like profanity.

It took Kayla a moment to realize why Dade had said the woman's name, but then she spotted the tall brunette who got out of the driver's side of the car. It was the paramedic who'd come to her estate right after the shooting.

"Your sister knows Carrie?" Dade asked, his attention fastened to the two women making their way to the porch.

"I don't think so." Yet, here they were together.

What was going on?

Kayla shoved the concho into her pocket and hurried to the hall where Connie was waiting. The nanny had no doubt heard the car engine and was wondering if they were about to be attacked again.

She handed Robbie to Connie. "I'll be back after I talk to my sister."

And by God, Misty better have some answers.

By the time Kayla returned to the living room, Dade was talking on his cell. She didn't know who he had called, but he clearly wasn't happy. He had such a grip on the phone that she was surprised it didn't crush to powder, and his eyes were narrowed to slits.

"Who says I'm at the Wellman ranch?" Dade barked. He paused, then cursed. "How the hell did you manage to follow Winston?"

Kayla's stomach dropped. If her sister and this medic had followed the D.A., then Charles's hired guns could have done the same. Oh, mercy. This had just gone from bad to worse.

As if he'd declared war on it, Dade paused the security system and threw open the door. Carrie tried to push her way in, but Dade blocked her.

"I need to check your arm," Carrie insisted. "You could get an infection. Or worse."

"My arm is fine," Dade insisted right back, and he jerked away from Carrie when she tried to check the bandage that was visible just beneath the sleeve of his black T-shirt.

Carrie's eyes narrowed as well, and she shot Kayla a glare. Kayla ignored it and saved her glare for Misty, who was practically standing behind the much taller Carrie.

"Why did you come?" Kayla asked her sister.

"Why?" Misty stepped to Carrie's side. "Because you believe I tried to kill you. I had to see you, to convince you of the obvious. I would never take money from someone who wants to hurt you."

It certainly sounded convincing, and Kayla wanted to believe her, but there was the issue of the money that Misty had recently acquired. There was also her sister's mere presence.

"Why did you come here?" Kayla asked. Again, she had to dodge a glare from Carrie. "You must have realized that someone could have followed you."

"No one did," Carrie snapped, and she repeated it to Dade. "I'm not stupid, Dade. I know how to watch my back—and yours."

"Winston was certain no one had followed him, either," Dade informed them. "But you somehow managed it. How?"

Carrie huffed, and her glare softened. "I figured Winston or Alan would be out to see you sooner or later, so I kept an eye on the parking lot at the D.A.'s office. I got lucky and saw them leave."

"You did all that so you could check on my arm?"

Dade didn't sound happy about that. Or convinced that Carrie was telling the truth.

That put some fire back in her eyes. "I care about you," Carrie snarled under her breath. And then she put that snarl into the look she gave Kayla.

Oh, so that's what was going on. Carrie had a thing for Dade. That was, well, reasonable. After all, Dade was a hot guy and no doubt a prime catch. Still, it made Kayla uncomfortable, and she didn't want to explore why she didn't like Carrie going to extremes to check on Dade.

Kayla walked closer until she was side-by-side with Dade and snared her sister's attention. "Were you watching the D.A.'s parking lot, too?"

The seconds crawled by before Misty answered. "Yes, and when Carrie spotted me, we got to talking. I asked her to bring me out here with her."

"She demanded I bring her," Carrie clarified to Dade. "I agreed finally because I didn't want her to do something stupid by trying to follow me."

Kayla figured the *something stupid* had already happened.

"You put Robbie in danger by coming here," Kayla told Misty. Her sister opened her mouth, but Kayla spoke right over her. "We can talk about your innocence after the trial. After Robbie is safe. But for now, I need you just to back off and stay away from us."

Misty flinched, and her eyes actually watered. Because Kayla had never seen Misty cry anything but crocodile tears, she had to wonder if these were genuine. If so, Kayla would owe her a huge apology. Later. After the trial.

"You both need to leave," Dade said. And it wasn't

a suggestion. It was an order. He started to close the door, but Carrie caught onto it.

However, the woman didn't look at Dade. She looked at Kayla. "You don't even remember me, do you?"

Kayla lifted her shoulder. "You were at the estate last night."

"Before that. I was with Preston the night you two met."

Kayla hadn't expected the woman to say that, and with so much already on her mind, it took her a few moments to remember that night.

"A charity fundraiser in San Antonio," Carrie added. "I was talking to Preston, and you interrupted us."

Yes, she remembered meeting them, and she vaguely recalled a woman next to Preston. Until now she'd had no idea it was Carrie. "A friend interrupted you," Kayla corrected, "so she could introduce me to Preston."

At the time, Kayla had thought it was one of the best moments of her life. And she continued to think that until she got to know the abusive man behind that million-dollar smile.

"Does this have anything to do with the trial or Kayla's safety?" Dade demanded. He clicked on his phone. "Because I have security arrangements to make."

"Yes, it does have something to do with the trial." Carrie had a death grip on the door to keep Dade from closing it. "Kayla was bad news then, and she's bad news now. She went to that fundraiser to meet a rich guy, and she succeeded. She didn't care that Preston and I were dating. She just moved right in on him."

Stunned by Carrie's accusation, Kayla pulled back her shoulders. "I wasn't aware you were seeing Preston. He didn't mention it."

"And I'm sure you didn't ask." Carrie paused and glanced away. "Preston ended things with me that night, and I figure you had plenty to do with that. I know your type, and I know you would have said and done anything to snag a man like him. All that money, all that power. You wanted it, and you didn't care who you pushed aside to get it."

Kayla could only shake her head. "You know nothing about me," she insisted.

"Kayla's right—you don't," Misty agreed. "And I didn't come out here so you could attack my sister."

Carrie ignored them and switched her attention to Dade. "Kayla could get you killed. You must know she had something to do with that attack last night. Why else would the gunman have called her?"

Because Kayla was right against Dade's back, she felt his muscles go stiff. "How did you know about that call?"

Carrie's eyes widened. For just a second. And then she shrugged. "I heard someone talking about it. Don't remember who." Her stare drilled into Dade. "How else would I have known? You're not accusing me of anything, are you?"

Dade cursed. "No, but I am telling you for the last time to leave." And to make sure that happened, he slammed the door in their faces.

"I'm sorry," Kayla said at the exact moment Dade said it, too.

Kayla managed a frustrated groan. Dade skipped the groan and made a call. To his brother, no doubt. They had to get out of there fast, now that seemingly everyone in Silver Creek knew their location.

While Dade was on the phone, Kayla looked out

the window to make sure their guests did indeed drive away. Her sister gave her one last glance before she got in the car. The glance was definitely one of disapproval. Maybe because Kayla hadn't welcomed her with open arms. Maybe because Misty thought Kayla should have defended her more.

It didn't matter which.

The bottom line was that she couldn't trust her sister. Coming here had been irresponsible at best and at worst, it had endangered Robbie.

Dade ended his call and looked out the window just as Carrie and Misty were driving away. "Get your things ready. Grayson will be out in a half hour to escort us to our ranch."

"Your ranch?" she questioned. "Your brothers aren't going to like that."

"My brothers are all lawmen, and they'd never put their personal feelings above the badge." But that troubled expression let her know that this would not be a laid-back visit. "It's only temporary, until we can make arrangements for another safe house."

Kayla turned to tell Connie the news, but she stopped. So did Dade, and he shook his head. "Think back to last night," he told her. "Was the gunman's phone call mentioned while Carrie was still there?"

Kayla tried to pick through the details of that nightmare. "I don't think so." And that led her to her next question. "You suspect her of something?"

He shook his head. "Don't know yet. I don't like that she brought up her connection to your late-husband."

Neither did Kayla. "She seemed to think I was horning in on her possible relationship with Preston. And with you."

Dade didn't deny it, and the suddenly tight jaw muscles confirmed it. "Carrie and I were together, but things ended between us months ago."

Kayla didn't doubt that Dade had ended the relationship. Nor did she doubt Carrie still had feelings for Dade. She only hoped that Carrie wouldn't risk their safety all for the sake of getting Dade back into her life.

"I'll tell Connie we're leaving soon," Kayla let him know. But the nanny had obviously overheard the news because she was already packing their things.

Kayla started to help, but then she heard Dade's phone ring again. She hurried back to the living room to make sure nothing else had gone wrong.

"Kayla's not available," Dade said. His voice and his face were tense, and she walked closer, wondering who had caused this reaction.

"Do your slimy lawyers know you called me?" Dade asked whoever was on the other end of the line. "Brennan," he mouthed to her.

Oh, God. She'd already had enough for one day without adding him to the mix. Why was the devil himself calling Dade?

Dade's mouth tightened even more. So did the grip he had on the tiny cell phone. "That sounds like a threat."

Threat. That word slammed through her like a heavyweight's fist. Charles was liberal with his threats, she had grown accustomed to them, but how dare he call now after nearly succeeding in killing her?

She marched across the room and held out her hand. "I need to talk to him."

Dade was shaking his head when she ripped the phone from his hand. "What do you want?" Kayla demanded from Charles.

"Kayla." Charles said her name in that sappy sweet way that only he could manage. "You're a hard woman to reach. I've been calling all around, trying to find you. Imagine my surprise to learn you're with one of the Ryland boys. My advice? Sleep with one eye open because the Rylands would love to slit your pretty little throat."

"What...do...you...want?" Kayla paused between each word because she was fighting to hold on to her composure. She wanted to scream. She wanted to reach through the phone and slap this vile man.

"I called to make sure Robbie was okay." The sappiness went down a notch.

"Well, he's not." She turned away from Dade when he tried to take the phone, but she did hold it so he could hear. "He's in danger because of you. Because of the assassins you hired to kill me."

"Kayla..." Silence, for a few seconds. "My differences with you would never extend to my grandson. Besides, I didn't hire any assassins."

She didn't believe him for a minute and judging from Dade's snarl, neither did he. "What kind of sick man endangers a baby just so he won't have to go to jail?"

Charles cursed. "I didn't endanger him, but I intend to find out who did." And with that, he ended the call, leaving Kayla to wonder what the heck had just happened.

"He's trying to trick me into believing he wasn't behind that attack last night," she mumbled.

Dade eased the phone from her hand and hit the end call button. He also turned so he could keep watch out the window. "Before that attack, had Brennan done anything to put Robbie at risk?"

Kayla didn't want to think of the past year or the

months before that when she was pregnant, but she forced herself to go back. To the bad memories. To the beatings that Preston had delivered. To the verbal abuse from Charles.

"No," Kayla answered. "When Charles learned I was pregnant, he seemed happy. And he was even happier when he learned I was carrying a boy. He warned Preston not to hit me when I was pregnant because he didn't want to risk a miscarriage."

That confession cut through her because it was a reminder of the life she'd led. Trapped in hell. She was so ashamed of what she'd allowed to happen.

"Don't cry," she heard Dade say, and that's when she realized there were tears in her eyes.

Kayla cursed the tears. She was tired of crying and just as tired of breaking down in front of Dade.

"I'm not a wuss," she mumbled.

"Never thought you were." He huffed and pulled her into his arms. "Shh," he whispered, his breath brushing against her hair.

It felt so good to have him hold her like this. His arms were warm and safe, but she couldn't do this. Dade was nothing like Preston, but she had to stand on her own two feet.

And that's why Kayla stepped back.

Dade looked at her, frowned and hooked his arm around her waist. He snapped her right back to him. "I'm offering you a shoulder to cry on. That's it. No strings attached."

"Oh, there are strings." And she hadn't meant to say that aloud. Dade was looking out the window, keeping watch, but she waited until his eyes angled back to her. "This attraction has strings."

"Yeah," he admitted. He brushed his mouth over hers. "I wish I could do something about that, but I can't. I want you. You want me. You're scared of a relationship, and I don't want my brothers hating you any more than they already do."

Kayla took a deep breath. "So our decision should be easy. We keep our hands off each other."

He raised an eyebrow because his hands were already on her. And he wasn't backing away. Dade leaned down and put his mouth on hers again. It was just a touch, but it blazed right through her, leaving her breathless. Making her want more.

Kayla couldn't have more. Not now. Not ever.

She put her hands on his chest to push herself back. To put some much-needed distance between his hands and her body.

But a sound stopped her cold.

Chapter 9

The blast ripped through the house.

Dade automatically drew his gun, but this wasn't another visitor. Nor were shots being fired.

This was an explosion.

"Go to Robbie," Dade told Kayla, but she was already heading in that direction.

Dade pressed the emergency response button on his phone to alert the dispatcher of a problem, and he hurried to the side of the window and looked out, not sure of what he might see. But what he saw sent his stomach to the floor.

His SUV was a fireball.

Dade knew this wasn't some kind of freak accident. No. Someone had put an explosive device in it. But Dade couldn't see that *someone*. He checked the yard and the pasture on both sides of the SUV.

No one.

It was too much to hope that the person had set the explosive and then left. In all probability, the bomber had moved to the back or sides of the house where he'd be out of sight.

And was ready to attack.

Dade did a quick check of the security system to make sure it was armed. It was. And he hurried to the kitchen so he'd have a view of the backyard and the outbuildings.

"Take Robbie and Connie and get into the bathroom," he yelled out to Kayla.

Judging from the sound of the footsteps, Kayla was already doing that. Dade hoped it would be enough to keep them safe.

He peered around the window frame and into the backyard. He didn't spot anyone, but there were a lot of places to hide. Two barns, trees and even several old watering troughs in the corral area. Because the troughs were metal, that would make them an ideal place to hide and then launch an attack.

But what was this attack about?

Had Brennan sent someone to kill Kayla?

That didn't feel right. Because if he'd wanted her dead, he could have instructed the bomber to toss the explosive closer to the house. Of course, that would have endangered Robbie. So, maybe this was some kind of ruse to get them to run. The thought had no sooner crossed his mind when he caught the scent.

Smoke.

Dade couldn't see any flames, but he could certainly smell it, and threads of thin gray smoke started to seep through the tiny gaps around the back door.

"The house is on fire!" Kayla yelled a split-second before the smoke detectors went off.

Their situation had just gone from bad to worse, because Dade knew how this was going down. He had to get Kayla and the others out of the house. Outside. Where that bomber-arsonist was waiting for them.

Later, he would kick himself for allowing this to happen, but for now he needed to take some measures to keep them all alive.

With his gun ready, Dade hurried to the other side of the house where Kayla and Connie were waiting in the doorway of the bathroom. Kayla had Robbie in her arms, but the baby was kicking and fussing.

"The fire," Kayla said, pointing through the open doorway of the second bedroom.

Dade could see the flames now. Bright orangey red, and they were licking up the side of the house. There wasn't much time.

"We have to get out," he told them, although it was clear from their faces they already knew that. The trick was *how* to get them out.

He snatched a damp towel from a hanging bar and tossed it over Robbie. Maybe it would give him some protection. "Stay low and follow me. Hurry," Dade added.

There were two exits, front and back. Plus the windows, but he couldn't use those because it would take too long to get them all out. Speed was important now. They had to hit the ground running and get behind cover. Not easy to do with a baby in tow. Maybe they would get lucky, and Dade could hold off an assassin until backup arrived.

Thank God Grayson was already on the way.

Keeping watch, Dade led them back through the living room, but he stopped to grab a backup hand-gun from his overnight bag. Unfortunately, they might need it.

"I can shoot," Kayla insisted, and she passed Robbie to the nanny so she could take the gun.

Dade wanted to say no, that he didn't want her to have to fend off an assassin, but right now he needed all the help he could get.

"We're going out front," Dade let them know.

It could be a wrong call. A gunman could be out there waiting, but his gut told him their attacker would be expecting them to leave through the back, as far away from that burning SUV as they could get.

Kayla's breath came even faster. Maybe because of the smoke that was drifting through the room. "What then?"

Another gamble. "I go first. Then Connie and the baby. We keep them between us." Protecting them from gunfire. He hoped. "Once we're off the porch, run out the gate to the right of what's left of the SUV and then drop down. There's a deep ditch out there, and we'll use it for cover."

Kayla gave a shaky nod, one that Connie repeated, but neither looked at all confident in his plan. Robbie peeked out at him, his head and body covered with the thick towel, and it nearly broke Dade's heart to think of the baby in danger. This wasn't right. No child should be in this position.

"It'll be okay, buddy," Dade whispered to the baby. He gave Kayla one last look. She was terrified, her hands shaking, but he saw the determination there, too.

She was a fighter, and that was exactly what he needed right now.

Dade hurried to the door and threw it open, not bothering to disarm the security system. Hopefully, the alarm would unnerve their attacker in some small way. He looked out, didn't see anyone waiting to attack, so he motioned for them to follow.

The blast of cold air came right at them the moment they stepped onto the porch. It was mixed with the stench of the fire, and the smoke from both the flames and the SUV. The SUV was already a goner, and it wouldn't be long before the wood frame house was reduced to ashes.

Dade moved quickly, maneuvering Connie and Robbie onto the porch and then the steps. Kayla was right behind them, not as close as he wanted but that's because she was keeping watch behind them. Good move. Because their attacker could come through the back of the house and ambush them.

"Hurry," Dade instructed Connie even though he doubted she could hear him over the clanging security alarms.

With Robbie in her arms, Connie stepped down into the ditch. Dade looked back to motion to Kayla to hurry as well, but she wasn't looking at him. Her body snapped to the right side of the house. So did her aim.

And she fired.

Everything happened fast. Dade got a split-second glimpse of the person dressed head to toe in black before Kayla's bullet sent the gunman ducking for cover on the opposite side of the house where the fire was blazing.

Kayla held her position. Her weapon raised and ready.

"Get down here!" Dade shouted to her.

He had already aimed at their attacker, and it didn't take long before the guy lifted his head again. He fired right at Dade.

Kayla yelled for him to get down. Dade did the same to her again, but she didn't move until a bullet came her way.

Hell.

She was out there in the open, too easy of a target. And she seemed to be frozen. Or maybe she was trying to use herself as a diversion so the gunman wouldn't send any bullets toward Robbie and Connie.

He didn't intend to let Kayla sacrifice herself.

Dade glanced at Connie to make sure she was deep in the ditch. She was. And she was using her own body to protect Robbie. They were away from the house fire and the SUV. The baby was as safe as he could be, so Dade did something about making sure Kayla didn't get killed.

He sprinted to her and hooked his arm around her waist. But he wasn't fast enough.

The bullets came flying right at them.

Even with the deafening noise of the security alarm, Kayla had no trouble hearing the shots. Or seeing their attacker as he leaned out and fired.

She returned fire just as Dade pulled her off the porch and to the ground. He scrambled to get them to the side of the house. Opposite the gunman and so close to the fire that she could feel the heat from the flames.

But she was also yards away from her precious baby.

Kayla wanted to run to Connie and him. She needed to make sure they were all right, but if she stepped out, their attacker would kill her. She wasn't afraid for her own life, but if she got killed, she wouldn't be there to protect Robbie.

"Keep watch behind us," Dade shouted to her.

Oh, God.

She hadn't even considered that the gunman might run to the back of the house and shoot at them through the flames and smoke. If he did that, at least he wouldn't be near the ditch, but again she couldn't take the risk of Dade and her being gunned down. She turned, putting her back up against Dade's, and Kayla held her breath, waiting. And praying.

Somehow, she had to get her baby safely out of this.

She cursed herself for coming back to testify, but sooner or later it would have come down to this. A confrontation with Charles was inevitable, and she'd only delayed things when she went into hiding.

The winter wind shifted and sent the black smoke right at them, spreading it all around—not just the house but also the yard. The gunman could use it as a shield, but worse, the smoke burned her throat and lungs. Kayla started to cough. Not good. Because that would give away their position.

"We have to move," Dade insisted.

Kayla knew he was right, but there seemed no place to go. The fire was directly behind them, and if they went into the front yard, the gunman would pick them off. That left the side. No fence. No buildings they could duck behind. However, there were some pecan trees about thirty feet away. If they could get to those, they could use the trees for protection and still be able to see the ditch.

"Stay low and move fast," Dade instructed, and he tipped his head to the trees.

Kayla nodded and prayed they could make it. Dade gave her one last glance, and he seemed to be trying to apologize to her. But Kayla was the one who'd gotten them into this mess. She hoped later she would have the chance to tell Dade how sorry she was for that.

"Now," Dade ordered. He, too, was coughing now, and she hoped the move would at least put them out of the smoke's path.

Each step was a victory, and she counted them off in her head while keeping watch over her shoulder. They only made it six steps before she saw the figure emerge from the smoke. She and Dade just kept running, but Kayla kept watch behind them.

At first their attacker seemed to be part of the smoke itself, but she realized that's because he wore black clothes. Only his face was visible. Definitely a man, tall and thin, and he had the cold, hard look of a killer.

The man took aim at them and fired. Just as Dade dragged her to the ground. The dirt was like ice, and the cold and adrenaline slammed through her. Her heart rate spiked when the bullet slammed into the ground just inches from her.

Dade pivoted and fired at the shooter. He didn't waste any time. He latched onto her wrist with his left hand and yanked her hard, shoving her behind the tree. Dade followed, readjusting his aim, but he didn't fire.

Kayla peered out from the pecan tree. She could no longer see the gunman, but thankfully the smoke wasn't obliterating her view of the ditch. Or the road—where she saw the approaching vehicle.

"There's a truck," she said to Dade.

His gaze whipped in that direction, but Kayla pinned her attention to the area where she'd last seen their attacker.

Where the heck was he?

As menacing as it was to see him step out of that wall of smoke, not knowing where he was chilled her to the bone. She kept her gun ready and tried to steady both her heart and her trembling hands.

"It's Grayson's truck," she heard Dade say.

Relief flooded through her, but it was short-lived. That's because a bullet slammed into the tree just inches from her. Kayla jumped back, bashing into Dade, but both of them somehow managed to keep hold of their guns.

Volleying glances between the direction of that last shot and the road, Kayla spotted the Silver Creek patrol truck that had come to a stop just twenty yards or so from the house. Grayson was behind the wheel and he was alone. She wished he'd brought the entire deputy force, but at the moment she would take whatever she could get.

"Keep watch," Dade ordered, and he took out his phone.

Because of the shrill security alarms, she couldn't hear much of what Dade was saying, but he'd no doubt called Grayson because she could see him on the phone, as well. She hoped they were figuring a way out of this nightmare.

There was movement just to the right of the smoke, and Kayla spotted the gunman again. He aimed and fired. The bullet flew past her, so close that she could have sworn she felt the heat from it.

Kayla reached out from the tree and fired back. With her shaky aim, she doubted she had hit anything other than the burning house, but she wanted to keep the shooter at bay. She didn't want to give him a chance to get closer to the ditch.

Dade slapped his phone shut and shoved it back into his jeans pocket. "We need to keep the gunman busy. Mason and the fire department are on the way, but Grayson's not going to wait for him. He'll go ahead and get Connie and Robbie away from here."

Kayla couldn't even manage a *thank God,* but she was beyond thankful that Grayson had put her baby first. She wanted Robbie far away from the bullets. Still, how did Grayson plan to get them into his truck?

"Stay here," Dade told her. That was it, all the warning she got before he dived out from cover and behind the adjacent tree.

The gunman fired at Dade.

Of course.

And she realized this was exactly what Dade wanted their attacker to do.

Dade moved again, jumping the narrow space between cover and the next tree. From the corner of her eye, she saw Grayson's truck speed forward.

The gunman saw it, too.

And he turned in that direction.

Kayla forced her hand to steady, and she fired a shot. The gunman jerked back as if he'd been shot and disappeared into the smoke again.

Grayson came to a stop, and the passenger's door flew open. Connie must have figured out quickly what was going on because it was only a few seconds before she came out of the ditch. With Robbie clutched close to her, she jumped into the truck. The moment the door was closed, Grayson sped away.

Kayla was so relieved that tears sprang to her eyes, but she blinked them back. Yes, her baby was safe, but now Dade and she had to finish this.

She glanced over at Dade when he motioned toward the backyard. At first Kayla didn't see the gunman, but she picked through the smoke and outbuildings and finally spotted him. He was crouched behind a large metal container in the corral area.

"You stay here," Dade mouthed. "I'll circle around behind him."

Kayla wanted to scream *no!*, that he should wait for backup, but Dade had already turned his back on her and was darting to another tree. He continued that way until he reached the last tree, and then he dropped to the ground.

When her lungs began to ache, Kayla forced herself to breathe, even though the air was clogged with smoke. She kept her wrist braced to help with the jitters, and she prayed her aim would be good enough to help Dade and keep him alive.

He was risking so much for Robbie and for her.

And the risks continued.

Kayla's heart started beating like crazy when she lost sight of Dade. The gunman was still there, lurking behind the container. He wasn't far enough out in the open to give her a clean shot, and she couldn't take one for fear of accidentally hitting Dade.

She spotted more movement. Not from the gunman, but from Dade. He was creeping along the side of the wooden corral fence. Because she could see him, she did something about creating a diversion. Kayla fired a shot just to the left of the container. It worked.

The gunman shifted in that direction.

It wasn't much, but it was enough. Dade vaulted over the fence and raced across the corral. Kayla was terrified and could only watch and wait. If necessary, she could fire another diversion shot.

It wasn't necessary.

Dade made it all the way to the container before the gunman whirled around. Too late. Dade knocked the gun from his hand and jammed his own weapon against the man's head.

Kayla broke into a run toward them, and she kept her gun aimed and ready. Dade made eye contact with her. Just a glance. Just enough to reassure her that this attack had come to an end.

But then she got a good look at the gunman's face.

A face she recognized.

And Kayla realized this wasn't over. No. This was just the beginning.

Chapter 10

Every muscle in Dade's body was primed for a fight. Yeah, Kayla and he had managed to capture the person who'd tried to kill them, but that person wasn't talking.

Danny Flynn, however, was smirking.

Despite the handcuffs and ankle shackles, the SOB *lounged* in the interview room while Carrie and another medic bandaged the graze wound on the top of his left shoulder. It wasn't a serious enough injury for him to go to the hospital. Besides, Dade didn't want this snake out of his sight.

"If this were the old days, I could beat a confession out of him," Mason mumbled. His brother was right behind Kayla and him, and all three of them were glaring at the hired gun who had refused to answer a single question, much less admit his guilt in nearly killing Kayla and Dade.

"I wish I could just slap that stupid smile right off his face," Kayla added, earning as close to an approving nod as Mason ever gave. "He put my baby in danger, and by God, he's going to pay for that."

Dade felt the same way. But Flynn had already lawyered up, and that meant Brennan would probably pay the bill for the attorney who was on his way from San Antonio. Somehow, they had to get Flynn to confess that Brennan had hired him to kill Kayla.

If that's what had really happened.

The pieces all seemed to point in that direction, but there was a niggling doubt in the back of Dade's mind. Maybe that had something to do with the way Carrie kept glancing back at him. Dade didn't trust her, and he was trusting her less and less with each passing second.

Kayla groaned again, and glanced first at Dade's phone, which he held in his hand. Then, she glanced at the dispatcher who was seated behind the front counter.

"Grayson will call as soon as he has Connie and Robbie settled," Dade reminded her.

That didn't soothe her. Nothing short of holding her son would, and Dade couldn't give that to her right now. Grayson hadn't wanted to bring Robbie and Connie back into town where they might be spotted by one of Brennan's cronies or someone who might inadvertently reveal their location. Instead, Grayson had decided to go ahead and establish a new safe house, somewhere, and Dade wouldn't know the location until everything was in place.

Kayla glanced up at him. There was no longer fear in her eyes. Just the anger fueled by what had to be a bad adrenaline crash. "I don't know how much more I can take of this," she whispered, leaning closer so that only Dade would hear.

"I know." And even though he knew it would earn him a glare from Mason, Dade slipped his arm around her and eased her out of the doorway and away from Flynn's line of sight.

But Mason didn't glare. Well, not at Kayla and him anyway. He glared at Flynn.

The medics finished and packed up their equipment. Tommy Watters came out first and nodded a farewell to them. Tommy was fresh out of his EMT training, and this was probably his first gunshot wound. He seemed in a hurry to get out of there.

Not Carrie, though.

She stopped, snared Dade's gaze. "How did this joker find you?" Carrie asked as if she hadn't already considered the possibilities.

"He followed you." And Dade didn't make it sound like a question. It was not only possible, it was likely that Flynn had followed either Carrie and Misty or Winston and Alan.

Carrie shook her head but not before sending a venomous glance at Kayla. Probably because Dade still had his arm around her.

"No one followed me," Carrie insisted. She looked around as if to see who was listening. "But her sister made some calls when we were driving out there. Why don't you ask her about it?" And with that toss under the bus, Carrie strolled away.

Dade cursed. He would ask Misty all right, but he hated the concern that created in Kayla's eyes. She had enough on her plate without suspecting her sister's involvement in these attacks.

"I'll find out where Kayla's sister is," Mason volunteered. "And I'll see if I can come up with something you can use for leverage to get this dirtbag to spill his guts."

The dirtbag was still smirking. If Flynn had any pain whatsoever from his injury, he certainly didn't show it. No fear, either. Probably because he thought his lawyers would be able to wrangle a deal, but there was only one thing that would make Dade deal with Flynn: for Flynn to hand them Brennan on a silver platter.

Kayla caught onto Dade's arm when he started to move around her and go into the interrogation room. "Can you call Grayson before you question Flynn?" she asked.

Dade didn't have to debate this, even though he knew Grayson was no doubt busy. Still, Kayla had to have some reassurance. It'd been nearly two hours since Grayson had driven off with Connie and Robbie.

Dade shut the door between Flynn and them and pressed in Grayson's number on his cell. His brother answered on the first ring, and Kayla moved closer so she could hear.

"Everything's okay," Grayson assured him before Dade could even speak. "I have Connie and the baby at a safe location."

"Where?" Kayla immediately asked.

But Grayson didn't give her an immediate answer. He hesitated big-time. "I'd rather not say. We obviously have some kind of breach in security. Maybe a leak in communication, and until I'm sure it's safe, I don't want to tell anyone where we are."

Tears sprang to Kayla's eyes. "But I need to see my baby."

"And you will," Grayson answered. "Just give me a few more hours to make sure I've made things as safe for Robbie as I can."

"How can you do that?" Kayla asked. Her voice was trembling now, and she was on the verge of a full-fledged cry.

"Nate is on his way there to the sheriff's building so he can run a bug sweep. I want to make sure Brennan or one of his henchmen didn't plant some kind of listening or tracking device. Then, Nate will interview all four people who went to that safe house because one of them could have leaked your location."

So that meant Winston, Alan, Carrie and Misty would all be brought back in. Good. Dade was to the point where he didn't trust any of them.

"When I'm sure it's safe to do so, I'll arrange to have Dade bring you here. Okay?" Grayson asked.

It took her several seconds to agree. "Okay." It certainly wasn't the arrangement she wanted, but it would have to do. Robbie's safety came first.

"I'll have Nate call you when he's done," Dade told his brother, and he ended the call. He turned to Kayla. "Why don't you wait in my office while I talk to Flynn?"

Her breath rushed out with her words. "I don't want to. I want to hear what he has to say."

Dade couldn't have her in the interrogation room with Flynn. He had to follow the rules. Well, the basic ones anyway. Plus, Kayla was on the verge of losing it, and if she went after Flynn and tried to slap that smile off his face, she might get hurt.

"You can watch and listen in the room next door," Dade let her know. "There's a two-way mirror."

Kayla looked as if she might argue, but Dade brushed a kiss on her lips. "I won't be long." And he ushered her into the observation room.

Because the camera was already positioned near the two-way mirror to record Flynn's interview in the other room, Dade went ahead and turned it on to start the recording. He was about to go back to Flynn when he saw Mason making his way back toward him.

"I just got off the phone with Nate's contact at SAPD," Mason explained. "Flynn has a teenaged son that he calls Little Dan. Apparently, he's the apple of Flynn's wormy little eyes. The kid just turned sixteen and has a juvenile record. When he was in lockup last year, Little Dan lost it. Had some kind of panic attack because he's claustrophobic. My advice is play dirty with that bit of info and see where it gets you."

Dade would. Flynn certainly hadn't minded the dirty play when he fired those shots around Robbie and Kayla, so Dade would give him a little of his own medicine.

Flynn sat, waiting. Oh, yeah. He was a pro at this. Dade knew the man was thirty-six and had been arrested four times for assault and breaking-and-entering. However, there had been no arrests in the past two years since he'd been on Charles Brennan's payroll.

"You're wasting your time," Flynn volunteered the moment Dade stepped inside. His smile widened, revealing tobacco-stained, chipped teeth. With the yellowy gray in his dark hair, Flynn looked much older than his years. "I'm not saying anything to you."

Dade read him his rights. Then, he swiveled the empty metal chair around and sat in it so that he could casually drape his arms over the back. He wanted to look as laid-back as Flynn, even though inside him there was a bad storm brewing. Dade really wanted to beat this guy senseless for trying to kill Kayla.

"You don't need to say anything," Dade said. "I'll just keep you company until your lawyer arrives. Then we'll process you and put you in a holding cell." Dade forced a smile. "Look at you. So relaxed. Not bothered at all by any of this. Nothing like your son. He's really making a fuss over at SAPD."

Flynn's smirk evaporated. "What the hell does that mean?"

Dade shrugged. Paused long enough to get Flynn to squirm. "SAPD picked up Little Dan about a half hour ago."

Flynn would have come across the table if it hadn't been for the shackles tethering him to the chair. "You got no right to touch my boy."

"Oh, yeah? Well, SAPD disagrees. An eyewitness tied Little Dan to the shootings." Dade shook his head, feigning concern. "Accessory to attempted murder. And from what I hear from my brother over at SAPD, they're going to charge your *boy* as an adult."

Flynn made a feral sound and violently shook the chains. "I need to call him *now.*"

Another headshake. "You got one phone call, and you made it to your lawyer."

"You can't do this." Flynn's jaw was iron stiff. "Little Dan can't stand to be penned up. He gets these fits, and he'll need his meds. He'll go crazy without 'em."

Dade made a sound of understanding. "Yeah, that probably explains why he tried to call you when he was picked up. But, of course, we have your phone in evidence, so his call went to voice mail. Too bad. I heard the officers had to get rough with him to put him in that cell."

Flynn opened his mouth again as if to make that animal sound, but then he squeezed his eyes shut and groaned. "He had nothing to do with this. Let him go."

"Can't do that. Attempted murder of a baby, a witness in protective custody and a deputy sheriff. Those charges aren't just going away."

Flynn's breath came out in short angry spurts, and the veins popped out on his forehead. The seconds crawled by, and Dade hoped Flynn would say something, anything, before the lawyer waltzed in and uncovered Dade's lie. The lie would hold up in court because cops were allowed to give false information during interrogation. However, the lawyer would no doubt advise Flynn to stay quiet.

"What do you want to hear?" Flynn growled.

"The truth, of course." And Dade waited and did some praying.

"My son had nothing to do with this," Flynn repeated. "So as soon as I've had my say, you'll make a call to get him released. Deal?"

Despite the time eating away at him, Dade pretended to think about that. "If you convince me that Little Dan is innocent, then I'll make that call."

Flynn's dirt-brown eyes narrowed. His mouth shook because his teeth were clenched so tight, but he finally nodded. "Charles Brennan hired me and Raymond Salvetti to scare his daughter-in-law. To do that, we had to find her, so we had someone watching her sister. I followed her out to the house where you and Kayla were hiding out."

Oh, that didn't help Dade's anger to hear it aloud, and

he wondered how Kayla was doing with this. Maybe she would come bursting into the room.

"Scare?" Dade challenged. "You fired shots at her. You tried to kill her."

"No," Flynn quickly disagreed. "The orders were to scare her, but Salvetti got trigger-happy and fired into the estate. That was his doing, not mine. Hell, I could have blown up the house today with her in it, but those weren't my orders. I was just supposed to grab that baby and get out of there fast."

It took a moment for Dade to tamp down the emotion, the anger. Nope, it was rage. He hated this slimy piece of filth in front of him.

"Why take the baby?" Even though Dade was sure he already knew the answer, he wanted this on tape.

Flynn dragged in a weary breath. "For leverage. Brennan figured his daughter-in-law would do anything, including keeping her mouth shut, to get that kid back."

Yeah, that was what Dade had expected, but he hadn't expected for it to feel as if someone had slugged him. Robbie and Kayla could have been hurt or killed.

"Why did Salvetti call Kayla's cell?" Dade pressed.

"To make her look suspicious." Flynn cursed. "But Salvetti wasn't too bright because he wasn't supposed to call me."

Well, that explained that, and Dade believed the man was telling the truth. "What about Kayla's sister? Was that call to set her up, too?"

"I don't know." Another quick answer. "Salvetti was taking his orders directly from Brennan, not me. So, I don't know why he'd call anyone. Now, it's your turn. Phone your cop buddies and get my boy out of lockup."

Dade met him eye to eye. "If I do that, you'll just recant all of this later. What I want is proof that links you and Salvetti to Brennan."

Flynn looked up at the ceiling as if seeking divine intervention. Dade just waited him out, hoping the lawyer or Kayla wouldn't come barging in.

"There's something that ties Salvetti to a crime. If you dig hard enough, I'm betting you can connect the dots from Salvetti to Brennan. But if I tell you, you've got to promise witness protection for me and my boy."

"You know I can't make a promise like that, but I'll see what I can do." And Dade would. Because as much as Dade despised Flynn, he despised Brennan more and wanted to put him away for life. "What proof do you have?"

Flynn swallowed hard. "There's a wall safe in my house in San Antonio. Inside there's a gun with Salvetti's fingerprints. That gun was used in a murder."

Dade heard the voices in the front part of the building and figured the lawyer had arrived. "Connect the dots for me," Dade insisted. "What does this gun and murder have to do with Brennan?"

Flynn leaned closer. "Salvetti has worked for Brennan a long time. Longer than me. And he was working for Brennan when this murder happened. My advice? Dig into it. Now, *please* call SAPD."

Dade heard the hurried footsteps coming down the hall. Two sets. One belonged to Mason, he soon learned, and the others belonged to Darcy Burkhart, an attorney who had recently moved to Silver Creek. But Darcy was no stranger to Dade. No. She had been one of Brennan's attorneys during the initial investigation.

"This interview is over," the petite brunette said. She

was a good foot shorter than Mason who loomed over her, but she still managed to have an air of authority. "I need to consult with my client."

Dade got to his feet. "Your client just confessed to an assortment of felonies."

Darcy stayed calm but fired a nasty glance at Flynn. "I need to speak to him *alone*."

Dade nodded and used the remote device on the wall to turn off the video recorder as he was required to do. Client-attorney privilege. But Dade thought he might already have what he needed without any additional statement from Flynn.

"Make that call," Flynn shouted out to him as Dade headed for the door.

"I will," Dade lied.

He stepped out into the hall with Mason. The lawyer went in, and Dade waited until she'd shut the door before he said anything.

"We'll need a search warrant for Flynn's safe," Dade instructed. "And we need Brennan back in custody."

"It's already in the works," Mason assured him. "SAPD will pick up Brennan, and they'll execute the search warrant the moment they have it in their hands. You think this will link us to Brennan?"

"I hope so." And Dade hated that he sounded so pessimistic, especially when he realized that Kayla was right behind Mason and hanging on his every word.

"Flynn did confess that Charles hired him," Kayla said.

"Yeah." And that would get Brennan back in custody. Temporarily anyway.

Because she looked ready to fall flat on her face, Dade caught onto her arm and led her down the hall toward his office. "This Darcy Burkhart is a tough attorney," Dade let Kayla know. "She could somehow get it all thrown out. That's why it's important for us to connect this so-called gun to a murder and then to Brennan. That's physical evidence and could be a helluva lot better than just a confession from a man with a criminal record."

"So-called?" she repeated. "You think Flynn lied about that?"

Oh, man. He hated to see her hopes smashed like this.

Dade took her into his office, made her sit in the chair across from his desk. He wished he could give her a shot of whiskey from the bottle he kept in his bottom drawer, but she would need a clear head because she still had to make a statement about the shooting. Instead, he handed her a bottle of water that he'd taken from the small fridge behind his desk.

"I'm sorry," Kayla mumbled. She drank the water as if it were a cure for what ailed her, gulping it down so fast that it watered her eyes. Or maybe that was just more tears on the way.

Dade wanted to pull her into his arms for a long hug. He wanted her to lean on him. But that would be a dangerous mix right now because of the attraction. He settled for skimming his fingers down her arm.

"Everything new we learn just seems to complicate things," she mumbled.

Yeah, it did. Dade would have preferred Flynn to give a clear, no-strings-attached confession, but instead he'd added this mystery gun to the mix. It might be critical, and it might be a smokescreen. But someone had to investigate it. That tied up manpower and resources when all those resources should be focused on picking up Brennan and canceling his bond.

Dade moved some things off the corner of his desk so he could sit. Not exactly touching Kayla but close enough. But Dade didn't watch where he was sliding a stack of folders, and they bumped into the framed photo, knocking it over.

Kayla reached out and picked it up. She started to put it back, but she froze, staring at the picture.

"It's my maternal grandfather, Sheriff Chet McLaurin." The shot had been taken outside a brand-spanking-new sheriff's office. Chet was smiling that good-ol'-boy half smile of his with his white Stetson slung low on his weathered face. "He was a legend around here before he was killed."

"Killed?" she said under her breath. Kayla continued to study the photo.

"Yeah. He was shot twenty years ago while investigating a robbery. His killer was never identified or caught." And after all these years, that sliced right through his heart. His brothers', too. In fact, it's the reason all the Rylands had gone into law enforcement. A case they couldn't solve.

A wound that couldn't be healed.

"I've seen this photo," she said, tapping it.

Surprised, Dade took it from her and had another look, even though he knew every detail. "There's one in Grayson's office."

She shook her head. "No, I saw it in Charles's office."

"What?" And Dade couldn't ask it fast enough. "What was Brennan doing with that picture?"

"I don't know." She had more water and licked her lips. "About eighteen months ago, I was sneaking around in his files. Looking for anything I could use to get Preston and him arrested. I knew that was the only way I could get out of…my situation. I'd just learned I was pregnant, and I was looking for a way to get out."

Dade felt it again. That jolt of hatred for the Brennan men who'd made Kayla's life hell.

"I remember the picture because it seemed out of place. I mean, there were other photos. Some mug shots. Some taken from a camera with a long-range lens. And then there was this one of the Silver Creek Sheriff's office. I looked at it a long time, trying to figure out why Charles had it."

Dade did the same now. He tried to see it with a fresh eye. His father was in the shot. His mother dressed in her Sunday best. Him, and all his brothers.

"Who's that?" Kayla asked, tapping the image of the person standing next to him.

"My brother Gage." Dade didn't want to feel the resentment for his younger sibling, but he did. "He left home not long after high school and didn't come back." Gage had run out on the family. Just like their father. "He joined the CIA and was killed on a deep-cover assignment."

"Oh, I'm so sorry," Kayla said softly.

Dade shrugged. "Thanks," he mumbled and got his mind off Gage and back on the picture taken all those years ago.

Next to Gage was Mel, the current deputy, who was then just starting her rookie year. Two deputies, long since retired. The then mayor, Ford Herrington, who was now a state senator. And then Dade's attention landed on the man at the far right of the happy group.

Winston Calhoun.

He was the assistant D.A. back then and had every right to be in the photo. After all, it was the grand opening of the Silver Creek law-enforcement facility. But because of Dade's recent suspicions about Winston, his presence in the photo seemed a little menacing.

"Where are the files that had this photo?" Dade asked.

"In the storage room off Charles's office. But it's no longer there," she quickly added. "I went back about a week later to see if I could find anything, and all the files were gone. I'm pretty sure Charles figured out I'd been snooping in there."

Dade didn't doubt it. Heck, Brennan probably had surveillance and knew what Kayla had done. It sickened him to think that the only reason Brennan had let her live was because she was carrying his grandchild.

The picture probably wasn't enough to get an additional search warrant for Brennan's place, but Dade would question the man about it when SAPD took him back into custody.

Which hopefully had already happened.

He reached for his phone to find out the status of that, but it buzzed before he could make the call.

"It's me," Mason greeted in his usual growl. "Brace yourself, little brother, because we got a problem. A big one. And the problem's name is none other than Misty Wallace."

Chapter 11

"What's wrong?" Kayla asked the second Dade got off the phone.

His mouth went tight, and he squeezed his eyes shut for a moment before he answered. "It's Misty," he finally said. "Grayson had flagged her bank account. It's routine when monitoring a suspect who might try to flee."

Kayla was about to argue that *suspect* label, but Dade's expression had her holding her tongue and waiting.

"About twenty minutes ago, Misty cleaned out her account. A detective at SAPD immediately tried to call her, but she didn't answer her cell. So, the detective called her apartment. Misty's roommate answered and told him that Misty had packed up and left." Dade paused. "Kayla, she stole her roommate's handgun."

Oh, mercy. Not this. Not now. What the heck was

Misty thinking? This would only make her look guilt-
ier. If that was possible.

"SAPD is looking for her," Dade added.

Of course they would, and then they would drag
her back in for questioning. Kayla didn't know which
she feared most—that her sister was in danger or that
Misty was running because she'd had some part in the
two attacks.

Kayla's breath broke before she could choke back
the sound, and just like that, Dade was there, gathering her into his arms.

"She's my sister," Kayla managed to say. And that
seemed to be enough explanation because Dade only
made a sympathetic sound of agreement. "I want her
safe. I don't want her out there running around with a
gun."

Dade nodded. "We'll find her."

The fear must have flashed through her eyes because
Dade shook his head. "Don't go there," he insisted.
"We'll find her and *talk* to her. That's all."

"Please," she begged. "Tell them not to shoot her."

"No need to tell them that because the cops know
she's scared and on the run. They're trained to handle
situations like this, Kayla."

His voice was so calm, so reassuring, and Kayla
believed him because the alternative was too hard to
accept.

"It'll be okay," he promised.

Dade brushed a kiss on her temple and pulled back
so they were eye to eye. That was always a dangerous
stance for them because it also meant they were close
to being mouth to mouth.

"I can't believe this is happening," Kayla whispered.

That included Misty, the attacks and, yes, even this bi-
zarre attraction to Dade. "I'm terrified for my sister.
And I miss Robbie so much. It breaks my heart to know
that he's in danger. He's just a baby."

"Yeah." He used the pad of his thumb to swipe a
strand of hair away from her face.

Like everything else, the embrace, the temple kiss,
the simple touch—all those things seemed far too intimate. Ditto for the way Dade dipped his head. Kayla
braced herself for a bone-melting kiss, but with Dade's
mouth and breath closing in on her, he only shook his
head.

"Let me call Grayson and see how close he is to
securing things with the new safe house." Dade took
out his cell, pressed in some numbers and then put the
call on Speaker. "Grayson, it's me," he said when his
brother answered.

"Everything is okay," he immediately said. "I have
two Texas Rangers en route, and once they're here, I can
head out to pick up some supplies. Then we can make
arrangements to bring Kayla out here."

She heard what Grayson said, but it was hard to concentrate because in the background she also heard her
son. Robbie was laughing.

"I need to say hello to him," Kayla insisted.

Grayson didn't argue, and soon the sound of Robbie's laughter got closer and closer.

"Hi, Robbie. It's Mommy." Kayla tried to keep the
fear out of her voice. Not easy to do. But she obviously
succeeded because Robbie squealed with delight.

"He's being a really good boy," Connie let her know.

That put a lump in her throat. "Tell him I love him

and that I'll see him soon." Kayla moved away from the phone so that Robbie wouldn't hear her cry.

Dade talked with his brother a while longer, and judging from the conversation, they were working out how she would be transported from town and out to the new safe house. Of course, she would have to be back in Silver Creek to testify.

If Charles didn't get another trial delay, that is.

"You okay?" Dade asked when he ended the call. He slipped his phone in his pocket and pulled her into his arms.

"No." Kayla didn't even try to lie to Dade. Besides, he could see her tears. He kissed one of them off her cheek.

"Kids are tough," he told her. "Robbie probably thinks this is some kind of adventure. He's safe, and right now that's all that matters."

Dade was right. Thanks to Grayson and him, they had her son out of danger. And she, too, was safe in Dade's arms.

"I keep ending up here," she whispered.

The corner of his mouth lifted. "Yeah. Eventually, we'll have to do something about that." But it didn't sound as if he intended for that *something* to include staying away from her.

Just the opposite.

Dade lowered his head. Leaned in—

Just as there was a knock at the door. They flew apart, but not before their visitor got a good look at their near lip-lock.

"Nate," Dade greeted his twin.

Nate nodded, but there was no greeting in his eyes or the rest of his body. He obviously didn't approve of what he'd walked in on. And why would he? Nate still lumped her in the same category as Preston and Charles.

"We located Brennan," Nate explained, sounding all-cop. "A Texas Ranger is escorting him here."

Funny, when Kayla had seen Nate on the computer screen during Misty's interview, he'd looked calm and in charge, but in person she could see the nerves right there at the surface. Nate had that Ryland intensity in spades.

"His lawyer has filed a motion to throw out Flynn's confession," Nate added.

Dade cursed. "On what grounds?"

"Ms. Burkhart claims that Flynn isn't mentally stable, that he's had several stints in psychiatric facilities, and that when you interrogated him, he was in need of his medication. She also says you exacerbated Flynn's condition by lying to him about his son."

Kayla wanted to curse, as well. "Please tell me he's not going to walk," she begged. "The man tried to kill us, and he put my baby in grave danger."

Something went through Nate's ice-gray eyes. Sympathy maybe because he, too, was a parent. "I'll do everything humanly possible to keep him behind bars." Nate wearily scrubbed his hand over his face. A gesture that reminded her of Dade. They weren't identical, but they were alike in so many ways.

"What about the gun Flynn mentioned?" Dade asked. "Is the lawyer trying to kill the warrant?"

"She wasn't fast enough." Nate didn't smile exactly, but there was some relief in his expression. "SAPD already has it, and officers are headed over to Flynn's place now. The warrant allows them to search only the safe, though, so let's hope Flynn wasn't lying."

Yes, and while they were hoping, Kayla added that maybe the gun could be used to put Flynn and Charles behind bars for the rest of their lives.

"Is this lawyer working to keep Charles out on bond?" Kayla asked.

"Probably," Nate admitted. "But until the question of Flynn's sanity is decided, we can act in good faith and hold Brennan. Of course, with his connections he might be able to find a judge who'll speed through the sanity decision."

So, they might not have much time.

"I'd like to be there when you interrogate Charles," Kayla insisted. "Maybe I can rile him enough that he'll admit to something wrong."

Nate shook his head and moved back into the hall. "Can't do that. For one thing, Darcy Burkhart won't allow it." He said the attorney's name like the worst of profanity.

Dade stepped out, as well, and when Kayla looked into the hall, she saw why.

Charles was there.

"We have to follow the rules to a tee," Nate said to her, his voice a whisper now. "I don't want to give Brennan a chance at a free pass." But then Nate stepped aside. "However, there is no law against you speaking to your former father-in-law if you happened to run into him. Like now, for instance."

Kayla nodded. "Thank you." It was a concession that Nate didn't have to allow her. Now, she only hoped she could do something with it.

She maneuvered around Dade and Nate and started up the hall. There was a Texas Ranger on Charles's right side, and he stopped when Charles did. Charles had the gall to smile at her.

"Kayla, pretty as a picture," he purred.

"I was nearly a dead picture. Someone tried to kill me again." She didn't wait for him to deny it. Kayla got closer and leaned in. "You might think you hold the cards, but you don't. If you ever want to see your grandson again, then the hired guns stop now."

Of course, she never intended for Robbie to be in the same vicinity as his grandfather, but her son was the only leverage she had.

His smile faded. "I would never endanger my grandson. And I will see him, one way or another."

"Not if you're behind bars," she fired back. "Your hired gun rolled on you, Charles. Danny Flynn said you sent him to kill me."

The anger flashed across his face. Then, quickly left as the smile had done. "Flynn's a lunatic and a liar. I fired him, you know. Weeks ago. And this is all to get back at me."

She hated that the lies came so easily to him. And hated the sound of the woman's footsteps behind her. Kayla knew it was the attorney, and the woman would soon put an end to this.

"Who helped you put these attacks together?" Kayla demanded. And she prayed he didn't say her sister's name. "Was it Winston Calhoun?"

"This conversation is over," Ms. Burkhart said before she even reached them.

But Kayla didn't give up. "Who was it?" She latched hard onto Charles's arm. "Carrie Collins?"

Still no reaction, so Kayla tried again. "Alan Bowers?"

Now, there was a reaction.

Charles's smile returned.

"Alan," he mumbled. "Now, there's a man with secrets." He leaned in, put his mouth to her ear. "Ask him if he's had anything to drink lately. I think he prefers scotch on the rocks."

Kayla pulled back, shook her head. "What the heck does that mean?"

But Charles didn't get a chance to answer. His attorney wrenched him out of Kayla's grip and marched him down the hall toward the interrogation room. Nate and the Ranger were right behind them.

"What was that about?" Dade asked her.

Kayla had to shake her head again. "I'm not sure. Charles could be trying to put the blame on Alan."

Or maybe that's where the blame should be.

"I'll talk to Alan again," Dade assured her. And he phoned the other deputy, Melissa Garza. Mel, as Dade called her. He asked her to round up the available suspects for another interrogation.

Good, Kayla wanted them questioned again, but this could all be part of the game. No accomplice. Just Charles and his two gunmen: Flynn and Salvetti. One of them dead, and the other was in custody. She wanted to believe that meant things were looking up, but they were dealing with Charles here.

Dade started down the hall, but first he grabbed the picture of his grandfather from his desk. "I'd like to try a little experiment," he explained.

He caught up with the others and ducked into the interrogation room where Mason and Nate were with Charles and his attorney. He handed the picture to Nate and then whispered something that Kayla couldn't hear.

"Let's watch." Dade caught onto her and led her into the room with the two-way mirror.

She watched as Nate set the photo in front of Charles. Nate didn't say a word, even when both Charles and Ms. Burkhart gave him questioning glances.

"What am I supposed to do with this?" Charles asked.

"Look at it," Nate explained. "See if you recognize anyone."

Nate suddenly looked calm and in control. Mason, on the other hand, looked like...himself. As if he preferred to beat a confession out of Charles. Kayla was in Mason's camp right now and wished that could happen.

Charles did pick up the picture, and a thin smile moved over his mouth. "Your grandfather," he said without hesitation. "A complex man."

Because her arm was next to Dade's, she felt him stiffen. Inside the interrogation room, Mason and Nate had similar reactions.

"You knew Chet McLaurin?" Nate asked.

"What does this have to do with my client's current situation?" Ms. Burkhart interrupted.

"Nothing," Charles assured her, and he pushed the photo away.

Dade cursed. "You said those files from his office were missing?"

Kayla nodded. "But I doubt he destroyed them. He probably has storage facilities somewhere."

"When things settle down here, I'll look and see what I can find."

That left Kayla with a sickening feeling. Everything Charles touched turned bad, and she hoped he hadn't had any kind of connection with Dade's grandfather. It was obvious Dade loved Chet McLaurin, and Charles shouldn't be able to hurt the few good childhood memories that Dade and his brothers had about the man.

She remembered the silver concho in her pocket and eased her hand over it. It was silly, but just having that piece of Dade so close to her made her feel better. But it was more than that. She was starting to feel protective of his family. As if she had some right to protect. Some need.

And she couldn't feel that way.

That was a sure path to a broken heart.

Charles's lawyer started the session with some legalese about the validity of Flynn's confession. Nate countered with some legalese of his own, and only then did Kayla remember that Nate had a law degree, as well. Kayla was trying to sort through what they were saying when Deputy Mel appeared in the doorway. She held out the phone for Dade.

"It's SAPD calling about that search warrant," the deputy explained. "I figured you'd want to talk to them."

Dade practically snatched the phone from her hand. "Deputy Dade Ryland."

Kayla moved closer, trying to hear the conversation, but the discussion being piped in from the interrogation room blocked out whatever was being said. Plus, Dade wasn't giving anything away. He was just listening.

"Do that ASAP," Dade instructed, and he ended the call.

"Did they find anything in the safe?" Kayla immediately asked.

"Yeah." Dade turned for the door. "Now, let's see if it's important to this investigation."

That's all Dade said before he turned the camera

on and darted out and into the interrogation room next door. His entrance grabbed everyone's attention, and the lawyer was no doubt on the verge of objecting when Dade bracketed his hands on the interrogation table and got right in Charles's face.

"SAPD just executed the search warrant of Danny Flynn's safe." And he waited, the seconds crawling by.

"So?" the lawyer and Charles said in unison.

Dade glanced at his brothers first. "They found a gun. A .38 and a spent bullet."

Kayla couldn't believe it. Flynn had told the truth. Well, about that anyway.

"What do you know about the gun?" Dade demanded.

Charles pulled back his shoulders. His only reaction before he shrugged. "I know nothing about it. And when you test it, as I'm sure you will, you still won't be able to link it to me. Because I didn't have anything to do with that gun or anything else in Flynn's safe."

Dade didn't pull back. "That's because you're a coward. You hire people to do your killing."

The lawyer objected of course. Nate countered that objection, and while they were engaged in verbal banter, Dade and Charles just stared at each other. Except Charles's expression was more of a glare now.

Good.

Dade had managed to hit a nerve and that wasn't easy to do.

Kayla went closer to the tiny speaker mounted on the wall so she wouldn't miss any of the conversation.

"If the gun's not connected to you," Dade said to him, "then why would your disgruntled former employee lead us right to it?"

Charles's glare softened, and the cockiness returned. "Do you want me to guess why a nutjob would keep a gun and a shell casing in his safe?"

"Sure. Guess." Dade had some cockiness, too.

"I think Flynn was hiding a secret," Charles calmly provided.

"What kind of secret?" Dade demanded over the protest of the attorney.

Charles waved off his lawyer. Then smiled a smile that only he and Satan could have managed.

"Just guessing here, mind you," Charles said, his voice low and calculated, "but I think it's a secret that could bring you Ryland boys to your knees."

Chapter 12

Dade felt numb and in shock. Yeah, it was stupid to put faith in anything Brennan said, but Dade couldn't shake the feeling that in this one instance, Brennan had told the truth.

It's a secret that could bring you Ryland boys to your knees.

Did that gun have something to do with his grandfather's murder? Maybe. And if so, Flynn might have handed them the evidence to solve a two-decades-old crime.

Darcy Burkhart cleared her throat. She didn't groan exactly, but she looked as if that's what she wanted to do. Dade could understand why. Brennan had just said way more than he should have.

"I need to speak privately with my client." Ms. Burkhart glanced at the mirror. *"Privately,"* she emphasized. She stood and motioned for Brennan to do the same. "Is there another room we can use?"

Nate and Mason exchanged glances, and it was Nate who escorted them in the direction of the other interrogation room down the hall.

"I've got calls to return," Mason mumbled and headed out.

Dade took a deep breath so he could go back to the observation room with Kayla, but she came to him. She caught onto him when he stepped in the doorway and hugged him. It seemed natural, and it was far more comforting that it should have been.

"Charles likes to play mind games," Kayla reminded him.

Dade didn't doubt that, but maybe this wasn't a game. "The gun might be connected to my grandfather's murder. We never found the killer or the murder weapon. But there's a bullet that was taken from his body. We can do ballistics to see if this gun killed him."

"When will you know?" she asked.

He shook his head. "I asked that the test be run ASAP. Nate can give them a shove, so we might know something...soon."

And Dade hoped they could live with the consequences of the truth. Oh, man. This could hurt bad. "In the back of mind, I always wondered if my father had something to do with that murder."

There. He'd said it aloud. A first. Probably all of his brothers had thought it, but it seemed too sick to put into words.

"I'm so sorry, Dade." Like her hug, it was the right thing. It soothed him as much as anything could have.

It also reminded him how deep the pain was from the loss of his father and grandfather.

It was a pain he didn't want to feel. But damn, that gun had brought it all back to the surface.

"My father left just days after my grandfather was killed," he heard himself say. "And he and my grandfather weren't the best of friends. Both of them could be hard men, and they clashed."

She eased back. Her eyes met his. "But what motive could your father have had for killing him? And then how would Flynn have gotten the gun?"

"I don't know." He scrubbed his hand over his face. "I just know that our grandfather's death left a big hole in the family."

Kayla just stood there. Listening. Waiting for him to continue. She was offering him a chance to talk this through, and Dade was surprised, shocked even, that he wanted her to hear it.

"It'll always hurt," Dade explained. "It was like being ripped apart, and then Grayson had to put us all back together again." Dade paused because he had no choice. "Grayson's the father that our real dad should have been. He raised us all. Mason, too. He helped raise us while he built the ranch into one of the best in the state."

"You helped with that," Kayla told him.

Dade shook his head and turned away from her. "I helped with roundups and picking up breed stock. Mason is the reason people respect the ranch. Grayson is the reason they respect the law and the family."

"You're a deputy sheriff," she pointed out.

"Right." Man, this hurt, too, but he thought he'd buried it deep enough. Apparently not. "Nate's a cop superstar at SAPD. And Kade, the youngest, he's made a good name for himself in the FBI. Gage did the same in the CIA before he was killed in the line of duty. Like I said, I'm ordinary, but that's okay. I've learned to live with that."

Kayla closed the door. Well, actually she slammed it. Then, she caught onto his arm and whirled him around to face her. Dade saw it then. The anger in her eyes.

"You are not ordinary," she insisted. "You saved my life. My son's life. You've bucked up against your family to protect me."

The anger faded, and there was a moment. One scalding moment where Dade thought he was going to kiss her again. Kayla must have felt it, too. That pull deep within her. Because she shook her head and gave a reluctant smile.

"Besides, you're too hot to be ordinary," she said. "Want to hear a schoolgirl-like confession? You're hands-down the hottest guy I've ever kissed. When you walk into a room, Dade, I have to remind myself to breathe."

Dade had to mentally replay that three times before it sank in. He waited for the punch line, waited for Kayla to say she was just kidding. But she didn't. She leaned in and brushed her mouth against his.

When her eyelids fluttered up, and he saw those baby blues, he knew this was no joke. Kayla thought he was hot. So, he kissed her, hard, just the way he'd dreamed of kissing her.

The rap on the door got rid of the cocky smile that Dade was sure was on his face.

The door flew open, and he spotted his brothers.

Nate looked hurt and confused. Mason looked ready to rip off their heads, especially Dade's.

"Before you have another, uh, private conversation, you might want to check the recording system. It's on." Nate pointed to the camera and microphone mounted just behind the two-way mirror. The very camera that Dade himself had turned back on before the picture confrontation.

Hell.

Kayla's face turned flame red, and she shifted her position so that her back was to his brothers.

Dade wished he could dig a hole for both of them, but he knew that groveling and looking embarrassed wasn't the way to go.

"Yeah, I kissed her," Dade admitted. "Either of you got a problem with that?"

Nate dodged his gaze, shook his head and walked away. Which meant he did have a problem with it, but he respected Dade too much to say anything.

Mason's mouth tightened as he pushed himself away from the doorjamb he was leaning against. "When you screw up, you don't do it half-assed, do you, little brother?"

No, he tended to go full-blown with it. And in this case, it was a screw-up that he knew he couldn't avoid. Kayla was under his skin, and Dade thought maybe that's exactly what he wanted.

"By the way, three of our suspects were just brought in," Mason let him know. "Winston, Alan and Carrie. Let's just say, they aren't so happy to be here, and because Grayson's not back to ask the questions, that means one of us draws the short straw."

"I'll do it," Dade volunteered. He wanted to do it because each question, and answer, could help get Kayla and Robbie out of danger.

"When is Grayson expected back?" Kayla asked, her voice wavering a little. Yeah, Mason could be intimidating as hell, but Grayson's return meant she could see Robbie.

"Not for a while," Mason told her. "Once the Rangers are in place, Grayson said he still needs to pick up some supplies. Plus, it's getting late, and it won't be a direct drive out to the safe house. That's a long-winded way of saying it might be morning before we can get you out there."

Kayla sighed, obviously disappointed. She was beyond anxious to see her baby, and once Dade finished the interrogations, he needed to call Grayson and see if he could hurry things along. Besides, Dade wanted Kayla at the safe house, too, so she wouldn't be under the same roof with Brennan and the other suspects.

"I'll bring the three in here," Dade told her. "So you can watch and listen. We already know the sound system is working," he grumbled. But he added a smile to that and landed a kiss on her cheek.

"It's SAPD again," Mel said, coming up the hall. She handed Dade the phone. "He says it's important."

Dade took the phone and also took a deep breath. Important could be code-speak for bad news. "Deputy Dade Ryland," he answered.

"This is Captain Shaw Tolbert, SAPD. I'm Nate's boss. We got an immediate match on that spent shell casing retrieved from Flynn's safe."

Oh, man. He was right, code-speak for bad news. "That means the casing must have already been in the system." Which meant it had been used in a crime.

"Yes." And that's all the captain said for several moments. "And your informant, Flynn, was right. Salvetti's prints were on the weapon. I figured it'd be best if I told you, and then you could break the news to Nate."

"Nate?" Dade questioned.

The captain mumbled another "yes." Then, he paused again. "The bullet is a perfect match to the one that killed Nate's wife."

To Kayla it felt as if everything was moving in slow motion and spinning out of control at the same time.

She'd watched from the hall as Dade told his brothers about the bullet. She saw the pain register on their faces—an old wound opened up again—and she felt that same pain deep within her.

The Rylands had suspected all along that Charles had been behind Ellie's murder, and they'd apparently been right.

Well, maybe.

"Only Salvetti's prints were on the gun," Dade explained, relaying what the captain had told him just minutes earlier during their phone conversation. "And there's nothing to indicate it's been tampered with. The prints are clean, in places they should be on a gun, so they haven't been planted. This gun is the real deal."

No one said anything right away. All stood there, obviously trying to absorb the horrible news they'd just learned. "The gun can't be linked to Brennan," Mason concluded, and he punctuated that with some raw profanity.

"Not directly," Dade agreed. "But we all know that Ellie's last assignment as a cop was to investigate one of Brennan's drug-pushing henchmen. And she was killed carrying out that investigation. Captain Tolbert said he was personally going to take another look at the case and see if he can make a strong enough connection between Salvetti and Brennan."

Because Salvetti was dead, that might be harder to do, but there was a bottom line here: Salvetti had been the one to kill Nate's wife, and the man had almost certainly been taking orders from Charles. Now, Nate had the gun that might eventually point to Charles, but Kayla didn't think it was going to make it easier for him to accept his wife's murder.

As if he knew what she was thinking, Nate looked up, snared her attention. "I'm sorry," Kayla said because she didn't know what else to say.

He nodded, mumbled something under his breath, and much to Kayla's surprise, Nate walked toward her. He closed his eyes a moment, but when he opened them, his attention was focused fully on her.

"I know Brennan is making it hard for you to testify, but please don't back down," Nate told her. "You might be the only person who can get him to pay for what he's done."

"I won't back down," Kayla promised. She repeated it so the others would hear. "One way or another, I'm putting Charles Brennan behind bars. Or better yet, in the grave. I want him on death row."

Mason nodded. So did Nate. Dade lowered his head, shook it, and mumbled something she couldn't hear.

Nate glanced back at his brothers. "We'll keep your son safe, no matter what. You have my word on that." When his eyes started to water, Nate quickly turned and moved away. "I have to get out of here for a while."

No one questioned that, and Kayla totally understood. She hated being this close to Charles, but now she had just one more reason to hate him—he'd hurt Dade and his family by taking the life of one of their own.

Dade glanced around as if trying to figure out where to start. He finally hitched his thumb toward the interrogation room. "I'll start with Winston and Alan," he told Mason. "I'll talk to them together. Why don't you deal with Carrie?"

"I'd rather deal with a PMS-ing diamondback." Mason's mumble was drenched in sarcasm. "What about Brennan?"

"Let him and his lawyer stew for a while." Dade caught onto Kayla's arm. "You can watch from the observation room while I chat with Winston and Alan."

"Remember to breathe, Kayla," Mason said when she walked past him.

She whirled in his direction, expecting to see Mason's usual scary glare, but the corner of his mouth hitched. It wasn't full-fledged, but it was a smile. He gave a half shrug as if he didn't want to expend too much energy for either gesture.

"I should probably tell you that you could do better than my little brother," Mason added. "But it sounds as if this is out of your control."

It was. She had already fallen hard for Dade, and nothing was going to change that. Unfortunately. That meant there were hard times ahead for her because this relationship with Dade wasn't just complicated. It was a potential powder keg.

Kayla brushed her hand against Mason's arm to thank him. She figured the subtle approach was better with this particular Ryland. He made a sound that could have meant anything and strolled away.

"Let's get something straight," Dade said to her on the trek to the observation room. "You won't take any unnecessary chances when it comes to Brennan. We'll get him behind bars."

"And my testimony will do that," she reminded him.

Dade had the same reaction as he'd had in the hall. A head shake and an under-the-breath mumble. "Just don't do anything stupid."

That didn't sound like his first choice of words for a warning, but Kayla couldn't ask for clarification. That's because Carrie came out of the reception area and walked directly toward them.

"Mason will interview you," Dade let her know.

Of course that earned Kayla a glare. She was tired of this woman's reaction and decided to go petty. Kayla leaned over, brushed a kiss on Dade's mouth. "I'll watch from here." Something he already knew of course, and she stepped into the observation room.

"Do I have to remind you that Brennan and she are family?" Carrie said to Dade.

"No, you don't have to remind me."

And much to Kayla's shock, Dade leaned into the observation room and kissed her right back. He added a delicious little smile that Carrie couldn't see because his back was to the woman. Then, he turned, caught onto Carrie's arm and ushered her down the hall where Mason was waiting for her. However, Dade didn't even make it back to the interrogation room before Darcy Burkhart rounded the corner.

"You have a problem," Darcy announced, zooming in on Dade. She glanced in the room at Winston and Alan. Winston was seated, reading something on his phone. Alan was pacing.

"What now?" Dade asked, sounding as frustrated as Kayla felt.

"I'm requesting a trial delay because there's a conflict of interest." She slapped some papers in Dade's hand. "That's the statement I just took from my client. I've already called the judge and the county D.A. I suggest you bring in the Rangers or some other impartial agency to handle the investigation."

Oh, mercy. Had something truly gone wrong, or was this another legal ploy?

Kayla stepped out in the hall to see if she could get a glimpse of the paper that Dade was reading. But he lifted his finger in a wait-a-minute gesture.

"What the hell is this?" Dade demanded, though he'd only had time to skim the page.

"Ask *him*." Ms. Burkhart pointed directly at Alan.

Alan sank down in the chair, head dropped into his hands, and he groaned. "I'm sorry," he said.

"Sorry?" Dade demanded. "Is it true? Tell me the hell it's not true." Dade was practically shouting by the time he got to the last word.

"It's true," Alan admitted.

"What's true?" Winston asked, getting to his feet.

Dade handed him the paper, and Kayla held her breath as the D.A.'s eyes skirted across the lines.

The color drained from Winston's face. "Oh, God."

Kayla repeated that and was about to ask what the heck was going on, but Winston glanced at her, then Dade.

"Does Kayla know?" Winston asked.

"No." And Dade said that with too much regret for this not to be really bad news.

"What is it? What don't I know?" she managed to ask.

But Dade didn't answer. He motioned for Mason who was still in the hall with Carrie. "I need to get Kayla away from this and upstairs. It's late, and she's been through more than enough today."

Mason nodded. "What do you need me to do?"

"Have Mel interview Carrie," Dade instructed. "You need to take Alan's statement. After that, he'll resign as the A.D.A., and then you can arrest him and have both Alan and Brennan moved to the jail. I want both in lockup for the night. Call Nate. He can help with that."

"Arrest Alan?" Kayla repeated, but she was the only one of the four who seemed surprised with Dade's order. "Did he do anything to Robbie? Did he hurt my baby?"

"Nothing like that," Dade assured her.

That didn't ease the knot in her stomach.

"We have to talk," Dade said to her. No longer a shout. Practically a whisper.

He caught onto her hand and started walking.

Chapter 13

Kayla didn't ask Dade what he'd just learned, which meant she no doubt knew this was not going to be news she wanted to hear.

Still, Dade would tell her.

It just wouldn't happen in front of Alan or any of the others. She'd had her heart bared enough today without having to go through a semipublic ordeal of hearing Brennan's latest. And there was no mistaking it.

This would be an ordeal.

With his hand still holding hers, Dade led her up the back stairs to the studio-style apartment. Once it'd been part of the jail, but when a new facility had been built five years ago, Grayson had converted it to a place where they could crash when the workload was too much for them to go home to the ranch. Basically, it was one massive area with a kitchen, sitting space, desk, bed and bathroom, but for tonight, it would be a safe haven where Kayla could hopefully get some rest.

Well, after she fell apart, that is.

Dade led her inside, locked the door and had her sit on the well-worn leather sofa that had once belonged to his grandfather. In fact, pretty much everything in the room was a family hand-me-down moved from the attic at the ranch.

"Tell me," Kayla said, and there was pure dread in her voice.

First, Dade poured her a shot of whiskey from the stash Mason kept in one of the cabinets. He handed it to her and motioned for her to drink.

She did. Kayla took it in one gulp. "Tell me," she repeated. "Was Alan working for Charles?"

"Not exactly." Dade took a deep breath and sat on the coffee table in front of her so they'd be eye to eye. "Alan committed a crime and covered it up, but Brennan found out what he'd done. Brennan insists he hasn't been blackmailing Alan, but it might take a while to prove if that's true or false."

Kayla swallowed hard. "And the crime? Alan's too young to have murdered your grandfather." She paused. Her eyes widened. "He didn't have something to do with Ellie's death?"

Because she was going to need it, Dade inched closer and pulled her deep into his arms. "According to Brennan, a little over a year ago Alan was drunk, and he was involved in a car accident. He hit and killed your husband, and then he fled the scene."

She pulled in her breath and didn't release it. Kayla held it so long that Dade eased back to make sure she wasn't about to pass out. "Alan killed Preston?"

"Afraid so." He waited for her to cry, but the tears didn't come. "Preston had a security camera in his car that activated during the crash, but when Brennan came upon the scene just minutes after it happened, he took the camera before the cops got there."

"So he knew all along how Preston died." Still no tears. She shook her head. "Honestly, I thought Charles had murdered him. They clashed more often than not, and I figured Charles got fed up and killed him or had him killed. This sounds horrible, but Preston's death was a relief to me. As far as I was concerned, he was no longer my husband. No longer anything to me."

He touched her cheek. "Are you okay?"

"Yes." But then just like that, something flashed through her eyes. "Oh, God. Charles will try to use this to throw out the case against him. That's why he told his attorney about it after all these months."

Dade wished he could disagree with that, but she was right. "Mason and Nate will be all over this. The Texas Rangers, too. Brennan will go to trial."

Now the tears came. "He can't get away with this. He can't."

Dade pulled her back in his arms. "He won't. It's true—the only reason he spilled all of this now was to call Alan's integrity into question."

"And it will," she insisted.

"It might. But I read through the case against Brennan, and I don't remember Alan's name appearing anywhere in the motion documents. This is Winston's case."

And while Dade might have some suspicions about the D.A., he wouldn't borrow trouble. Eventually Brennan had to run out of luck and dirty little secrets that had so far kept him from doing any serious jail time.

Plus, there was something else. "Brennan implicated himself today when he gave that statement to his attorney about Alan. Brennan obstructed justice by removing that camera from his son's car. That's another charge we can tack on to the others, and we can use that to revoke his bond and put his sorry butt back in jail. Well, for tonight anyway."

Kayla groaned softly. "That's something, I guess." She eased back a few inches and faced him again. "You've been good to me through all of this. I won't forget it."

Dade stared at her. "That sounds like some kind of goodbye."

She looked ready to say yes, it was. But Dade wasn't about to accept a goodbye. So, he kissed her. Yeah, it wasn't fair. It was ill-timed. But it was also what he needed. Hopefully it was what Kayla needed, too.

"Remember," he said against her mouth, "I'm the guy that makes you forget to breathe." He meant to make it sound light, but it sure didn't come out that way.

Her eyes came to his again, but there was no humor, no teasing. "That's true. And if you don't think that scares me, think again."

He brushed his mouth against hers. "Fear is the last thing I want you to feel when it comes to me."

"Too late." Her words ended in a kiss. A kiss that melted right through him.

Dade returned the favor. "Funny, you don't sound afraid." She sounded aroused, and looked it, too, with her heavy eyelids and flushed cheeks.

He felt her muscles go slack, and she slipped her hands around the back of his neck. "I'm afraid you might stop," she whispered.

Oh, man.

That did it. He was a goner. He hadn't brought Kayla up here to have sex with her, but that was an invitation he couldn't resist.

Dade could think of at least a dozen reasons to quit doing this. Damn good reasons, too. But he couldn't come up with any reason that was stronger than the simple truth. He was burning alive, and Kayla wasn't just the source of the fire, she was the cure.

"Dade," she said, her voice mostly breath, barely a whisper.

But he heard her loud and clear. "Kayla," he managed to say, even though it seemed too much to have the sound of her name leave his mouth.

"Your arm," she reminded him and eased back a little. "Be careful."

Careful and his arm were the last things on his mind right now. Dade didn't think he could keep this together very long. He'd never been a patient, gentle lover. Never had a partner who was interested in anything but hard and fast. He didn't think that was true of Kayla, though.

Restraint, he reminded himself in the same motion that he reached for her.

His hand slid around the back of her neck, and he dragged her to him. His mouth went straight to hers, and in that one touch, that one breath, he took in her scent and taste.

So much for restraint.

"Sorry," he said, taking her mouth the way he wanted to take the rest of her.

"Sorry for what?" she snapped back and stared at him. Her mouth was already swollen from their kisses.

Her face was flushed. And her heavy breathing pushed her breasts against his chest.

The sight of her melted him. "Sorry for not giving you an out, for not seducing you the old-fashioned way."

Dade kissed her again. Too hard. And yet it wasn't hard enough. He pressed against her, snaring her in his arms, and dragging her even tighter against him.

"I don't want an out," she mumbled through the kiss. "Old-fashioned is overrated. And I just want you."

He didn't have much breath left, but that pretty much robbed him of the little bit in his lungs. So did the maneuver she made by brushing her sex against his.

Hell.

The bed wasn't far, just a few yards away, but the desk was closer. Grappling for position, they landed against it, the edge ramming into Dade's lower back.

The kisses got crazy hot. Dade couldn't figure out where he wanted to kiss her most, so he settled for any part of her he could reach. Which wasn't easy. Kayla was doing some crazy kisses, too, and she was trying to rid him of his shirt. Dade helped. He ripped it open.

She made a sound of relief and lowered her head to plant some kisses on his chest. It was torture. Her hot, wet mouth moving over his body as if she knew exactly what turned him on.

And she obviously did.

Because she made it all the way to his stomach. And lower. Especially *lower*. When she dropped one of those fire kisses on the front of his jeans, Dade figured this was about to get crazier.

He caught onto her, dragging her back up and turning her so that she was pinned against the desk.

"I want you naked now," he guttered out.

Kayla apparently agreed because she started to do battle with her top. Dade did more than battle. He jerked it over her head and discovered a woman with a flimsy lacy bra. It was barely there, but he removed it anyway.

Kayla was beautiful everywhere. Certain that his theory was correct, he shoved down her pants and pulled them off her. Then, her panties.

Yeah. Beautiful everywhere.

He leaned in, slowly, and touched his mouth to the pink heart tattoo on her breast. She sucked in her breath and froze. She had that deer-caught-in-the-headlights look. She was waiting. And Dade made sure the wait was worth it.

He kissed his way down her stomach. Her skin was like silk. And that scent. Not that he needed it, but it pulled him right in. Dade caught onto her right leg and lifted it over his shoulder so he could kiss her exactly the way he wanted. The way she apparently wanted, too, because she gasped. Moaned. And then cursed.

Dade was positive it was a good sign.

So was the fact that she thrust her hips forward and shoved her hand into his hair.

He would have finished her off then and there, with the taste of her burning like fire through him. But Kayla obviously didn't want things to play out this way.

She jerked her leg off his shoulder, and with her hand still in his hair, she yanked him back up. Not gently, either. Nor was she gentle with his zipper. Kayla was a woman on a mission, and she batted Dade's hand away when he tried to help. She got his zipper down and shoved her hands into his shorts. Dade could have sworn a freight train rammed through his head.

Restraint, he reminded himself again.

It was as useless as the last reminder. Kayla freed him from his shorts and wrapped her legs around his waist.

Dade did try to ease into her, but that didn't work, either. She was tight, wet and hot. And she used those long legs to push him deep inside her.

She made a sound. Not a gasp or moan this time. Her breath shuddered, and the sound came from deep within her throat. Dade recognized it. It was something beyond pleasure. It was a sound he would have made himself if he could have figured out how to breathe.

The moment seemed to freeze. They were there, their bodies fused together. Their gazes locked. And maybe it was because of that intimate position, Dade knew exactly what she was thinking.

This felt good.

No. Not just *good.* It felt *way too good.* He'd figured sex with Kayla would be extraordinary, but this was a million steps beyond that.

"We're so screwed," he managed to say.

"Oh, yes," she managed to say right back.

They didn't take the time to weigh the consequences of this beyond-sex moment. The moment unfroze. The heat roared through them.

And they dived at each other.

Dade caught onto her hips. Kayla caught onto his back and his neck, digging her fingers into his skin and completing the thrusts inside her.

He felt her closing in around him. She was so near climax. This was usually the part when he buried his face in his partner's neck and went to that dark primal place where the only thing that mattered was finishing what he'd started. First her, so he could rid his body of this fire that was consuming him.

But he didn't do that this time.

Dade never took his eyes off her, even though his vision was blurred. He knew this would be over too quickly, and he wanted to see every moment. Record every touch, every sensation.

He wasn't disappointed.

And he wondered how many times in life reality lived up to a man's fantasy.

Kayla sure did.

She met each of his thrusts, but her grip went gentle on his neck. Her fingers stilled but not her body. The climax wracked through her and she reached for him, pulling him closer. So he was careful.

Gentle.

And it was that gentle coaxing and that look in her eyes that ended it all for him. Dade thrust into her one last time and let himself fall.

Right into Kayla's waiting arms.

Chapter 14

If Dade hadn't kept a grip on her, Kayla was certain she would have slid right to the floor.

All in all, that might not be such a bad thing because Dade and she were half-naked, but with the climax high already starting to fade, Kayla knew that sooner or later they would have to talk.

Best not to be naked on the floor when that happened.

She was out of breath again. Felt as if her bones had dissolved to dust, but Dade obviously had a burst of energy. He scooped her up, deposited her on the bed that was only about twenty feet away. He had the good sense to fix his jeans so that at least one of them would be semipresentable if someone knocked on the door.

Kayla got a good look at him while he was dressing. Mercy. No man deserved a body like that. Lanky but with just enough muscles to make him interesting. And then there were the tattoos. A small dragon on his left shoulder blade and a badge on his hip. Appropriate because he was a lawman to the core.

"I know," he mumbled, sounding disgusted with himself. He dropped down on his side next to her. "I'm sorry."

Well, that took care of any shreds of a sexual buzz. Kayla just stared at him until Dade cursed.

"Hell, I'm not sorry for *that*," Dade amended. But that didn't clarify anything until he leaned down and kissed her. "I'm sorry I didn't use a condom."

Oh. Kayla might have cursed too if her throat hadn't snapped shut.

"I'm not on the pill," she was finally able to let him know. Mainly because it'd been a year and a half since she'd had sex. "But I think we'll be okay. It's the wrong time of the month."

She didn't want to get into a discussion about her irregular cycle. Nor did she want to think about this one-time sex with Dade making her pregnant. Good grief. She wasn't a kid, and even though this need for Dade had consumed her, she still should have remembered to take the simple precaution of using a condom.

He got on the bed with her, slid his arm beneath her neck and drew her closer. Just like that, her thoughts about the unsafe sex faded, and Dade—and his incredible body—took control of her mind.

"For the record, you're not as delicate as you look," he whispered.

"Delicate?" Again, she wasn't sure how to take that. "I hope that didn't disappoint you."

"Nothing about you disappointed me." And yes, there

was some frustration in his voice. She understood that. Kayla was frustrated at the strength of all of this. "Besides, I wouldn't be a good fit with delicate. You're more my match."

He dropped a kiss on the top of her breast. Right on her tattoo. He might as well have poured warm wax over her because the heat went through her entire body. A slow hunger that was still there despite what had happened just minutes earlier.

"Why a tattoo?" he asked, kissing her breast again. This time, he used his tongue on her nipple.

It took a moment to form words, and her fingers found their way into his hair. "A way of rebelling."

"With a pink heart?" he mocked.

She dredged up a smile. "My rebellion has a feminine side. I wanted something pretty." And it was impossible to concentrate with his hand trailing down her back. The slow hunger suddenly wasn't so slow.

"You've got *pretty* nailed down." His breath was hot when he blew it over her nipple that he had wet with his mouth.

Kayla's breath broke, and that hunger suddenly became hot, slick and all-consuming. "What are you doing to me?" she begged.

"Post-sex foreplay." He flashed a grin that could have seduced her all by itself. But that wasn't necessary because Dade had other lethal weapons in his arsenal.

Kayla knew this would lead straight to a broken heart, but she pulled him to her anyway. She wanted his mouth. His body. She wanted all of him, all over again.

At first, she thought the buzzing was in her head, but then Dade cursed and snatched up the phone on the table next to the bed.

"Dade," he snarled.

Kayla, too, wanted to curse at the interruption, but then she forced herself to remember that one floor beneath them in the sheriff's office there was a major investigation going on. One that was a matter of life and death—*hers.*

Dade put his hand over the receiver. "It's Misty. And she says that she has to talk to you now."

Kayla didn't even try to choke back a huff. She wanted to hear from her sister, was worried about her, but Misty's timing wasn't good. Kayla got up, sandwiched the phone between her shoulder and ear so she could dress while she talked.

Dade lifted an eyebrow at that, but he, too, put his shirt back on. Bedtime was over, much too soon, and it hurt to think this might be the one and only time she would get to have Dade.

"I'm here," Kayla said to her sister.

"I've been trying to reach you," Misty fired at her. "When you didn't answer your cell, I called the sheriff's office, and some woman said she'd connect me. Are you really at the sheriff's office?"

"I'm here." And Kayla decided to get straight to business. "Where are you and why did you take all that money from your bank account?"

Misty made a sound. Maybe surprise. Maybe outrage. It was hard to tell. "Someone's following me. I'm afraid Charles or someone is after me."

Kayla was worried for her sister, but she wished she had more energy to deal with this. "Why would Charles have someone follow you?" She reached over and put the call on speaker so Dade could hear the answer.

"I don't know!" Misty practically yelled. "Why does Charles do anything?"

"I could say the same about you," Kayla countered. "Explain why you took the money from your account and the gun from your roommate."

Her sister made another of those sounds. "Because I'm scared. Didn't you hear what I said? Someone's following me. I need to see you. *Now.* And I don't want any of the cops around. I want us to be alone, so we can talk."

Dade shook his head.

Kayla knew he was right. The last thing she needed was to be out and about to meet with Misty. "We can talk at the Silver Creek sheriff's office," Kayla pointed out.

"No, we can't. The cops think I've done something wrong, and I haven't. Well, not intentionally anyway."

Kayla groaned and sank onto the edge of the bed. She was a hundred-percent certain she wasn't going to like this. "What did you do?" she demanded.

"Nothing!" Misty hesitated after that outburst. "I didn't know it was Charles who bought that painting, okay? I didn't know."

Kayla didn't even bother to choke back a groan. This was not what she wanted to hear.

"When did you find out Charles was the buyer?" Dade asked.

Misty made another sound. This one was definitely from outrage. "He's listening to us? Why would you do that, Kayla? Why would you let him hear a private conversation?"

"Because there's too much at stake for this to be private," Kayla explained. "Now answer Dade's question— when did you learn Charles had bought the painting?"

Her sister took her time answering. "I figured it out a few days ago. Someone called, a man who didn't identify himself. He said he'd bought the painting as a favor and he wanted me to tell him where you were. I didn't know, but when I told him that, he didn't believe me."

Kayla could only shake her head. "The man who called was likely Danny Flynn, who's in custody for attempted murder. Or maybe it was Raymond Salvetti, who's dead."

"Like I said, I don't know because he didn't give me his name," her sister insisted.

"Did you specifically see someone following you?" Dade pressed.

"No, but I can feel it!" Misty snapped. "And I'm done talking to you. Kayla, I have to see you now."

Kayla took a moment, not because she was debating her response—she wasn't—but she wanted to word this as clearly as possible. Even though any wording would cause Misty to pitch a fit. "It's too dangerous for me to meet with you anywhere but here."

Her sister used some raw profanity. "I can't believe you're choosing that cop over me."

Kayla was about to explain this had nothing to do with Dade, or choices, but Misty slammed down the phone.

Dade pulled in a hard breath, took the phone from Kayla and tapped the receiver. "Mel," he said to the deputy who apparently answered, "did you get a trace on Misty Wallace's location?"

Kayla couldn't hear the answer, but she saw the frustrated look on Dade's face. "All right. Thanks."

"Where is she?" Kayla asked.

"In town. The call came from the hotel at the end of Main Street."

Oh, mercy. Why hadn't Misty just told her that? Maybe because her sister was genuinely worried that Charles or someone else would find her location?

Or maybe Misty had sinister reasons?

"Don't go there yet," Dade said in that I-know-what-you're-thinking tone. He slid his arm around her. "Focus on the good."

The good. Well, she certainly had some of that. Her son was at the top of that list. The fact that he was safe with Dade's brother was another *good*. And then there was Dade. A *good* of a different kind.

The question came to her, and Kayla didn't even try to stop it. "What will happen when this is all over?"

He tipped his head to the bed. Smiled. "More of that, I hope."

Kayla didn't want to smile. But she did. "Your brothers won't approve."

"They're coming around." He brushed his mouth over hers. Instant heat.

"And in the meantime?" Kayla kissed him back.

"We just remember to breathe when one of us walks into a room."

She laughed. Couldn't help herself. "You're never going to let me forget that, are you?"

"Never," he promised.

Kayla felt herself floating and realized Dade was easing her back onto the bed. She would have gone willingly, but the phone buzzed again.

"Misty," she snapped.

Dade growled something much worse but answered

the call. "This better be important," he warned the caller.

But it must have been important because Dade went still. He just listened for what had to be a full minute and then finally said, "No. I'll escort Kayla there."

That brought her off the bed. "You're not taking me to see Misty," she challenged.

Dade shook his head. "Brennan's request for another trial delay was denied. The judge wants you at the court-house in the morning so you can testify."

Morning had come way too soon for Dade. The night had flown by despite neither Kayla nor him getting much sleep. Both of them had tossed and turned.

And ached.

Well, he'd ached anyway, and he was pretty sure Kayla had done the same.

Despite the great sex they'd had on the desk, his body had kept on burning for her even after Misty's call and the news that Kayla would be testifying soon. But Dade had finally managed to show a little restraint. There were no condoms in the apartment, and he hadn't wanted to leave her alone to go get any. Besides, she had needed rest.

Not sex.

Except somewhere in the night, sex had felt like a need more than sleep. More than common sense. More than anything. Thankfully, Dade had kept his hands off her so they wouldn't have a repeat round of amaz-ing but unsafe sex.

Kayla had started her morning with a breakfast sand-wich and coffee that Mason had delivered and a phone call to Robbie. Despite the gloomy cloud of the trial hanging over her, talking to the baby had helped her mood. It'd helped Dade, too, though he felt a little guilty for stealing some of her parenthood pleasure.

Now, Dade finished up some emails and made some calls while Kayla showered and dressed in the bathroom. They had plenty of time to get to the courthouse, almost an hour, and it was just up the street. Still, Dade knew he would breathe easier once he had Kayla in the witness room where she would remain until she testified against Brennan.

"And then what?" he mumbled to himself.

With luck, the trial would end soon. Brennan would be behind bars. And the reason Kayla was in his protective custody would end, as well.

Dade refused to dwell on that. He had to focus on getting Kayla to the courthouse and up on that witness stand. After that, well, he'd deal with all of that later. However, he couldn't dismiss that he had complicated the heck out of their situation by sleeping with her. Not just sex.

But making love to her.

Cuddling with her in bed was not a good way to sort out his feelings for her. It was just another complication.

She stepped out from the bathroom, and there was complication number three. She looked amazing. So beautiful. And it wasn't the clothes. The gray top and skirt that had been picked up from her estate was pretty much nondescript. The kind of outfit someone would wear to court. It was the woman wearing the clothes that made them look amazing.

Dade mentally cursed.

All this *amazing* junk had to stop. He had to clear his head so he could concentrate on getting Kayla through her testimony. He was doing a decent job with his concentration until she crossed the room and dropped a kiss on his mouth.

"You look like a cop," she muttered.

Dade glanced down at his usual black shirt and jeans with the badge clipped to his belt.

"That's a compliment," Kayla assured him.

Oh. Suddenly he felt *amazing* again, so he gave in to it and kissed her. Not a peck, either. Dade made this one long and hard. When he finally let go of her, they both were smiling big goofy smiles.

Oh, yeah.

This concentration stuff was working well.

"It'll be okay," she assured him. But then Kayla blinked. "It will be okay, right? You didn't get any bad news when you were on the phone?"

"Nothing bad," he assured her. "In fact, some of it is actually good news. Flynn was transported to the county jail last night, and he begged Winston for a deal. Flynn will testify against Brennan in exchange for a reduced sentence."

Her smile wasn't so goofy now. Her nerves were showing. "Because Flynn tried to kill me, I hope it's not a too short sentence."

"It won't be," he promised. And he would make sure of it. "Winston told Brennan's attorney about the deal with Flynn. Let's just say Brennan is not a happy camper."

She blew out a breath of relief, then stared at him. "You're right, that is good news. But does that mean there's bad news, too?"

He made a so-so motion with his hand. "Alan is out of jail on bond," he continued. "But a deputy from a neighboring town is keeping tabs on him."

Her eyes widened. "You think Alan will try to run or something?"

The *or something* hiked up her nerves. "No, Mason said Alan was ready to take his punishment. He'll be charged with intoxicated manslaughter which is a second-degree felony, and we'll also tack on leaving the scene of a crime. There's no way around it. He'll see some jail time, and he'll lose his law license."

Kayla nodded. "I'm betting Charles planned to use Alan to help him get out of this trial."

"No doubt, but it didn't work." He ran his hand down her arm, hoping it would help soothe her.

"And Misty?" she asked. "Any word from her?"

Dade had to shake his head. This fell into the bad news category. "No other calls from Misty. The Rangers traced her call to the hotel, but she wasn't there when they arrived just minutes after she finished talking to us."

Another hitch in the nerves department for Kayla. Her mouth trembled a little. "Once I've testified, I'll see if I can get in touch with her."

Dade didn't try to talk her out of that. He wouldn't have succeeded anyway because, for better or worse, Misty would always be her sister.

Kayla moved away from him and picked up the pants she'd worn the previous day. The ones that Dade had practically ripped off her. She reached into the pocket and retrieved something.

His silver concho.

"For luck," she said, and she slipped it into her bra, probably because she had no pockets in the outfit she was wearing.

Dade couldn't imagine the concho being lucky, but he wasn't about to argue with her. Whatever got her through this morning was fine with him. He only hoped it didn't set off the metal detector in the courthouse. His brothers would have a field day with his trying to explain why Kayla had his concho in her lacy pink bra.

"Ready?" he asked, checking his watch. "Mason should be waiting for us."

"Mason?" she questioned.

"I wanted two of us to escort you to the courthouse." He tried to toss that out there casually, as if going outside a single block was no big deal. But her safety was the biggest deal of all to him, and Dade wanted to take every precaution.

"Thank you," she whispered as they walked out.

They went down the stairs where Mason was waiting for them. He had his shoulder propped against the wall while he read something on his phone.

"A problem?" Dade asked.

"Just ranch business."

Yeah, the ranch ate up a major part of Mason's time, and Dade didn't want to think of how many hours they'd all spend playing catch-up when this was done.

The building was quiet for a change. Grayson was on his way back from the safe house with Robbie and Connie. Mel was at the jail with Brennan and his attorney. That left the other deputy, Luis Lopez, and the dispatcher, Tina Fox, to man the sheriff's office. But hopefully nothing else would go wrong before they had their full staff back in place.

"It's only a block away," Dade let her know. "But we're driving." With Misty unaccounted for and Alan out on bond, he wanted to be careful.

Mason and Dade put her between them and hurried to the cruiser that Mason already had waiting. They didn't waste any time, and as soon as the three of them were inside the vehicle, Dade drove away.

It took him longer to get out of the parking lot and onto Main Street than it did to drive the block. Dade didn't let down his guard, and in fact his guard sky-rocketed when he pulled up next to the courthouse and spotted Brennan.

"Charles," Kayla mumbled, obviously spotting him as well.

Brennan was in handcuffs, and Mel was heading to the side entrance of the courthouse. Probably to avoid the photographers and news crew out front.

Dade and Mason got out first, positioning Kayla behind them. Out of Brennan's line of sight. Or rather that was the plan. But Brennan saw her anyway because he came to a dead stop. No smirk or smile today.

Brennan shot them an ice-cold glare.

"Happy with yourself, Kayla?" he called out.

She didn't answer, but Dade hated that she had to be this close to the devil himself. Dade looked back to reassure her, but then he heard Mason.

"Hell," his brother growled, and from the corner of his eye, he saw Mason reach for his gun.

Dade automatically did the same. He drew his gun and took aim.

But it was already too late.

Despite the cuffs, Brennan rammed his elbow into the deputy's stomach. His motion was seamless. And fast. Too fast for Dade to get off a clean shot.

Brennan grabbed the Glock from Mel's holster and put it to the deputy's head.

Chapter 15

Kayla was too stunned to move and could only stand there and watch in horror at the nightmare happening right in front of her. Charles had finally lost it, and he looked ready to kill the deputy on the spot.

"If anyone moves, she dies!" Charles shouted.

Mel froze, and Dade and Mason stood there with their guns trained on him.

"Stay behind me," Dade whispered to Kayla.

She did, but she hated that once again Dade and his brother and now Mel were taking the ultimate risk to keep her alive.

Charles kept the gun pressed to Mel's head, and he inched back until he was right against the brick exterior wall. He probably did that so no one could sneak up on him and grab the gun, but he had to realize that he couldn't escape.

Or maybe not.

Kayla got a sickening feeling. Was this some kind of calculated escape plan? Maybe he had someone nearby ready to assist.

Kayla's gaze darted around the crowd of people who, like her, had come to a dead stop. No one looked ready to spring to Charles's aid, but that didn't mean he hadn't managed to pay off one or more of them to help him escape.

Or even kill her.

The crowd and the buildings on each side of them essentially meant they were trapped, literally in the parking lot between the two-story courthouse and the town's mortuary. They weren't close enough to either building just to duck inside. Of course, there was the cruiser and a few other vehicles they could take cover behind if it became necessary.

"Drop the gun, Brennan!" Dade ordered.

Now Charles smiled. "Not on your life. Or I should say, not on Kayla's life, because we both know she's the one I want." He dug his gun into the deputy's head. "The cop here is just a poor substitute."

Oh, God. Was he going to try to trade Mel for her? Kayla didn't want the woman hurt, but if she traded positions with the deputy, Kayla figured it would be like signing her own death warrant.

"Mr. Brennan?" his attorney, Darcy Burkhart, called out. She was in the crowd but was making her way toward them. "Stop this, please. And put down the gun."

"Stay back," Mason warned the lawyer, and thankfully she froze. Kayla didn't want Charles to have any excuse to go on a shooting spree.

"What now?" Mason tossed out to Charles. "We just

all wait outside until we freeze to death or your hand gets tired?"

The corner of Charles's mouth lifted again. "I like your bedside manner, Deputy. No, we don't wait. Kayla will walk toward me, and I'll let the good cop here go."

Kayla felt everything inside her turn to ice. She couldn't stand there and let Mel die.

"You're not going anywhere," Dade warned Kayla when she took a step forward.

Mason and Dade closed ranks, stepping closer to each other so that it created a barrier between Charles and her.

"But Mel…" Kayla protested.

"He's not going to kill her," Dade whispered to her from over his shoulder. "Right now, Mel is the only thing stopping him from dying."

Even though the blood was rushing through her, causing her pulse to pound in her head, Kayla forced herself to think that through. Dade was right. Charles was too narcissistic to commit suicide, and that's exactly what he would be doing if he killed Mel.

"Well?" Charles challenged.

"There is no *well*," Dade challenged right back. "You can't escape. The only thing you can do is give Deputy Garza back her gun and then go into the courthouse so we can get on with this trial."

"It's not a trial," Charles argued. "It's a lynch mob. I know what you did—talking that idiot Flynn into telling his lies so he could get a lighter sentence. You should have offered the deal to me, Deputy Ryland, because Flynn has blood on his hands."

Kayla shuddered. Even though she knew Flynn was

a criminal, she couldn't imagine anyone dirtier than Charles.

"Thirty seconds," Charles added. "That's all the time you boys have. If Kayla isn't over here by then, I'll start shooting."

That caused a ripple of chatter through the crowd, and even though Kayla didn't want to risk looking back, she heard some of them running. Good, because she was afraid this could turn ugly very fast.

"No deal," Dade answered. "Kayla stays put."

Charles lifted his shoulder. "Then in twenty seconds, I'll kill someone, and I'll keep killing until I have Kayla."

"Get ready to jump behind the cruiser," Dade warned her in a whisper.

But Kayla didn't get ready. She stared at Charles from over Dade's and Mason's shoulders. She had only one thing that she could use to reason with Charles, and it turned her stomach to have to do it.

"Charles, think this through," Kayla called out to him. "Preston is dead, and if you kill me, then Robbie will be an orphan. You'll never get to know him because you'll be on death row. Is that what you want for your only grandchild?"

"Robbie," Charles repeated, and there seemed to be some regret in his voice. "It's unfortunate but necessary. Besides, I have good lawyers, and that death penalty might not even happen. You'd be surprised how many legal loopholes gobs of money can find. In fact, I think I feel an insanity plea coming on."

Kayla's heart dropped. She'd held out a shred of hope that she could reason with him if she used Robbie, but Charles was too far gone to listen to any reason.

"Jump behind the cruiser," Dade ordered her.

"You and Mason, too," she insisted.

But the words had hardly left her mouth when the sounds cracked through the air.

Oh, God.

Charles fired the gun.

Dade turned, hooked his arm around Kayla's waist and dragged her behind the cruiser. Mason went the other direction and ducked behind an SUV.

"Get down!" Dade shouted to the crowd who all thankfully seemed to be scrambling for cover.

He couldn't tell if the bullet had actually hit anyone. There were shouts, screams and the sounds of all hell breaking loose.

Brennan's lawyer was still begging for him to surrender, but Dade was pretty sure that wasn't going to happen. Her client had just attempted murder in front of dozens of witnesses, and Brennan seemed to be in the mode of last resort.

Unfortunately, *last resort* could get someone killed.

Dade peered around the cruiser. Brennan now had his handcuffed wrists looped around Mel's neck, and the gun was aimed outward, toward the dispersing crowd.

And toward Kayla.

Mel looked pale and shaky. Rightfully so. She'd been a deputy for twenty years now and had never faced anything like this.

Behind him, Kayla wasn't looking steady, either. Her mouth was trembling, teeth chattering, breath gusting, and she was praying.

"Grayson can't come driving into this with Robbie and Connie," she mumbled.

"He won't. By now he's already gotten a half-dozen calls and is arranging for backup."

Dade was sure of that, but what they needed was a hostage negotiator. Nate, preferably. This was one of his areas of expertise, and Dade hoped like the devil Nate was nearby or on his way.

"Kayla?" Brennan yelled. And he shouted her name several times in that same mocking tone.

Each shout made her tremble harder, and Dade wished he could slam his fist right into the man's face to shut him up. He was sick of the games Brennan was playing and even sicker of the effect it was having on Kayla.

"You planning to die today, Brennan?" Dade yelled back. He didn't figure for one minute that would put any fear in the man, but he needed to do something, anything, to rattle this SOB.

"Not me. No plans to die," Brennan assured him. "The deputy here probably didn't have plans, either, but that's exactly what will happen if Kayla doesn't get over here. Now!" he shouted at the top of his lungs.

"Oh, God," Kayla mumbled. She inched closer to Dade. "I have to go out there. I can't let him kill Mel."

Dade had to get his jaw unclenched before he could speak. "This isn't up for discussion. You aren't going out there because Brennan will gun you down before you make it to him. Then, he'll use Mel as a human shield to escape. If he manages that, he'll kill her, too, and anyone else he can take out in the process."

Dade glanced at her to make sure that had sunk in. It had. She nodded. And Kayla got a new look in her eyes. "I have to do something."

"Brennan will make a mistake," he assured her. "And when he does, Mason will have him."

Dade tipped his head to his brother who was about ten yards away. Mason wasn't looking back at the crowd. He had his attention nailed to Brennan, and his gun was ready. Thank God Mason had a steady hand and a deadly aim.

"Kayla!" Brennan shouted again. But this time, it wasn't just a shout. Brennan fired another shot, and this one slammed into the cruiser.

Dade cursed and pulled Kayla lower to the ground, but he wasn't sure that was any safer because a bullet could go underneath the car and hit her.

"How many bullets does he have?" Kayla asked.

Too many. Mel's gun was a full-sized 9 mm Glock, and it held seventeen rounds. That meant Brennan had fifteen more chances to try to kill as many of them as possible. But Dade kept that to himself.

"Mason, if you get a shot, take it," Dade shouted, although that order was just for Brennan's benefit. To remind him that any second now he could have bullets flying at him. Mason certainly didn't need permission to take out a would-be killer.

"How many bullets does he have left?" Kayla pressed.

Dade huffed. "Fifteen."

She huffed, too. "We have to do something to make him use up those rounds."

Yeah. Dade's mind was already trying to work that out. He could maybe move Kayla to another vehicle for cover and put the cruiser in gear and send it Brennan's way. Of course, that was a long shot because Brennan might realize the cruiser was driverless and not fire.

Then, there was the danger of moving Kayla. He needed her out of this parking lot.

And then Dade saw a possible game changer.

Nate.

His brother was at the end of the morgue and was peering around the corner of the building. Nate wasn't exactly concealed, and Brennan would no doubt be able to see him if he looked in that direction.

Hell.

He hoped Nate didn't do anything stupid, especially considering his state of mind. After all, it had been only hours since Nate had learned that Brennan was almost certainly the man behind Ellie's murder.

Dade glanced at Mason who was motioning for Nate to get back. Brennan couldn't have seen Mason, either, but something must have alerted him because he turned his head in Nate's direction.

"No!" Kayla shouted, obviously aware of what was happening.

Dade couldn't risk firing a warning shot because it could ricochet and hit someone. But he had to do something before Nate stepped out and offered himself in exchange for Mel. Brennan would only kill him.

"Give me the concho," Dade said to Kayla.

Kayla's eyes widened, but she took it from her bra. The moment that Dade had it in his hand, he tossed it straight toward Brennan.

It worked.

Brennan's attention snapped in the direction of the silver concho when it plinked onto the concrete parking lot. He fired at it.

And then everything went crazy.

Mel must have realized this was her chance to get

away because she dropped to the ground, and since Brennan's handcuffed wrists were looped around her neck, she pulled him down with her.

"Stay here. I mean it," Dade warned Kayla, and he rushed out to help Mel.

Nate and Mason did the same, all three of them converging on what was now a fight to save Mel. The deputy had her hands fisted around Brennan's wrist so that he couldn't aim the gun at her.

But that meant the gun was aimed pretty much everywhere else.

Dade ran toward the scuffle and kept his own weapon ready. Mason did the same. They could only watch as Brennan kicked Mel, trying to wrench her hands off his wrist.

A kick to her stomach did the trick.

Mel fell back, gasping for air, and her hands dropped from Brennan's. However, she wasn't completely out of Dade's and Mason's line of fire.

Brennan grabbed at Mel, no doubt to use her again as a human shield, but he blindly fired the gun in Dade and Mason's direction. The bullet went into the air, missing them, but Dade knew once Brennan had control of Mel that the next bullet would almost certainly find a target.

Hopefully not Kayla.

Dade prayed she was still behind the car where he'd told her to stay.

Brennan latched onto Mel's hair, and Dade cursed when he realized he still didn't have a clean shot. He was so focused on finding a solid shot that it stunned him when he heard the sound.

The familiar thick blast.

A bullet.

The shot slammed into the side of Brennan's chest, but it didn't bring him down. Brennan stopped, and his attention zoomed to his left.

To Nate, the man who'd just shot him.

But it was too late for Brennan to duck and take cover. Nate fired a second shot directly into Brennan.

Brennan mumbled something.

Then he dropped to the ground.

Chapter 16

Kayla held her breath and prayed those shots hadn't hit Dade.

She'd obeyed Dade's order to stay put, but she couldn't stay down. Kayla peeked over the cruiser to make sure Dade and everyone else was all right.

So far, so good.

Thank God. Dade, Mason and Nate were all still standing. Mel, too.

But she couldn't say the same for Charles.

He was on the grassy strip by the exterior courthouse wall, and Kayla watched as Mason went to him and put his fingers against Charles's throat. Mason shook his head.

"Is he dead?" Kayla asked, but there wasn't enough sound in her voice for it to carry.

Still, Dade must have heard her because he said

something to Mason, turned and hurried toward her. He holstered his gun and pulled her into his arms.

"It's all right," he whispered. "Charles is dead."

"Dead," she repeated. Despite Dade's grip on her, she started to walk toward the body. She had to make sure.

"He's dead, Kayla," Dade tried again.

But Kayla kept going. Of course Dade was plenty strong enough to stop her, but he must have sensed that this was something she needed to do.

As she approached the body, Mason stepped away to go to Nate. Nate didn't look any steadier than Kayla felt. Probably because he'd just had to kill a man. Kayla leaned down and as Mason had done, she put her hand against his neck to feel for a pulse.

Nothing.

But when she drew back her hand, she saw the blood, Charles's blood, on her fingers.

She stared at the blood and braced herself for whatever emotions were about to slam through her. But Kayla was surprised that she felt nothing but relief. Maybe that made her a sick person, but for the first time in years, she felt free, and she could give her son a safe and happy life.

Some of the crowd came forward, as well. Charles's attorney was at the front of the pack and kept mumbling how sorry she was to Nate and Mason. Winston was there, too. But Kayla picked through the people and caught Nate's gaze.

"Thank you," she mouthed.

He nodded, but this had to be a bitter relief for him. He'd finally gotten his wife's killer. However, that wouldn't give him back his wife.

"You don't need to be here," Dade told her, and he

would have ushered her out of there that very moment if Kayla hadn't held her ground.

Kayla walked closer to Mel. The deputy was bruised and scraped up, but her physical injuries didn't look serious. "What did Charles say right before he died?"

Mel glanced at Dade as if seeking his permission, but Kayla stepped between them and looked Mel straight in the eyes. "Tell me, please."

For several moments, Kayla didn't think the deputy would do it, but Mel finally lifted her shoulders. "He said, 'Tell Kayla it's not over.'"

Both Dade and Mason cursed, but it was Dade who got Kayla moving. This time digging in her heels didn't help because Dade scooped her up and carried her to the police cruiser. The moment they were inside, he drove away, leaving the chaos of a crime scene behind them.

"Brennan said that to get in one last jab," Dade insisted.

No doubt, but it made her sick to think that he hated her so much that he wanted her to be tormented even after his death.

"Grayson will be back soon with Robbie and Connie," Dade reminded her.

She nodded, thankful that soon she would be able to hold her baby. But even now, just minutes after Charles's death, she was already thinking, what was next?

Where would she go, and what would she do?

There would be no trial, so there was no need for her to stay in town. Or Silver Creek for that matter. She cringed at the idea of going to her estate because there was probably still blood and shot-out windows from the attack where Salvetti and Flynn had tried to kill her.

Besides, there were no good memories there.

But where?

It surprised her to realize her best memories were those with Robbie and Dade. The oatmeal breakfast in the kitchen at the ranch safe house. The phone conversation Dade had had with Robbie after Grayson had gotten her son to safety. How had her life, and her heart, become so tangled with Dade's that it was hard for her to imagine a future without him?

"Are you okay?" Dade asked her.

"Yes." But they both knew it was a lie. The adrenaline was roaring through her, and the thoughts and images were firing through her head.

Especially the images.

She didn't want to close her eyes and see Charles, or his blood on her hands, but she did, and Kayla wondered when this part of the nightmare would finally go away.

Dade parked behind the sheriff's building and ushered her in. Judging from the deputy and dispatcher's somber faces, they'd already heard the news.

"Grayson needs to talk to you," Tina, the dispatcher, relayed to Dade. "Nothing's wrong with your baby," she quickly assured Kayla. "He just needs to go over some police business with Dade."

Dade reached for his cell, but then stopped. He glanced down at her hands. "Why don't you go upstairs and wash up? Once Robbie is here, I can take all of you out to the ranch."

Kayla blinked. "The ranch?"

"For some downtime," Dade clarified. "The town will be buzzing with reporters and gawkers for the next couple of days."

Of course. Because this would be big news. It was possible the entire thing had been caught on film by a camera crew and would be replayed over and over on the news channels.

Dade nudged her in the direction of the stairs, and Kayla forced one foot ahead of the other. Each step seemed to take way too much energy, probably because she was in shock, but she would get this blood off her hands.

The apartment was just as Dade and she had left it, and her attention went straight to the bed with the rumpled covers. The place where Dade had made love to her. Or maybe it had just been sex for him. Later, she would sort all of that out, but for now she needed her son. Once she had Robbie in her arms, she didn't intend to let go for a long time.

She made her way to the bathroom and turned the water on full blast in the sink. Kayla grabbed the bar of soap and started to scrub.

The tears came.

They sprang to her eyes so quickly that she didn't have time to try to blink them back. She hated Charles for what he'd done, but she couldn't completely dismiss the waste of a human life. Robbie's blood kin. His grandfather. A man her son would never know.

Kayla stared into the sink as the blood-tinged water and soap suds spiraled down the drain. She reached to turn off the faucet, but she saw something out of the corner of her eye.

A gun.

She got just a glimpse of it before the arm curved around her neck, and the barrel of the gun jammed against her back.

"Like Charles said, it's not over, Kayla," the person growled in her ear.

* * *

"Tina said we needed to talk," Dade greeted Grayson when his brother answered.

"You okay?" Grayson immediately asked.

"Yeah." And that was mostly true. Kayla and he had come out of a dangerous situation without a scratch, and that was nothing short of a miracle. Still, it would be a while before he wouldn't think of how close Kayla had come to dying—again.

"How's Kayla?" Grayson continued.

"Shaken up more than she'll admit. Seeing Robbie will help. How long before you get here?"

"About fifteen minutes. I kept Robbie and Connie at the sheriff's house down in Floresville."

No wonder it was taking Grayson so long to get here. Floresville was an hour and a half away from Silver Creek. But it was smart for his brother to take them that far away. As bad as the ordeal with Brennan had been, it would have been much worse if Robbie had been put in danger, too.

"What are you going to do about Kayla?" Grayson wanted to know.

Good question, but Dade didn't have an answer that his brother would like. "I want to keep seeing her," Dade confessed. "Do you have a problem with that?"

"No, and neither will anyone else in the family," Grayson said as gospel. And it would be. Even though they were all adults now, Grayson was still head of the Rylands, and what he said was pretty much a go.

"Thank you," Dade mumbled.

"Don't thank me yet. We've all got some long hours ahead of us to tie up this Brennan mess."

Yeah. And the mess that Alan had left them. "I'll let Kayla know that Robbie will be here soon."

Dade ended the call and hurried toward the stairs. Despite the fact he'd just witnessed a man's death, he was feeling darn good. The green light from Grayson was no doubt responsible for that and so was the woman waiting for him in the apartment. Dade only hoped that Kayla wasn't standing up there trying to figure out how to tell him that it was over between them, that she couldn't stay in Silver Creek any longer.

His good mood faded a bit.

And then it vanished completely when he opened the apartment door and saw Kayla's expression. She was in the doorway of the bathroom, and her face was paper-white.

"What's wrong?" Dade asked, and he went to her so he could pull her into his arms.

But he froze when he saw the gun.

His stomach crashed to the floor, and every muscle in his body went into fight mode. He reached for his weapon.

"Don't!" someone warned. It was the person on the other end of that gun.

It was a woman's voice, and one that Dade instantly recognized.

"Carrie," he spat out. "What the hell do you think you're doing?"

"Tying up loose ends," Carrie calmly answered. "I thought I'd be finished doing that before you got here. Guess not. I really hadn't planned on killing you, too, but you got here a little sooner than I figured. Now, take out your gun using only two fingers and toss it onto the counter. Do anything stupid, and I'll kill her where she stands."

Dade believed her. He didn't know why Carrie was doing this, but there was no hesitation in her voice.

"Your gun," Carrie repeated. "Put it on the counter. Now."

Dade hated to surrender his weapon, but he had no other choice. He couldn't stand there and watch Carrie kill Kayla. So Dade did as this nutjob asked and laid his gun on the counter.

Carrie inched Kayla forward but not too far. Carrie's back stayed to the bathroom where there were no windows and therefore no way for anyone to sneak up on her. That meant Dade was going to have to figure out how to disarm both Carrie and this situation.

"Brennan is dead," Dade told Carrie.

"Yeah, I saw it happen. When I realized he'd been killed, I sneaked in the back. Tina was busy on the phone and didn't see me so I came up here and waited. I knew you'd have Kayla wash the blood from her hands."

Even though her every word was critical, Dade listened to make sure no one was coming up the stairs. Grayson would be arriving soon, and Dade didn't want Robbie coming into this.

Dade looked past Kayla. Or rather, tried. Hard to do with that look of stark fear on her face. God, she didn't need to go through anything else. But Dade pushed that aside and snagged Carrie's gaze.

"Is this about me? About us?" he asked. "Because if it is, then this isn't the way to win me back."

Carrie laughed, a quick burst of air, but there was no humor in it. "No, it's not about you. Well, maybe just a little. Let's just say I probably wouldn't have taken the job if you hadn't dumped me for her." She gave Kayla a hard jam to the back.

Hell.

"We broke up months ago," Dade reminded her, although he doubted she would listen to reason. After all, Carrie was holding Kayla at gunpoint. "And if this isn't about me, what is it about?"

"Money," Carrie volunteered.

"Charles is paying her off," Kayla provided. She still had some fear in her expression, but now there was anger, too.

"Hard to pay someone off if he's dead." Dade kept his attention fastened to Carrie. Especially her trigger finger. If it tensed, then he was going to have to dive at the women and pray for the best.

"Charles set it up before Nate killed him. One of his offshore lawyers is holding the money for me. All he has to see is Kayla's death certificate, and the cash is mine." Unlike Kayla, there wasn't a shred of emotion in Carrie's voice. All ice. "He sent instructions through one of his employees for me to help him. First, I took Kayla's phone from her car and made it look as if she'd been in touch with Salvetti."

Well, that was one mystery solved, and it probably had been easy because Carrie had come to the estate in her official role as a paramedic.

"And then Brennan told you to do this?" Dade tipped his head to her gun.

"Yes," Carrie answered. "He said I was to tie up loose ends if he could no longer do it."

"I'm a loose end," Kayla added. Her gaze drifted to the door, and Dade knew she was thinking about Grayson's arrival. This had to end before his brother came up the stairs with Robbie and Connie.

"So Brennan paid you to kill Kayla?" Dade asked. "Why would you agree to do that? Is this really just about the money?"

"The money...and her." Carrie glared at Kayla. "I was in love with Preston, and she took him from me. She didn't care that she broke my heart. Heck, I'll bet she didn't even love him. She just didn't want me to have him."

"I didn't know about you," Kayla insisted. "Preston never even mentioned you."

"Liar!" Carrie practically shouted. "He loved me, and he would have kept loving me if you hadn't gotten in the way. I should have been the one married to him."

"I wish you had been," Kayla mumbled.

Dade remembered the photos of Kayla's battered face and knew that was true. Carrie clearly had no idea of Preston's true nature.

"So, you're going to kill Kayla because Preston dumped you?" Dade pushed. He wasn't sure he'd get a sane answer, but he wanted to hear it anyway.

"Damn right," Carrie spat out. "I should have been Preston's wife, living with him in a fancy house. I should have had all that Brennan money. Not her. Well, now I'll have some of it, and I'll rid the world of this man-stealing witch who got in my way."

Dade couldn't believe the rage he was seeing and hearing, but he had to keep his own rage in check and get Kayla out of this. "How much did Brennan agree to pay you?" Dade asked Carrie. "Because I can match it."

"A million dollars." Now, Carrie smiled. "Is she worth that much to you, Dade?"

"Yes." And in that moment he knew that was completely true. Kayla was worth that and more.

She was worth everything.

And that included dying for her.

Even if he had to trade his life for hers, he was not going to leave Robbie an orphan.

"Yes?" Carrie challenged.

"Yes," Dade repeated. "I'll make the call and have the money sent anywhere you want. Better yet, I'll double Brennan's offer."

Carrie hesitated, and Dade said another prayer that she would jump at the chance for blood money. But then something flashed through her eyes.

Not just anger.

This was one step beyond that.

"You barely know her," Carrie spat out. "And you're willing to give up so much for her? The witch has brainwashed you. Just like she did Preston. Can't you see that?" She cursed, not waiting for his answer. "You've changed, Dade, and not for the better."

Dade disagreed with that. He had changed. He no longer felt like the bad boy of the Ryland clan. He was the man who was going to save Kayla's life.

"The money?" Dade reminded Carrie. "I'm offering you two million dollars." And he adjusted his feet so he would be able to move better.

"No deal," Carrie told him. "I'd rather have Charles's money."

"You mean you'd rather kill Kayla," Dade fired back.

"That, too."

When Carrie smiled, Dade knew he couldn't change her sick mind. Maybe if she thought she had Kayla out of the way, she would stand a chance with him. And maybe she just wanted him to suffer because things hadn't worked out between them.

Dade glanced at Kayla and gave her a look that he hoped she could interpret—brace yourself.

He lowered his head and launched himself forward.

* * *

Kayla didn't have time to react.

One moment she was standing with Carrie's gun jammed to her back, and the next moment Dade dived right into them.

All three of them went crashing to the floor.

Something rammed hard into Kayla, maybe it was Carrie's gun, but whatever it was, it knocked the breath right out of her. Not a good time for that to happen because she needed to help Dade get that gun. It wouldn't be long, maybe just seconds, before Grayson walked in with Robbie.

Gasping for air, Kayla managed to roll to the side, and she got a better look at the life-and-death struggle. The three of them were wound together, and her right arm was hooked between Dade and Carrie.

Thankfully, Dade had managed to get his hands on Carrie's arm, and he had a death grip on her. That was the only thing that prevented the woman from aiming the gun. Unfortunately, Carrie's finger was still on the trigger, and she made use of that.

She fired.

The blast echoed through the room and through Kayla.

It was deafening, probably because the gun was so close to her ear. Certainly someone downstairs had heard it and would come up to investigate. Kayla didn't know if that would be good or bad because it would be impossible for anyone to get off a clean shot.

Kayla tried to move away, to untangle herself, but Carrie must have noticed what was going on because the woman kicked Kayla right in the chest. Her breath was already in shreds, and that didn't help. But it did rile her to the core.

She couldn't let Carrie get away with this.

Kayla rammed her elbow into Carrie and used the leverage to force herself out of the mix. But Dade was there in it, his hands still locked around Carrie's wrist.

Another shot slammed into the ceiling.

Even though it didn't come close to Dade or her, Kayla couldn't risk a shot ricocheting off something and hitting Dade.

Frantically, she looked around the room for anything she could use as a weapon. The first thing she spotted was a heavy silver-framed photo of Dade and his brothers. Kayla snatched it from the counter and brought it down, hard, on Carrie's head.

Carrie made a sound of outrage and tried to turn the gun on Kayla.

Dade cursed and held on despite Carrie kicking any and every part of his body that she could reach. She also managed to get off another shot.

"What's going on in there?" Deputy Lopez yelled from the other side of the door.

"It's Carrie," Kayla shouted. She didn't know whether to tell the deputy to come in or stay put.

"To hell with this," Dade snarled, and he rammed his elbow across Carrie's chin.

The woman's head flopped back, but she didn't stop fighting.

Kayla could only watch in horror as Carrie managed to maneuver her body, twisting it, until she broke free of Dade's grip. For just a second. In that second, Dade grabbed at Carrie again, but Carrie's attention was focused only on Kayla.

"You're a dead woman," Carrie threatened. And she brought up the gun.

Just as Dade latched onto it and Carrie's hand.

He bashed both against the floor. But not in time. Carrie pulled the trigger again.

Kayla immediately knew something was wrong. The sound was different this time. Not so much of a blast but a deadly sounding thud. And she knew.

Someone had been shot.

"Dade!" Kayla yelled. She grabbed him by the shoulder and dragged him away from Carrie.

She saw the blood then.

So much blood.

And Kayla felt her heart stop. God, had she lost him? Had Carrie managed to kill Dade?

The timing was horrible, but the only thing that kept going through Kayla's head was that she hadn't gotten the chance to tell him that she loved him.

"Dade," Kayla said through a sob.

He turned his head and caught her gaze. "I'm okay," he assured her.

But Kayla shook her head and stared at the blood.

Dade climbed off Carrie, and in the same motion, he hooked his arm around Kayla to move her away from Carrie. But Kayla still saw the woman.

Lifeless, the front of her green scrubs soaked in blood.

Carrie still had a grip on the gun that she'd fired. And when she fired that last bullet, she'd accidentally shot herself.

"It's over," she heard Dade say.

And he pulled Kayla into his arms.

Chapter 17

"Are you sure this is okay?" Kayla asked—again.

Dade tried to give her a reassuring nod—again. It had only been two hours since Carrie had tried to kill them, and he figured Kayla would need a lot of reassuring until it was nothing but a bad memory. He took Robbie from the infant seat in the back of the cruiser. Robbie flashed Dade a big sloppy grin and babbled some sounds. Happy sounds. Unlike his mom, Robbie had no apprehensions about coming to the Ryland ranch.

"Da da da," Robbie babbled.

Dade knew he was just trying to say his name, but it melted his heart anyway.

"The ranch is big," Kayla commented as she stepped from the front passenger's seat. She looked up at the sprawling two-story redbrick house.

Dade took a moment to try to see the place through

Kayla's eyes. Yeah, it was big and getting bigger. Three thousand acres, but Mason was constantly in "buy" mode when it came to adjoining land. And the house, well, it had gone through changes over the years, too.

"Grayson and Eve are having a new wing put on so they'll have more room for their baby," he let them know. He tipped his head to the addition that had already been framed. "Nate and Kimmie live in the left wing with Kimmie's nanny, Grace. I already called and talked to Grace, and she said she'd help out taking care of Robbie."

"That's kind of her," Kayla said softly.

Yeah, and it might become a necessity because Connie had decided that she needed a break. Dade couldn't blame the woman because she'd spent the last couple of days in danger, in hiding and on the run. Before that, she'd been in hiding with Kayla. Hardly the best employment situation.

Kayla's gaze went from the left wing to the porch that extended across the entire front of the main house. Unlike her estate, the ranch was homespun and didn't have a high-end decorator's touch.

"It's really beautiful," Kayla said, looking back at him. She smiled both at Dade and Robbie, but her smile couldn't hide her nerves. "But I probably should have gotten a room at the hotel while my place is being repaired. Especially because I don't think I'll be going back to the estate."

Dade stopped. This was the first he'd heard of this, and Kayla and he had spent the last couple of hours talking.

"Too many bad memories," she added.

He didn't doubt that, but he didn't like that Kayla was making plans that she hadn't talked about. Of course Dade had done the same.

Her attention drifted to the other vehicles in the drive. Mason's truck. Nate's Lexus. Grayson's SUV. "Your brothers are here."

"Yeah." Dade had made certain of that. It was part of the *plan.*

And that led him to his next thought.

This might be a mistake. A huge one. But sooner or later he wanted his family to meet Kayla and Robbie— *really* meet them—not with bullets flying or while neck-deep in an investigation. That investigation was over now. The danger, too. And it was time Kayla faced his brothers under normal circumstances.

Normal.

Finally.

It wasn't perfect, but they were getting there. No more threats to Kayla's life. No more Brennan. No more Carrie. Heck, Kayla had even managed to reconcile with her sister. Over the phone anyway. In a day or two Dade would see about getting them together face-to-face for a little mending time because they now knew that Misty hadn't had a hand in the attempts on Kayla's life.

"Kade, my youngest brother, is at work at the FBI office in San Antonio, but he'll be here later tonight," Dade let her know. "They won't bite," he whispered and nudged her onto the porch.

"Even Mason?" Kayla questioned.

Dade shrugged. "He'll behave." He hoped. With Mason you were never quite sure what you were going to get.

The front door flew open, and a silver-haired woman came rushing out onto the porch. Kayla would have taken a step back if Dade hadn't caught onto her arm to anchor her in place.

"Kayla, Robbie, this is Bessie Watkins, the woman who takes care of us."

"I do at that. I cook, clean and give 'em you-know-what when they need it." Smiling from ear to ear, Bessie went straight to Robbie. "Now here's a handsome little angel."

Robbie approved of the compliment and gave her a grin.

Bessie scooped the baby right out of Dade's arms, kissed him on each cheek and then hugged Kayla. "Welcome to the Double R Ranch."

"Thank you," Kayla managed, but she still didn't sound comfortable.

"The others already had lunch," Bessie let them know. "But if you're hungry, there's plenty of roast beef and pecan pie left. And I'm fixing a big pot of chili for dinner."

Yeah, and Dade could smell it. Walking into the house was always like coming home for Christmas, and he would never take that for granted.

With Robbie cuddled in her arm, Bessie ushered them inside, past the foyer and into the massive family room. Again, no fancy stuff here. Hardwood floors, leather furniture and a floor-to-ceiling limestone fireplace with some log simmering in the hearth. The only artwork was family portraits and paintings of some of the ranch's prize-winning livestock.

To Kayla it must have been like walking into the lion's den.

There was a basketball game on TV, volume blaring, and Mason, with a beer in his hand, had claimed one of the oversize recliners. Nate was stretched out on the floor while Kimmie, his daughter, arranged little plastic horses on his stomach and chest. Grayson and Eve were on the sofa making out.

Well, kissing anyway.

"Newlyweds," Dade whispered to Kayla, and he cleared his throat so it would get their attention. It did. Everyone stopped, even Kimmie, and stared at Dade and their visitors.

For one bad moment, Dade thought this had been a mistake to spring Kayla on them and vice versa, but then Eve leaped off the sofa and hurried to them. Like Bessie, she gave Kayla a hug. Dade, too.

"Thanks," Dade told Eve, returning the hug. Eve might have been only his sister-in-law, but he loved her as much as he loved his brothers.

"Kayla and this handsome little angel are staying with us a few days," Bessie let them know.

She sat Robbie on the floor next to Kimmie, and the little girl—God bless her—immediately offered Robbie one of her toy ponies. There was only two months difference in their ages, with Kimmie being slightly older, but they were almost identical in size.

"Mason will get your bags from the car," Bessie insisted. "Won't you, Mason?"

Mason stared at them. And stared. Before he finally grumbled something and climbed out of the recliner.

"I'll help," Nate said, getting off the floor.

"The bags can wait," Dade insisted, and that drew everyone's attention back to him.

He swallowed hard. It was a do-or-die moment. And everything hinged on what happened in the next few minutes.

Dade took a deep breath and turned to Kayla. "I'm in love with you," he blurted out.

Other than the TV, the room went stone-cold silent. Even Robbie and Kimmie quit babbling.

"I didn't know," Dade continued, "until I saw Carrie holding that gun on you."

"Now, that's romantic," Mason snarled.

Dade shot him a scowl. So far, this wasn't going well. He could deal with Mason's snark, but Kayla's mouth was partially open, and she was staring at him.

A dozen things went through his head, none good. She was about to run for the hills. Or laugh. Or tell him that it was the adrenaline crash talking. After all, it'd been only a couple of hours since Carrie had tried to kill her.

Kayla caught onto his arm. "Uh, we should probably talk about this in private."

Dade held his ground. "I considered that, but I figured sooner or later, preferably sooner, I wanted my family to know how I feel about you."

She nodded. Got that deer-caught-in-the-headlights look. And nodded again. "Okay." She scrubbed her hands down the sides of her dress. "I'm in love with you, too."

That hit him like a sack of bricks.

Oh, he'd wanted the words, but he hadn't expected Kayla to admit it without some prompting. He also hadn't expected to feel this way after hearing those words come from her mouth.

Yeah, it was a shocker. His knees were weak. His thoughts spinning a mile a minute. But most of all, Dade was over the moon.

"It's true?" he checked.

"Yes," she verified and cast another uncertain glance at his gob-smacked siblings.

That *yes* was enough for him. Dade put his arm around Kayla's waist and hauled her to him for a kiss. And not just a peck. He wanted this to be a kiss they would remember for the rest of their lives.

He caught the sound of her surprise with his kiss, and he moved into it, letting the taste of her slide right through him. Like hot whiskey. And sex.

Especially the sex.

But he tried to put that on hold for a moment even though the kiss was a reminder that he would like to drag her off to his bed and soon.

Someone cleared their throat—Bessie, he realized. "Why don't I take the little ones to the nursery?"

"In a minute." Dade figured he might as well go for broke. He looked at Bessie, Eve, his brothers and the babies. "I'm going to ask Kayla to marry me. I just want to make sure nobody has a problem with that."

More stares.

Except for Kayla.

She made another of those happy melting sounds of surprise and launched herself into his arms. Dade realized then that her response was the only one that mattered. And Robbie's, of course, but Dade and the little guy seemed to be on the same page because Robbie clapped his hands and babbled, "Da da da."

The baby was clearly a genius.

"I love you," Dade reminded her.

Kayla kissed him. Again, not a wuss kiss. This one had Mason growling, "Get a room, all right?"

Both Kayla and Dade were smiling when they finally broke the kiss. "And your answer to that marriage proposal?" Dade reminded her.

"Yes." No hesitation whatsoever, although she did cautiously eye the rest of the clan.

There it was again. The feeling that he'd just been hit hard and loved hard all in the same moment. Dade never considered himself a gushy kind of guy, but he suddenly felt like gushing.

"Well, it's about time you got a good woman in your life," Bessie declared. She hugged them both again.

So did Eve. "Welcome to the family," she told first Kayla, then Robbie.

Nate came next, and Dade knew this was a huge concession for his twin. Nate was still reeling from the news of Ellie's killer, but that didn't stop him from pulling Kayla into his arms.

"You'll be good for Dade," Nate whispered to her.

"He'll be good for me," Kayla whispered back.

And Dade hoped like the devil he didn't disgrace himself by getting misty-eyed.

Nate pulled something from his pocket. A silver Double R concho. "I picked it up from the parking lot," Nate explained. And he took Kayla's hand so he could put it in her palm. "I would give it to Dade, but he might throw it away again."

Dade just shook his head. Throwing it away just wasn't working because this was the second time it'd turned up. "Kayla can decide what to do with it," Dade let her know.

Her hand immediately closed around it. "Then, I'll keep it."

Eve pulled her neck chain from beneath her blouse to reveal her own concho. It was a gift Dade had given her for Christmas. "It makes me feel like part of the family."

"You are family," Dade clarified.

Eve smiled, brushed a kiss on his cheek. "Soon Kayla will be family. Robbie, too."

Grayson was waiting right behind Eve, and when she stepped to the side, his big brother was there to give

Kayla his own welcoming hug. This was like the Ryland version of a receiving line.

"This family can always use some more females," Grayson teased. "And apparently another wing of living quarters." But his expression turned more serious when his gaze met hers. "Welcome to the family, Kayla."

Oh, man. That put some tears in her eyes. Eve's, too. This was going much better than Dade had expected, but then, this was his family. There was a lot of love in this room.

Then, Mason stepped forward. He didn't snag Kayla in his arms. He just stared at her. And stared.

"You could do better, Kayla," Mason told her. He lifted his shoulder. "But not much."

Coming from Mason, that was a warm fuzzy welcome, and much to Dade's surprise, Kayla leaned in and kissed Mason on the cheek. Dade couldn't be sure, but he thought Mason might have actually blushed. It was hard to tell under those multiple layers of stubble.

"I'll get the bags," Mason said, strolling out. Nate was right behind him.

Eve scooped up Kimmie. Grayson took Robbie. "We'll show Robbie the nursery. It's like a toy store in there."

"And I'll check on dinner," Bessie piped in, following the others out.

Dade knew it was a ploy to give Kayla and him some alone time, and he was thankful for it. He didn't waste even a second before he pulled Kayla to him and kissed her.

"Marry me?" he said against her mouth.

"I've already said yes."

"Yeah, but I wanted to hear it again."

Kayla smiled, and he caught that smile with another kiss. "Yes," she repeated. But then she pulled back, blinked. "Are you sure about this?"

He didn't blink, but he did frown. "You're not sure?"

"No, I'm positive. I love you. I *really* love you. But I have so much baggage with a bad marriage under my belt."

"Then it's time you had a good marriage. To me," he clarified, causing her to smile. "Because I *really* love you, too."

But again, her smile faded. Because there was nothing she could say or do that would make him change his mind, Dade decided to end her doubts with another kiss.

He backed her against the wall, next to the portraits of his family, and he put his mouth to hers. Dade didn't stop there. He pressed his body against hers, until there wasn't a sliver of space between them. And he kept kissing her until he heard that sigh. That little sound of surrender and pleasure. Kayla melted against him.

"Well?" he challenged. "Got any doubts now?"

Kayla eased back, her chest pumping for air, her heart racing. "None. I love you, Dade Ryland, and more than my next breath, I want to be your wife."

Good. That's exactly what he wanted, too.

Dade smiled and pulled her back to him for another kiss. "Welcome home, Kayla."

* * * * *